everyone in silico

by jim munroe

four walls eight windows, new york

EVERYONE IN SILICO

Copyright © 2002 by Jim Munroe.

Published in the United States by:
Four Walls Eight Windows
39 West 14th Street, room 503
New York, N.Y., 10011

Visit our website at http://www.4w8w.com
First printing October 2002.

Library of Congress Cataloging-in-Publication Data on file

ISBN 1-56858-240-4

10 9 8 7 6 5 4 3 2 1

Printed in Canada

Book Design: beehive

for Susan

When Paul sat down on the bench, the young man moved over a bit without looking at him. His gaze was fixed on something in the sky.

Paul crossed his arms and looked down the tracks.

The young man made a quiet noise. Paul looked at him, and then followed the young man's eyes up. All Paul saw were the gleaming buildings of Frisco's business district, several stretching higher than the eye could register.

"Yeah, they've built them big here," Paul said. "They're not just scraping the sky — they go up forever."

The young man looked at him for the first time. Paul's face was an indistinct blur of features, his suit fashionably cut. "Oh…" the young man said, looking up again. "No, I was watching the ad." He pointed at the empty sky.

Paul turned the dial on his watch, and the blue sky turned into a giant man running through a forest with a six-pack of Pepsi strapped to his head. The buildings obscured some of the ad. The man stopped, pulled off a can, and opened it. "Ah, yes," Paul said. He noticed movement to his left — a giant panda with a fedora was parachuting to the ground. Paul recognized the panda as the mascot for an insurance company. He turned the knob on his watch and both waving panda and Pepsi ad disappeared. The young man was looking at him.

"So you guys still wear the scramblefaces, even here," the young man said.

Paul shrugged. "You get used to it. Same as the ties."

The young man looked at his own tie. "Yeah. I never thought I'd get used to it," he said, twisting it around like a noose. "But you do."

Paul laughed, looked down the tracks. Far off in the distance there was a trolley car almost too tiny to see.

"If you don't mind me asking," the young man said.

Paul looked back, his face a flurry of faces, a cipher.

"Uh, it's none of my business," said the young man. "But…" he pointed to Paul's watch. "If you're platinum, why are you taking the trolley car?"

"Oh," Paul laughed. "I just enjoy it. Clears my head. Gives me time to think."

"I see," the young man said, the blank look on his face clearly communicating that he didn't.

Paul started to look back at the approaching trolley car.

"I'm actually silver," blurted the young man.

Paul looked back at the young man, who was smoothing his hair back.

"Lot of people assume I'm bronze, because I take the trolley car. But it's just that I can't port. There's a technical glitch."

"Really?" Paul said. "That's too bad." He got up. The young man jumped up too.

"Yeah, check this out. I'm going to try to port home," the young man said. "Watch."

The young man turned into a black silhouette of himself. Around the edges of the silhouette, light and image bent inwards.

"Wow," said Paul, stepping away. "That looks bad."

The young man returned, his face agitated. "I know. It only happens when I try to port, though. Otherwise, I'm fine. They say it should clear up soon."

Paul nodded.

The trolley car stopped, and the doors opened.

It was never good to work on an empty stomach, but Nicky had procrastinated to the point where there was no other choice.

At least I'm just hungry, not hungry and wet, Nicky thought as she wandered down Commercial Drive, welcoming the sun on her face like a long-lost friend. The rainy season was over: Vancouver had finally shucked off winter's grey cloak and the strip of stores and restaurants seemed cleaner, newer, reflecting Nicky's small smile back at her.

"Nicholas!" said someone coming out of the Safeway.

"Hey, JK," Nicky said, turning. "Little shopping?"

JK lifted his bulging bags as he backed away. "Lotta shopping. Gotta go. Like the new cut. Looks like an octopus is sitting on your head."

Nicky smiled and shook her thin ponytails. "Why thanks, Joseph Kindertoy." She tried not to stare at his bags as she waved goodbye.

In the first Starbucks she saw she noticed some kids she knew, so she waved and kept on going. The Starbucks a block down looked clear, however, so she held her watch on the rusty plate until the door buzz-clicked.

Breathing a silent relieved breath — she hadn't been positive she had enough for a coffee — she threw her stuff at a table near the window and went up to the counter. As the machine filled her cup, she watched the people bustling by. Spring was all over their faces, as obvious and gleeful as strawberry jam.

Nicky put sugar and two Milkbuds into her coffee and watched the door. Mostly tourists, since the kids from the Drive favored the outlet she had passed by. The steam from her cup curled around and coalesced briefly into the Starbucks logo, then dissipated.

An older masked couple came in and tentatively looked around the café. Nicky rifled through her watch for something to read. She found an article on using EasyCut for amphibious splicing and got her watch to project it on the table instead of her retina. After a minute, she checked the couple out over the rim of her coffee cup. They were at the counter, waiting for a couple of boys to finish filling their soup-tureen mugs. They were as noisy as their clothes.

The boys finally touched their watches to the payplate, bouncing them off it in a perfunctory way.

"Next time, ask him where's his body at!" the kid said on his way out the door, and his red-capped friend exploded in a honk-laugh that made the masked man step back briefly, place a hand to secure his mask, then square his shoulders

3

and pretend he was rubbing his face.

Nicky strained to hear what the man was saying to the woman in his quiet voice, noticed that he touched his bare fingers to the payplate. Nicky smiled inside. *Loaded.* Only the utterly destitute and the fabulously wealthy did without watches.

After casually pressing a black pellet onto the surface of the table next to her, Nicky leaned away from it and absorbed herself in her article. The woman stood for a second with the classic lattes, holding them well away from her white smock, and surveyed the room before nodding the man towards the table next to Nicky. *Good,* Nicky thought, tapping a protein DNA graphic in her article and pretending to watch it unravel.

There was a movement from her backpack, and Nicky's heart rate suddenly spiked. Moving her legs slowly, she placed one of her feet on the opening of the bag, then the other one. She could feel pushing against the side of her shoe. *Settle down, you little shit,* Nicky thought, *you're not the only one who's hungry.* She nervously glanced at the couple as they draped their coats over their chairs, but they seemed comfortable. The man even took off his mask despite the woman's disapproving clucking. He had a square jaw and full lips, which he pressed against her ivory fingers. She had had her nails coated in mirror, and he pretended to stare at himself in them. She hit him and giggled.

Nicky, not looking up, lifted her foot. For a second, nothing, and then, just as she was considering kicking the bag, a brown blur. It had crawled up the man's leg and launched itself onto their table before the couple registered what was happening.

Luckily the woman's mask muffled her scream, because even then it bored into Nicky's ears. Nicky snatched the brown animal to her chest and surreptitiously slipped a black pellet into its mouth. "I'm sorry, ma'am. I don't know how it got out, my bag was closed…"

The man's mask was back on his face, and a halo was starting to generate around the two of them. Nicky stroked the head of the tiny pug-faced little bulldog with a single finger and murmured reassurances to it. The animal, however, was fully pacified by the pellet and stared at the couple with honey-liquid eyes.

"Oh, what a beautiful little… creature," the woman said, holding out her hand. "Turn off that silly thing, Alex," she said.

The halo disappeared. "Sorry," Alex said, to both Nicky and the woman. "It's just…"

Nicky looked down, kept petting the bulldog.

"It's just *nothing*. He's paranoid," the woman said, reluctantly taking her eyes off the bulldog to look at Nicky. "He's been watching the news too much. I apologize for his rudeness." She looked back at the bulldog. "Can I…"

Nicky glanced at her. *Go on, beg.*

"May I… hold him?" she said.

"Her," Nicky stated firmly, as if she cared.

The woman leaned back, a little beaten. Nicky noticed the lines around her eyes and worried she'd pushed too hard.

"May I hold… her?" she said, finally. Nicky paused for effect, looked down at the little critter, and then slowly extended her hands.

"Oh… oh, she's a frisky… oh!" the woman said, her exclamations echoing in her mask. The little bulldog was trying to climb out of her hand and up her smock, its little paws gripping the red cross design printed there.

"Heh heh, careful Simone," said Alex, his eyes watching Simone's rapturous face as much as the little dog. Nicky noted the emotions washing over his face and thought, not for the first time, that some couples might as well have *childless* stamped on their foreheads.

The dog was gnawing on her finger, and Simone was delighted by this. "Oh, Alex, look. It thinks my finger is a bone."

"Heh heh," Alex responded, looking at Nicky with an assessing eye. At this, Nicky held out her hand for the dog, and Simone reluctantly returned it. "So warm…"

"Where'd you get it?" Alex said, trying to sound conversational, taking a sip of his coffee.

"I made her," Nicky said.

"With what?" Alex said dubiously.

"You know those do-it-yourself kits?" Nicky said.

Simone nodded. "I had one of those when I was a kid. Mine didn't work…"

"They never did," Alex said. "They always turned out wrong… messes."

"Yeah," Nicky agreed. "She was my fourth try. I bonsaied her. It took the better part of a year. Even then, it was kind of a fluke. That's her name, actually — Fluky."

"Fluky, oh, that's cute," Simone murmured. She looked at Alex.

Nicky let the dog chew on her finger, trying not to lose her nerve. She thought about JK's bulging grocery bags and forced herself to smile. "Yeah… I've seen a bonsaied tiger go for ten thousand, and it wasn't nearly as unique. It just looked like a cat."

"Ten thousand dollars, huh?" Alex said, almost to himself. He glanced at Simone. "I couldn't see paying more than five…"

Nicky frowned outwardly, while a joyous melody of cash registers *ca-ching!*-ed in her head.

By the time she got back to her place, the sun was dropping behind the mountains. In the dim light, she could still make out that her front door had been flashed — Can You Afford *Not* To Upgrade? Go For Self! — but Nicky ignored the giant block letters and let herself in. She had to swipe her watch twice before it snicked open. *Cheap piece of shit.*

She went into the kitchen and put away her groceries, stuffing the empty bags into a space between the counter and the wall, and remembered she had muted her watch when she went into Starbucks. She checked her messages. One was from her mom, inducing the familiar twinge of mom-guilt. The rest was spam that her filters didn't catch, one of them advertising the next generation of spam filters.

She stopped for a second and debated whether or not she should call her mom back now. She decided she didn't want it hanging over her head when she was in the lab and knew that the longer she waited the greater the chance her mom would go snooping around. She'd know she was home. She'd know Nicky got the message. She kept meaning to disable her mom's ability to track her watch's position, but she knew that would mean a shitstorm of drama. If she needed to be untraceable, she could always take it off and leave it at home, as high school a manoeuvre as that was.

She stood in her kitchen, paralyzed by indecision. She looked at the groceries, unappealing since she had eaten almost a whole packet of Sandwich Fixin's on the way home. She watched a fly loop around and land on her garbage lid. She checked it — three-quarters full. *Well, if it's attracting flies I better get rid of it…*

She tied it up and lifted it out of the can, watching for a second to see if there were any drippings. As she left her house she realized that the depot closed in 15 minutes, so she picked up her pace, walking the plank to the sidewalk and step-swinging the bag. The setting sun stretched her shadow out, making her look like a lurching zombie coming out to feed.

She admired a grand old house done up in canary yellow. It was similar to her own — at least a hundred years old, a walkway stretching out to the sidewalk to compensate for the fact that it was built on a slope. Nicky loved the style; it made her feel like she was living aboard a pirate ship. *Too bad the False Creek flood hadn't happened here*, Nicky thought sacrilegiously, *I'm sure these things are seaworthy.*

She got to the depot and went right up to the scale and plopped the bag down on the belt. It came to $8.343, so she held her watch up to the payplate 'til it dinged and the belt started up.

"Mmm, thanks!" The voice echoed in the empty depot as the stained belt moved the bag towards its black maw. She headed for the door, happy to leave the stinky and somehow creepy place. The recorded voice sounded hungrier than it had when there were even a few people lined up in there. She waited unconsciously for the "That was delicious!" recording to play as she pushed the door open.

Instead she got, "Pee-yoo! Don't you wish you could have just said, Empty Garbage?" followed Nicky out on to the street. The "Go for Self!" tagline was cut off by the closing door.

She smelled her hands (fine) and glanced back at the green garbage can icon glowing in the half-light. As she headed home through the empty streets, she felt a little lonely. Since she had moved here, most of the kids her age who hadn't left Vancouver had moved to apartments around Commercial Drive. But Nicky felt that moving to the Drive, still busy with people, would be kind of living in denial. Plus, there was no way she could afford as much space there.

She heard squeaking when she got in and remembered she hadn't fed the flukes. Nicky walked into her living room and looked in the fluke cage. Two of them were sleeping, but the other one was doing his best to wake them up.

"How-are-you-my-little-meal-tickets?" Nicky said in her best imitation of Simone's baby-voice, reaching into the bag of Critter Kibble. She fed the one that was running around, panting with his big eyes glazed over, and the other two blinked awake. "Oh yeah, *now* you're awake. Where were you when I was taking in the groceries?" The flukes looked at her and started to whine.

She chucked the other two pellets in the cage and rolled up the food bag. Checking the time, she decided to get something done before JK arrived, so she headed up to the third floor.

She caught a glimpse of her new haircut in a mirror. *Do I look like an idiot with this hair?* she wondered. She had had a shoulder-length ragged cut for ages, and she needed a change — but she half suspected she'd done it to dramatically mark the end of her relationship. *Kathy would have hated it*, she thought giddily.

On the top floor stairwell, she stepped up on the wooden chair, pushed open the hatch and pulled down the well-oiled ladder that led up to her laboratory.

The lights came on gradually as she stamped down the hatch. She looked up with some regret at the covered skylight and window, even though it would have been pitch black outside by now. She remembered being excited by the skylight when she had first found the house, figuring it was perfect for a bedroom. But Kathy complained of having to climb down in the middle of the night to go to the washroom — it was a pain, but still, it would have been so cool to wake up to the sun — and so the lab ended up here instead. When Kathy ended up moving to Frisco, Nicky couldn't be bothered moving all the lab equipment out. What had started out as a small operation with an EasyBake and a shaky table had expanded into quite a bit of stuff.

Wedged against the slanted roof was a long silver counter with tons of beakers and vials and other antiques that Nicky had a soft spot for. Her computer setup was also outdated, but stable — like the rest of the equipment, she had scooped it up when the genetics department was phased out.

She called up her active in silico experiments — two had been birthed alive. One was a three-headed fluke she had called Cerberus, and the other had a single eye in the middle of its forehead. She focused in on the Cyclops fluke first, noting with satisfaction that it was blinking normally — the last version had been birthed with a messed-up eyelid. She called up the Cerberus fluke. It wasn't doing as well, only one of the three heads breathing normally.

She zoomed in on the organs and got the computer to diagnose. The heart glowed red, 125% the normal rate. The lungs were within normal parameters this time, although still a little off. Nicky sighed. *Maybe three heads* aren't *better than one…*

She went back to the Cyclops and introduced different stimuli. The model fluke barked happily when it was introduced to food pellets, sexual partners, and petting. It looked good to Nicky, so she decompiled the dog into its spawning ingredients. To free up some memory, she went back to the sick puppy and deleted it. The computer, as it always did when deleting, made a tinny scream. It was just a morbid thing the EasyCut programmer put in, but it always reminded Nicky of the first time she heard it.

It had been in the first week of classes, when they were all getting trained on the equipment. Her professor, a tiny outspoken Asian woman, was showing them how the in silico programs were used.

"Now when I was a little girl, we were still dealing directly with the meat. None of this computer simulation crap. We'd use in vitro fertilization, being very very careful. But things still went wrong. And when it did, you'd have to take the sick little creature and terminate it." She deleted the current experiment and the computer screamed. She smiled as the small crowd of students jolted back. "Newbies," she mocked. As Cho pushed by them to the next piece of equipment, Nicky noticed her earlobes kicking.

Nicky remembered being more surprised by Professor Cho's highly modified earlobes than she was at the scream. She'd never seen club kickers in real life — the early body modification that pulsed with sound had been unfashionable for more than 20 years. After she got over the shock, Nicky decided it was gutsy — still later, she thought it hinted at why Cho stayed in genetics when it had ceased being scientifically relevant. She just didn't care what people thought.

At the end of Nicky's second year her department was shut down, and Nicky had made an appointment to see Cho supposedly for direction on which stream to take now.

Cho had been working on an in silico experiment of a tri-lunged horse when she came in. She had waved Nicky into a chair and made a few more adjustments before closing the horse. When it blinked out, Cho leaned back in her chair and tilted her head.

"I'm kind of surprised to see you here," Cho had said.

Nicky just looked at the professor's small smile, trying not to stare at her dancing earlobes.

"You struck me more as someone who knew what she wanted to do," Cho continued. "While the people who've been in this office lately are a mess. But this's been coming for a long time. There haven't been any jobs in genetics for a decade… except teaching jobs. We're lucky the school is allowing students to transfer some of their credits. When the arts were phased out, they didn't even get that."

Nicky wondered at the prof's defensiveness. Was it because she'd been dealing with angry students all week, or was it the knee-jerk reaction of the professional know-it-all? She decided to cut to the chase. "What's going to happen to the lab equipment?"

Cho looked like she hadn't considered it. "It's too outdated to be of use to any other department," she thought out loud. "They'll junk it, I suppose."

Keeping her face neutral, Nicky said, "I've got a couple of experiments I'd like to finish, and I don't have access to anything like that."

Cho nodded, her eyes suddenly hard. She touched the bridge of her nose. "Hmm. Yes, well… I'd be putting myself at risk if anything unorthodox was to happen to them…"

Nicky was suddenly very glad that she hadn't ever talked to Cho about personal matters. "I looked at the prices for them used, and they're way too much. I'm going to have to move out of my place as it is."

"My situation isn't very good either," Cho said with discomfort. "Your parents?"

"They've cut me off," Nicky said, preferring not to elaborate.

Something in Cho deflated. "Yeah, me too. There're no jobs in a digital world for us dirty meat-workers," she murmured. "Information Architecture, young lady, that's what I suggest."

"Yeah," Nicky said, trying to keep her voice respectful. "That's what my mom said."

A few weeks later, Nicky had a fully functional lab in her attic. A little slow, but it was a stable system with Genome 2035 installed. The EasyBake oven was handy to have — no more having to send out her experiments to be compiled. And if the beakers and test tubes she had scored cluttered up the place a little, they at least gave her a sense of history.

Not just ancient history, either. They reminded her of first year, working late late late to finish an experiment alongside other students. Someone would inevitably cook up something in one of them to break the tension — and there was a lot of that, with the stress of deadlines, the limited equipment, and the egos. At some point, for incentive, someone would come from the chemistry lab and set a steaming beaker of something yummy and narcotic within everyone's sight.

Thinking of those long nights and fucked-up mornings, Nicky felt a wave of nostalgia. To fight how suddenly alone she felt, she asked the computer for some fast and melodic music. She started a new Cerberus fluke and began to work on its organs, hiding everything except the problem lungs and heart. *Maybe I could get a little more room by getting rid of the spleen...*

A few hours later her watch spoke. "Hey Nicky, I'm at the door."

"Oh, hey JK. Down in a second."

A ladder and three flights of stairs later, she could see his big frame silhouetted in the lace-curtained window beside the front door.

"Sorry I'm late," JK said as he stepped in. He looked around her place in his characteristic way, stooping and peering intently through his small spectacles.

"No biggles, I've been chipping away in my lab."

"Man, you've got a hall. I wish I had a hall," JK said, looking for a place to hang his bike.

Nicky took it from him and arched her eyebrow as she hung it on a coat rack, saying "Were you in a big hurry or something?"

JK grinned. "Naw. I just felt like riding."

Nicky shook her head on their way upstairs. "You're a reckless fool, JK."

He shrugged. "It's not dangerous anymore. Who's going to hit me now — man, you've got a living room. I want a living room," JK said as they passed through it.

Nicky couldn't resist showing off the spaciousness by spinning, her arms extended. "Gotta move to Strathcona, son."

"Your hair looks great when you spin like that," JK said, laughing.

They climbed up into the attic and, as JK squeezed his shoulders through the hole, Nicky cleared out some dishes from the EasyBake. She got an empty one and handed it over to him.

He set it down on the silver counter and pried it open. He took a small metal box from an inner pocket and removed some seeds from it, and while he was painstakingly placing them in the container's compartments Nicky wondered why he didn't just get rid of the muscles when he was constantly dealing with tiny things. And if he was going to spend money on body mods, why didn't he correct his vision first? But watching him focus on the task, Nicky decided she didn't want to ask. It was more interesting, in a way, not knowing.

He clicked the box closed and passed it to her. She put it in the EasyBake and set it to organics only. "You don't need the box copied too, do you?"

JK shook his head. "Nope. I put 'em in there so they're separated enough. Last time I did them loose, there were a bunch that fused together."

"A hundred of each enough?"

JK licked his lips, looked pained. "That'd be great, but I don't know how much extra you have…"

Nicky cut him off with a raised hand. "S'okay, I got the machine pretty much fully loaded. And my projects are one-of-a-kind rather than mass produced, so I don't need that much." She set the machine to working.

"The job will take about eight minutes," the EasyBake said. "And it will use under 1% of remaining toner."

"See?" Nicky said. "I'm going to get a cup of tea. Want one?"

JK's face lost its anxious look. "Ah!" he said, nodding and rummaging around in his bag. A few seconds later, he produced a jar full of dark leaves. "I brought tea!"

Nicky, halfway down the ladder, looked at the jar and raised a quizzical eyebrow. JK just smiled and put the jar under his arm, followed her to the living room and through to the kitchen. Nicky was already reaching up for a tetrabox of Starbucks Earl Grey.

"Oh, come on," JK said, unscrewing the jar and taking out a leaf. "I just need a pot of boiling water, and then we'll have tea."

"Sorry, no pot," Nicky said with a smile, whacking the box against the counter and peeling it open. She set two mugs beside it and when a spiral of steam slid out of the opening, she poured one for herself. She looked to him to see if he wanted one, and he nodded with defeat, twisting the lid back on the jar. "Oh come on." She handed him the balloon-festooned mug ("Lordy lordy look who's forty!") and slapped him on his shoulder. "You remember what happened that last time I had one of your herbal potions."

JK's face cracked in a mischievous smile. "You *said* you wanted to get wasted," he said. "If it hadn't been after a keg of beer and a genderbender, it would've been fine."

Nicky let her silence be the response, although really she was pleased it got her out of trying whatever it was he had. She settled into the big quiltwork armchair and stretched her legs out. JK put the tea down on the coffee table and put a finger into the fluke cage.

"So you still passing off these ratdogs as canine bonsai?" JK said.

"Yep," Nicky said, taking a sip of tea and resting the mug on her belly. "That's where I was headed when I saw you on the Drive today, actually. Got enough to get me through next month."

"Sweet," JK said, finger-wrestling with the little creature. "And they never catch on and come back?"

Nicky shrugged. "Your average person doesn't know the difference between a simple ratdog splice and a bonsai. Other than the life span and the jaw strength, there's not much to tell them apart. Plus, I always sell to tourists, so I know they'll be on a plane pretty soon, and it'll get confiscated."

"Yeah, the Drive's filthy with tourists these days. Lots of people doing a final tour before they upgrade. Easy pickings."

Nicky took another sip and looked up at the ornamental ceiling, water stained but still grand. "Yeah. I feel kind of bad about it, but there's no real harm done. If they have the money to fly or upgrade then they can afford to support the local culture."

"Desperate times require desperate measures," murmured JK. "Can I feed them a tea leaf?"

"Don't, you freak, they have a very strict diet." Nicky looked away from the ceiling and straight at JK. "The thing is, though, I don't feel like these are desperate times. I've been living off this scam for a half-year now. But…" She lolled her head again. "Just because I'm clever enough to find ways to live decently in this shitty world doesn't mean the world isn't shitty."

JK turned away from the cage and ran a hand through his shaggy hair. "Well," he started, a tea leaf sticking out from a corner of his mouth. He sucked on it thoughtfully. "It's not that things are getting worse. In some ways… they're getting better. Easier, anyway. Less hassles. It's just that the world is… losing relevance." He pulled the leaf out from between his lips and dropped it into the mug.

"I don't want you tripping out on my living room floor," Nicky warned. "This is a respectable place."

"It's seriously just tea, Nicky," JK said. "From India."

"How did you get a hold of raw organic stuff?" she challenged. "Not from your mail-order club?"

"It's not through the mail, anymore," he said vaguely.

"Your job is completed," said Nicky's watch. "Would you like to…"

Nicky shut it up with a tap and set her tea down. "I'll grab it, just stay here."

She made her way up to the attic, opened the EasyBake and carefully took out the sheaves of seeds. With minor spills, she was able to slide most of them into the original container (hoping that was what JK wanted) and seal the lid. Then she made her way down, telling the system to save and shut itself down, feeling her body complain as she climbed down from the lab. She was too tired to do any more work tonight. The tea had failed her.

JK was back at the cage, looking at the flukes.

"Want one? Only ten grand!" Nicky cracked as she handed him the container.

"Fantastic," he said, looking inside.

"Yeah, the machine doesn't divide by color," Nicky said. "You'll have to do that by hand."

"You wouldn't believe how much stress this saves me, Nicky, you're an angel."

"Not an octopus?" Nicky said, tugging on her pigtails.

"Same difference," JK laughed. "Seriously, last time I had to go to Kinko's —"

"They don't have EasyBakes there," she said.

JK nodded. "I know, but they do organic duplication. But I was incredibly nervous the whole time, assuming they'd make me fill out an intent-of-use form —"

"What are you doing with them, anyhow?" Nicky said, hoping to stop the waves of gratefulness before they built into a tsunami.

"Another new growth party. Hopefully you'll be able to go to this one."

"Well, hopefully you'll tell me about this one," Nicky said, poking his big chest.

"I know, sorry about that."

"Mmm-hmm."

"But now you're practically a patron. So I'll send you the coordinates."

"Excellent," Nicky said, stifling a yawn.

JK grabbed his backpack from where he had laid it beside the couch and opened it up. He noticed something there and pulled it out. "Oh yes." He took a little holocoin out and tossed it on the floor. A unicorn crawled out of it and pranced in a circle, stopped, seemed to notice Nicky and said in a whinny, "Come to see Mike Narc's show!"

JK was putting away the container. "I figured you're working with similar themes..."

Nicky gave a one-shoulder shrug. "Sorta." The show invite was a floating, large-bosomed woman now, who was intoning the time and place. "I met him once, and he struck me..." She looked at JK. "Do you know Mike?"

JK made the finger gesture for *a little*.

"I dunno. Maybe I'll go," Nicky said, picking up the coin projector.

"He's a bit arrogant," JK said, putting on his backpack.

"*Yes.*"

They laughed at her vehemence.

"It might be the fact that we're working in similar territory, though," Nicky admitted.

JK shook his head. "It's so different though, in terms of treatment."

Nicky squinched up her mouth, nodded. "*I* think so."

JK noticed the time. "Holy yikes, I gotta scram." He reached for the door. "Seeya!"

Nicky turned and walked into the living room, grabbed the jar of tea. "Not without this you're not."

"Shit!" JK said, shouldering off and opening his backpack. "Can't forget that. OK seeya for real this time," JK opened the door and left.

"Later," Nicky said and shut the door. It wasn't until she was coming back from the living room with the empty mugs that she noticed the bike, still hanging from the coat hook.

Doug flicked through the numbers again, his long fingers jerking spastically. *Nope. No way to do it.* He sighed and leaned his head against the palm of his hand, placing it there like a crystal ball on a silk pillow.

And although it wasn't giving him any answers, Doug's head was somewhat crystal-ball-like: the bald top of his head gleamed softly, ringed by a well-kept monk's fringe. His long face suited his current depressed state: thin-lipped misery accompanied by a thin moustache.

Doug stood up, stretched, and gazed out his window. Through a tiny square patch — about one foot by one foot — he could see the mountains. Just the tips, but that was enough. He had no idea how the patch had peeled off, nor why it remained unfixed. He had considered telling someone, but it wasn't like his bosses made money off of the billboards that covered the outside of the buildings. That was the building owner's lookout.

It was a bit creepy, however, that prime ad space would be left to waste. It was the clearest indication Doug had had that things were really changing, of the emigration, or whatever the pundits were calling it these days. He really should have known that, of course, but Doug had felt his concern for such matters diminish steadily over the years, a leak he felt incapable of fixing.

He looked at his watch. Quarter to 12. *Shit.* He sat back down in his chair. Tapped the armrests, looked at his patch of sky. Stared at the finance sheet floating before him in his cubespace. *Oh, fuck it. It's close enough.*

He got up, waving off the spreadsheet, and elbowed his way into his black greatcoat. He headed out the door, checking his watch to see if he had enough for Pilar's. *Damn. Not enough for a decent meal and a tip.*

Striding past people in the hallway, he hid his disappointment.

Fuck how I hate the day before payday — "Hi Gloria."

"Early lunches for the execs."

Nosy — "Well. We don't get to chit-chat on the phone all day, so we need a proper break."

"Ha ha."

What am I doing, sparring with the secretary —

"Doug! How goes it ol' chum."

"Maintaining, Mike, you know how I do." *No! Don't get on the elevator ah shit*— "...So where you off to?"

"Pilar's. Can't get enough of that kelp piñata stuff. You?"

It's paella, moron. "Oh, McDonald's."

"McDonald's?"

Don't act like you've never heard of it, you fat bastard — "Sure. I force myself once a week at least. Keeps my ear to the ground."

"Hmm."

"It's all the same food, I mean — Pilar's a McEatery." *God, that was desperate.*

"True, true. Well, watch those McNuggets, ha ha."

"Ha! Never touch 'em." *Can these doors open any slower?* "Well, take care."

As the elevator whisked Mike away to the underground mall, Doug fished around in his pocket for a handkerchief. He pushed through the (barely) revolving doors into a fairly nice day, but Doug had his polka-dotted hanky firmly pressed to his mouth as he headed towards the golden arches.

He caught a flash of his mountains between two massive buildings and almost knocked into an old man carrying a rather wet-looking garbage bag. "Fug you," he said through swollen lips, and Doug nodded his agreement, getting away from the cloud of stench as quickly as possible.

The McDonald's sign loomed above, inaccurately stating 99 Billion Served. It had been frozen there for as long as Doug had been alive, and he had actually written an essay on it for a class in corporate history. "Obviously, there was the practical consideration of the costs involved in adding new slots for higher numbers," he had written with the self-assurance native to cocky teens. "And there was also the zeitgeist of the '90s and '00s to consider — a last-gasp reaction against the unlimited growth model. So McDonald's upper echelons sat tight, knowing that their point had already been made — that everybody loves their delicious flame-broiled burgers."

Standing in line, the greasy smell reminded him that they weren't flame-broiled at all. He had lost marks for that, although he had gotten top marks for analysis — that's what mattered, since he was sure (even then) that his future lay in coolhunting.

Doug thumbed a burger and fries, having to press the worn fries icon twice before it registered. He pressed his watch against the payplate, held it there. It dinged its approval, and the relief Doug felt at this was quickly followed by self-loathing. *Worried about the cost of lunch at Mickey Dee's...*

The tray slid toward him. He picked it up and headed to an empty table surrounded by other empty tables, as far away from the cluster of youngsters as he could get. A younger Doug Patterson would have tried to get a little closer and eavesdrop on the conversation and make mental notes of the slang, but Doug Patterson at 37 unwrapped his burger and watched them with dull indifference fortified with caution.

"But the two lanes were merging, right. So-so-so, I was like," the kid took a toke, "Let's go, shitarse. You wanted to race, so let's race." He had huge gaps between his teeth and the full attention of his crew. "Onetwenty-oneforty-one*sixty*... the motherfucker didn't stop, I'll give him that. Should have though. Ended up as the window display at Macy's. *Totalled*." He toked and blew a smoke stream at his gun finger, listened to his crew make impressed noises. "My Camaro had not a scratch."

One of the kids, a girl of about nine, screamed. Then, stopping entirely, pulling her knees up to her chest: "Oh see, so-so-so, that's my bullshite alar-um."

"Verify. Fuck you little — go! Just go verify. Last night. Granville and 7th." The kid crossed his arms, made cartoonishly big by his white puffy jacket, and jerked his chin. "Fuckin' — go! Look stupid."

The little girl exaggeratedly spoke into her watch. "List fatalities —"

"Did I say he died?! No, I *didn't*..."

"Cancel. Did a car accident occur yesterday at Granville and 7th?"

The kid and the girl locked stares as they waited, eliciting hushed giggles from the others. Finally the watch verified an accident. The kid spread his hands out, a gap-toothed smile on his face. "An that's —"

"Cars involved with this crash?" the little girl continued, her face a curl-framed study in innocent curiosity.

"Two cars, a Camaro Extremis and a Lightfoot, were towed from the site."

One kid covered his face in his hands, moaning, and the sounds of misery-induced hilarity beat down the gap-toothed braggart.

"Stung," pronounced the little girl, a small hint of a smile on her lips.

"Who cares, I picked up that Camaro for like, a hundred fifty —" he started. Singsong: "*Stung*."

"Ah, I'm makin' money all the time," the gap-toothed kid said, shoving himself upright, moving towards the counter.

"How much of the tow charges have been paid off?" the little girl asked her watch as he moved away.

"Zero dollars." Hilarity. "Accruing 13% interest per annum."

One of the kids stood up and called, "Yo, Zero! Get me a burger motherfucker!" Then he seemed to notice Doug. "So-so-so, chicken hawk. You like this?" He motioned to the six-pack of abs on his prepubescent body, visible through a sheer t-shirt.

Doug shook his head and looked away, finishing off his burger and starting on his fries. He emptied the packet on the tray and doused them liberally with ketchup, focusing on the motions, willing their attention away from him as an escaping convict wills away a searchlight on the yard.

Doug lifted large handfuls of fries to his mouth in an effort to inconspicuously eat more quickly. He could only swallow the potato derivative so fast, however, and he looked up to see the gap-toothed kid veering towards him on his way back from the counter.

"So-so-so," the kid said, getting out a pack of tokes and sliding in beside him. He sparked up and gave Doug the once-over, pausing at his expansive bald pate. Doug realized that what he'd thought were gaps were teeth tattooed black. "How you doin', guy?"

"I'm fine." Doug raised his eyes to the kid's, but the kid was already glancing over at his friends, who were talking amongst themselves. Only the little girl was really paying attention. Doug steadily mowed down his pile of fries.

"You know, guy," the kid said. "These Marlboros are really smooth. It's a perfectly balanced mix between tobacco and marijuana that packs a punch while staying really flavorful."

"Really," said Doug, happy that the kid was just pitching at him rather than something else. "Marlboros, you say," he said in an interested voice, mopping up the last of the ketchup with the last of his fries.

"Yes! Why not try one?"

Doug took one of the tokes from the green and white pack and set it on his tray, "Thanks."

"Yes, Marlboros. Marlboros are…" the kid was checking his watch.

Hopeless, Doug thought, *out of pitch ten seconds into it and checking his account in front of the mark.* "Tasty?" he prompted. "With a high that lasts all day long?"

"So-so-so, with-a-high-that-lasts-all-day-long," the kid said, more to his watch than to Doug. A second later, "Fuck. Why didn't I get anything for that?"

Doug got up. "I said it first. You should have also offered me a light."

The kid went for his pocket.

"I don't smoke. But you get a few extra bucks for offering a light," he dumped his tray into the garbage, the mat sticking for a second before obeying

19

gravity.

"Whattaya throwing the toke away for," the kid said bitterly.

"They're not cool any more," Doug said, walking away, taking his handkerchief out of his pocket and rubbing the grease off his fingers.

"Whatta fuck you know about cool," the kid muttered. "Bald-ass."

Doug pushed through the door, heard the kid yell "Money, alla time making money!" as he rejoined the group. Through the window, his glance caught a tableau: the kid in the white jacket showing someone the bank balance on his watch; the person being shown looking contemptuous; the little girl with the curls staring at the gap-toothed kid, her face as placid and as lazy as a viper a few seconds before striking. There was something about her face that reminded him of his own daughter, and Doug walked away quickly, trying to distance himself from that thought.

After lifting the hanky to his nose, he decided to pocket it. Better unfiltered air than air filtered through french-fry grease. As he walked around the bums littering the sidewalks, he remembered an article he had read yesterday about Frisco — supposedly a few bums had been introduced in select locations "to ease the psychological transition." Doug thought the whole article was probably cooked up by Self for marketing reasons, but still... he might have admired it, except that he was unable to think about Frisco without a ball of anxiety spinning to life in his gut.

So naturally there was an ad in the elevator that made him think about it. The Self logo pulsated to life. "If you had upgraded already, you wouldn't have to be wasting time in this stupid box. Hours of your life are spent shuttling your meat from location to location, representing thousands of lost —"

Doug made an angry sound.

The Self ad emorphed. "Trouble with aggressive impulses? We all have them, but wouldn't it be nice if you could control your emotions and just mellow out? With the Self silver package —"

A shuddering sigh from Doug emorphed the ad again. "Feeling blue? Are your sad days lowering your productivity? If —"

"Shut up," Doug said, as levelly as he could muster.

The ad paused for a second, and Doug almost thought it had listened. But, no.

"Sick of ads bombarding you every second of every day? Getting the Self gold package means that ads are optional!"

The doors slid open, and the ad called cheerily after him "Go for Self!" The guitar lick reverbed until the doors mercifully closed.

Doug made his way through the hall back to his office, feeling more defeated than he had when he'd left. He'd barely sat down when a man with short white hair poked his head out of an office doorway. "Ready for our two o'clock, sport?" he asked Doug.

"Will be at two o'clock, boyo!" Doug shot back in what he hoped was a hearty tone.

He got up and shut his door behind him. *His* door. The one (and only one) upshot of the company's expansion was that at least that idiot Stevens had been moved out two months ago.

Stevens wasn't so bad, Doug chastised himself as he got behind his desk. It was more that having to share with him sent a message — he was no longer worthy of his own office in the eyes of the management. No longer the young shark he had been in his prime, pulling in so much data they'd needed —

Ah, it was dumb luck. The fact that he had been there at the beginning of the Ripper thing, that he had slid so easily into the community there — hell, that it had started in Vancouver. It was dumb luck. But it had been good for at least ten easy years at the company, years where his words were gathered like sacred fruits as they dropped from his lips.

Doug checked his schedule to see what Lauden wanted to confer on. Consumer Trends — Tobacco. Lauden was a traditionalist, and wanted something good to feed Philip Morris, to keep them as a client even though they were having serious problems with the current transition. *I know how you're feeling, Phil ol' pal,* Doug thought as he scanned through the conversation he'd had with the kid at McDonald's.

There were only two or three snippets he could use, but he made the most of them. He worked on his analysis, happy to focus on something for a while, and pretty soon Lauden's white spiky head poked in. Doug nodded, rose, and sucked the info back into his watch and followed Lauden down the hall.

"So I've asked the new kid in on this," Lauden said, his face blank.

Doug felt something nasty shoot through him that he couldn't quite identify. "Fuck. Could this day get any better?"

"Oh, buck up, Patterson. You used to love a good fight!"

Doug bit his tongue. "That was before home office started hiring scum off the street." He glanced at Lauden's doughy face, which revealed nothing. "I mean, at least with you and me there was some point to it."

"Ha ha," Lauden said, holding the door open for him.

Oh fuck. Not just the new kid, but the boss too.

Doug rounded the board table and beamed at his boss. "Mr. Harris!"

Mr. Harris stood up and stuck out his hand for a shake. Doug almost fell for it, but "Oh no you don't you old bastard," Doug said, stopping just short of falling for it, waving his finger at Harris. He had noticed something a little too symmetrical about his boss's hair.

"How'd you know?" Harris said, "Is it the resolution?"

"God no," Doug said, choosing a seat opposite his boss and two away from the kid, whose emanations of scorn he could already almost feel. "The resolution's fan-*tas*-tic. Upgrading suits you, sir. No, it was just that I knew that you hadn't entered the building."

"Looks really good on my end too. Right down to the wood grain," Harris said, slapping the table.

"Wow, the sound on this set-up's pretty yum," the kid said.

God, not a minute into it and he's already dropping slang, part of Doug's brain raged. The kid was, as usual, dressed in the latest styles of the 12–17 set, his face so fresh it looked uncooked. "Well, it's good to see you, sir," he said. And it was true, partly. Harris was the only coolhunter that Doug could talk more than trends with, someone he could talk high-concept and theory with. But he also knew Harris was getting a little impatient.

"OK, well…" Lauden started. "Whattaya got for us, Doug?"

Doug started to pull up the files, silently thanking the gods for his poverty. "I collected a little data on the subject," he said, looking over his notes. "I don't know if we're going in the right direction with our assumptions that smoking is a dying trend. We might be being hasty."

"Look, all the studies so far have shown it's in final phase," the kid started in a tone that sounded rehearsed to Doug. "There's no danger-appeal, no vice-appeal — the smart money says it's on its way out. Philip's had a long run, but it's time to close up shop."

"Our job isn't to advise it on operations," Lauden said. "We're here to analyze its product's current cool quotient and produce usable data for our client. CCQ is only one factor in their decision."

The patronizing tone Lauden was using on the kid soothed Doug. "A 12–17 year-old male pitched Marlboro's Ganja Lites to me." Doug played the audio clip from his watch, handed transcripts of the sessions around.

"That's one of the lamest pitches I've ever heard…" scoffed the kid.

Doug pretended he hadn't heard him, since he more or less agreed. "We know that the teen demographics are very-to-extremely reluctant to pitch products they don't associate with strongly. And the subject was clearly the leader of his social group." That last part was a lie — the little girl with the curls was alpha, putting him at beta at best — but there was no way they could tell that from the audio clip.

It was like Lauden read his mind. "Was this recorded under controlled fieldwork conditions?"

Fucking T-crosser, Doug thought. *Fucking I-dotter.* "Well…"

"I don't think there's any doubting the validity of Doug Patterson's research," Mr. Harris said with a little laugh. "Question is — what can we bring to the client from this?"

Out of the corner of his eye, Doug caught the kid steepling his hands and nodding wisely. Doug gritted his teeth for a second, pretended to be scrolling through his notes. "The vice-appeal and danger-appeal aren't going to work with upgraded consumers. But people also smoke to do something with their hands, to differentiate themselves from the crowd, to take an introspective break, to punctuate their angst with plumes of smoke —"

"Whatareya, copywriting here?" the kid mumbled.

"— and that won't change when the market upgrades. Look at it this way — the fact that their product was lethal didn't kill the industry. This transition isn't a roadblock, it's a speed bump." This last bit was a favorite phrase of Mr. Harris's, and he was rewarded by a soft grunt from his boss as he closed his notes.

Lauden backed him up. "That's relevant analysis."

Harris nodded, his eyes off in middlespace.

The kid was smiling as he went through the transcript. Then he cleared his throat. "Subject A: 'Whatta fuck you know about cool, bald-ass.'"

Both Lauden and Harris laughed. On another day, Doug would have had more energy, but today he really had to struggle to even muster up a thin smile.

"You're a little piranha, aren't you?" Mr. Harris said with a wry smile.

"Very little," Doug added, keeping his voice even.

"Oh, untwist, would ya," the kid said, with a lazy grin that said *I've got you on the ropes*. "These old guys. First thing to go is their sense of humour. Uh, well, second thing," he said, indicating hair.

More chuckling from Harris. Lauden was looking down at the table.

"Let's finish this up," Harris said. "Doug, I'm definitely picking up what you're putting down. But there's the reputation of the agency to consider. We'd be putting ourselves in a very vulnerable position if we were the only dissenting voice. The feeling I get from Philip is that they're definitely scaling back their tobacco operations until they can find something to attach their brand to that's going to be viable in Frisco."

Doug nodded, a little stunned at how badly he had been beaten, and on how many fronts.

"I'd like to do some research on that, sir," the kid was saying, all mockery gone from his voice, all professional. "My own findings were more along those lines than Patterson's."

Mr. Harris's smile showed awareness of the kid's ass-kissing, but he nodded his approval. "Why don't you get started on that now. Get back to Lauden early next week... Tuesday latest."

Doug stood with the other two and moved towards the door.

"Doug..." Mr. Harris was standing now. "How are your preparations going? Ready to make the move soon? Things are heating up in Frisco..."

Doug nodded wordlessly, forcing himself to walk no faster than the other two.

Harris's brow furrowed.

"Couple..." Doug started, actually gulped, and went on, "Couple of loose ends." He was at the door. He reached for the doorknob, and slowly pulled it closed. "I'll be there ASAP."

Harris gave the slightest of nods.

Doug shut the door with a click. When he turned around, Lauden and the kid were striding down the hall, chatting. Lauden glanced back once, gave him a *Hey, what can you do?* look, and disappeared into an office.

The SkyTrain was still pretty crowded at rush hour. As it slid along on its monorail track, Doug peered out the window at an even older rail system — a train yard cluttered by cars that looked like cast-aside beer cans.

Was that a tent? Doug thought, seeing a flash of olive green fabric in the yard. *Probably some kind of garbage.* It was hard to imagine someone living in the open, having to wear a mask all the time.

He kept staring out the window, although there wasn't much to see in the quickly dimming light. It was better than watching the advertisements, especially since most of them were for Self packages. Luckily they were broadband ads, unable to emorph with this many people.

Doug closed his eyes and willed himself home, trying to imagine himself in the seat of his sedan, trying but failing… the babble of ads just slightly louder than the squeaking and clicking of the SkyTrain ruined the effect. *Death and ads,* he thought to himself in an effort to drown his irritation in philosophy, *the two constants of our free market society. Maybe ads are more constant, if upgrading is all it's cracked up to be…*

The SkyTrain hit a rough curve that jolted Doug, and he gripped the bar harder. He caught a child staring at him and he stared back, until he noticed that the adult with the child had been staring just as rudely. The adult, however, when confronted with Doug's arched eyebrow, looked away. *It's not like you've never seen a balding man before, moron. The kid at least has an excuse.*

He looked away. He knew that most people considered his decision not to regen his hair as eccentric at best and lazy at worst, but until he sold his car, he hadn't had to confront this on a daily basis. Now, with the little shit at work drawing attention to his lack of hair, Doug felt his credibility eroding away.

Not that he had ever doubted that he had a timeless, indisputably cool look. Even when he had realized why he had chosen this style, it didn't shake his faith — although the realization had been traumatic for other reasons.

His father had been dying for the better part of a year, and he had gone to see him at the hospital after work. The sour-smelling room was big enough to house the life-support machines and a chair, upon which Doug had spent many an hour. Since the second stroke his father hadn't been very communicative — well, he hadn't spoken — and so Doug was left to his own thoughts, which often strayed to figuring out how much it was costing him per second to keep the decaying man alive.

"…you leave…" his father had said. His eyes, rheumy slits, were locked on him.

After a moment of complicated shock, Doug had licked his lips and replied. "…You want me to leave?"

"Why did you leave Pop?" the old man wheezed.

"I didn't leave, Dad," Doug had replied.

"Pop why did you leave?"

That had been the most coherent conversation they had had in months, but it wasn't until they were going through his stuff after the funeral that Doug realized that his delirious father had mistaken him for his grandfather.

"Honey," Cheryl had said, coming into the basement. She had taken on the job of going through the mounds of decaying print photos for ones worth scanning. "Is this a relative?"

He had looked up from the box he had been sorting through and taken the picture from Cheryl. His grandfather was in the middle of a sax solo, looking suave and dashing. His solid dome head with a well-kempt monk fringe had substance, dignity.

"Yeah…" he had said. "I haven't seen this in years." When he had seen it as a boy, he hadn't recognized the family features at first, assumed it was someone famous. When his father had told him who it was, the glamour of a relation had thrilled him. His father's dismissive and abrupt descriptions had just deepened the mystery.

The SkyTrain stopped at Main Street-Science World and a bunch of people got out, including the family of starers. Doug took a seat and ignored the little boy pointing at him through the window, although it naturally attracted the attention of those who'd just entered.

Brat. Doug felt his jaw clench and forced himself to unclench it. Apparently he ground his teeth in his sleep, according to his dentist, and he occasionally wondered if this indicated anxieties so deep that they only surfaced in dreams. He made a mental note to ask his dentist if this had increased, now that his anxieties skittered freely over his consciousness at all times of the day.

Tired of watching lights flash to and fro outside the window, his eyes wandered cautiously to the other patrons. All but a few of them were watching media beamed from their watches. The middle-aged woman opposite him was particularly immersed, her mouth slightly agape. She blinked, and Doug caught an inverted flash of the guy-on-guy pornography that was being beamed onto her retinas. He quickly looked down at his own watch. *That'll teach you to be nosy, Doug ol' pal.*

He didn't select anything to watch, though, since he was pretty close to home and he had lost that apparently psychic ability that SkyTrain regulars had to prevent them missing their stop. When he was young, of course, he had had it, as well as an uncanny ability to predict where the next free seat would appear. He had lost a lot of instincts since then.

Since settling into his first car at 17, a ride befitting the prodigy at the agency, and selling his car before the bottom totally dropped out of the market at thirty-seven, not much had happened. Twenty years had passed in a comfortable but not excitement-rich bubble. Oh, there had been moments — the birth of his daughter, the death of his father, hot accounts — and mostly, these little moments, coupled with security, had been enough stimulation for him and Cheryl. But now that his security was as low as his bank account, he wondered if he had been living life too conservatively...

The doors slid open, startling him. *Was this it? Yes!* Out through the doors and, moving with the flow, through the turnstiles. A few went down the escalator here, fumbling for masks before entering the night, but Doug strode across an enclosed walkway. He loved the glass walkway, especially in the morning when it glinted with the sun, clouds looming above, safe from the torrent of traffic below. How, if you timed it right, you could see the SkyTrain gliding out of the hills and get there just in time for it to whisk you away. There was something Doug found intensely satisfying about that; it helped lighten the bitterness he felt over the loss of his car.

Maybe I could buy a used one — that kid said he got a Camaro for $150. But Cheryl had been expecting to leave since August, when they sold the cars, and would take his buying another one as proof that they were staying. She'd want a car herself, then, for her and Olivia. Probably another one of those ridiculous 6x6 SUVs that kept growing each year. Doug could tell her that it was a pointless arms race, but the mother in her would look at Olivia's fragile little body and opt for the reinforced titanium frame.

Doug walked into the condo foyer and waited for the elevator. In the doors' mirrored surface, he looked at his slightly rumpled suit with disapproval. Another lady, slightly familiar, joined him in his elevator vigil before he could smooth himself out.

"Seems like I spend half my life in these things," the lady said.

"Mmm," said Doug.

The elevator arrived. On the way up, a Self ad started up with an exaggerated yawn.

"Is there anything more boring than shuttling your meat from location to location?"

"Nope!" the lady chirped, laughing at herself. Doug put on a polite smile and glanced at her, hoping she was simply talkative. He watched the floor indicator, waiting for his number to come up. The ad droned on.

Finally, the elevator slowed. Just as the doors were opening, both the ad and the lady said, "Go for Self!" The bubbliness of her pitch and the fake-downbeat tone of the ad combined in a nauseating way, but Doug didn't turn around. He knew exactly what he'd see: the half-apologetic, half-smug look. Although she was probably a freelancer, even the professional pitchmen had that look — it wasn't actual shame then, but it was effective in defusing anger. But Doug wasn't so much angry as stunned.

Doug walked through the corridor, absorbing the experience, filtering it. Trying to ignore the cold sweat that had broken out on his brow, the metallic taste in his mouth. The fact that it had happened in his building was a bad sign. *How did she get in? Could she actually be a tenant?* Things were getting desperate.

He stood in front of 1712, wondering if he should tell Cheryl. He held the doorknob, waited for the locks to tumble, one thought racing through his mind.

We've gotta get out of here.

The little old woman stood beside the phone, stooped slightly, her ear to the receiver. The foyer was dim, with dust motes visible in the weak shafts of light. *I should really vacuum that rug,* Eileen thought vaguely.

She thought she heard a click, but no, it was still the hold jingle. She sighed and made her way around to the chintz-cushioned chair beside the phone. She lowered herself onto the chair, still listening carefully.

The music stopped. "Hello?" said Eileen.

The next song started up. Eileen sighed. She hated using the phone, always had Jeremy do those kinds of things. He always liked using the phone, accessing sites, connecting to things… even before he could talk he played with that toy phone. She smiled to think of him holding the receiver in his two chubby hands, drooling on the numbers. *Of course, maybe that was what got him into this trouble in the first place…*

"Self Technical Service," said a slightly bored voice. "Could I have your passport number please?"

Eileen had to think for a moment what the man wanted. *Self service passport?* "Well hello, I'm not sure if you're the right person to talk to…"

"What's your passport number, ma'am?"

"My Canadian passport? I didn't think they used those —"

"The passport number issued with your Self purchase ma'am, not an official document, but a reference number which we use to serve you better."

"I haven't made any purchase. I have a question about —"

"No problem ma'am, I'll redirect you to our FAQ system —"

"I was just — hello?" Eileen heard the hold music again, followed by a cheery recording.

"Welcome to our Frequently Asked Questions system. If you have a browser installed, launch it now. Otherwise, press one now."

Eileen leaned forward and pecked the worn button.

"If you have an inquiry about our special offers on Self packages, press one. If you're having problems upgrading, press two. If you have successfully upgraded and are having difficulties adjusting to your new reality, press three."

Eileen sighed, trying to remember what number it was that she had pressed before on her previous call. *Was it three?* She tried two.

"If you're having a lot of trouble, please come in person to our office in… Vancouver… at… 783 Robson Street." The address was spoken by a different voice. "Press one to —"

Eileen hung up the phone. *783 Robson.* That was near enough, and she could use the walk anyway.

It took her awhile to find her hat, even though she had stuck it in her sleeve as always. As she fumbled with her keys, she thought back to how Jeremy would always huff and fuss at the delay, saying she should get touch locks put in. She always told him it was too expensive, even though the real reason was a movie she had seen where the villain had cut off someone's fingers to unlock a door. *No thank you, I'll stick with my little keys.*

It was always like that, with them: Jeremy pushing her towards the future. She didn't mind, it was what young people did — assuming newer meant improved, seeing the flash but not the burn. But Eileen knew better.

She started off down the road, taking a pull from her o-tube every now and then. The houses in this part of town were stately old ruins, not unlike their occupants. She came up to the gate and waved at the little guardhouse — the windows were opaque, but she knew Jack was in there. Or Helen, one of them anyway.

She palmed out and pushed through the turnstile, ignoring the computer voice: "Goodbye, Eileen Ellis." There were a few taxis outside the gate, as always, and she looked for one that wasn't idling and got in. She gave the others dirty looks. What was the point of barring cars from the community when there were a dozen gas-guzzlers out there spewing fumes right outside the gate? She remembered, as she approached the humming cars, that there wasn't any gas left to guzzle, and that they were rechargeables.

Still a waste of energy, she tutted to herself as she got settled, setting her purse next to her. There was a hiss of static. "Where to?"

Eileen blinked. *Where — Robson Street. What was the number?* "Uh…"

Hiss, pop. "Sorry what was that?"

She couldn't remember the number. She stared at the speaker, not wanting to tell it that, yes, once again, one of the old biddies from Sunset Beach had forgotten where she was going. "The Self offices on Robson Street," she blurted suddenly, hoping that he knew where they were.

The taxi started to pull out. Eileen sighed, relieved. She decided that she was going to jot down some notes, while she was relaxed, to ask those Self people. She opened her grey, somewhat ratty purse (she knew she should get a new one but couldn't be bothered — anyway, who was she trying to impress?) and pulled out a notebook.

She turned it on and jotted down some notes:

1. Where is my grandson!!!

She stopped there. That was the question, and it wasn't even a question — she more or less knew the answer. So she deleted it and started again.

Why You Should Return My Grandson

- he's too young (12!)
- he's easily overstimulated
- he's my grandson

That was about it, but Eileen thought her reasons were pretty convincing. The taxi pulled up to the curb, and she fished her card out of her purse. It was a new taxi, though, and it just had a payplate.

"Driver?" she said, waving her card.

The slot snicked open, and a young woman in her twenties handed her a card reader. "Oh!" said Eileen, sliding through her debit card. "I thought you were — you sounded like a man."

"Mmm," said the girl. "Voice modulator. Less robberies that way."

"Oh," said Eileen, handing her back the reader. "Sorry for the trouble. I'm always telling my grandson: the only thing I want my watch to know is the time!"

The driver smiled, shoved the reader under the seat, and adjusted the elastic on her ponytail.

"You watch yourself, young lady," said Eileen as she slid out of the car. "I could have slit your throat easy as pie, just there." She smiled in at her and slammed the door.

Oh, do I have my — oh yes, it's right here, she thought, patting her purse. The taxi pulled away, leaving her in front of a storefront. The facade was a tasteful white and blue, with Self Technologies set in small, assured type. She took a breath and entered the building.

Inside was a plushly carpeted room with large desks. At one of the desks, a young man leaned back in a round swivel chair as he spoke to an attractive young couple. An older man was just finishing up at another desk, nearly colliding with Eileen as he waved his goodbye on the way to the door.

"Oh —" said Eileen.

"Pardon me!" the old man said. When he looked at Eileen, a twinkle came to his eye. "Just in time for folks like us, hey?"

"Well," said Eileen, but the man was past her.

"See you over there," he said with a laugh Eileen didn't like.

The woman who had been tending to the old man walked up to Eileen. Her hair was swept into a stylish bun and pinned in place, her face was fresh and inquisitive.

"Can I help you, ma'am?" she said.

What a lovely girl, thought Eileen. *She looks a little like Mary, when she was younger.* "Well yes," she began. "Maybe we should sit down," Eileen said, indicating the desk. The chair for visitors wasn't as plush, but it still looked awfully comfortable. The woman nodded and slid around to her seat, and they both sat down.

"Now. What can I help you with?" the woman said with serious eyes.

Eileen was glad it was a woman. The men could be very dismissive, especially of someone her age. "My grandson…" She stopped herself before it all came spilling out. She remembered the notes she made and started to root around in her purse for them. "My grandson is missing. Ah!" She pulled out the notebook.

The young woman looked at the notebook and then back at Eileen. "Well, that's terrible… has it been for long?"

"No, just a few days. But I received a bill from your office. I've tried to get in touch with him using the address you gave me, but there's been no answer. He had mentioned something about it being free…"

The young lady leaned back a little and nodded. "I see. Well, we do have a no-strings-attached test drive offer, but the person must go back of his or her own accord." She stopped and let that sink in. "You see? If they don't, they're charged for the time."

Eileen shook her head. "That's not like Jeremy."

"I'm sure it's not… could you slide your hand on the desk, ma'am? We need a skin sample for DNA matching." Eileen obeyed.

The young lady paused for a second, her eyes moving up and down. "Ma'am, I'm not getting any descendants of yours on the system."

Eileen smiled uneasily. "He's not my grandson, really, I suppose."

"Ma'am, of course you know we can't —"

"Can you do a search for clones?"

The young lady's eyes widened.

Eileen tilted her chin. "I call him my grandson because it's easier than explaining." *And dealing with reactions like yours. Wonder what you'd do, though, with millions of dollars and no uterus?*

The young lady blinked suddenly. "Here we are. Jeremy Ellis."

Eileen nodded, relieved. "Did you give me the wrong contact address on the bill, perhaps?"

Slow shake of the head. "No… that's correct. It says that he arrived six days ago… transferred immediately to Gamerz Heaven… and then nothing. No transfers, no data requests, no hits of any kind."

"Oh yes! I've heard of the Game Players Heaven, he wanted so badly…" Eileen stopped when she saw how puzzled the young lady looked.

"I've never seen… ma'am, could you hold on a moment? I should ask my manager about this." She touched her ear nervously and disappeared.

Eileen realized that she had been speaking to a hologram. She tutted and felt stupid that she hadn't noticed, of course a place like this wouldn't have meat help. *This manager better know —*

The young lady came back, her face composed, and a thin man even younger than the woman stood behind her. "Here you go ma'am, he'll help you." Then she blinked out.

The thin man slid carefully into the chair, and Eileen noticed how natural it looked. *They must practice that,* she thought.

"I'm Gerald, and you are…?"

"Eileen. Eileen Ellis. My… boy…"

"I've been filled in on your situation, Ms. Ellis." He rubbed his chin. "I wish I could say it was unique."

"A little boy disappearing isn't unique?" Eileen said, leaning forward.

"Well, first of all, Ms. Ellis," the thin man said, pursing his lips. "Jeremy isn't a little boy. He's entitled to all the consumer products aimed at the 12–17 demographic." He fixed her with water-blue eyes. "And he agreed to the contract."

"No one reads those things," Eileen snapped. "They just click on the I Agree button."

"Nevertheless, Jeremy agreed to the trial hour of the bronze package, and when he didn't logoff after that, he was automatically registered as an active user and charged accordingly."

"Well. I want him back." Eileen felt the skin around her cheekbones tighten.

The thin man sighed. "Ms. Ellis… we get a lot of missing people complaints, or allegedly missing people, here. Usually it's husbands and wives. And we say, if it isn't charged to a joint account, that there's really nothing we can do. In your case, if you like we can stop the payments, but they're really extraordinarily reasonable. It's practically free."

That was strange. "Why… is it so cheap?"

The thin man smiled, and began a practiced spiel. "The bronze package is subsidized by a number of corporate patrons in exchange for it being a delivery system for stimulus-rich promotion."

Eileen worked her way through that, unravelling it. "You mean... it has advertising."

"Well, yes. It's a lot more dynamic than traditional —"

Eileen felt a sweat breaking out, under her arms. "He can't have... he can't have advertising."

The couple in the desk next to them got up, looking happy. The dark-haired man looked over at Eileen, his smile failing a bit as he noticed her agitation. He followed his blond boyfriend out.

The thin man watched her, plainly debating if the time for decorum had passed.

Eileen took a big breath and tried to calm herself down. "Because of a problem when he was... born... Jeremy has an extreme sensitivity to stimulus. He even has to wear special glasses when he plays games."

The thin man nodded. "The contract he agreed to clearly states that anyone with a medical condition —"

"He's slipped into a coma before," Eileen said. "What if he's in a coma — in there?"

"The contract —"

Eileen just looked at him.

He stopped. "Ma'am, I've got to ask you to leave. There's nothing I can do about this. When your grandson wants to get in touch, he will."

She looked at him, laid the words out as carefully as she could: "Where is his body."

"You know that for security reasons, the location of our clients' bodies is a matter of the most confidential —"

"Where."

The thin man whispered something and then lifted his hands in supplication. "Ma'am, I'm afraid I'm going to have to contact a security team if you do not vacate the premises immediately. I am truly sorry about the problems between you and your... your —"

"*My grandson!*" Eileen screamed.

The thin man took a step back and disappeared.

Eileen looked at the other desk, and saw that it was empty too. She was alone. She looked at the notebook that she still clutched in her hand and slowly put it in her purse.

She got up and moved through the empty office and pushed out the door, feeling like every cell in her body was dragging her down. Outside, it was a grey-yellow twilight, and she hailed a cab. Across the street, a cube van burst open, and security men in riot gear piled out. They charged into the Self office just as she got into a taxi. She watched them mill around, her purse feeling too heavy in her lap.

Jeremy.

The next morning, Eileen got up and felt her way to the bathroom — *go to bed when it's too bright, get up when it's not bright enough.* She was halfway through relieving herself when she remembered about Jeremy, and it hit her hard, a flashfreeze. It was a few seconds before her pee started again. She sat there, feeling the cold tiles even through her calloused soles. It made her remember about how Jeremy thought she was inhuman because he couldn't tickle her feet no matter how hard he tried, while he screamed and howled at the lightest of brushes.

It was the memory of his laugh that finally drew it out of her. She bent her head and let the tears drip on her legs, a painful sound coming from her lips. She squeezed her eyes tighter, tighter… then wiped, got up. "Stoopid," she said, her sinuses having filled instantly. She splashed some cold water in her face and stared at herself in the mirror. "Don't be stupid, Eileen."

She tottered downstairs and got herself a cup of tea. She forgot to shake it first so it was pretty weak, and she wondered for the thousandth time what was wrong with teabags? Why did they have to meddle, these companies, in things that were better left alone? They pretended like they knew better, so you went along with it… even with her old job it had been like that. There were a few missions that she had had that were obviously poorly thought out, disastrous, enough so that she stopped reading the papers. The missions were supposed to help those people in the long run, help them adapt to the world market by eliminating key bad apples, but more often than not, the violence raged on like a forest fire. If you believed what you read.

By the time the caffeine really kicked in, Eileen had worked up a heart-pumping anger. And then it struck her. *Of course.* She forced herself to finish off her tea before she got up and made her way to the phone.

Her co-worker's number jumped to mind immediately, and it wasn't re-routed to some fancy new address, two good omens. Eileen was still shocked by the voice at the other end.

"Who is it?"

"It's… Eileen. Eileen Ellis."

"Eileen!" Mary squealed. "Oh my god! It's been years — decades! How… how are you?" Her initial excitement had curved down into caution.

"*I'm* fine. But… Well, it's a long story. Maybe we could meet. But I need to ask you something right away. Mary…" Eileen's eyes were squeezed closed, as much from the dust as from the tension. "Do you still have your suit?"

Eileen dabbed her cookie into what was left of her tea and took a nibble, listening intently to the glamorous woman in blue seated across from her.

"…And even if he did come back, I wouldn't want him. I'd show him the door so fast his head would spin." Mary said.

Eileen shook her head, dabbed. The waitress came around to offer tea, and Mary took some, smiling brilliantly at the waitress. *She still has her looks,* Eileen thought, amazed that the years had hardly withered her, barely streaked her hair white. Eileen's hair had gone completely white over ten years ago. The waitress moved towards her cup, but Eileen put a hand over it to stop her, and she glided away.

"Oh, you're better off without that… jerk," Eileen said. She chose her words carefully, since Mary was one to take offense rather easily. She would be telling horror stories about a man one day and then come back at you for agreeing with her the next, once he was back in her good books.

"So…" Mary said. "You ever meet a fella…" She lost her mischievous smile when she saw Eileen's face. "Better off without them. It's like they said in the company, XYbother?" She laughed at her own joke, and Eileen smiled, if just to see her old friend in good form.

"I never knew why you wanted a boy. When I heard, I said 'What? Did something go wrong?'" She was laughing again, and Eileen's answering smile was much weaker. She thought about the cloning rep advising her, in a bored tone, that the gender alteration would increase the chances of flaws. They didn't call them defects. She wondered if that could be connected to the stimulus seizures.

"I figured he would have more advantages as a man," Eileen said.

"Well, how is he?" Eileen said.

"Fine, good," Eileen said guiltily, taking the last cookie and changing the subject. "This is really a beautiful hotel."

"Yes, isn't it grand?" Mary said, looking around at the nearly empty dining room, the round ground floor of a coliseum-shaped building. "You can just smell the history. Used to be a library or some such. Terribly expensive, but I get over to Vancouver so rarely… you should come to visit! The island's so cosmopolitan now… it's no Frisco, but we try!"

"Maybe when I get my affairs sorted out," Eileen said.

"I brought what you asked me for, by the way," Mary said.

Eileen had seen the small bag immediately, but she smiled gratefully. "Thank you."

The waitress buzzed past, and Mary dropped her voice. "I'll just leave it here when I go…"

"Great." Eileen paused. "How did you keep it after —"

Mary smirked. "Well. That's a story. Remember how they were withholding my bonus? Because my facemask was 'damaged'?"

Eileen remembered it. While most of the operatives had put on any decorations with removable flash prints, she had drawn on hers with, among other things, lipstick.

"So. I was so mad. I *needed* that bonus! So I hid it, and told them I destroyed it. They were mad, but I'd already been paid up, so they couldn't dock me. And they were being dissolved by their parent corporations, so they were too busy trying to save their jobs to bother following up with me."

Eileen felt a little queasy thinking of the risk Mary had run. She tried to cover it up by sipping her tea, but noticed her hand was shaking a bit.

"I had planned to sell it — get the bonus money they screwed me for. But…" Mary shrugged expansively. "I guess once I had settled back into normal life I didn't want to, you know, get back into… that. It was going good with Larry at the time… so I just packed it away. Oh!" She covered her mouth. "Listen to this. Larry, about a year after I put it away, finds it in the bottom of a box somewhere. He takes it out and says I'm keeping secrets from him. He confronts me with it. He says, 'I can't believe you never told me you were … a scuba diver!'"

Eileen giggled.

"A scuba diver! It was a riot. I just about killed myself trying not to laugh. I was so scared I'd have to tell him the whole thing…"

"Oh, there's no point in that," Eileen said, sipping her tea. "No point at all."

"Exactly." Mary looked at Eileen, smiling sadly. "It's so good to talk to you, Eileen. I'm sorry if I'm talking your ear off."

"You're not. You're just being Mary."

Mary smiled, and her eyes landed on the bag with the suit. "Please be careful, Eileen. I'd feel so guilty if anything were to happen. Oh! And don't uplink, whatever you do. I'm sure that would set all sorts of alarms off." Her hands fluttered in demonstration. "Will you get in touch with me when you finished with whatever you're doing? So I know you're OK?"

Eileen nodded. She'd want to return the suit, anyway. "You'll be at the same number?"

"Well, if it's — if not, there'll be a forwarding service." Mary's eyes dropped, moved over the linen.

"You're going?" Eileen said dully.

"Well… of course. For the next few weeks, there's a seniors' special. You're not seriously considering… staying."

Eileen hadn't, although since this business with Jeremy the idea of trusting Self certainly wasn't appealing. She hadn't really expected to stay — she'd just assumed that they'd go when the time was right.

She hadn't considered staying, but all these presumptions about what she would want, how she would act, were making her want to dig her heels in.

"I suppose I'm not really thinking about anything beyond getting my affairs in order," she said to simplify things.

Mary nodded and smiled at her. "So you're really not telling me what you need it for?"

Eileen shifted in her seat uncomfortably, took a sip of tea that wasn't there.

"Tell me this, oh mysterious one," Mary said, her eyebrow arching. "Is it a man?"

Eileen thought, decided that it was factually true, and nodded.

Mary looked over her shoulder. "Well," she said conspiratorially, nodding at the package. "It wouldn't be the first time that suit's come out of retirement to deal with some cheating little shit."

That night in her bathroom, Eileen used a small silver mirror to look at her back, wishing that the mirror's makers had been more concerned with surface area than ornate detailing. But a few angles later, and crouching slightly, she was able to see it.

Although the skin around it was blotchy and greyish, the small black hole hadn't changed at all. The knob of spine that it was drilled through was different, less symmetrical. She was worried that it might have grown over, sealed up like her belly-ring hole had. But no, it looked solid. But was the rest of her solid enough to withstand the connection?

She opened up the Nordstrom's bag that the suit was packed in. Mary had also wrapped it in brown paper and tied the whole thing up, so it took Eileen a few seconds to free the blacksuit. She rolled it out on the bed.

Uniform was what they had been trained to call it — there weren't any logos or anything — and the technical name was some military mumbo jumbo that had sounded impressive but that Eileen had immediately forgotten.

Forgot what a trial it was to get this thing on, Eileen thought, stepping into the jet-black neoprene bodysuit, pulling it up past her bare, blue-veined legs. She stuffed her bare arms in, and, holding her white hair in place, pulled the head mask over and waited in the pitch darkness.

The sealing sequence started immediately, and Eileen felt the zipper slowly crawl up her back. She felt her sagging breasts barely bumping the bodysuit's surface and thought that she — *ow!*

The zipper had caught some loose skin. Feeling blindly, Eileen found and yanked the zipper down, holding her back straighter this time. The zipper resumed its crawl. Eileen hoped that Jeremy would see the note she had left for him in the unlikely chance he made it back on his own. *He'll open that fridge sooner rather than later,* was her thought as the suit plugged into her central nervous system.

The familiar triumphant chime. The sudden rush of electrically induced adrenalpro. The brightening of surroundings, first in low rez blocky shapes and then high, higher, perfect rez. "System speed," Eileen mouthed, and her heart rate showed normal.

She walked around the room, trying the eyes in the back of her head, moving her body in some limbering exercises she hadn't thought about in years. Her body sent sharp little reminders of this fact to her joints, and it took a lot just not to cry out.

"Pain Mute on."

The numbness settled over her like gauze, and she was able to stand up straight, even arch her back. Her sharper vision noticing it, she wiped the dust off the full-length mirror, leaving a grey streak on the edge of her matte black hand.

Glove, Eileen corrected, knowing that it was futile to resist thinking about her suit as part of her. She let out a bark of a laugh as she focused on her face — *mask, I mean.*

Mary, you silly girl. She had forgotten the outrageous face Mary had drawn on: large red lips, blue almond eyes, a cartoon femme fatale painted on her mask. Eileen had preferred the unadorned black, had felt that the smiley faces and such were a bit inappropriate — not to mention a good target — but she herself couldn't help tittering a little as she looked at how the vamp face contrasted with her bony pelvis and bulging knees.

"Set system speed to 500%," she mouthed. Nothing happened. *Was it working?* She reached forward and flicked the mirror. Nothing.

She looked around at her room. *Well, it had been years —*

The mirror, where she had flicked it, had an indent. Then, as if someone was sketching them, crack marks leisurely spidered out from the indent.

Eileen felt relief. She left her room and went into Jeremy's. His cubespace was on — as it always was — and the Self contract was floating there, a sinister writ. Beside it was another subcube, something else he was working on. She stared at the strings of numbers and letters. *He was so clever.* As she focused on it, her suit said, "Decrypting document Deep Inside Lois Lane...10% decrypted..."

"Cancel job," Eileen said, feeling an odd flutter in her chest. *That wouldn't help me find him,* she told herself. *What I need is to be uplinked! I could get his current coordinates from his watch...*She opened a file.

"New target file opened. Data?" the suit whispered in her ear.

"Name: Jeremy Ellis. Primary occupant of room." Eileen leaned over his desk and sniffed. The suit needed more, so she took another, deeper sniff, her facemask almost touching the desk.

"Cloned 2025. Hair black, eyes —"

Eileen stopped the flow of data the DNA sample had provided. "Evidence of other occupants?"

There weren't any. Self hadn't sent out agents to take Jeremy away — or at least, not organic agents. That would have been too easy.

Gently closing the door with its *Gamerz Only!* sign on it, she thought about the time that he had explained to her, so seriously, that she was an honorary gamer and thus was admitted past the threshold.

The suit asked, "Would you like to uplink? Yes or No."

"No," she said, jogging down the stairs.

"Not uplinking means that you might be depriving yourself of critical information regarding your target. Are you sure? Yes or No."

"Yes," she snapped.

She opened the door and stepped out into the chilly night air. The suit automatically adjusted. "Track Jeremy," she said. Blue blotches appeared here and there, solidifying into a trail going down their garden path and stopping at the sewer.

As she shut the door behind her, she realized that she'd left her keys upstairs, and even if she went back for them she had no pockets to keep them in. She walked away from her house with one last anxious glance at its unlocked state. *Don't be stupid. If someone breaks in, you can track them down and —* she stopped it, the voice. It was the voice that always accompanied the suit, as much a part of it as the nagging whisper. But it was her, this voice — a harder, stronger, colder her.

She reached the street. Jeremy's traces stopped at the sewer. They may have dissipated naturally, or the Self agent may have... she lifted the sewer grate set into the middle of the road, as if it were a pot lid, and climbed down. Reaching up, she snagged it with a few fingers and slid it back into place. The clank it made, slowed down, stretched over a few seconds.

The tunnel glowed with grey-green infrared. There were no traces of Jeremy, but she knew where she was heading. The walls were thick with the filth of centuries, the few inches of water equally fetid. She imagined a spider sentry with Jeremy in tow, scuttling down the tunnel. *They dragged my boy through —*

She put the adrenaline that the rage fed her to work, jogging down the tunnel. By the time the shattered glass had finished dropping from her bedroom mirror, a crystalline snowfall, she was several city blocks away.

The two men stood together on the little knoll, hands in pockets. The taller man wore blue knee-length shorts and an unbuttoned golf shirt, while the shorter man was overdressed, holding his blazer in the crook of his arm as he made his case. It was hard to say for sure, because both men had scrambled blurs where their faces should be, but by his body language the taller man seemed more interested in watching the children play.

"Now you see, this is what I'm talking about," the tall man said, pointing a beefy finger at the blur-faced children. "This is the second time that kid has fallen down in that exact place. This picnic doesn't even have a decent loop rate."

"Paul, c'mon, you know we have a budget limit on these things —"

"But you're not even trying. Your heart ain't in it. It's all work work work with you guys. Look at you, Al — with your tie on. Come on!"

"It's just... I've got a meeting after," Al mumbled, deleting his tie and loosening his collar. "Better?"

"Pathetic," Paul said, turning around and looking at the adults swarming around the barbeque. "I mean, we're in the culture industry, the ones the ordinary joes look to to spice up their lives, and this is the best recreation you come up with?"

Al lifted his hand to the sky. "Whattaya talking about? It's a beautiful day. Look at those clouds! Those are high-quality clouds, Paul. Not a chance of rain."

"My point exactly!" Paul said, taking his hand out to point at the shorter man. "No chance of anything. Where are the ants, Al?" He shook his head. "Now the Branders picnic, that was something. They had some terrorists come in and shoot the place up. Pitchmen screaming, people running everywhere." He laughed.

Al made a sour noise. "Aw, that's in poor taste. Especially in light of the Exxon Massacre..."

"Creative. That's what it was. Everyone shitting their pants, even though they knew they couldn't be killed. All it took was a few holo's getting their heads perforated to accessed that fear. It's hardwired into us, even if we are just software."

"Well, I remember a time when we didn't have to wear scramblefaces," Al said. "That dates me, but it's true."

"Well, the cutting edge sometimes cuts back," Paul said with an easy laugh.

Al shook his head and chuckled. "That's what I admire about you, Paul —

you can turn anything on its head. Make crazed terrorists seem like they're keeping us sharp. Our firm, on the other hand, has been the bedrock of the industry for longer than you've been alive. And that's why I think we'd make a great team to go for the Self account."

"Oh, good lord! Not you, too, Al!" Paul said, making a gesture of pulling his hair out that was obscured by his scrambleface. "Don't tell me you're going on this wild goose chase, too!"

Al turned away, seemed on the verge of giving up. Then he turned back. "It's not a wild goose chase. It's the biggest single account in the history of business."

"I don't even believe that Self's operations are generated by an artificial intelligence, Al. It's all a scam to convince the end users that it's all top secret and totally secure. But even if that wasn't a scam, don't you realize that it's the same old story? In the old days they'd dare kids to hack their code, and kids would spend man-years finding ways to get in — which the company would then patch."

Al laughed. "I think it's a little different than that, Paul. Our profession consists of the finest cultural analysts and data miners on Earth."

"Self gets us to exhaust our resources to simply give them information about their operations that they already know and are promising an undisclosed exclusive deal in return... If you can't see the connection," Paul said. "Then I guess you can't."

A phone floated by in mid-air, between them, but Al didn't notice and started to say something. Paul held up a hand. "I've got a call."

He turned away slightly, holding his hand in a phone shape to his ear. The connection was made immediately.

The voice was warbly from the strain of several filters. "There's something going on at the Robson Street Self office. Do you want me to check it out?"

"Definitely, Honey, eight sounds good."

"OK, contact me when you're alone. I'll have more info then." Click.

"You were right to give this picnic a miss, Hun," Paul continued, looking over at Al's slumped form. "These fellows don't know how to loosen up." A laugh.

Al raised a timid hand goodbye and went back to the barbeque. "All right sweetheart," Paul said to no one. "Yes, I'll remember."

Alone on the knoll, he held his hands behind his back and watched the children. As one of them tripped and skinned her knee for the third time, he disappeared, leaving the little girl to her eternal fate.

Nicky got to the launch about an hour after the invite said it started, entering the brightly lit Molson's Gallery to be immediately caught in the staring crossfire. Trying not to scurry, Nicky moved towards the art. She held JK's folded bike in front of her where it was less obvious in an attempt to minimize her oddness level, feeling the tiny feet of her little creature crawling over the back of her jean jacket. *Maybe the gecko was a bit much.*

She looked at the boxed holo. It was a cavern, an underground mine, judging by the little railcars.

"Well you know what *they're* like. You're lucky you got out of it with your scalp intact," said someone behind Nicky.

Someone else replied in a tone too low to hear. Nicky leaned forward to examine the box, picking out tiny figures hacking away at the cavern walls. *Dwarves?*

"I think you're right," said the first voice, which was quiet but distinct. "He's just the type. Too young to be that intense, but he's staring at your stuff pretty hard."

Nicky glanced back. The guy with the distinct voice had a large grey afro in which he had stuck mirrored sunglasses. The mumbler was the artist — Mike something — who looked uncharacteristically nervous. Nicky moved away before Mike recognized her, even though it was unlikely with her new hairdo.

There was a cash bar with a kind of cute bartender. She looked at the price list — $10 for a Coke, $15 for a Molson Ex, $17 for Evian, $20 for a Tropicana — and she almost considered treating herself to an OJ, seeing as she just got paid. *I can get a whole box for the same price at Safeway,* she thought. *I'll get some on my way home.*

She walked away, returning the bartender's smile nervously, wondering what kind of clothes he wore when he wasn't in his tux t-shirt uniform. She imagined herself asking him that, and a thrill of terror passed through her.

She stationed herself in front of another box. This was the one that had been on the invite — the unicorn trotting around the distressed woman with the heaving bosom. Nicky noticed that the artist had spent more time on the princess' erect nipples than on the unicorn's whole head, but that was typical. He had done a not-bad job on the field, though...

"Who do you identify with more?" said a familiar voice.

Nicky turned to see a middle-aged man who she'd never seen before. She inwardly sighed as she looked at the guy's blank stare, his almost empty Molson. *JK, where the fuck are you?* "Uh… neither." She looked back, and, sensing he wasn't going away, challenged: "What about you?"

"Probably the unicorn," he said with a smile that loosened up the severity that his short grey hair gave his features. "I feel more… fancy-free than stressed out these days."

"You think unicorns are free?" said Nicky, not meaning to be challenging, just genuinely surprised.

"Well, look at that one," he said. "Trotting around all over the place."

"He's anxious. Constantly on the move. He's hunted," Nicky said, plucking the gecko from the cuff of her jacket just as it was on the verge of slipping up her sleeve. "Doomed," she said as she placed the gecko back on her shoulder. "And she's probably in on it, with her exaggerated damsel-in-distress routine. She's probably the bait."

The man laughed. "Huh," he said. "I'm going to get another drink," he said with a waggle of his empty bottle. "Want one?"

"Sure," Nicky said, figuring that since he didn't make the obvious virgin-unicorn crack he'd do until JK arrived. She scanned the room, which had filled up a bit with the usual suspects since she had arrived. She caught the eye of a tall blond girl across the room and waved.

"*No thank you*," Mike said, his voice suddenly crisp and carrying all over the room. He leaned forward and shoved a business card back into a young man's blazer pocket. The young man — the one that had been spotted earlier, Nicky supposed — smiled ruefully and left the gallery. Mike, his sneer not entirely covering up a grin, turned back to his friends. His crony with the afro squeezed his shoulder, nodded approvingly.

The buzz in the gallery increased noticeably, and Nicky tried not to get angry. She moved to the next box and stared at it, not absorbing anything.

"What was that?" said the short-haired man, who had returned with a beer for her.

"Thanks," Nicky said, taking a sharp pull on the cold bottle without even looking at it. "That was the first step in the dance known as Artistic Success."

"Wha — who was the stiffy?" the short-haired man asked.

"Recruiter. Probably freelance. Offered to rep Mike as a creative."

"And he turned him down?" said the man incredulously, his ample eyebrows raised. "Wow."

"No. Yes," Nicky said, taking another pull at her bottle, tasting it this time.

"Ahhhh… it's so fake and stupid."

They looked at the box for a moment. It featured a man lying on a slab.

"How is it success if he —"

Nicky sighed. "It's just the first move. If an artist doesn't reject the first offer vehemently enough, then he's not the real thing. The coolhunter loses interest."

"Ah," said the short-haired man. "Hard-to-get."

They watched as an astral projection struggled out of the man on the slab and flew off. The short-haired man leaned back and read out the title of the piece. "Goeth for Self." He laughed.

Nicky rolled her eyes.

He noticed her reaction. "Oh come on, it's funny!"

"It's *easy*," frowned Nicky.

"Well," he said, pointing his bottle at it, "Not everything has to be difficult. It's like… commentary. On how we've attained the ability to do something we've dreamed about for centuries."

"So they keep telling us," Nicky said, something about black magic bouncing around in her head but not getting out. "But… I mean, why be an artist if all you're going to do is echo?"

"Whoa!" said the short-haired man. "I'm just a code monkey, ma'am. What do I know about that? Let's ask this guy," he said, nodding at the door.

JK had just walked in, a big smile on his face as he greeted a few people. He waved and made his way towards them.

Nicky looked at the short-haired guy through slitted eyes. "Hey! You know JK?"

He shrugged innocently.

JK was briefly chatting with Mike, then plucked the mirrored sunglasses from the guy with the afro and put them on. Their owner checked him out and approved with an a-ok finger circle. JK finally made it to them.

"Chase! Nicky!" he said. "You found each other!"

Nicky watched her scowl melt in the giant mirrors on JK's face.

"Well, there weren't too many octopus-haired gals carrying bicycles…" said Chase.

Nicky snickered. "Those sunglasses…"

"Are they working for me?" he said, his smile cranking up even higher.

"And how," Nicky said, feeling her mood pull out of the dark concentric spiral.

"I wish I could see something in them," he said, looking around the room. He took them off and returned his normal specs to his face, poking himself in the eye with the handle as he did so.

Chase arched an eyebrow. "What are you on, man?"

"Do you guys wanna go… somewhere?" JK said, waving at someone.

"Uh huh!" Nicky said. *Yay JK!*

Chase shrugged. "OK. Where?"

JK gave them the thumbs-up, and started heading towards the exit.

They followed JK as he cut a cheery swath through the room, now dense with humanity. Nicky gave Chase an encouraging smile, sensing he seemed a bit irked by JK's choppy conversation, and answered for him.

"Somewhere interesting, probably."

By the time they got there, it was pretty late.

"This is perfect," said JK, indicating the expanse of asphalt. "Let's hang out here for a while."

They were in the shadow of Science World. It was a giant sphere lodged on the brink of the inlet, its mirrored structure divided into triangles by a metal frame. Nicky remembered the first time she'd entered it, how disappointed she'd been by the regular box shapes of the buildings it housed. But the wonderful exhibits soon distracted her.

JK was unrolling his bike, the tires hissing and the joints clicking into place.

"Do you guys remember coming here as a kid?" she said.

"Uh huh!" said JK. "I remember one time I was here on a class trip." He got on the bike and started riding around. "They had this thing where you could experience what it was like to be a seed. Like the growth cycle. You got into this jelly box…"

Chase, sitting on the soft asphalt, leaned back on his palms and grinned. "Jelly? Oh, you mean that biomass stuff?"

Nicky was watching JK weaving back and forth in circles that seemed on the verge of collapsing. "You sure you're OK on that thing?"

JK ignored her. "Yeah, biomass jelly. Tricked your body into thinking it was something else. It was kind of messy, but we loved the stuff."

Nicky gave up and sat on the ground, crossed her legs. She remembered something really impressing her at Science World, but couldn't put her finger on it. A color wheel? No, a prism. A giant prism hanging from the rafters, refracting.

All colors coming from white. Black being the absence of color.

"Something similar in Toronto," Chase said. "Science Centre, I think it was called. Real original."

They laughed at that for a while. "Well, it beats Science World II I guess."

"Science World II: Back to the Lab," Nicky said. JK snickered at this, and Nicky felt her annoyance at being ignored lighten. "You from Toronto?" she asked Chase.

JK rode away towards the edge of the water.

Chase shook his head. "Nope. About an hour outside it. Closer to Montreal, really." He was making finger imprints in the asphalt. He looked up at her. "Where are you from?"

"New West," she said, trying not to look at JK as he climbed up on the frame of his bike. "Oh man!"

Chase turned to see what she was gaping at. JK was standing on his frame as the bike rolled briskly along the edge of the waterfront, his broad shoulders making an absurd silhouette. Chase smiled and shrugged.

"He's not even on the asphalt anymore, it's just concrete along the water…" Nicky said. *And what if he fell in the water?* "Those things make me nervous." She focused on her gecko, which was leaning off her jacket to tongue the ground.

"Ah, they're not as dangerous as all that. I'm an old guy, so I remember when you could still ride them around," he said with a smirk. "Kids fell off them all the time… it was only in the ads that they fell under the wheels of passing convoy trucks."

Nicky felt queasy, remembering an ad of that kind where a woman was riding her bike with a baby seat into traffic. It was in slow motion — you fully expected her to be broad-sided and her and her baby to be brutally mangled. Instead, a car swerving to avoid her causes a three-car pile-up, and she rides off unscathed. It ends with a close up on the window of one of the wrecks where someone's scrabbling to get out just before it explodes.

Chase saw the look on her face. "I mean, people rode them for a hundred years before those ads came on," he said.

People did a lot of stupid things, Nicky thought. She wished he'd change the subject. That ad had given her nightmares for years.

"Bikes are good fun," Chase continued. "Right JK?"

JK came up, riding on one wheel. He balanced there for a second, and then, with a quick move with his heel, hit the lever that disassembled it. He landed squarely on his feet in what Nicky had to admit was a pretty neat move.

"Where'd you learn how to do that?" she said.

"Where'd I learn how to do anything?" JK said with a smile.

"Everyone used to know how to ride a bike," Chase said. "But traffic got so bad people were always getting in accidents or collapsing from smog and then getting hit… it was either change the automotive industry or make a bunch of scary public service announcements…"

Nicky shrugged. She'd heard conspiracy stories all her life — she'd been a fan of the genre, when she was, like, 12. The whole air thing seemed exaggerated as well. Her eyes started to sting after a few hours outside, it was true, but she had allergies.

As it hissed and clicked closed, Chase asked, "There's no smart parts in there at all? Not even in the rollup mech?"

JK shook his head. "Nope. The Czechs are geniuses at simple machinery. Wanna give it a try?"

Chase declined.

"Nicky?" JK asked.

Nicky was on the verge of refusing when she heard Chase's bark of a laugh. A potent mix of contrariness and annoyance forced her to her feet.

"Yeah, OK."

JK smiled with delight, unrolled the bike with a flick of his wrist. He adjusted it to her height. After placing the gecko into her pocket — it was nearly still, seeming to know something was happening — she lifted her leg over the frame. Grabbing a handful of JK's shirt for balance, she stood up on the pedals and sat on the seat.

Then, gritting her teeth and bracing for a fatal accident, she pushed off.

Wobble wobble wobble straight straight straight! Nicky felt victory rise from her belly as real as the night air on her face. She kept on away from them, smiling as she heard their cheers, and headed around the Science World structure.

The lights across the inlet, the commercial district, were bright enough to easily navigate by, but as she rounded the sphere it got decidedly darker. She looked up at the mostly residential hillside and tried to figure out if there were less lights now than a year ago…

Shit is that a pole? Nicky swerved a little too tightly, and the bike fell over on top of her. "Fuck…" she said, struggling to extricate herself from the stupid thing. She got up quickly — she had fallen hip first, but the asphalt had cushioned her fall — and glanced backwards to see if she was within sight of the guys. They were hidden by the curve. *Good.*

She started walking the bike the same direction she had been riding. Her hip was fine, probably wouldn't even bruise. Her face was still burning, though, and she remembered an incident in the second grade, after a classmate had pushed her down. The playground security guard just lectured her about the playground being hard as stone when *he* was a kid — obviously having long forgotten the sting of humiliation that the new bouncy substance was powerless to reduce.

It was a long way round, so Nicky decided to get back on the horse. A little more tentative than she had with her annoyance-fuelled first try, she nonetheless was able to pedal herself to a straight line. She kept her eyes in front of her this time.

By the time Chase and JK were in sight, her eyes had adjusted to the darkness, and the relative brightness strained her eyes. She rolled up and swung off the bike.

"There she is," said JK. "Thought you found a way to ride on water."

Chase was lying down now, head propped up on one hand. "So you *have* ridden bikes before."

Nicky was trying to kick the same place where JK had. "Nope. First time." She hit the lever just as JK was about to help, and it rolled up. She handed it to him, a little relieved and a little reluctant to be giving it up.

"So is it the same kind of exhibits?" JK asked Chase.

"Uh… kinda," Chase said. "They have a Science World thing in Frisco," he explained to Nicky.

Nicky sat down and hugged her knees. "A *Science* World? That doesn't make any sense!"

"There's no science there," added JK.

"I know, it's kind of… they call it the Science and Technology Pavilion. They have these pavilions that they suggest you go to on your free hour. It's a similar set-up though… you know the ball that when you touch it and your hair stands on end?"

Nicky nodded. "To demonstrate static electricity, yeah, but there's no —"

"Don't ask me," Chase protested, "I know. Anyway, they have the same thing except that when it sticks out it starts to grow. So I did it, and everyone's laughing, and when they turn off the ball my hair's, like, super long."

JK laughed. "You with long hair. Ha! How long?"

"Like, down to my butt. And I could swish it around and feel it on my back and stuff—"

"But what does it have to do with science? It's all a software demo," Nicky said.

"It's a theme, I guess. Showing people familiar things. They had a zoo, too, and a shopping mall, that was really the most impressive —"

"A zoo, huh?" Nicky said, staring at her little creation. "Any geckos at this zoo?"

"No," he said. "A giant lizard of some sort though."

"All cute or impressive, though, right?" she said. The gecko was flicking its tongue at her nose. She had given it a double-forked one, and it fanned her nose.

"I guess so. I don't remember any ugly and unimpressive animals, but I probably wouldn't." He laughed. "There was a unicorn there, I remember that."

Nicky hissed in response, and the gecko scuttled to the far side of her hand. "Unicorns suck. Why would it have to be a zoo? If they can do anything there, why not have the animals mixing with the humans? Why does it have to be the same old shit?"

"It's true, it's pretty uncreative at the moment. It's improved a lot, though," Chase said. "I used to live there."

"Chase was in Frisco before it was Frisco," JK said.

"Oh yeah?" Nicky said, surprised. "Were you coding there?"

"I think so..." Chase said, squinting his eyes in a pantomime of remembering.

They all laughed.

"Yeah. It was still a relief effort for those crippled by the Quake, and they were looking for anyone who could code... back in those days you actually had to go down to San Francisco — what was left of it — to uplink."

"Huh!" Nicky said. The brother of a friend in high school had gone as well, and she had thought he was brave. "How long were you there?"

"For most of 2031, I guess. Ten or eleven months. Of course, it was just a blink of an eye to me — if I hadn't been flashbacked in a different room from where I'd been processed for uplinking I wouldn't have even noticed anything had happened."

"Wow," Nicky said. She'd heard about the revert-to-saved transition but she'd never met anyone who'd been through it. It seemed so unfair.

"It's not so bad, now," Chase said. "They make a full recording of your time in Frisco — although past a certain point..."

"Who wants to sit through eleven months of life?" JK said.

"Exactly," said Chase. "You're invested in Frisco, once you stay a certain length of time."

"I guess you could fast-forward past the embarrassing or boring parts,"

Nicky said, poking the gecko awake.

"Your little guy wishes he could fast-forward this part," JK said. "'Let's go home, Nicky, I'm hungry!' he's thinking." JK did the gecko in a soprano voice that made the little creature look at him.

"One of my plans was to set up a service to edit people's lifecordings for them," Chase said. "But..."

"No one comes back, practically," Nicky finished. "You're the first one I've met."

"Yeah," JK said. "You freak of nature. What's wrong with you? Everyone else's having a great time over in Frisco!"

Chase just shrugged.

"Tell her what you do now," JK told Chase. When the older man rolled his eyes, JK said, "He does the menus for all the Ristwatch products." JK mumbled into his watch.

"Please hold your Ristwatch up to your eyes for retinal positioning," Chase's calm voice said from JK's watch.

"Please hold your Ristwatch up to your ass for rectal positioning," the real Chase mimicked.

They laughed, and the sudden noise startled the gecko.

"I knew your voice sounded familiar!" Nicky said.

She had plotted her walk home for maximum pleasure and minimum danger. Although the air would be cleaner with a little more rain, Nicky was happy to have a stretch of rainless days after the wet winter, taking shallow breaths and wondering for the thousandth time about getting a mask. *Too damn geeky*, she concluded for the thousandth-and-first time.

She was walking along the edge of the Pleasant Acres neighborhood, the leafy trees poking out from the bars of the 20-foot high fence. A few blocks in she could smell the green — imagined the oxygen sliding into her bloodstream. *Better than an o-tube,* she thought, *but then stolen oxygen always tastes better.*

She passed the guardhouse at the entry gates, curiously looking in. She saw the outline of a KrazyCar in a driveway, its fins giving it a distinct silhouette. The first time she'd seen the tiny car advertised — it showed a dozen or so clowns bouncing out of it, although it was clearly only big enough for one — she had figured it'd be dead in the water, regardless of getting eighty miles to the charge. *Guess that's why I'm not a coolhunter...*

A block or so beyond the guardhouse she saw a person beside the gate, a big pile of something on the ground beside him. There was the familiar *krac!* and the pile, which was a person covered in blankets, jerked with the flow of electricity.

Oh shit, thought Nicky, stopping in her tracks. The guard was putting his taser gun back into its holster and lazily heading back to the guardhouse. He noticed her and kept his hand on the laser.

Nicky looked at the person-pile, who glowed and jerked. "They, you know, they're just here because the air's better. Two people died last year from oh-two deprivation, you know," she said, repeating herself in her nervousness.

The guard stopped in front of her, the brim of his hat shadowing his eyes. "She's not allowed to camp on the property, miss." He walked away.

Nicky continued, numb. Then she whipped around. "As if electrocuting her is going to help!" she yelled, feeling lame.

Her words had no noticeable effect on the guard's lanky strides.

As Nicky passed the twitching body, she could hear a whimpering, but she kept walking. *At least she's not dead...*

Pleasant Acres was ending, and it was separated from Joy Enclave by a freeway. She decided to walk along the side of the freeway, since otherwise she'd have to pass under it through a creepy and stinky underground tunnel.

Fucking security. Torturing an old woman to protect a bunch of empty houses.

She followed the little path for a couple of nervous minutes beside a flow of whizzing metal until it dipped down and under the freeway. She told her watch to turn on her halo field, and for a second she thought she had used up her minutes... but then it glowed bright enough to see. She was glad she had it, for the light as well as the protection — there were usually a few people sleeping there. No one tonight, though.

As usual, Nicky was glad to get out from the shadow of the freeway bridge, even though the train yard wasn't the safest place either. But she could keep to the wide open spaces out here, where there weren't that many places for hypothetical attackers to lunge from. She figured she'd be able to turn on the protective field in time if someone came running across the field, so she turned off her halo.

It's not even that dark, Nicky said scornfully to her scared half. In fact, it seemed brighter than normal. She could see the individual rocks blackened to coal in between the long dead tracks, the strands of a weed that looked like wheat.

Ahead, she saw a boxcar that had a faint aura around it. She walked up to the boxcar and stopped, listening. She couldn't hear anything, so she decided to proceed fieldless to save her minutes.

She rounded the rotting artifact and discovered a spotlight trained on it, lighting up a strange design. The design looked new: a colorful image of a fat man sitting on a basketball, smoking a huge joint. *Give it up, fatty, give up the fatty, give it up for the b-boyz and b-girlz* were some of the words that Nicky read uncomprehendingly.

What it meant was a puzzle; who had put it there was a bigger one. She couldn't recognize any brands. Maybe Nike, with the basketball... maybe Marlboro, but they always spelled it "phatty" (something about the negative connotations of obesity, she remembered from class). And the image was so rough, the paint wasn't solid in places...

Fear pulled her out of her reverie when she remembered where she was. She turned around quickly, the solid wall of the boxcar at her back, and looked around as best she could with the spotlight in her face. A bit to her right, she noticed another spotlit boxcar and what looked like two figures facing it.

Were they the people behind these things? she thought, apprehensive but curious. "Protective field," she said, and as the halo surrounded her, she headed towards them. *What were they doing?*

They looked like they were working on a picture similar to the other one. As she got closer, she could hear a hissing sound starting and stopping, and the murmur of their voices. The bearded one stopped and shook something that made a clicking sound, noticing her as he did so.

"Good evening," he said with a mock formality.

"Hi," said Nicky, stepping into the light pool.

The other one looked at her, his angular black face showing nothing.

The first one, who had his hair in thick brown ropes, asked "So you enjoying the show?"

A show? She noticed that they weren't painting from scratch, but instead tracing over a design. "Why are you doing this?" she asked, feeling stupid but asking anyway.

"We're restorin' some of Vancouver's finest art," the bald black man said, his face serious. "These pieces date back to the early nineties."

"They're paintings," Nicky said, understanding. She was glad she hadn't asked if they were ads. The painting of interlocking shapes they were working on took up the entire surface, except for a small patch where it wound around the letters CN. But then Nicky realized that they weren't interlocking shapes after all

— they were letters.

"Virus," she read aloud. "Virus CN?"

"Canadian National is the brand of the boxcar," the bald man said. "Virus is the tag." He tossed the can he was holding and walked away.

"Graffiti artists had codenames, or tags, that they used to sign their work," said the man with the beard. "Get me another orange, willya Andre?"

Andre was unzipping a small green tent beside the boxcar. "If we have one."

"These paints are really hard to find. Krylon stopped making them when flashing got big," the bearded man said. He yawned and pulled at his ropes of hair as if to keep himself alert.

"Why don't you just flash these things?" Nicky said. "You could just scan it in and adjust the color levels."

The bearded man laughed, a glimpse of tattooed teeth. Andre came back and handed a can to him, popped the cap off his own. "Hey Andre, she wants to know why we don't just flash these things."

Andre snorted through his nose. Nicky felt her face begin to burn.

The bearded man held his hands up, as if he detected her growing annoyance. "OK, so there were these graffiti artists. In the eighties, nineties. They used the city as a canvas. Made these murals, sometimes with permission of the wall owners, sometimes without."

"Usually without," Andre interjected between his can's hissing.

"Yeah well, some of them decided that it wasn't fair to keep all this talent and art in the city — so they snuck into the train yards at night." He thumbed back to the painting. "And did up some freight trains."

Nicky waited for the point. "Uh huh."

"Well, I mean, they did up ones that were active. And the people who drove the trains didn't have the time to paint over them — they couldn't just flash them blank like nowadays. So imagine this. You're on your way to, I don't know, your grain silo, you're in your truck in the middle of Saskatchewan. You come to the train tracks and you stop cause there's a train coming."

"And these boxcars are on it?" Nicky guessed.

"Exactly!" the bearded guy said, slapping his hands together. "So this guy's sitting there, getting a surprise art show. So these graffiti artists basically exported urban culture to the countryside."

Andre looked at him, his even white teeth showing in a slight smile. "Exporting urban culture. Exporting ego, more like."

Nicky laughed.

"I'm serious!" the bearded guy said. With his eyes bright like that, Nicky saw that he wasn't as old as he had seemed at first. She wasn't used to seeing young guys with beards. "I know it was ego too, and they didn't think of it like that, exactly — but that's the beautiful thing about it. It was all accidental, kinda. And to get to your question, the traditional graf scene died out with the flashing technology. 'Cause it was super hard to get paint, and even if you did get a piece up it'd be flashed off in a second. There were a few writers who got into flash pieces—"

Andre shook his head. "Not the same. Not the same."

"Yeah," the bearded guy shrugged with one shoulder. "It was pretty much over."

"So it would be kind of sacrilegious to flash them," Nicky guessed.

"Exactly. *Exactly!*" the bearded man said. He held his hand flat to his chest. "My name's Simon," he said. "This's Andre."

"Nicky." She waved, not ready to turn off her field to shake hands.

"Well Nicky," Simon said. "I'm glad you came across our art show. Where are you coming from?"

Nicky smiled as she realized it for the first time. "An art show."

They laughed at that. "You *must* be an artist," Andre said, not turning around.

"Kinda," Nicky said. "Not like this, really. Not painting. I make little animals." She would have shown them the gecko but it always hid when her field was activated. *Not really representative of my style, anyway.* She felt a need to impress this strange pair, but ended up tongue-tied. *As usual.*

"Oh yeah," Simon continued, when it was clear she wasn't going to elaborate. "Splicing, cloning, that kind of thing?" His eyes seemed interested.

"Yeah. I've got this series of ratdog splices that has a kind of mythic theme," she said, trying not to wince. *God, that sounded pretentious.*

"Sounds yum," he said appreciatively. "Are you showing somewhere?"

"No no," Nicky said, already wishing she hadn't said anything. "I'm just fooling around. I haven't got a chance at sponsorship. No one'll touch biologicals."

"Good for you," said Andre. "That means you're the real thing."

Nicky was afraid he was mocking her, even though Simon was nodding at her, and she didn't have the energy to sort out what the hell they were talking about. "I gotta go," she said suddenly with a lame smile. "Bye."

She walked away, out of their weird circle of light and towards home.

As soon as Doug shut the door behind him, he felt something hit his lower body. Something soft. He pried her off and lifted her up. "Olivia," he said, looking into her green eyes. "Trying to kill me?"

"Hi Dad," she said with a calm smile that belied her projectile state just moments before. She lunged forward and planted a kiss. "Whatja get me?"

He dropped her.

"JJ Dad, JJ," she said, hugging his leg. Just Joking or not, it was not what he wanted to hear with McDonald's gas still roiling in his belly. *Should have picked her up one of those toys there.*

He walked into the living room, pretending like Olivia wasn't clinging to his leg. His wife was watching some comedy show. "Hey Sweetie," she said, glancing at him briefly.

"Looks like I picked up a parasite somewhere, Cheryl," he said in a serious voice. Olivia quietly giggled.

He had Cheryl's full attention now. Her face, slack from watching her show, now cycled through amusement and feigned worry.

"Down here on my leg," Doug said, putting his hands on his hips.

Cheryl leaned over on the couch arm and saw Olivia. "Uh oh," she said with a smile. "That looks really bad, Doug. Why, it almost looks... it almost looks like a little girl."

"I *am* a little girl!" said Olivia. "Not a parachute."

"Yes," Doug said. "I believe it's the littlegirlus parasite again. I'm going to have to operate." He wiggled his long piano-player fingers and descended on Olivia. He tickled her methodically and mercilessly.

"Daaaaaaaaaad!" she screamed.

"My, the parasite certainly makes a lot of noise," said Cheryl with a grin.

"It's probably just gas being released," explained Doug, stopping for a second. Olivia took the moment to hold on tighter. "Hmm. This is a tough one. Would you give me a hand with the operation?"

"Certainly!"

Seeing her mother rise from the couch, Olivia ceded defeat and let go.

"The growth has apparently dropped off on its own," noted Doug.

"The growth," Cheryl snorted, heading for the kitchen.

Doug immediately went to the television and turned down the zoom — Cheryl would always fill the room given her own choice, but Doug liked it small.

The stand-up comic shrunk down to about a foot. He strutted around on the table as the unseen audience roared. When it died down, he said, "...And that's why I always date locally." The audience exploded, and Doug turned the volume down a bit.

Olivia had flumped down on the couch. Doug sat on the other side. Her tiny body stretched out to take up as much room as possible. It wasn't very much.

"Well?" he said. "What happened today?"

"Stupid stuff," she said. "Nothing." With her white-blond curls framing her face and her arms at her sides, she looked like a doll.

Doug waited.

"Just like... we went to school. There was a new kid today, a girl with ugly shoes."

That was strange. Middle of the term. "Did her school close down too?"

"Maybe. I don't know. This new school is so stupid. They don't even have any games at recess, the kids have to make their own."

"That's too bad," Doug said lamely. He remembered reading in the parents' letter they had gotten that after the move to Frisco, the school would be expanding their recess game options. *The move will allow us to engage your children, both at work and at play, in a manner heretofore unimaginable!* Doug had told himself it was just ad copy (and overly wordy ad copy at that), but he still felt guilty.

There was a new stand-up comedian on, a really old guy with a slight hunch. "What is up with Self?" he was saying, holding out his palm. Doug realized, more from the voice and the body language, that it was Jerry Seinfeld.

"So you sign up for this *plan*, and you're instantly transported to this *place*... this place that looks like San Francisco, sounds like San Francisco, but is actually just a box in some room somewhere. I got that part. It's like e-mailing your brain." The audience roared at Jerry's old-man shtick, and he held up a hand to quiet them down.

Doug sighed.

"But what happens to your body? Supposedly, they take your body away to some *secret location*... and *do* something to it. I'm sorry, but doesn't that sound like something they should be paying you to do? Back in my day, you'd get dinner and a couple of drinks outta it at least!"

Doug laughed, despite himself. Olivia looked at him, stone faced.

"He's funny, hey?" Doug said.

"Funny looking," Olivia said, echoing one of Doug's favorite lines.

They cracked up. "Delivery," Doug's watch said.

Doug got up, wondering what it was. He asked his watch to show him what was out there, and he got a still of a young Chinese boy with a box beamed to his eye.

He opened the door and, for a horrified moment, realized he couldn't pay him. He nearly shut the door but instead stood frozen as the boy handed him the box and left.

Cheryl paid for it already. Thank god. He shut and locked the door behind him. He took off his shoes, numbly, mechanically. As he walked with the box to the kitchen he started to get mad at Cheryl. *Why was she ordering out for dinner? She didn't have anything else to do but make dinner! Was it cutting into her TV time?*

He handed the box to her wordlessly and watched as she emptied it into the wok. Thick black noodles slipped around with the hissing mix of veggies. "I just had the skinny noodles," she said.

Doug nodded, breathing through his nose. "Looks good," he forced out. He wanted to say something constructive, something like *You know Cheryl, I'm happy to pick up something on my way home. Delivery's so expensive.* But delivery had never been expensive before. She cooked because she liked to and because she had the time, not to save money. What if she began to suspect the financial trouble they were in, how badly he had fucked things up?

"How was work?" she asked, looking up as she sprinkled cashew bits into the pan.

"Stressful," he said. "That new kid Chan's a real twerp."

"Still?" Cheryl said, surprised. "They're usually kissing your ass by now."

"Mmm," Doug said, picking a cashew out of the pan. *Chan smells blood in the water.*

"It'll be fine," Cheryl said with a confidence that nearly broke Doug's heart. "You've got 20 years of experience under your belt."

"Well, the ol' belt's getting a little tight," Doug said.

"You'll have to cut a new notch, then," Cheryl said with a distracted smile.

"Heh," said Doug, annoyed. He waited a few seconds and then said, as if it was entirely unconnected, "You know, someone pitched to me in the elevator today." He knew it was wrong, but he couldn't help spreading the anxiety a little.

She was looking for something in the fridge. "At work? Your work elevator. Not *our* elevator."

"Our elevator. Just a few minutes ago."

She didn't say anything. Doug felt a twinge of guilt, and got a couple of plates out.

"Probably nothing," he said.

"Hmm," she said, spooning out the food onto the plates.

"Wow, this smells great," Doug said, hoping to lift the cloud over his wife's face. "I'll talk to security about it," he said. He rummaged through the cutlery drawer for some chopsticks.

She nodded. "Olivia," she called. "Dinner."

Why do we have to have these fucking things on Fridays? Doug thought, knowing the answer. The weekly meetings used to be scheduled on Mondays, but Harris met with the Frisco team Mondays now. But it's not like there was commuting time. He could have practically been in both places at the same time, wasn't that the beauty of it?

Doug pushed his chair back from his desk and leaned back as far as it would go, waiting to be called in to the meeting. Stretched out his legs, but didn't quite dare put his feet up on the desk. Arms folded, head lolling to one side, he looked through the missing patch at the mountains. *Could you climb up that far?* He imagined the crisp air, the winding paths, and the view — the view! The city would look like a ridiculous thing, put in its place by distance and monolithic geography. More than the silence, more than the clean air, it was thinking about this place shrunk to nothing that made Doug calmer.

"Patterson," Lauden said, poking his head in the door. "Harris is here. Let's do this."

His smile might as well have fallen off and rolled to somewhere unreachable, because Doug's face was grim for the rest of the day. He looked through his documents quickly — *twerp won't catch me with my pants down again* — and threw one look back at the mountains before he shut the door.

What was stopping me from going there? It was ridiculous that he'd lived here his whole life and had never even gone for an afternoon. *Drive up there one day with Olivia and Cheryl, just see how high you can go. Presuming they have roads… presuming you still had your car, dumbfuck.*

He walked down the hallway, almost reeling, numb and deaf. *Of course, you never thought to go when you had your car.* He was amazed to feel a shortness of breath… *was this a panic attack? Ridiculous.*

He felt a bump at his elbow. It was the kid, also walking to the meeting room. "Sorry Doug," he said, with almost a shy smile, his hair looking a little messy. It reminded Doug of his nephew's bedhead. "Hey, I was being an idiot last—"

"Yep," Doug cut him off, pulling the door open and holding it open for him, staring at him, his numbness wearing off. *The twerp is smartening up. Harris probably straightened him out.*

By the time he took his seat his breathing was back to normal. He looked around at his co-workers and noted the higher tension levels. *Why couldn't these things be on Tuesday, at least?* He remembered the old Monday morning meetings, people pulling apart muffins as they gave their reports, a whole week ahead of them to fill in any holes.

Stevens was the last to get settled, flicking in and getting into a chair. Doug hadn't seen him since he relocated — he looked considerably slimmer but not so much that it was really obvious. He'd slim off gradually. Stevens knew the appropriate thing to do. And as much as he used to sneer at him for it, Doug knew that that was the difference between him being here and Stevens being in Frisco.

He remembered a conversation they'd had, when Frisco was just a novelty vacation for the rich. Stevens was complaining about his wife bugging him to go. "Thinks we're made of money. She doesn't understand we have to turn a profit as a couple — we can't just break even. The market's good now, but..." He'd looked at Doug with envy. "Can't understand how you make it with your wife not working."

Doug had just smiled mysteriously, ignored the nervous flutter that always appeared in his stomach whenever he thought about his finances — it'd work out, always did. But now, Stevens looked at him as if he'd been lied to. *Why aren't you in Frisco?* he seemed to be saying. *What've you got going here?* Stevens wasn't very smart.

But Harris was, in an offhanded way. He'd figure it out soon enough. Really, he didn't know why he didn't just come clean with his boss. It wouldn't take very long. *My wife quit her job to raise our child, and when she wanted to go back the jobs had gone to Frisco. So we decided to wait until we moved there. But I don't have enough savings for the down payment on a gold package, and there's no way we'd get decent jobs without it. No more than you'd get a decent job in a cheap suit wearing bad cologne...*

Stevens was halfway through his report already, and Doug hadn't noticed he'd started. It was mostly numbers, and numbers always bored him. *Part of the problem, wasn't it Patterson?* Billion dollar accounts had been impressive when he was a 17-year-old punk like Chan here, and certainly the twerp had a look of interest on his face. Looked tired, though, as he scrolled idly through his notes.

"You still haven't told me if we're hitting our numbers in terms of meat-clients versus Frisco-clients," said Harris. He smoothed the hair on the side of his head, and Doug noticed that he had no ears.

"Well, just barely. Our income split is 80/20, but our workforce split is still 75/25," Stevens said, holding up a caution hand. Doug couldn't resist a glance back at Harris. He'd heard that it was a popular look among Frisco execs, and it did give him a sleeker, harder look. Had he changed his eyes, too? Had Harris's eyes been grey? Doug felt that knowing this, commenting on this, could mean the difference between keeping and losing his job.

Lauden gave his report next. "Of the four subcultures in the Vancouver area we've been amassing data on, we're seeing a 10% return…"

Harris looked unimpressed, making an occasional note.

Stevens took a call, his mouth moving silently as Lauden continued, discreetly flicked out.

Lauden went on for a while, ended with his "bears further investigation" mantra.

"Can you come in tomorrow to finish the investigation?" Harris said, not looking at Lauden. "We're looking for profiles, not ongoing studies."

Another reason Friday meetings sucked. Saturday was sitting there like the trembling vestal virgin, waiting to be sacrificed to the gods of completion.

Lauden's lips were slightly open as if he couldn't believe his weekend had been yanked away from him again. Numbly, he nodded. "Sure." Doug admired the note of cheerfulness.

Harris trained his eyes directly on Doug. "OK. We're not taking on any new non-Frisco accounts as of next month. To handle the ones we have, we'll be keeping a skeleton staff — Lauden will be heading up the team here — and it'll strictly be research, no analysis."

Lauden licked his lips. "Well," he said in a let's-be-frank tone. "If there're no clients, there's very little left to research."

Harris nodded. "True. There are a few older groups, however, that our clients in Frisco can use information on. Infiltrators, for instance."

The silence was uncomfortable. Chan's eyebrows had arched incredulously, but he kept quiet. Doug just smiled bitterly. *Infiltrators. Perfect.*

Harris's gaze swept the room like a machine gun. His usual jovial manner was nowhere to be seen. Doug had only seen him in this mode during mass firings. *Which this could be...*

"Things are getting hot in Frisco," he said, looking directly at Doug. "Things are very interesting and very competitive. Subcultures are manifesting themselves in new and unclassified ways, and it has the industry in an uproar. Alex says we need all our analysts in Frisco." He paused. "By next week."

Oh fuck.

"Doug?" Harris said.

Doug shook his head. "There's still some loose ends —"

"There always are," Harris said dryly. "David?" he said, looking at Chan.

Chan smiled broadly. "I'm there. Tomorrow if you need me."

Of course, Doug thought, staring at the pine table's texture, *Of course the little fuck is ready. No dependents, no wife, just that saucer-eyed tart he drags around to—*

"Monday's fine, David," Harris said. He sighed, and Doug was amazed at the level of exhaustion in it. His face was fresh, his eyes were sprightly — but then, holograms never had to look tired. *How had it changed negotiations,* he wondered, *now that body language isn't a factor?*

"We'll need at least one experienced man if we're going to do any kind of decent research here," Lauden said, nodding and looking at Doug.

Good old Lauden, Doug thought. *We're two sick old wolves watching each other's butts.*

"All right then. I've got another meeting to get ready for. Meetings stacked for the next 12 hours, actually," Harris said, with an undecipherable chuckle. "I won't be checking in with you weekly anymore, but we'll meet next Friday to work out the details of your new research objectives."

Our new diminished objectives, you mean to say, Doug thought. Almost immediately he chastised himself. *Don't be so fucking proud. You're lucky you still have your job.*

"OK, have a good one," Harris said, flicking out. It wasn't until he did this that Doug realized how careful he'd been at other meetings to wait until they had left to disconnect. *Wonder if he's getting used to it or just doesn't care about shocking us any more?*

"Have a good one," Lauden said. "Not too likely."

"Crackers for you, guy," Chan said. "Still though, probably something to do with the fact that everyone's working 14-hour days there."

"Seriously?" Doug said.

Chan got up. "Yeah. So-so-so, we gotta be competitive, everyone else's

63

working 14 hours, you don't need to sleep, like that," he said on his way out the door. Gone was the shyness of an hour ago, as gone as Chan himself would be by Monday.

"I don't envy you, Chan," Lauden said after him. "It'll be tough."

Chan laughed. "S'future, guy. Move it or lose it." He disappeared down the hallway, leaving Lauden and Doug alone.

Lauden just shook his head and rolled his eyes. Doug laughed — for Lauden, this was the equivalent of character assassination.

"All right, ol' wolf, we gotta couple hours left," Doug said, leading the way back to their offices.

The SkyTrain pulled away from the station with a bit of a jerk, shoving everyone in a choreographed fashion that no one resented. *Maybe you could be that way with life,* Doug pondered. *Take the hits as if they're delivered unintentionally by a machine.*

Certainly he felt a bit like that now — as the SkyTrain trundled along its tracks, none of the day's disasters troubled him. He had gotten a seat on the train, even a bit of a view out of the window opposite through a serendipitous mix of short people with arms angled just right. A faint smile played on his lips as he watched sun glint off the buildings, the cables of the bridge over the water. Maybe it's just that I got paid, he thought, the golden oldie Eric B. & Rakim song "Paid in Full" running through his head. He remembered the derision Olivia had expressed when he had busted a few rhymes a while back: *Daddy, hip hop is* so *old man music.* Guilty as charged.

Thinkin' of a master plan, ain't nothing but sweat inside my hand.

The next stop blocked his view, but a bunch of kids got in and they were just as entertaining. This stop was near St. Edmond's, an absurdly expensive school that was hemorrhaging students to Frisco — Doug could tell this just by the diminishing size of the groups that got on at this stop — but was resolutely continuing. *While other schools folded faster than a house of cards*, Doug thought, although he knew why — Olivia's school was a good value, while St. Edmond's would turn a profit with three students per class. They could afford to run two schools concurrently.

He didn't like it, though — he remembered how it felt to be the new kid, how hard-won identity points were reset to zero. His mom had moved him from one of the last publicly-funded schools to Kits North, and it had taken him a year to recalibrate. When his old school was shut down, the influx of old classmates made it worse — he fit into neither clique, too poor for one and too rich for the other. It had, however, given him the beginnings of a career in observing and analyzing youth culture.

My career, thought Doug, looking at the kids in front of him, automatically noting their little indicators. *Some career. Sucking the blood of innocents and then having my stomach pumped.* But he thought this with a certain equanimity — he recognized that he was only critical of coolhunting when work was going badly. But the idea of being the parasite in the food chain was harder to dismiss the older he got. Maybe Harris knew this, that was what was behind the urgency.

But because of his financial negligence — his gross negligence — he'd been unable to take the hint. Really, it was a miracle that Harris had stooped to giving him this make-work job, as ridiculous and laughable as the Infiltrators assignment was. A younger Doug would have sneered at his manager's sentimentality, maybe even exploited it, but now he felt only the gratitude of a mangy animal thrown a bone. And really, he'd be an idiot to expect that Harris wouldn't expect some kind of return on his investment.

He looked at the kids in front of him and wondered if they'd ever heard of Infiltrators, or if this had become obscure knowledge of his profession. Infiltrators were a probably-mythical subculture that invented subcultures to sell to coolhunters, and then flipped the money into making those subcultures a reality. Then, later, they sold the proof that the subcultures were fakes to the highest bidder. When Doug was coming up in the '20s, a lot of his colleagues had been burned, worried that every new lead led to a camouflaged tar pit. Just as the industry had gotten used to a level of stability as cultural commentators, a collection of malcontents had put the fear of God into them: their tag, an "i" with a circle around it, appeared everywhere, and made their numbers seem infinite. Doug, with no reputation yet to lose, dismissed it as a covert branding campaign and was brazen and fearless where his colleagues were cautious. Harris had liked his moxy and had promoted him quickly.

Doug thought of Harris's face today and sighed.

"Kinsey's just being an assbutt," said a plump kid, his face speckled with red freckles. "If he can have those stupid spikes in his eyebrow, why can't I point my ears?"

The boy he was talking to nodded, a slender, big-eyed kid with an absurdly large knapsack. On his left, a tall girl said, "Well, Mr. Kinsey doesn't wear a uniform either. It's uniform regulations."

65

"I know, but *why*," said the plump kid. "On the one side, you have the all-knowing teachers who get to do whatever they want —"

Another girl, beside him, put in "Yeah, like Mr. Randall and his sword —"

"Exactly," said the plump kid, "A perfect example! Randall gets to carry around a weapon —"

"You could put out an eye with your ears," the tall girl said. The plump guy made an exasperated sound.

"...Or you could put out an ear with your eye," the slender kid put in with a timid smile.

The tall girl tossed her head and giggled. The plump kid's eyebrows beetled a bit with the conversational derailment, until the girl beside him elbowed him. "S'a joke, Steve. Don't be such a stiffy."

Steve touched his arm where she had elbowed him, looked at her, smiled reluctantly.

"It's unfair, though," said the slender kid, "The school is too strict."

The train stopped and the foursome bowed forward a bit to allow for the flow. Doug carefully looked elsewhere, glancing only occasionally at the group. He was glad he'd worn his hat — his sharp-rimmed fedora wasn't nearly as stare-worthy as his shiny pate.

Steve looked at the girl beside him. She might have been his sister, they had the same blond hair and freckles. "Did you do all right on the history test?" she said, looking down. She had a few inches on him.

"Yeah. Multiple choice was easy. But the essay question was hard, though. What necessitated the dismantling of government during the '20s? What'd you put?"

The girl ticked them off on the hand not holding the bar. "Need for a more efficient economy, it was riddled with corruption, not willing to take military action against ecological terrorists... uh... I think that was all I got."

"Shit, I forgot the corruption one," said the slender kid.

"I forgot them all," said the tall girl, and they all laughed. "But that was such an unfair question! We hardly did any government stuff in class. It was mostly International Monetary Fund. Yeah, when did the IMF become the United Corporate Interests Council?"

"2023," said Steve.

"No, that was when UCIC moved into the White House," the freckled girl said. "They changed the name in 2008."

The slender boy nodded. Doug had pegged him for the new guy — the crispness of his uniform, and his general timidness, gave him away.

"Well, the UCIC is of no importance today…" Steve said expansively. "Today, it's all about EWBF!" He looked around at the others, nodding and grinning.

There was a few seconds before the blond girl figured it out and said, "*Elven Warrior: Blood Feud.*" They all laughed.

"Ah ha," said the slender kid.

"I was going to say!" said the tall girl. "I didn't remember that on the test!"

Doug noticed an older teen, dressed in a ball-specked jacket, sneer at the mention of the popular fantasy series. None of them caught his look, and Doug was strangely relieved.

He couldn't really hear the teenagers now, but their body language was just as interesting. The tall girl and her exaggerated cluelessness, her obvious grabs of the slender kid's arm. Steve, and his soft glances towards the blond girl. The blond girl's serious watchfulness. The slender kid — the slender kid was actually looking right at him.

Doug held his gaze until the kid looked away, and then avoided looking at them. Steve sprang up, mock brandishing a sword, and said, "Come, brave ones!" The hipster teen rolled his eyes at this, and the slender kid caught it. Doug watched, almost sadly, as the kid glanced back at Steve with new eyes, eyes that suspected his new friend Steve was not cool. Doug looked at the hipster teen, wondered if he knew how corrosive he was, wondered if he was corroded down to a core of cynicism himself. He wanted to grab the hipster, shake him, tell him that he knew someone who worked for the person who designed the campaign to make those stupid jackets the new wave of urban chic. Instead he walked out the door.

He followed the kids, feeling slightly foolish but mostly right about following his urge to get off several stops before home — equal parts being attracted to the untainted enthusiasm of the Elven Warriors and being repulsed by the jacket-hipster's pre-packaged snideness. He made a mental note to get something for Olivia afterwards. He lifted his hand to his head in the watch's shorthand for phone and said, "Cheryl."

By the time he stepped off the escalator she'd answered. "Working late?"

"Yeah," Doug said. "Why don't you and Olive just go ahead. I'm gonna pick up something here." The teenagers headed towards the theatre.

"All right," his wife said agreeably. "Lucky you called before I started cooking."

"Oh, I know," Doug said, scanning the food marquees. "I know what's good for me." He said goodbye and disconnected, trying to decide on dinner while people milled around him. KFC was giving away a toy with their dinners, so he punched in a quarter chicken meal — using his handkerchief because the screen was greasy — and waited. He had to wait just long enough to contemplate how unhygienic the inside of the machine probably was if the outside was this nasty, when the steamy box jutted out for him to take. He almost forgot the toy, which dropped down into a separate container.

Sitting down at an orange and beige tablette with a view of the theatre, he sat his fedora on the round textured seat beside him and began his meal. While he chewed on a chicken leg, he read the fine print on the side of the box. MAY CONTAIN TRACE AMOUNTS OF PEANUTS AND HUMAN DNA, it warned. Doug rolled his eyes. *What didn't?* He looked at the toy, which looked more or less like a plastic bag of white cotton. *Picked fresh from the Colonel's plantation!* Doug's brain spat out.

Flipping it over, however, revealed that it was a wig, beard, and black framed glasses. *Oh perfect*, Doug thought sourly. While Olivia might look cute as the Colonel, just a few weeks ago she had asked Cheryl to pluck her eyebrows because they looked "like a boy's." He sort of liked the glasses, though. He took them out and slipped them on — they had clear lenses, too, which he naturally smudged with his chickeny fingers.

He noticed a man a few tables over, drinking something and watching him. When he stood, he saw and recognized the attentive look on the ruddy old man's face, and instead of taking his box to the garbage he left it there. He walked to the theatre, pausing to take in the *Elven Warrior: Blood Feud* holoclip above the entrance. A tiny figure is hunched over a slain comrade. The camera zooms in slowly as the figure stands, framing his anguished, shadowed face, zooming closer. When only his gleaming eye is visible, the zoom stops. Only his ragged breath is heard for a moment, and then, within the eye, a fire explodes to life.

Doug didn't watch the hack 'n' slash revenge sequence that followed, just lifted his watch up to the payplate. He glanced back at the food court and noted that the man had made it over to his table without the security guard noticing. There was a soft ping, and the cash register informed him that the campaign was already underway, was that OK? Doug said it was, and there was a flash of light as it took his picture. A rotating elf-version of Doug appeared, glasses and all. It was amusing, but not quite what he wanted. He cycled through the default settings to find one that wasn't so elderly.

He settled on a young grey-eyed elf with buckskin shorts and a bow across his chest. The register asked if he wanted extra weapons with that, but after checking them out — you could get anything from a catapult-armed truck to an electroscythe — he stuck with his bow and silver dagger. There were a bunch of other questions about outfitting and food, but he just chose the defaults.

It told him the booth number and he found it, using his watch to unlock it. The door closed behind him and the darkness was so complete he had to feel with his hands for the helm that hung from above.

As he adjusted the helm to his height, he could hear voices drifting over the open-topped booths.

The sun was just rising as the band of adventurers walked through the forest clearing. One of them, a stocky elf with a crossbow, held his hand up. The others — a cloaked mage, a female warrior elf with chain mail, and a willowy female elf with an Uzi — stopped.

The stocky elf pointed his crossbow at a faintly rustling bush and flicked on the laser sight. "Come out or be killed."

The bush rustled some more and finally parted to reveal a slim and young elf, hands held apart in supplication.

"What weapons have ye?" said the stocky elf.

The elf plucked the bowstring and turned around to show the dagger tucked in the back of his buckskin shorts. "Please, warriors, my name is Doug. I wish to join your party."

The stocky elf looked around at his comrades. They shrugged. He was plainly not satisfied by this. "How do we know he isn't an agent of the Orc Overspawn?"

"Why don't you try your Reveal spell, Mike?" asked the female elf in chain mail.

"Yeah OK," said the hooded figure, dipping into a leather pouch and throwing glittering dust on Doug.

Doug felt a little uneasy, hoped it wouldn't show his real face. He almost felt like he could feel it as it whisked around him, but he knew that couldn't be the case. When it got to his head, words of fire appeared above him: NEUTRAL. HOME TOWN: Brentwood Mall.

"Well met, fellow Brentwoodian," said Steve, slapping him on the shoulder. Doug's character stumbled with the impact, although Doug in the booth remained still. Steve put his fists on his hips and nodded as he surveyed the smaller elf. "You shall have to come with us, because we have just come from Brentwood. Or, rather, we have just escaped Brentwood."

"Escaped?" said Doug. "What mean you by this?" He put on an alarmed look and glanced from face to face.

"The bastard Overspawn murdered every last one of our fair townspeople," the female elf in chain mail said. "And then, before we could give them a proper burial, he caused them to attack us — as the undead."

"Great Zeus!" Doug said, knowing he was fudging his mythologies and hoping they didn't care. "You mean — zombies?"

"They kept coming and coming," the other girl elf said, firing a burst of her Uzi into the air. "It was totally awesome."

"Conserve your ammo," Steven said severely as the others laughed. "Awesomely *terrible*, that is. Our own children, friends, family, twisted by evil forces to the point where we had to... put them down..." He shook his head, and turned to Doug, his fists still on his hips. "That's Elsie, by the way. Our magic user goes by the name Mike, the pigtailed amazon by Christina and I am Steven. We can always use a brave soul."

Doug nodded, careful not to smile. The helm picked up facial movement uncannily well.

Having done the introductions, they continued the way they had been heading — Christina and Steven took the lead, and the other three walked together.

"Have you played much before?" said Elsie. "I haven't. That's why I got the Uzi. To, like, make up for how crappy I am."

Doug shook his head, looking around the forest. "No, not since — not much. None of the *Elf Warrior* series." The detail was very crisp, and while the people had an occasional quirk or stutter they were entirely believable.

"I've done two of them," Mike said. "Steven's done them all."

"How did you become a magic user?" Doug asked. Ahead, Christina was checking her compass and saying something to Steven.

"Well, Steven said it suited me. He says I'm mysterious," Mike said, laughing a bit. "I sort of like it."

"Yeah, I was going to be a magic user too," said Elsie, looking at Mike. "They're so cool. But then Mike showed me all the casting stuff," her hand twitched spastically. "And I was like, forget it, too complicated."

Mike's hand moved in quick gestures, and a fireball slowly glowed to life.

His eyes sparked as the spell completed.

"Cool," Doug said.

Mike undid the spell with the same gestures backwards. It faded out.

Elsie clapped, her hands ghosting a little with the speed. "Awesome!"

"It's way more sensitive on site," Mike said with a smile. "When I cast from home I have to try like three times before it works. My set-up is so crap and the ping is, like, forget it."

The forest had thinned, and there was a city of twisting towers in the distance. Doug stared at them, thinking about the mountains he could see from his office. *Was there smoke coming from them?* Doug lifted a hand to shade his eyes and felt his real hand knock into the helm. His body did a weird jerk.

"Careful," Mike said. "You can reset it if you knock it hard enough, they're pretty sensitive."

It wasn't smoke; it was something flying. Flying towards them. "Hey, uh, do you guys see that? Hey, Steven," Doug said, but Steven was already on it. He had removed a bronze telescope from his pack and extended it. He stopped and raised it to his eye. Everyone stopped.

"What is it?" Christina said, her voice grave. Steven was closing the telescope, packing it away. He said nothing, and it seemed like the *shing!* as he unsheathed his broadsword would be his only response.

But then he said, "Orcs." A second later, as the winged animals were almost discernable, he looked around into the faces of everyone. "Orcs mounted on dragons."

As everyone around him readied for battle, Doug realized that he hadn't bought any arrows for his bow. He took the dagger in his hand, a tiny silver fish scaler, and waited for death.

Eileen was in the dark. Not literally — her suit would never stop feeding her retinas crisp and well-lit visuals of the pitch black tunnels she was running through. But she had none of the other datastreams that she was accustomed to — without uplinking, all she had to go on was the information she herself had collected.

She followed the tunnel, picking a direction at random. Once it had intuited what she was doing, a prompt had come up and offered to take over the repetitive leg movements. She had let it, but now she almost regretted it — it left her with nothing to do. Unlike when she was uplinked, there was no fresh information about her targets to peruse, no maps to look at, no co-agents to chit-chat with.

Not that she was much of a one for chit-chat — Eileen had always been more of a nose/grindstone type — but she liked to have the murmur of human voices in the background as she combed through the new data. She was always happier when she was occupied, when her hands were busy.

Now, with nothing to watch but the walls sliding by, she started to feel a little disconnected from her body, as if it were a strange contraption she was riding on. She forced herself to focus, to feel her limbs pumping, to notice the shape of the puddles in the ground ahead.

Silence was better than pointless chatter, she supposed. She remembered a mission in Uganda — destroying some bottling plant that wouldn't comply with the new regulations — where Mary had been talking to a tough newbie called Karen, riding her a little.

"Why did you paint a skull on your mask, Karen?" she had said over the comm.

There was no response.

"Is it because you like to fuck skulls, Karen?" Mary said in a sweet voice.

Karen ignored this, too. The four of them ran in silence for a few seconds, a thin black line.

"I mean, it's OK if you like that kind of thing, Karen —"

The skull spun her way. "Shutthefuckupbit—"

There was a sickening *thwock*, and everyone's suit sped up to 500%. Everyone's but Karen's, since she was on her knees with a machete splitting her head. As Eileen routed and gutted the knife-sniper, she felt numb. Whose fault was it? It wasn't Karen's fault for looking away. It wasn't her boss's fault for protecting their investments. It wasn't the Ugandan's fault for protecting his interests. It wasn't Mary's fault for being born with a big mouth. And it wasn't her fault for not telling Mary to shut up. It just was.

Nothing had seemed clear-cut to Eileen, and she had assumed it would always be that way. But it had grown inside her. When the doctor had told her that the baby had been successfully embronned as a boy, that was the first kick inside her. When she saw it struggle to breathe in the cloistered atmosphere of the clone incubator, she started to believe. And when they had wiped off the gel, none too gently, and passed her her very own crinkle-eyed baby boy — flesh of her flesh — she *knew*. There was one thing in life she was sure of.

Jeremy needs me. And if they think they can keep him in some electronic hell while I'm still alive —

An alert popped up and the electrical impulses contracting her leg muscles slowed her to a stop in front of a grungy ladder. WHICH WAY? the alert was flashing, and she blinked it off. *This is one of the times when having a map to cross-ref with would be really useful,* Eileen grumbled to herself, looking down the continuing tunnel.

She'd never flown blind before and remembered that there had been something in their training about it — what was it? *That's right — an internal odometer.*

"Distance covered?"

"Eight point four kilometers," her suit responded.

"Direction?"

"Due northwest."

That's good. Not too far off target. Up and out, she decided, gripping the grimy rungs.

Eileen emerged from the tunnel, feeling the night air and sounds rush around her. She was at 200% of normal speed, keeping to the sidewalks and curbside, thankful that she wasn't in a neighborhood with dog walkers and joggers. The ragged woman she passed thought she was a memory and smiled a perfect smile after her.

The moment she hit the sidewalk she cut back to 150%, glancing around for prying eyes. None. The van completed the turn and caught up to her, and she locked on it and kept apace. She glanced at a sign: DOWNTOWN — 1KM.

She smiled under her mask. "Chickens heading home to roost," she said in Megan's voice. Or more specifically, Megan's voice as it had sounded coming through the comm link — flattened and digitized, something to do with certain sound ranges being more detectable by the enemy. Eileen suspected it had been to make them sound like robots, even to each other. There were a lot of things they did like that, things that had seemed silly to Eileen at first, but after a few missions she began to see that they helped.

She was in the retail sector now, and she had to vie with sidewalkers, parked cars, and brighter lights. She — or more specifically, that damn mask Mary had drawn on — was turning heads. It was against protocol to be so visible, but she didn't care. She was pretty much unstoppable in a crowd like this, even if a security team was activated to deal with her.

She caught sight of the Self outlet she'd been at yesterday. She had a sudden fantasy of catching that little bastard of a manager there in the flesh. She'd get information out of him. She'd enjoy doing it. She slipped into the alley beside the outlet and concealed herself behind the stacks of boxes lining the building. They struck her as strange given that Self had no actual product. She flicked her razors out and sliced one open. Empty.

Her suit, noting her proximity to a door, told her that it was an easily breachable magnetic combination lock. She did so and slid into a fairly bare room. It had a few of the boxes she had seen in the alley; a few taps showed they also were empty. She increased her audio input, heard no voices.

She entered a well-carpeted hall that led to the front office where she'd been earlier today — she could even see people passing by the front window and felt vulnerable in her blacksuit against the mostly white interior.

But she crept along the hallway, looking into the doorways that lined it. SELF DEMO BOOTH #3 and #2 were empty, entirely plain rooms, but #1 was an office with a man sitting at it. She slowed down to normal.

His back was to her, but he waved her in.

"Come on in," he said. He was flipping through some pages. Hungry for data, Eileen scanned them but they were either gibberish or encrypted. She looked around the room, taking in the bookshelves, the giant oak desk, the view as it would be from a fifty-storey building. *Was that the Statue of Liberty beside the Golden Gate Bridge?*

The man at the desk chuckled. "Quite a view, huh? Especially from the first floor."

She turned to look at him. He was a broad-shouldered man with his sleeves rolled up to show beefy arms. His face was a constantly shifting pattern, a blur of features. She asked her suit to descramble it. Her suit told her that there was no one there.

"Why don't you have a seat? That one's pretty comfy," he said.

She touched it to make sure it was there. *No one there.*

"So, having trouble with Self?" said the man, getting up from his seat.

She felt like she had with the manager. This was ridiculous. She didn't come here to be shunted back and forth between middle management.

"So are we," the man finished. He placed his hands palms down on the desk. "Maybe we can work something out."

She sat down, opening audio out.

"Who are you," she said, her digitized voice flattening the question into a statement.

"My name is Paul," he said.

"Do you work for Self."

"No."

Eileen paused. He crossed his arms and waited. She balled her fists and continued.

"Then why are you here."

"We're gathering data about Self. One of my people spotted you at the back entrance, and I decided it would be good to meet you."

Eileen looked around, scanned for bugs and came up empty. "This location will be monitored by Self."

Paul shook his head. "These outlets are shells with no connection to Self's actual operations. I've been using this as a base of operations for a month, now. It's rather convenient — these rooms are very expensive to install, and they attract attention. Hiding in plain sight."

Eileen looked around, trying to figure out if Paul was of any use to her. Her eyes resting on the Statue of Liberty, she noticed a small "i" in a circle on the books the lady held.

"I don't trust you," she said.

Paul laughed, a raw little chuckle. "Strange bedfellows. If I had known 15 years ago that I would be striking a deal with one of you midnight marauders… you psychotic strike breakers…" He cut himself off, laughed that little laugh. "But here I am. And here you are. And I know you didn't bring that blacksuit out of retirement for a jog around the block."

She froze up at the mention of her blacksuit.

Paul made a dismissive gesture. "We know a lot about you now that would have been… very useful to know then." Paul looked out the window. "You see, it's all about information. We presumed you were ex-soldiers. If we had known you were civilians — a constantly changing group, at that — we would have had an entirely different strategy."

Eileen was gazing out the window, focusing on a section of the city. She zoomed in and the illusion was destroyed — the tiny dots of cars remained dots, just got larger. *Strategy? Was he trying to convince her that he was part of —*

"But soldiers would have been too expensive. Because they knew the suit's speed had a cost — they'd be losing years of their lives. You didn't know that, though. You didn't know that you'd be a withered hag at forty." Paul paused, and Eileen could feel his eyes on her body, bony and sagging. Shame and rage pulsed through her.

"So that's why they used civilians. But that's not why they used infertile women."

She forced herself to respond. "We were better at multi-tasking than men, and we didn't have the family demands that… normal people had," she said, hating herself for using the word normal.

"The family demands."

Eileen faltered. "Yes."

"What was special about barren females, Eileen, was that you were easily manipulated. By the time you were in your twenties you were almost OK with the idea that you couldn't have kids. But there was something missing."

That was true. Eileen had been on a career track, working as a manager-in-training for the Gap. She had even outgrown her teenaged sullenness to the point where she could go to her friends' baby showers. It was her doctor who had told her about the position, when she had gone in to see if her body had changed enough in the last year to make a uterine implant viable.

"It's some kind of security job," he had said. "They're looking specifically for childless women of your age." He shrugged. "Be different from folding sweaters. And they pay incredibly well. I actually thought it was a mistake the first time I read it."

She had been sitting on the examination table. "Can I put on my clothes?"

"Yes, yes," he said, scrolling down his pad while she dressed. "Eileen?"

"Yes?" she said, imagining he saw some hope there, waited anxiously.

But he wasn't thinking about her uterus. "If you get in touch with them, be sure to tell them I told you about it. I get a commission."

This had been only one of many indignities that being born without a uterus had exposed her to. But when Jeremy's skin had dried enough to touch, skin soft like nothing on earth…

"It was worth it," she said out loud. Her robotic voice carried authority that she didn't feel — if she didn't get Jeremy back, would it still be?

Paul, also lost in reverie, looked up. In an angry, measured voice, he said, "I suppose you have to believe that. How else could you live with having killed — I don't know, what was your kill tally at the end of your ten missions?"

"I didn't keep track," Eileen said. Others would talk about it a lot, but she never took a particular pride in it. But all this talk about how could she live with it was silly. The targets were people she'd never heard of in countries she'd never heard of. They were always serious threats to the free market, dictators who were taxing more than the corporations could afford. Sometimes the market needed a little help to keep balanced, and they were that little help.

"Didn't keep track." Paul's voice was thoughtful. "We didn't either. It wasn't really the numbers. It was the fear. Every time we'd get something going somewhere, the suits would show up. Because, of course, we were riddled with moles. But we've learned. We've learned to give moles tapeworms. Did you know that if you give one mole a tapeworm, that its owner will destroy up to 25 perfectly healthy moles?"

Eileen didn't know what the hell he was talking about and remained silent.

Paul pulled an outsized calculator from his desk. "How about this, then... did you know that the odds of being born without a uterus when conceived in a 50 kilometer radius of a hot landfill is a hundred to one? Works out to a pretty sizable employment pool..."

She was tired of this. "Where does Self store the bodies."

Paul set the calculator on his desk with a click. "Looking for someone?"

She nodded, a quick snap.

He assessed her. "Is it a son or daughter?"

"Grandson. Jeremy Ellis —"

Paul waved her silent. "I don't know where he is. Self probably doesn't know where he is. They log hundreds of missing persons complaints a day. But rarely from parties as capable and focused as you, Ms. Ellis."

"Eileen," she said automatically, felt ridiculous for doing so.

"Eileen." Paul perched on the desk, folded his hands over one knee, studied her. "Eileen, I have a proposal. You continue your search for your grandson, and you let us help you."

"Why would you do that."

"You're looking for the same information we are, but have a unique skillset — thanks to your suit and experience — and motivation. If you let us, we'll hook up a datafeed to your suit. See through your eyes. Hear through your ears. Because we want to find out more about Self, we have a vested interest in guiding you towards your grandson. Plus, you'll be able to uplink through one of our dummy portals."

"There's no such thing as anonymous portals," she said.

Paul chuckled. "No, you're right. It's better — it disguises you as a totally average user. Believe me, we don't want your old employers knowing that you're active. You're more useful to us alive."

Eileen didn't want to consider what this ominous "us" would do with the information, if they were in any way connected with the insurgents in the '20s — but whatever their aim, they were well organized and serious. This Paul had the easy and authoritative manner of Oscar, her field liaison in black ops. And, the truth was, she didn't really have any more leads — Jeremy's trail had dried up, and without uplinking, she was pretty limited.

"All right," she said. "Hook me up."

When Eileen emerged from the office a while later, she felt like she hadn't negotiated very well. She didn't even really know if there had been an opportunity to barter — this Paul fellow had treated her as if he were hiring her for a job.

She left the way she came, holding the device that looked like a tiny round adaptor in her hand — she didn't have any pockets — and she scanned the alley. Nothing besides a few rats. *Should I do it here?* She scanned the device, and her suit told her that it wasn't in its database, and said that installing it before uplinking was extremely dangerous.

If I could uplink, I would be able to identify it... partially, at least. It's probably not standard issue. For all I know it'll slave me. But I won't be able to uplink before I install it.

Eileen revved up and took off down the street. There was still a good amount of pedestrian traffic so she went to 250% and stuck to the road. It was dark enough for her mask face to be taken as a figment of imagination.

An interesting man, though, Eileen thought. Didn't treat her like a useless old woman. He knew her worth. The talk about barren women hadn't been pleasant, but for all she knew it may have been true. By the time she'd finished her tenth mission, she'd felt less like a veteran commando and more like someone who had escaped a meat grinder by accident. But they had given her the money and even urged her to consider part-time.

She had thanked them but said that she wanted to focus on her new life as a mother. She would have filled in the spinal socket but that was irreversible, and besides, she didn't really have to look at it everyday or anything. It itched occasionally, but that was it.

The street changed to an even wealthier section, tiny car dealerships and high-end clothing stores like Salvation Army and her old workplace Gap Authentic. A young girl with red hair pushed out the door of the Tommygirl outlet and walked briskly away, her eyes darting around. A smile spread across her face a few seconds before the bra she'd stolen burst into flames. At the speed Eileen was going, she saw the smile turn into a scream in minute detail.

Eileen did what she was trained to do when people were dying around her — kept running. After a few agonizing seconds, the Tommygirl door opened and a slowly running employee came out with the extinguisher. The burning girl disappeared behind a white cloud, but Eileen knew it was too late. The antitheft chemical had done its job.

Eileen was a block away, wishing she hadn't seen the girl's face. She could imagine the girl's mother, also with red hair, launching a suit against Tommygirl. If she had money to waste. Or even if she didn't. The most that would come of it would be that Tommygirl might get a slap on the wrist for excessive measures. The fine would pay for the funeral, and the rest would go to court costs.

And if she was guilty of the shoplifting, her friends and neighbors would get to watch the tapes of the theft over and over again. See that you couldn't afford nice clothes. See that you didn't raise her right.

Eileen saw that Burrard Bridge was ahead and saw her cubbyhole. *Perfect.*

Underneath the bridge she found a ledge jutting out of one of the massive girders and climbed down onto it. Out of sight, she listened to the wind and the reverberation of the cables and tried to figure out how she was going to do this. The tiny device sat like a dangerous seed in her hand. Paul had said that all she had to do was get it near her socket and it would do the rest.

She set the adaptor in a hairline crack in the girder, moving her hand away cautiously. Just as she relaxed, a gust of wind rolled it towards the edge. Luckily she was still revved up, so she caught it in time.

Would it have been so hard to put pockets in these things? she wondered, looking around for a better spot. She ended up putting the device under her bumcheek, presuming that if it were very delicate Paul would have warned her.

She wasn't looking forward to the next part. She remembered unplugging quite vividly from her younger days, and she was in more pleasant surroundings then — a few steps away from a bath. Or, after particularly challenging missions, a hospital bed.

Well, Jeremy isn't likely in terribly pleasant surroundings, either.

After she slowed down to 100% and changed all her other settings to as close to human as they'd get, she removed her mask. Her view of the water changed from digitally vivid to her nearsighted smear, but a tangy smell of metal and sea hit her. She took a few breaths and arched her back, feeling for the plug.

Jeremy might be marinating in some tank somewhere. Or worse. Quick now, like a tooth —

Yank.

Immediately, she had to stop breathing: it was like fire. But she couldn't stop breathing. Fire fire *oh my god*

my arms my joints oh god oh god

The wind was like a thousand ice lashes, and her eyes now, her eyes felt *two coals burning oh shit ofuck*

She felt her bladder give way, she hadn't known she had to go.

can't pee because princess

When the suit had muted the pain, it stored it away for her, a diver coming up and getting the worst bends in the history

princess and the pea can't pee on the pea

Her hand, searching under her buttock, lifting it like a piece of meat

starting to see white can't let the white eat me Jeremy don't let it

Taking the pea and dropping it down the back of her suit, her elbow doing a marionette twist and *the pain hitting her face a giant white truck*

The pea rolled down between suit and socket, dropped in like the eight ball.

"Connection established, transmitting..." said a quiet voice. Paul was sitting in his office, watched several windows pop up at once. One graphed the data received, a spike on the increase. Another reported her vital signs, quickly being medicated back to stability. The window with her visuals showed concrete and girder — Eileen's mask was still crumpled and flattened under her. He heard the faint caw of and splash of the ocean.

An angel appeared above his shoulder. "Remember," it cooed, "You have a meeting at Yellow Belly with —"

Paul waved the reminder off and took a moment to deactivate his scrambleface. After it resolved into his earless face and grey eyes, he ported to a bustling restaurant.

A tremendously fat waiter set a drink down on the white linen. "Welcome back, sir."

"Thanks. I'm waiting for someone."

The waiter nodded and left.

He lifted the drink and had some. It tasted like cranberries and iron. Across the way, there was a pair of women chatting intently. One of them had a flat console that she was pointing to, a physical thing with a touchscreen. She gave it to the other woman and pointed something out to her.

Paul watched the body language of the woman who had first had the console and decided she was sales. When he looked at the other woman, he noticed her lips were changing. She put her fingers to them and smiled with them. She cycled through a few more lip options, finally looking up with a question in her eyes at the saleswoman.

Paul took another big sip of his drink, thinking about how interesting it was that a Frisco version of the makeup mirror — and makeup consultant — had been created. Even the design of the thing was interesting — it looked like one of those old bookreaders, rather than the normal mid-air windows. He wished he had the time to follow these things up instead of meeting with a Marlboro exec about how to upgrade their ancient product.

Doug Doug Doug. I need you here, Patterson. Too much to juggle here on my own. At first he just thought he was holding out for a raise, but he was acting too weird for that. Was he planning to defect to another agency?

Maybe it's a simpler reason, Paul thought, immediately pulling up a file on

Doug he'd had compiled by a third party years ago. The bank account PIN was still the same. He scrolled through it and found a litany of financial sins, lapsed payments and negative numbers.

Just a money issue. Paul thought about just giving him the cash for moving expenses, but that could cause tension with the other employees. And Doug could take offense pretty easily. So it looked like he'd have to go about getting him the money in a left-handed fashion.

And once he had Doug in place here, he could really get going on preparing for the Sesquicentennial.

"Whattayou smiling at there, Paul?" a man sitting opposite him said with an impish grin, pretending to look at the windows in front of Paul. "Dirty pictures?"

Paul, knowing that the Marlboro exec saw nothing, opened a time window so he could see how late he was.

"I know, I know," he said. "Sorry."

"Caught in traffic?" Paul said with a wry smile, sliding Eileen's visuals to one side and Doug's finances to another.

"That was one of my favorites," the exec said with a laugh. "I'm too old to come up with a whole new set of excuses."

Nicky woke up in a good mood. It was just one of those days where the sun redeemed any chipped-paint bedrooms, suffused the sketchiest places with a contagious glow. She lay on her futon for a few minutes, drifting in and out. Eventually her watch exploded.

"You lazy bitch! Get up! Do you want to sleep your —"

She slapped the alarm quiet. *God, my voice is shrill. Who would want to wake up to that?* Glancing back at her empty bed, *I guess no one does.* But her mood was such that she grinned at her self-pity.

She told her watch to play Eyes Absent, a dimecore band with a sweet-voiced boy angel for a lead singer. She got it to play from its speaker instead of directly to her cochlea — she found that heavy bass rattled her ear bones something nasty. She converted the futon into a couch, grunting with its weight. She left it unmade in the hope that somewhere, somehow, it was driving Kath crazy.

Still, I'd like to have Kath's fingers in me right now... Nicky cupped her groin, sliding her panties up and down, giving herself a cameltoe. She walked out of the room, bouncing with Eyes Absent and her own electricity.

She turned on the shower and stripped down, stepping in when the water was warm enough. She caught an eggy whiff of her hair before she soaked it and had to think for a minute where she had been last night. *Walked around a lot,* she remembered, feeling guilty thinking about what her mom would think about her carefree maskless existence. Mom had even worn her mask around the house on smog warning days.

She did a quick wash of the normal areas and took a while longer soaping up her naughty bits. Kathy had introduced her to the wonderful dexterity of finger play — when they had the masturbation film in health class, her 14-year-old self had rolled her eyes and wondered at the lengths the school would go to to keep them from fucking. But Kathy was older, and it had still been dirty when she was young. Nicky closed her eyes and tilted her face into the shower head, getting into a nice nice finger rhythm, imagining the singer of Eyes Absent looking like he sounded, moving as he —

The shower clicked off.

"Fuck!" Nicky said. She leaned against the wall of the stall, eyes still closed but tightly now, in frustration. Her skin immediately goosebumped. "Fucking —" she said, grabbing her towel and drying off.

Man I mean there's less people using water now so why don't we get a little fucking bit more? Cheap motherfuckers. Ten minutes a day had seemed enough at the rental office, but in reality they flashed by.

She scooped up her clothes and went back to her room, trying to recapture her mood of a few minutes ago, but the light from her window now seemed more demanding than inviting. Grabbing her bra off the desk chair, she slipped into it while looking out the window, daring anyone to look — her daily ritual, equal parts indifference and exhibitionism. There was often someone walking by out there — like that guy there with his dog — it was just that no one ever looked up. She pulled on a yellow t-shirt and some shin-highs.

She braided her hair, her fingers moving deftly. Seeing the dog made her think about working on her flukes. *Yeah, I should get to it... right after breakfast.* She finished her braids, checked to make sure they were fairly even. They seemed to go over well, boys thought they were cute and girls were impressed by her braiding skills — it was easy for her, but not for everyone.

She headed downstairs, thinking about the night before. Those two art shows... she sighed, getting out some cereal and bread. *The weird thing is... they didn't inspire me at all. They were draining.*

She flashed the bread and poured herself some Lucky Charms. *That awful Mike Narc show, fuck. Is that what you have to do? Couldn't they just give you money based on your work, not how well you spin your image?* She sat down at the kitchen table and stared in at her gecko, flicking his tongue at her through the cage. She spooned in a mouthful of cereal and stared at the box.

Collect All the Colors and Win! the cereal box suggested. Before she could read further she noticed the gecko had a paw out, trying to hook in a stray piece of cereal. She pushed it close enough with her spoon, watched it try to eat it.

And those guys in the train yard... it was cool but... kind of psycho. She just couldn't imagine her work just — out there, with nothing and no one behind it. *Kinda like what JK does, though.*

That was what appealed to her about JK, originally, but she never thought about putting her own work out that way. *Fine for him, I mean he's obviously got someone paying his rent...*

When she finished her toast, she left her dishes in the sink and grabbed a can of coffee out of the cupboard. Her watch started ringing just as she sat down on the couch in the living room. *It's probably... yep, Mom, right on time.* Her mom called a couple of times a week, almost always right at 11. It was almost as if she waited around for the few times that she could call without seeming needy, but the exactness of the calls was unnerving.

It must be hard to deal with all that extra time, not having to sleep, she thought guiltily. Her watch had stopped ringing, and she opened her coffee. She put her feet up on the end table and watched the flukes scramble around in their cage, their yipping irritating.

"Oh, I'll feed you soon," she said. She wondered if she should make the myth flukes mute and decided it'd make a gallery a little hard to bear, even harder than usual. *Not that they'd ever be shown in a gallery,* she thought sourly. She wondered why seeing Narc's show, which *was* similar thematically even though she hated to admit it, hadn't given her hope. *It'll seem like I'm imitating him...* The thought made her sick.

Nicky spent the rest of the morning feeding her animals and cleaning up a bit. Then she decided that she'd surprise her mother with a visit to Frisco, and, with a defiant look up at her lab, set off towards the SkyTrain station.

Family first, she thought as she pulled the door closed, *I mean, she's been there for months, and I haven't given her a proper visit.*

The SkyTrain station was a few blocks from her house. There was yellow tape across the entrance and a sign saying that service was being cut back to rush hour only at this station.

Nicky sighed and stood for a moment, weighing the 30-minute walk with the prospect of heading back to the lab. *Mom'll be happy to see me... and maybe I can hit her up for a cab ride home.*

She almost went up through Gastown but decided against it. She would have liked to see her old neighborhood — JK told her it was really different now that there wasn't any construction — but she didn't want to walk through Hastings and Main to get there. She'd have to step over people lying all over the sidewalks, sick and sad people with no money left, waiting to die. Nicky could never harden herself entirely to them — sure, they'd made stupid investments, but they were unlucky too.

Her dad was a real hardliner — it was one of the first things he'd said about Frisco, "None of those bankrupts come begging when you're trying to walk somewhere — it's like I remember when I was a kid." It bothered Nicky, but she couldn't exactly argue with him when he was handling her investments, her just-in-case money.

Nicky was starting to get hot despite the cool air, the midday shadows too short to offer much relief. She was in a residential neighborhood that was fairly well off — not quite a gated community but pretty close. In the window of one she saw a sign in bold letters: Locked and Loaded Theftproofing. A few houses down, there was another one — looked like a popular choice for those leaving for Frisco. It sounded familiar — *did Mom go with them?* She couldn't remember, she just remembered the description of high-caliber overkill that seemed to persuade her mother.

She wished she had peed before she'd left — she could feel that can of coffee now. Well, she'd just have to hold it. She recalled, as she often did in these circumstances, Mave Slamstein's *Perfection*. It was one of the first genart pieces she ever saw, as part of a high school class on applied art trends.

It was a human baby, a pink little newborn, lying on a giant purple cushion. Kicking around, flailing its tiny acorn fists, but completely silent. The camera POV rotated around slowly and focused on its face. The class gasped in unison — the baby had no orifices at all. No mouth or eyes, a bump where the nose should be, smooth expanse of groin.

Then, the teacher went to the next video — it took awhile with those old machines — and the baby faded in again. "Finding it a little hard to breathe?" a knowing voice asked. A chic little mask popped on the baby's face, and two cartoon eyes were drawn in. The class had laughed. "The GE Smogmaster fits… well, just about anyone!" A baby's giggle was heard.

Instead of learning the salient parts of that lesson — namely, that marketing played a big part in redeeming even shock art, and how that campaign in particular swayed public opinion on clone experimentation — Nicky had been hypnotized by the first image of the baby.

Perfection. She had researched the artist's history for a clue as to whether it was a sincere or ironic title, for details on how long the baby survived, how she funded a project with human DNA. Nicky would have loved to work with the original clay, as it were, and she was bitter that only billionaires could afford to license the genome.

But that was when she was 15 — she was old enough now to appreciate the beauty and achievability of a small canvas. *Give me a fluke any day.* Maybe one day, but for now she'd take minor miracles over frankensteins. She knew she'd have to work up to it — she felt bad when a fluke wasn't healthy, how could she cope with a human clone? And human clones were never entirely healthy.

Is that a — yeah! Nicky saw a pair of golden arches on the horizon, and mentally inverted it to be a W. *Washroom ahoy!* She sped up, trying to see if there were people inside.

She crossed diagonally to the restaurant, relieved to see people moving about inside. *Weird — no door on this side...* Then she saw the sign: "This McDonald's is for the exclusive use of the Maple Acres community. Underground entrance only. Sorry for the inconvenience!"

Nicky stared a hole through the old biddy sedately drinking her tea by the window and kept walking. She heard the *Perfection* baby giggle in her mind: *I never have to pee! No garbage in, no garbage out!*

By the time she grimly turned onto Robson she was near bursting. "How much further?" she asked her watch.

"The Self office is approximately 65 meters away," said her watch.

"How close is my bladder to bursting?"

"The Sports Ristwatch doesn't monitor that organ in this version. Would you like to be notified if this feature becomes available?"

Nicky turned into the Self office. She marched up to the first empty desk she saw and pushed a smile out onto her face. "Hi," she said. "I'm here to have a talk session with my mom, but first I need to use your washroom."

The woman behind the desk smiled apologetically. "I'm sorry —"

I'm sorry you don't understand the word "need," bitch. Nicky didn't speak, just walked towards a door that lead to a white hallway with rooms on either side. They were empty, so she continued through the backroom. "Miss," a voice called. "There's no —"

Nicky pushed through the last door and stumbled through into the alley. *Oh.* She looked back, saw the counter lady flickering a little in the doorway before it hissed shut.

Guess Friscans don't need toilets.

She looked down the alley towards the street. Not a lot of people, no one seemed to be looking down between the stores. She deliberated a few seconds, and then squatted behind some boxes.

She watched her piss creep across the asphalt, around large rectangular boxes all embossed with the Self logo. She zipped up and stepped carefully down the alley and around the front again. She took a breath and walked in the office. *Take two.*

Luckily, the woman was busy with some clients, a whole family. Nicky went up to the man, who looked up from the documents he was scanning to offer her a seat. "Actually, I'm here to talk to a Friscan. My mom. She's given me a coupon."

"I'll just see if we have any free slots," he said, holding up his hand.

Nicky smiled, decided against telling him that there were three rooms free

— he'd obviously totally missed her the first time.

"Ah, well, you're lucky, we do have a booth available right now. They're usually booked. Could I have the coupon please?" He indicated the payplate.

Nicky called it up on her watch and held it up to the payplate.

An older man, about sixty, came in. The salesman greeted him. "I'll be right with you as soon as I get her set up."

Nicky didn't look at the saleswoman but heard her falter in the middle of her spiel as the man lead her through the door to the booth. One of the rooms was in use now, a convincing office suite with a man and a woman in it. "Interviews," her guide said. "For businesses without a proper set-up."

He pointed to a door. "I've put the call through to the coupon issuer — you have 15 minutes."

He makes it sound like a prison, she thought as she sidled by — she felt it was rude to walk through him — and entered the white room. She shut the door and was alone in the empty room with a chair. She waited for a second for it to start, and just as she was getting restless, a voice said, "Node contacted, resolving environment."

The room flicked to life, scanning the room for objects. The chair and Nicky were bathed in scanner crossfire for a few seconds each. Nicky heard the clinking and burble of voices. "I can't see her," she heard her mother's voice.

Then, everything was awash with color. A few seconds later the resolution crisped and her mother, who was looking around anxiously, suddenly saw her. "Nicky! Over here."

"Hi Mom," Nicky said. She took a seat and looked around. They were in a jungle-themed café. A parrot landed on the table and squawked, "Welcome to the Rainforest Café! Awk!" When it fluttered off, a feather drifted down, and Nicky thought that was a nice touch.

"A new hairdo, I see," her mom said.

"And you've gone blond," Nicky said. *And about 20 years younger.*

"I was so glad you called, I thought you'd never use the coupon!"

Nicky ignored the chastising tone. She looked around at the other tables — a few families, a few couples. There was even a table of people playing bridge. Everyone looked young, but then, so did Mom. They might have been sisters. "So this is where you hang out?"

Mom laughed. "Yeah, for a few hours a day. It's big for ex-Vancouverites — the rainforest thing and all."

"A few hours, eh?" Nicky said, smiling. "Sounds like my life."

Her mom smiled sardonically. "I suppose…"

"Dad working a lot?"

Mom nodded. "More than before the move. Last week he didn't come home at all. Transition, expansion. He has two secretaries now," Mom said, with a little laugh. "Seems really… energized by it all, though."

Nicky didn't want to hear any more about it. The way Mom said "secretaries" reminded her of when Dad had told her about his affairs, though she didn't understand him at the time. "Sometimes mergers are exclusive deals," he had said, holding her hand. "And sometimes they aren't." He had looked towards the bathroom door where her mom had locked herself in. "But it doesn't mean the original merger isn't profitable." He had squeezed her hand, and Nicky had nodded, remembering something she had heard in Grade 6 business class. "Always read the fine print," she said. He had smiled hugely then and hugged her.

A chimp loped over with a teapot, but Mom declined. The chimp made an offended shriek, threw up his hand, and stalked off. "How's your mah-jongg group going?" Nicky said.

Mom's eyes lit up. "Oh, it's great. We're playing in this fantastic environment now — we're giants in ancient China or somewhere. When we put the pieces down they crush these peasant villages, and if we're tired, we just lean against a mountain! It's so funny. Actually, I was right in the middle of a game when you called, that's why it took a while for me to get here. Everyone was annoyed." She laughed, and when she saw Nicky's guilty look, she said, "Not for me leaving the game — we're a bunch of old-timers, they have kids too — they were just jealous."

"How do you know," Nicky said, "That they're old? Weren't you saying you met them over here?"

"Oh, you can tell in the first five minutes. Just what they talk about. Even the styles, sometimes. No one would have a haircut like you, for instance. And not everyone wants to look young. Jonah — he's a stubborn old goat — says he looks exactly the same. I believe him too. He's distinguished, though, while we women just look old." Another laugh that drained Nicky. "You look wonderful, though, Nicky, even with that… unique haircut. It's been so long since I've seen you face-to-face I was beginning to worry. With your lifestyle."

Nicky sighed. *Here we go again…* "Mom, my lifestyle is nothing to worry about. It sounds boring, compared to destroying peasant villages."

"It's just that you sound like your uncle… with the artist lifestyle, thinking it's fine to just to get by. You know what happened to him."

"Aw, Mom," Nicky said. "I'm not exactly starting a revolution."

"Neither was he," her mom said quickly. "He was just in the wrong place at the wrong time. Socialized with the wrong type of people."

"Ah c'mon," Nicky said, smirking at her mom's denial. "I mean, he worked at the company where they got the shuttles." She had always enjoyed the idea of Uncle Max being part of the insurgent group. There had even been a movie made a few years ago about the Harmless Cranks.

"Do you really think," her mother said, poking at her, "that a relative of your *father* would be a part of a terrorist group who destroyed millions of dollars worth of equipment and endangered hundreds of lives? Just to stop a billboard going up?"

Nicky arched an eyebrow and shrugged. "Well, it wasn't just another billboard. It was the moon."

"Still," Mom said. "You —" she was cut off by a sudden roar.

"Uh oh folks," an announcer said. "Looks like there's gonna be — a Rumble in the Jungle!"

Across the room, a wall of vines parted to reveal a huge expanse of savannah. There was a pride of lions off to one side, and approaching them with a casual lope were several grey apes. A lion roared again, and a gorilla answered it with a fearsome teeth-baring scream.

A weasel leapt up on their table. It had a peaked cap and a notebook. "Place your bets," it squeaked around a stubby cigar. "Odds are two to one against the greys."

"Ooooh, I like those odds," Mom said. "I'll put $500 on the lions."

The weasel nodded curtly and leapt off.

"You have one minute left," a voice said.

"Oh, Mom," Nicky said, getting her attention. "My time's up. Gotta go."

She tutted. "You're going to miss the show. It's really good — you can choose a champion to ride with and everything. See the fight from their perspective."

"Next time, I guess."

"Betting is closed folks. Those with heart conditions are advised… to get the hell out!" said the announcer. Nicky noticed it was a python that had slithered up the mike stand. She kind of wanted to see the beginning of the fight but she was worried that if she stayed for longer that it would automatically begin charging her. *And that just wouldn't do…*

Hand in front of her, she walked towards where she remembered the door to be and then slid her hand along until she found the knob. She brushed through the bridge group doing it, and she apologized. They didn't seem to mind.

Gassy Jack still reigned over Gastown, Nicky was glad to see. The shabby and leaden statue watched her wander to JK's apartment. She was struck by how quiet it was — JK hadn't lied about the lack of construction.

She got to his lobby and called him. "Hey, I'm downstairs."

"Hey, so am I!" JK walked into the lobby carrying a huge bag and his bike slung awkwardly over his elbow.

"Bad time, I guess," Nicky said, lifting the bike off his hands.

"Actually, a really good time." He carried the burlap bag out onto the street and set it down gently next to the curb. He thumbed his watch and then tapped it to hers. "Directions for tonight's festivities."

"It's tonight?" Nicky said. "Great!"

"Tell everyone you know," he said. "I'm going to be running around getting everything ready." He checked his watch. "Chase is supposed to be coming by."

"By car?" Nicky said, trying to help him look down the road.

"I don't know, that's why I brought m'horse," he said, indicating the bike she was holding. "Shit, should I bring..." he looked up towards his apartment. "No," he decided, smiling slightly at Nicky. "Sorry, I'm a bit of a wreck. I'm always a spaz before these things. What's up?"

"Nothing, just thought I'd come by and check out the old neighborhood. Crazy how quiet it is."

"Yep. Especially at night. This was one of the neighborhoods that emptied right out." JK sat down on his burlap bag. He had on baggy overalls and his hands were dusted brown.

"Are those the seeds?" she asked.

He slapped the bag, nodding. "It was a push, but there's enough."

"Man, you get a lot done," Nicky said. "I'm jealous." She thought about her flukes and the elaborate ways she'd avoided working on them today.

"I'm jealous of you," JK said, "Wandering around the city. Cranking sweet styles." They both laughed at his teenage slang. "I mean look at me!" He noticed his brown hands and slapped them clean. "I been too fucking busy to eat, never mind dress. It's been a while since I walked around beholden to no-one, like artist slash conwoman Tricky Nicky."

Nicky smiled. "Yeah. I know. I've got it good. It's just, I don't know, frightening to see people getting their art out there. It feels like there's a huge gap between working on my flukes and getting them shown somewhere."

JK nodded. "It's a balance thing." He looked down the road, pushing his glasses back on his nose. "Between having not enough time and having too much time. You just gotta work on it."

Nicky noticed a crack on one of the lenses she hadn't noticed before, but didn't ask him about it in case it made him self-conscious. She looked down the road instead and noticed a car. JK was standing up. It was a Nissan Piranha, blue and sleek, and it pulled up. *At least it isn't one of those stupid KrazyCars.*

He hefted his sack. "All right, see you tonight, Tricky."

Chase's window went transparent and he clicked on the outside speaker. "You need a ride somewhere, Nicky?"

She shook her head, and realized she still had JK's bike. She caught his eye and lifted the bike questioningly.

He was putting the sack in the back seat. "Uh, would you mind hanging on to it, Nicky? I don't wanna fuck up his upholstery…"

"I'm gonna have to start charging you a storage fee," she said with a grin.

"Great!" he waved and disappeared into the car. "Just invoice me."

Chase was still waiting to see if she needed a ride. "No thanks," she said, pointing at the bike. His surprised look was extremely satisfying.

She didn't actually have any intention of riding the bike, but a few blocks later the quiet streets and its slight awkwardness convinced her that it was silly to carry it. She unrolled it and, after a car passed, got on and began to pedal.

She watched the grey road slide beneath her, delighted at the speed. *The hell with the SkyTrain.* She tilted her head up and felt the wind whip by, yanking at her pigtails. She heard a car coming behind her, and she pulled off and stopped as it passed. It slowed slightly as it passed, but she put on an innocent look, balancing on the bike on tippytoe, conscious of her oddity. *Where did JK get this thing, anyway?*

Feeling bold, she decided to head down through Hastings and Main, the most direct route home. She stole glances at the bike as she wound her way down to Hastings: springs flanking the wheels, a silvery black frame so convoluted and squiggly it made her dizzy to look, two big buttons to brake and two more beneath them to — *hey, what were those for?*

"Ahhhgg!" the old man yelled, hands in front of his face, his body five feet from being run over by Nicky. Thumbs convulsed and punched the closest buttons, the mystery buttons — *not stopping not stopping starting to sink* — she released them and the bike popped up in the air! Over the old man by a good five feet! The bike landed, and Nicky's crotch got even closer to the hard seat. *Ow fuck!*

Thank god I'm OK ow bruised but OK, she thought as she thumbed the brakes and stumbled-slid off the bike. *How embarrassing, did anyone see?* The side street, within sight of Hastings, had a few homeless people littered here and there — overflow from the main strip. Nicky looked around and rolled up the (*stupid deathtrap of a*) bike, but none of the human heaps were even slightly interested in her — even the man who she nearly hit had merely rolled over and stared at her through muck-rimmed eyes.

Nicky turned onto Hastings and checked out the scene. Not as bad as she'd seen it, a few dozen lumps on the street but just a couple of zombies shuffling around. *Maybe the more mobile ones find some shade during the day...* she thought but then realized what had really thinned out the herd. There was a black debtor van with three or four security people outside of it.

"Eric Palmerson, your debt has been purchased by Sony Holdings Ltd.," one of them was intoning in a bored voice. "Are you capable of paying it off today?" The man, presumably Eric, a sad, bewildered look on his face, tried to walk away but was restrained. "In that case, Sony Holdings Ltd. has requested that you be relocated to a factory of their choosing until you've worked off said debt. Thank you for your cooperation." Eric was helped up into the back of the van, saying something that Nicky couldn't hear.

Nicky walked by, and one of the guards, the woman, looked at her for a moment too long. Nicky scratched her eyebrow significantly, showing her watch, and the woman immediately looked for another likely candidate.

Just when she relaxed, she felt a hand on her shoulder. The stories she'd heard about solvent people getting snatched by security people trying to fill their quotas flooded her mind, made her rear back her bike into swinging position and whip around...

"Nicky, right?" The security guy took off his black sunglasses and grinned.

"Yeah." It was a guy from her last year at UBC. *What was his fucking name?*

"It's John. John Steiner."

"Oh I remember. How's it going?" Nicky immediately felt stupid asking the automatic question.

He shrugged, fiddled with his sunglasses. "All right I guess. Hoping to make the move in a few months, working towards that. A buddy got me this extra job,

I'd like to get a silver package at least."

"Oh yeah," Nicky said, looking behind him when he thumbed towards his buddy. The other security people were lifting up a heap on the street. "How is it?"

"Oh," he said, shrugging. "It's OK. Good days and bad. They're getting relocated to a factory in the West Indies nowadays — beautiful climate there, even the smog is low because of the air pressure systems or something. A free vacation if you ask me."

"A working vacation," Nicky said.

"Well, exactly," he said, missing her sarcasm entirely. "Makes you think, though. Lots of them are there because they put all their eggs in one basket, made foolish investments. 'Diversify or die' isn't just a catchy ad slogan."

Nicky made a non-committal sound, her gut twisting between scorn and anxiety.

Someone called him over, an angry bark. "Gotta go," he said, pausing awkwardly. In his eyes, Nicky saw the signs of an impending invitation to dinner, a drink, as clearly as clouds gathering. Before it broke she smiled and nodded goodbye.

"See you around," she said, turning and walking away. "Good luck in Frisco."

"It's not how often he's there," Doug said, tossing some more Peanutz into his mouth. "I mean, the office runs smoothly enough without Harris. It's what it *represents*."

Lauden was nodding. "I entirely agree. He's definitely more in Frisco than here. Still, he got the meeting room wired for face-to-face meetings, and that's not cheap. A lot of companies aren't even doing that." He finished his beer and pointed at his glass. The bartender nodded, nearly imperceptibly.

"Me too," said Doug, looking at the Peanutz in his hand. *How did they get the salt to stay?* he marvelled. The salted peanuts he'd had as a kid had made his hands salty and greasy for hours afterwards…

*"…*don't you think?" Lauden asked.

"Sorry, man, I missed that," Doug said, guiltily. *There you go, Patterson, ignoring Lauden again.*

"Chan doesn't know what he's getting into," Lauden repeated.

Their beers arrived. "Enjoy Coors Silver Bullet," the bartender mumbled.

"Oh. Yeah," Doug agreed. "The higher the rise, the harder the fall." He paused. "I should know."

Lauden patted his back. They were both at the bar, so he had to look in the mirror to make eye contact. "It's not like that, Doug. People are talking, but most people just figured you wanted off the fast track. Most of us figured you'd have gone months ago."

Doug realized he had almost finished his new beer. *Better slow down.* He didn't want to end up crying on Lauden's shoulder. "Yeah, well. Research is my first love, anyway. Good honest work." He'd have dismissed it as data-mining five years ago, but now he was glad for the soft landing.

"Well, you know, I've always thought so," said Lauden. "Even if the smelter does a lot of the work."

Doug winced inside as he realized that this was probably something he'd said in the past. He glanced at Lauden, working steadily at his beer (he'd never known him to be such a drinker!) and looked at the backwards window signage mirrored back legibly: Coors Bar and Tavern.

He scraped the bottom of the bowl. "Can I get another bowl of Peanutz?" he said to the bartender's back. The bartender seemed to consider it before nodding. *Gimmie a break buddy, you're not the only one who hates your job*, Doug thought.

Did he hate his job? He wasn't sure. He hated his life at this point, that he knew. "Lauden," he said. "Do you love your job?"

Lauden finished off his beer and ordered another for them. "No. No, I don't love it. But no job's perfect."

"No, no job's perfect," he thought back to the research that he had started today, cross referencing all the conflicting data and loose ends they had on the Infiltrators. "Do you think the Infiltrators exist?"

Lauden was chewing. "Well, it's hard to tell," he said when he swallowed. "I mean, when I was last digging, they were still pretty strong, image-wise. But that was six, seven years ago. Now you don't hear much about them."

"Yeah, the CHA buzz rating's about four. Less than four," Doug said. "Do you think they could have been assimilated by the companies they were working for? Instead of going underground, going aboveground and legit? Why else would they have been so quiet for so long?"

Lauden smiled. "Maybe they're planning something…" he said in an ominous voice, raising a puffy eyebrow.

Doug snorted at his colleague's teasing, looked towards the door thoughtfully. *Should be getting home, soon.* He was about to look away when it opened and an attractive young woman came in.

Doug looked away, nevertheless wishing she'd come up to them. Just to talk. *I could ask her if she'd heard of the Infiltrators,* he rationalized. *It'd be work related.*

She came up to them.

"Hey Sam, sorry I'm late," she said, getting up on a stool with a cute little hop. She had ebony hair with stars in it and a school bag. *Lauden, you sly —*

"That's OK. Doug, Cara, Cara, Doug," Lauden said, leaning back and introducing them politely. Then he took out a recorder. "OK, whattaya got for me today?"

She's an informant, Doug realized. He was disappointed.

Cara pointed at Doug, a question in her (*lovely*) eyes.

"He's a co-worker, it's OK," Lauden said to her. "Have you read up on the Ephemerals yet?" Lauden asked him.

"Looked it over," Doug hedged.

"I've got something really good today," Cara said, fairly bursting. "A *party*. A totally *secret* party. Tonight. My friend Amy's coming too," she said, looking at Doug.

Doug excused himself to go to the washroom. While he was there, he let Cheryl know that he'd be working late tonight.

Maybe really late.

Nicky took a pinch from the sophisticrat's tiny box. "Thanks!"

The boy inclined his bowler hat. "My pleasure. Not the most complementary of drugs for a party like this, but…" he shrugged. "Snuff's my vice."

Nicky breathed in lilac, took a snort. "Ah, I don't mind letting my nose work twice as hard for one night of the year," she said, feeling all chipper.

The boy laughed. "Is this an annual event?"

She shook her head, barely connected to her body with all the drugs. She looked around at the swirl of people, moving her hand with the flow.

"It's wonderful, whatever it is," the boy said, realizing he wouldn't get an answer. "The sponsors are miraculously restrained… there aren't even any vendors here. I was at a MAC party last night — so crass."

"You were at a MAC party?" Nicky said incredulously.

"Friends insisted," he said, pulling at his collar. "And I try to keep an open mind. But they had models prowling the audience, kissing people at random — ostensibly to show off the lipstick. It was terrifying."

Nicky bust out laughing, imagining the poor sophisticrat so besmirched. She caught a new whiff. "Oh, wow, roses?" She looked across the huge hangar and saw a circle of people around a rapidly growing rose bed. JK was striding proudly away, his bags of tricks hanging off his arms and shoulders. "Keep watering!" he yelled at the rose bed people.

"He's the sponsor," she told the sophisticrat.

JK caught her eye and headed her way. "Tricky!" he said, smothering her against a bag that smelled like soil when he hugged her. "So you found our secret lair."

"Yep," she said. "It's a great place for it. Was it expensive to rent?"

"My pal Simon found it… he thinks it's an old airport hangar… but I think they used to grow pot here at some point, because the soil inside here is too good."

"Just hope it doesn't rain!" said the sophisticrat, poking with his brolly up at the roof, burned away except for a single windowed arch.

"Just hope it does!" JK said with a huge eyebrow wiggle that made Nicky giggle. "Time for my next set. Talk to you soon." He walked away, dipping his hand into one of the small sacks.

"You know…" JK pronounced to all, cocking his nose to the wind. "I think it's just about time for... orange blossoms!"

There was a smattering of excited applause as JK started spreading seeds in front of him. Then he walked over them, stomping them into the ground, and waved at people to follow him on his spiralling journey. Eight or nine people joined him, a lot of them with plastic jugs, clapping in a rhythm and stomping together.

Nicky and the sophisticrat stood back on the periphery of the circle. "They seem to know what to do," he said.

In stepping away, Nicky bumped into someone behind her.

"Sorry, whoa," said a shaggy-haired guy. He stopped what he was doing to watch the conga line of seed stampers. Nicky thought one or two of them looked kind of familiar, especially the guy with the bandana. *Was he at some art show?* When JK got to the center of the circle, he threw a handful of seeds up in the air and then the conga line scattered to the edges of the circle, where already, some sprouts were unfolding.

Then JK said in a stage voice. "Looks like it's going to rain!"

Everyone who had jugs started to throw water. Nicky leaned forward to give her little bottle a squirt. The plants sprang up wherever the water hit, practically crackling with energy. JK rubbed his chin with satisfaction and shuffled off.

"That's a cool shirt!" The shaggy-haired guy said, his lips smacking with some gum that was giving him a big grin. "Where'd ya get it?"

The orange blossoms burst into bloom, getting a big *ah* from the crowd. "Smell!" someone yelled, and someone else giggled.

Nicky looked down at her shirt to remind herself. It was pink and featured an angry monkey trying to shake off the double helix that was binding his fingers together. "It's an old design from, like, 2010? I forget where. I flashed it on myself." The guys looked at it for a few seconds more than necessary, and she remembered why she'd considered flashing the design on the back.

"Want some gum?" Shaggy asked, offering her an open pack of Body Buzz.

"Shore," Nicky said, taking a piece of narcandy.

As she did, someone yelled, "Swoosh!" and a black object flipped through the air. Shaggy jumped up to head it.

Nicky found it hard to continue the conversation with the sophisticrat, distracted by Shaggy's little jumps. One energetic lunge to elbow the swoosh back to his partner showed off a tastily muscled stomach.

"Nike!" he called, as it arced towards his partner.

Lean, energetic, and not a lot of mess, Nicky assessed.

"Swoosh!" his partner said, doing a tricky back-kick. Nicky remembered having seen some article about how swooshers can make enough on pitch-money alone, if they're good enough to draw a crowd.

Helps if they're a couple of hotties, Nicky thought, noting how many more girls were watching than boys.

"Never been one for games, myself," the sophisticrat said with a sniff.

"Not even mindgames?" Nicky said, realizing she said that out loud. She laughed to cover up the embarrassment, and the feeling of laughter through her body was delicious. *Oh god, I've got to get laid.*

"Hey it's the scientist girl," a dark figure said as he reeled past. He had his dreadlocks tied up in a bandana, but when he smiled she recognized him, even without his beard. He was carrying an open wine bottle and had it corked with his thumb.

"Hey, skulls on your teeth! I met you in the train yard!" She poked him in the arm.

"Wow," he said, "That sounds like a song." He stared at her for a second and then grabbed her arm. "I have to show you something," he said, pulling her away. Nicky stumbled along and looked back with an apologetic smile, but the sophisticrat had already turned away. She could practically hear him sniffing, *skulls on your teeth indeed.*

"This is the coolest place in the history of cool places," he declared as they walked across the hangar between groups of people and riotous flora.

She grabbed the wine bottle and took a slug. "And you found it?"

He looked at her and grinned. "Yes, just a few days after I met you actually. Me and Andre were… I told you we're here because the scientist's thing is happening here, right?"

"You told me no such thing," Nicky said. They were going up the stairs now, at the edge of the building where there was a second floor to go to.

"Big symposium here in the summer. Biiiig thing. Watch your step."

"You're a scientist?" she asked, wobbling a little and grabbing his shoulder. She had to move even closer to him to let a pair of girls squeeze by on their way down. One of them was wearing exceptionally sheer purple pants that drew eyes like flies, in part due to the way her metal underwear held her parts spread apart.

"Those rigs are really big in Detroit," he said.

"When were you in Detroit?"

"Like last week — two weeks ago now, I guess." They got up to the second floor, where people were sitting in clumps here and there. "I finally escaped the

Motor City."

"And now you're here scouting out locations for aromatic symphonies," Nicky said. "Nice life."

"Well, it just so happened I found this place, I wasn't actually looking for it. Me and Andre were camping out here — the train yard was a little exposed — and no one came to kick us out so..." he shrugged and spread his hands in an expansive gesture, presenting the party.

The view from the second floor shelf was phenomenal — different-sized circles of plants in various states of bloom and decay, people milling about between them. From this vantage point they looked like cells to Nicky. She sat down on the ragged edge of the floor, dangled her feet down, almost lost a sandal. When she was tugging it on tight, something clicked.

She whipped around and looked at Simon. "You mean." She dropped her voice. He clambered down beside her, and she grabbed his bandana and whispered in his ear. "You haven't rented this place."

His skull-smile seemed all too appropriate now, as she imagined what would happen when the owner's security team arrived. It would be a massacre, like those old documentaries about the '20s...

"Don't worry," he said, a hand on her shoulder. "Whoever owns this building is in Frisco right now, scrambling to make a living on the new frontier. They didn't ever bother to put a lock on the door. If they're not going to buy a lock, would they hire a security team?"

This fiscally based argument calmed Nicky down, but she was still mad. How many people would be here if they knew? She imagined the entire floor beneath panicking, screaming, the stampede for the exit... *Jesus! How fucking irresponsible!*

She turned to the person on the other side of her, ignoring Simon. He was a very drunk but affable-looking man, a bit older than most of the crowd.

He met her eye. "I was thinking that I'd like to make a trip to the mountains," he said all at once. He nodded in their direction — it was too dark to see them now, but the lines of lights for the ski lifts were clearly visible. "Have you been up in the mountains?"

She nodded, meeting his serious gaze. He was balding and with his thin little moustache he reminded her of someone from an old movie.

"They're nice," he said, swinging his gaze back. "Are they nice?"

She thought about her skiing trip — her dad flirting with the instructor, bad cramps from her period, shabby patches of fake snow. "I saw a deer," she lied.

"It had a little white tuft, right here," she said, indicating her chin.

"Ha ha," he laughed. "Like a little beard." He touched his own chin.

She laughed too. She looked, but Simon had left. His wine was still there, though, so she snagged it.

"Whattaya think of my hair," he said, having moved from stroking his chin to stroking his head.

Nicky stared at him, the wine making her bold. "It's kinda neat," she decided. "It goes with your face and moustache and stuff."

"Chan doesn't know what he's talking about, does he?" At her questioning look, he elaborated. "Guy at work. Thinks I look like a… loser. Like I should… fix it."

"Ah, Chan's full of shit," she said.

When they finished laughing, he looked down at his battered suit, and the look of resignation slowly settled back down around his shoulders.

Near one of the circles she noticed Andre and Simon talking to JK, who was busily digging. There was a girl with them, too, and they were looking up at the second floor. She pointed in Nicky's direction, and Simon looked and nodded.

Nicky just looked away, a little alarmed by the attention. Then the man next to her waved. "My little friend," he mumbled.

"Ah," she said.

She took a slug of wine, the silver wrapping rasping her lip, and caught a whiff from the plants below. "Mmm, is that rosemary?"

His aquiline nose quivered, but he didn't say anything. She offered him the bottle. He shook his head in the convulsive way that shows that the body knows it's had much too much.

A few seconds later, he spoke. "A shared sensory experience is an integral part of a party or gathering. Most subcultures use music, but the Ephemeralists use a selection of plants to create an atmosphere with the sense of smell."

Nicky, baffled, leaned over to look to see if he was talking to someone beside him. There wasn't anyone. She felt the bottle being tugged out of her hand.

"Hey!"

"Hay's for horses," said Simon. "Security bust up the party yet?"

"Ha," she said, but couldn't help smiling back at him. He smelled faintly of something, oil, musk? "How'd you know JK?" she demanded. "Mr. Detroit."

"We corresponded for a long time," he said, handing her the bottle, wiping a red dribble off his chin. "Through the mail." He clambered back into his spot, which was suddenly empty. The balding guy was gone.

"Letters? Why would you —"

"Not letters, objects. Let's see… he sent me a pen with a naked guy on it, I sent him a pineapple tuft. He sent me a quick drawing of an inside-out can, I sent him a queen from a chessboard carved in ice."

"I had one of those," Nicky said. "They don't last very long."

"I doubt this one did either. I should ask him about that."

"Go on."

"OK. I sent him the runt of the litter, he sent me… I forget… no, it was a receipt from 2036."

"So we're definitely not dealing in antiques," said Nicky. "This is not some kind of antiques-dealing club."

"No, it's just stuff," said Simon. "Next time it was a subatomic particle I sent — he said it never got there —"

"Ha!" Nicky said. She looked down on the party below, looking for the swooshers. They must have packed it in. *Too dark maybe. Too many people to knock into.*

"—and he returned the empty box with something invisible inside."

"Jokers the both of you."

"In our small ways. Then—"

"You sent him tea leaves, for 'T.' But not through the mail," she said, taking out her tasteless gum.

His eyebrows shot up. "That's right! How'd you…" He noticed her looking around for somewhere to put her gum, and he held out his hand. She smacked it into his palm before he could change his mind. He calmly put it into his mouth.

"Eeeeew!" she said, swinging her legs in disgusted delight.

He shrugged.

"It's even *tasteless*," she said, finishing off the wine.

"Oh, it's not tasteless," he said with a huge grin. "It tastes like wine. And the inside of your mouth."

She giggled, shoving the bottle into his stomach.

"But there's only one way to know for sure," he said, and he leant over her and gave her a kiss.

Nicky sighed, happy, but not wanting it to degenerate into a go-nowhere makeout session she didn't let him go for seconds. "Go get us some more wine," she said, tugging at one of his dreads. "Or something."

"All righty," he said, hopping to his feet. He had on some industrial-looking shoes. *What did he do for money, anyway? He wasn't sending shit through the mail for free...*

Nicky looked around her, realizing that this event hadn't cost anything. She grinned as she watched her boy trip down the stairs. He walked toward JK, and Nicky said, "No, *he* doesn't have any drugs," she murmured. *Other than the ones he seems to permanently be on, that his brain creates for itself...*

She wished she hadn't used all her water on the plants — her throat was dry now. She looked around her for easy marks. She didn't want to get up and lose her spot. Or her balance, for that matter.

Simon was nodding at JK, heading for the corners of the hangar where people were putting up black sticks of some sort. She noticed Andre, his black face almost invisible in the growing darkness, after Simon clapped him on the back.

"Yes, well of course most of my people are over there already..."

Nicky turned her head at the familiar voice — it was the sophisticrat.

"Made it up, huh?" she said chattily.

"Hey Nicky," said Chase, who it turned out was the one talking to the sophisticrat. "George and I were just talking about friends we've lost to Frisco." He hunkered down into what she had begun to think of as Simon's spot. He had a bright red shirt and a yellow frost on his hair, making him a lot younger-looking than when she'd last hung out with him and JK. "I'd say I'm 50-50 — half there, half here."

"That many here?" said George the sophisticrat. He didn't deign to sit, just loomed there with his hands resting on his umbrella handle. "I feel practically stranded. Every other phone call I get is from some fabulous new club or restaurant there that someone feels compelled to rave to me about."

She looked at Chase to see that he was waiting for her numbers. "I lost a lot of my friends when I went into genetics," Nicky said, surprised that there was still bitterness in her mouth after so many years and her current up mood. "Thought I was wasting my time. So staying here is just the latest in a series of unpopular decisions."

"So most of your friends are here," Chase said.

She shrugged and nodded. Nicky remembered Chase's time in Frisco — or whatever they'd called it before the Self consortium took over. "Did any of your friends get caught in —"

Chase was nodding. "Yeah, quite a few died in Quake II. Or that is, their bodies were destroyed. Some people say that that was the turning point for Frisco

103

— a lot of very talented people who had gone over for temporary relief coding found themselves there permanently."

"Stranded forever. My lord," exhaled George.

Chase shrugged. "Naw. Most of them were OK with it. These are coder freaks, remember. They probably would have stayed, anyway."

"You didn't," said Nicky.

"Yeah. Weird, huh? That's why I went back — remember I was telling you about the Science Pavilion? Just for a day or so."

"And?" Nicky said.

"And... it was strange. Being approached by strangers who considered me their friends. Trying to figure out if the ones whose bodies had died were different because of that, or because time had passed. They were complaining about Self, mostly, about the way that things had become more restrictive... but they were also complaining about all the newbies and how watered down the communities had gotten... I had three people tell me that people from San Francisco hated the name Frisco. So it was hard to tell if they were genuinely discontented or just being elitist."

Nicky resisted giving George a pointed look. "Well, at least they're coders. They didn't waste their time learning an obsolete skill like genetic engineering."

"Learning's never a waste of time, even in a science most consider archaic," George pronounced in a manner that would have been irritating had he not clearly been under 20. "Though genetics in this day and age is a little like knowing how to hand-letter books after Gutenberg came along."

"I understand your little creatures are actually really good," said Chase. "JK was saying that he should have asked you to bring them along to be, you know, part of this."

"*He* said *that?*" Nicky said, shock and terror and delight meeting in a huge three-way collision inside her.

"Yeah!" Chase said, chuckling. "On our way in the car."

"What are they up to now?" said George, leaning forward on his brolly, looking down his nose with an amused smile at the action below. The sticks had turned out to be torches, and pretty soon all the corners were flickering with light. JK was still working away at the patch in the middle, and Nicky stared at his hunched-over figure, the stunned feeling starting to melt.

She had never thought of it — it was stupid, really, but she hadn't — but this environment would be the perfect place for her flukes. Just running around, surprising people with their oddities, impressing the couple of people who saw their common theme… *Wow.* She wanted to ask Chase what JK had said, exactly, but she felt silly about it.

Chase put his hand to the top of his head, and then Nicky felt the first drop. She heard the moans and sighs around her, the ruffling and *snap!* of George's umbrella — maybe even heard his satisfied smile — and scanned the crowd for JK. *He'll be disappointed, oh well, it's been fun…*

She spotted him in the flickering torchlight, his big moonface tilted up to the rain, those glasses still bravely hanging on. A second later she saw why — all around the hangar, the plants were growing. If they were coming up fast before, they were coming up furious now. One girl screamed as a vine curled up her leg, but her friend tore her free, and they dissolved into a fit of giggling — until the next frisky vine set off another scream. Nicky thought it was the girl with the sheer pants. *So much for that aloof poise…*

The air was rich and sweet, and the ground was practically covered by greenery. "We'll have some problems getting out of here," George noted.

"Does that thing turn into a weed-whacker?" asked Chase, nodding at the umbrella.

"A machete would be just the thing," George said.

Nicky laughed, watched him make chopping strokes with far-off eyes. *He'll bring one next time, no doubt about it.* Simon burst into sight, looking soaked enough for two people, his bandana gone and his hair sticking every way but down.

He gave her the *c'mon c'mon* gesture.

"What?" she said. He just jumped up and down. She got up and excused herself to Chase and George. "What?" she repeated, but he grabbed her hand and pulled her down the stairs.

Down on the ground, it felt like a forest, mud and still-writhing plant matter forming a floor. Simon, kicking water bottles out of the way, took her around a few twists and turns until they got to the patch in the middle.

JK was there on his hands and knees, smiling ecstatically, his mouth and teeth stained with crimson. He smeared his red hand on his overalls. "It worked, Tricky!"

Nicky looked around at other mouths, red and laughing mouths. *What the fuck?*

From behind, Simon shoved something big and hairy into her mouth. Before she could get it out, the juice trickled down her throat. *Strawberries!* She munched down and swallowed. "Yum!"

Simon took time out from gorging himself to hand her another choice one. She bit off and spat out the stem and took this one in two bites. She started looking through the brush for her own, saw one go from green to red, and her hand reached for it.

Simon grabbed her wrist. "Too green. Wait, wait, wait," he said as it grew riper and riper. She struggled and elbowed him, and he let her go. "OK!"

Her hand shot out and plucked it, but before she put it in her mouth, she knew it had turned bad. She turned and popped it in his mouth. He chewed, bravely at first, and then reluctantly, swallowing with a titanic effort. "Just perfect."

Nicky was looking through the bush, aware now of more hands everywhere. *Lucky Simon had tipped me off early.* He picked beside her, and she gave him a hip bump and a smile. She found another one, a little one with a lovely tartness. The rain was coming down hard now, washing the juice from her face onto her shirt. She was glad it was a pink one.

After being cuffed and blindfolded, Doug drifted off. He was exhausted and barely felt his cock being ridden. But every so often his nipples would be pinched or fingers shoved into his mouth, pulling him back.

"You're getting soft, you worthless shit," she said.

Take it easy. "I'm sorry."

"You're sorry, what?"

"I'm sorry, mistress."

"That's right, you snivelling worm," she said, slapping his chest.

Ow. Fuck. Doug closed his eyes under the blindfold and tried to figure out why the pretty standard taunts felt like insults. They'd always struck him as a little funny and cliché, just sexy tough talk. It used to excite him to see Cheryl get this aggressive, so different from her normal self.

He could feel tits sliding up his body. His chin was grabbed and forced up, hard kisses on his neck, and the blindfold got pushed up a little. He could see a sliver, Cheryl sliding down his body. *I should tell her, she hates it when I watch...*

Cheryl flicked at the head of his penis with her tongue, and Doug moaned. His wife smiled a little to herself, squeezing the shaft and dragging the flat of her tongue slowly over his hole. Her face was calm and peaceful, and for a second, Doug was able to relax and enjoy it.

"Mmm, honey, that's awesome," he said.

She looked at him and noticed that the blindfold was askew. Annoyance settled on her face, and she crawled over him to pull it down, planting one knee on his elbow. *Ow ow ow...*

He heard her feet hit the floor.

"You know what happens to Peeping Toms," she said. A drawer opened.

"Yes, mistress. They get punished," Doug said, his voice contrite.

"Turn over."

Doug did so, crossing his arms as he awkwardly flipped over, wincing as his dick was flattened to one side. *No need for you, son. You're out of the game.* He listened to Cheryl rummage through their toybox, thinking about two Christmases ago when he had given her the starter kit. At the staff party, Doug had been bellyaching about the shopping he still had to do for Cheryl, and Lauden suggested a Japanese brand called DominaTrix Aplenty — good value, considering how well built they were. A bit of a cliché, Doug supposed, but what the hell. But as it turned out, she got him *The Complete Idiot's Guide to*

Bottoming. It wasn't that huge a coincidence, he supposed — S/M was big that year, with that movie out — but damn, did it ever make him look like the best husband!

Even though it was pretty softcore, Doug enjoyed seeing his wife get into a good whipping session. But the past few months it had been different. He was *feeling* it more, somehow. When she called him names, he would think about his financial bungling and wonder if those names weren't accurate. When he had been on top at the agency, the idea of being treated like a slave was funny, even appealing in its novelty. But he wasn't on top anymore.

By the sound of it, Cheryl was strapping on the Double Header. There was a snap and an *oh* as she turned it on and eased it inside her cunt.

"No mistress, please don't ass-fuck me," Doug begged sincerely. It was times like these that he was thankful that the toys were self-lubricated — by the abruptness of her movements and her silence, Cheryl was pretty mad.

He felt the bed move as she got on and into position. Then he felt a touch on his back. The Double Header snapped off.

"What — what's this?" Cheryl said quietly, her voice shaky and out of role.

"What's what... Cher—mistress?"

She was rubbing the spot on his back. "Is it a — tattoo? A brand? What — what is this, Doug?"

Hearing his name meant playtime was over. "I don't know."

"What do you mean, you don't know?" Her voice was fraying frantic. "Did you not think I'd see it?"

"I honestly don't know what —"

"Oh, Doug," she said, her voice heavy with disappointment. She got up from the bed. He heard her removing the Double Header.

"Will you at least tell me what it is?" Doug asked.

Cheryl made an annoyed tutting sound as she left the bedroom.

Doug flipped over and tried to pull the blindfold off with his thumbs. *Too tight. Shit. What is that thing on my back?*

She had said brand. Was that what it was? Doug recalled, a few years ago, when Cheryl had suggested that they brand each other for their anniversary. She had seen an episode of Oprah about it and thought it would be romantic. Doug hadn't been so hot on the idea, though — he remembered someone talking about someone getting it done and the name being spelled wrong. And, unlike a tattoo, those things were permanent.

Of course, he knew when whatever it was had happened. That night he and

Lauden and that girl had gone to that party.

"Honey?" he called. *What time was it?* Maybe she was putting on some breakfast. He could hear voices — Olivia was up. He hoped Cheryl would tell her not to come in — it wouldn't be the first time she'd seen Daddy trussed up, but he didn't feel up to a lengthy explanation before he'd had some coffee.

Maybe he could call up Lauden and ask him what happened. He remembered that after they'd left Coors they'd gone to Pilar's — he remembered the girl being impressed with the food, but she was probably easily impressed. She had certainly laughed a lot at his jokes.

His watch buzzed. Cheryl answered it — another delivery boy. *Goddamn her*, he fumed. *Breakfast too?!* But then he guiltily remembered wrestling Lauden for the bill at Pilar's and winning, and then insisting on buying some dope before they went to the party. Beer and beauty always made a big spender of him.

After the dope, the evening was cut up into tiny clips. Lauden, staying in the cab, waving goodbye to him and the girl; walking down a road with her to the strange location, telling her how pretty her hair was (*oh god had he fucked her?*); at the party itself, standing still in the swirl of all kinds of odds and sods, watching the plant-mural thing grow, breathing in the fumes of something...

The bedroom door opened and shut. He waited for Cheryl to say something, but he just heard her getting dressed. Finally, she said, "Are you asleep?"

"No."

"That's a change," she said, trying to sound light but coming off as bitter.

Doug heard the jingle of keys.

"You know Doug," Cheryl said as she unlocked him, each word distinct. "I've had offers."

His hands fell and he let them fall. *Job offers?* He forced himself to breathe. *What if she wanted to go for a job in Frisco now?* They had always wanted to go as a family, but Doug knew she was anxious to get back into the workforce... *What if she wanted the money to go upgrade now?* He frantically scrambled for an excuse. He pulled off the blindfold, squinting in the bright morning light.

Cheryl, fully dressed, was throwing the cuffs in the toybox. "You're just lucky he was a scumbag," she said, her face clumpy with sadness. She closed the toybox and pushed it out of sight.

Oh. That *kind of offer.* He watched her face, didn't know what to say. He sighed again.

"Oh, stop that shit," Cheryl said, leaving the room.

He got up, absently rubbing his raw wrists, and padded to the washroom. He turned around and looked at his back to see what all the fuss was about, having to go on tippytoe to do so.

It was a small circle with a lower-case "i" in it. It took Doug a few seconds to place it as the Infiltrators tag. He rubbed it — it was a tattoo, more than likely flashed on when he was out of it at the party.

He lifted the lid and took a piss. He tried to piece together his memories of the party, but all he had was fragments. He could picture the building it was in — the roof was mostly destroyed and you could see some stars. The floor was covered with dirt they'd brought in, either that or they'd removed the floor.

There was a kind of music too, but he couldn't remember where it had come from, whether there were people making it or what... and the fumes, the smoke, it was everywhere but it didn't sting or choke — just the opposite, it made his lungs feel infinite, like he could breathe this cold, delicious air forever.

As the water swirled around down the bowl, he remembered the plant-mural. How you could only see it from a distance, how it didn't make sense close up. You had to go to a ledge far above, and then you could see the spiralling design.

He had the thought that maybe, if he found a ledge high enough, he could see the patterns in his life.

Doug stepped briskly through the mall, trying not to drag Olivia. "C'mon, kid," he said, "We have to meet Mom in an hour."

"That's lots of time," Olivia sulked, trying to stop at a window displaying the latest boy band, dressed in checks. One of the members was mooning the audience with his tongue sticking out, and Doug frowned. *Charming,* he thought, realizing that his parental irritation meant the agency who put Pole Position together had done its job well.

"There'll be time for window shopping after Daddy does what he has to do," he blithely promised. He scanned the store names, saw one that looked promising: Brand XXX.

He paused at the display, promising Branding, Skin Work, Muscling, Bod Mods of All Kinds, and after a few seconds a tall blonde dressed in a housecoat walked into the display. "Hi there," the hologram said untying her belt, "I just got some work done at Brand XXX that I'm just dying to show you..."

They walked on. It didn't specifically list what he needed, and it looked like it was going to raise all kinds of questions in Olivia's nine-year-old mind. A second later: "Daddy?" she said.

"Yes Oliveoil?" he said, wishing they hadn't stopped.

"When are we going to Frisco?"

"Why do you ask?" he said, trying to keep the edge from his voice, wishing it had been an innocent question about sex. He led them onto an escalator. *Come on, it's here somewhere...*

"'Cause Savana — the new kid — left a few days ago. She's so lucky. My school is so crappy."

Crappy is all I can afford, my sweet little girl, he thought. The escalator moved slowly, but Doug didn't have the energy to walk. Avoiding Olivia's eyes, he noticed the store he was looking for.

"There it is," Doug said, pointing.

Olivia turned her head. "Where?"

The window display at Dr. Bodmodz was comparatively austere, more like a hospital than a brothel. Inside, not much had changed since he'd been here with friends — probably 20 years ago, he realized with a start. *Jesus.*

The counterperson leaned against the entrance door frame, a lady in her late sixties with a conservative brush cut. Doug was glad — he always felt silly discussing these things with someone younger than himself.

"Uh, hi," he said to the lady. Her eyes were solid black, but she had a welcoming smile. "I'd like to get a tattoo removed."

She nodded, and Doug appreciated her professional manner — no sarcasm here. "You can use booth one. And for the little lady?"

Olivia giggled at that but was too shy to talk to the woman. "Daddy, can I get a tattoo?" she whispered.

"Sure, honey," he said, glad she would be occupied. Before he entered the booth, he looked back at her gleeful face, "But no implants!"

She shook her head, blond curls bouncing. The lady was showing her how to choose a design.

Doug closed and locked the booth. A round little cartoon fellow in a smock flickered on. "Hi there! I'm Doctor —"

"Remove tattoo," Doug said, to see if he could skip the intro. The cartoon chirped, "No problem! Please expose the tattooed area." Doug did so.

A beam of light quickly scanned his body and threw up an enlarged image of the tattoo. *Man, I wish Lauden had come to the party, I could ask him what happened.*

"The diagnosis: to treat this tattoo, it will cost you $130.54 and take less than a second. You should know that the tattoo is not actually removed. The area is flashed the same color as the surrounding skin. Do you want the operation?"

I must have been babbling about my Infiltrator assignment, Doug thought. *And some kid thought it would be funny to tag me with a circle i.* Yeah, he thought, squinting at the enlarged image, *it's even smudgy... did it with one of those cheap handhelds.*

Just as he was starting to feel better, he noticed that the smudging was strangely regular. "Enlarge image to 500%," he said.

The image took up most of the wall of the booth now, and it was clearly made up of numbers and letters, so densely packed that they resembled a solid image. *Holy shit, what the fuck is this?*

He stood there for a second.

The cartoon doctor started tapping its foot. "Well?"

Struck by inspiration, he used his watch to scan in the image.

His watch said. "This image appears to be an encrypted file. Decrypting…"

"I have other patients you know," fumed the doctor, "And frankly, I'm losing my patience with —"

"OK," Doug said.

The tattoo was flashed away.

"Decryption complete. Connecting…"

Connecting?! To what?

His watch projected an office onto his retina. There was a man at the desk, a man with features that were blurred and shifting.

"Hello Doug," he said, looking up from something. "I'm glad you got in touch."

"Disconnect," Doug said in a panic.

The silence in the booth was sudden and complete. The doctor cartoon was gone. He waited for a second for his watch to bleep, but it didn't. *Who the fuck was that?*

He put his clothes back on and opened the door. "Remember to pay the nurse at the door!" the cartoon doctor's voice called after him.

The nurse looked up when he shut the door behind him. "Everything all right?" she asked, looking concerned at his stricken look.

"I'm — everything's fine," he said.

Olivia turned around and beamed at him. She had a vivid long-lashed third eye tattooed on her forehead. "Isn't it pretty? Just like Ultragirl Supreme!"

"Very pretty, darling," he said with a fatigued smile.

The counterperson had punched up the total. Doug touched his watch to the payplate, already tasting the Big Macs he'd be eating every day next week.

"Thanks for coming to Dr. Bodmodz — the funnest surgery in town," she said.

They walked out of the store and took their time getting back to the meeting point. Naturally the newest Pole Position album (*What Position Would You Like Mi Pole?*) was purchased along the way. They were a few minutes late, but Cheryl was still shopping. He scanned the thin crowd for her, imagining every additional minute draining money from his account.

"Ooh, I'm just a dirty grease monkey," Olivia was quietly singing along to her watch. "Ooh, if you look at my bum you can see," she said. "Wanna hear, Daddy?"

"No baby," he said distractedly, leaning against the railing. Downstairs in the lower level there was a bit of a commotion. Mall security was trying to herd someone out the door, a young flashily dressed woman. She was yelling something, and Doug strained to hear what she was saying.

"You can't control me!" she was saying, her lipsticked lips twisting with rage. The security guard held up a placating hand, the other hand on his gun. "No, fuck you! I'm not leaving 'til I get what I want!"

The security guard, a smile on his face, stepped towards her with his hand still outstretched. She grabbed his wrist and, with a scream, twisted it around until she had him in a headlock. Suddenly, she had the other guard covered with a gun that looked absurdly big in her hand. She frantically waved it around, sending the mall patrons scattering.

Doug grabbed Olivia and yanked her away from the rail.

The woman hit the guard she had in a headlock with the butt of her gun, and he stopped struggling. The other guard lifted his hands, his eyes wide in shock. "I want it for free!" she screamed at him.

Doug sighed and let go of Olivia, feeling silly. Olivia scampered back to the rail and watched.

The guard shook his head, and the woman shot him in the eye. His body folded like a house of cards. His head hit the ground with a wet *splick!* and blood seeped around his head. It looked, from Doug's top-down angle, like a red halo.

The woman, kicking the gibbering heap at her feet, walked towards the exit. "You fucking sheep!" she yelled at the mall patrons, flicking the laser sight across their huddling mass. "You do whatever they tell you!"

The other security guard had pulled himself together and was rising to a crouching position, sliding his gun out with excruciatingly slow caution while the woman harangued the crowd.

"You pay whatever they tell you to pay. Well, fuck that —" she took a second to whip around and shoot the guard, who fell to the ground with a gaping throat wound. "Free yourself!" she yelled, shooting her gun into the air, one shot for every word: "Free — Your — Self!"

Each of the three shots loosed a silver banner that unfurled from the domed ceiling of the mall. The banners said: Self Silver Package — Now Free! — Restrictions Apply.

The woman had disappeared, and the crowd had mostly dissolved, but there was a healthy buzz in her wake. People were pointing up at the banners and smiling — whether because of the surprising new offer or because they were proof that the whole thing had been a performance, it was hard to tell.

"Why are they still lying there, Daddy?" Olivia said, her voice annoyed.

He looked over the railing at the two guards, who really were rather convincingly dead. He entertained the disturbing thought that they'd decided to take the rubbernecking marketing strategy to a new extreme, but didn't voice that. "I think it's to keep your attention," he said. *They'd probably have a whole second scene with bodybags or zombies or mourning widows.*

Mainly, though, he was mulling over the offer. *Silver wasn't so bad.* It didn't have any of the frills, but it wasn't the equivalent of plastic clothes that bronze was. It had a kind of dignity, and maybe after a few years they could work their way up to a gold…

"Olivia, what the —" Cheryl exclaimed. Her arms were full of packages from Gap Sports and Safeway.

"I'm Ultragirl Supreme!" piped Olivia. She rubbed the temple around her third eye with her fingers. "I predict… there's some chocolate for me in that bag!" she said.

Cheryl smiled wanly. "Maybe when we get back to the car — well, home," she corrected.

Doug felt a twinge of guilt — *who goes to the mall in a taxi?* — and sublimated it by taking some packages from her.

"Something in there for you," she said nodding at one bag from Victorian Secrets. "It's an exact replica of the ones they used in brothels in the 1900s."

He looked in it and saw the handle of a bullwhip. "Yeeow," he said, waggling his eyebrows. *Period sex toys. Cheryl was such an 18–34.* They started walking out of the mall.

"Any trouble with your —" Cheryl started.

"No, no, it was just a prank flash job," Doug said, desperate to move beyond it. He couldn't think about it now. "Must have happened at the party."

Cheryl took Olivia's hand, shook her head as she looked at the tattoo. "School pictures next week, you know."

Doug slapped his forehead. "Oh, damn."

They got on the escalator. Doug nodded at one of the banners. "Didja see the ad —"

"That's why I was late, I was cowering in fear," she said with a grimace. "Those stupid things get me every time."

They arrived on the level where the bodies were lying, and Cheryl shook her head. "Too far."

Doug normally would have pointed out the teenaged boys hovering around the bodies, and told her that their positive reaction outweighed her slight disapproval — demographically speaking. But he didn't want to talk shop right now. He wanted to test the waters.

"Yeah," he said. "But it's a pretty great offer. I'm tempted to sign us up."

Cheryl's eyebrow spiked. "Sign us up? For silver? You're joking. You're joking, right?"

Doug smiled bravely, quivering on the inside. "No, seriously," he said lightly, "Think of the money we'd save." He smoothed down Olivia's curl as she listened to Pole Position and swung from Cheryl's unresponsive hand.

"What happened to your job needing you here?!" she said, an hysterical edge creeping into her voice. "I mean, the *money we'd save*? If we were in Frisco, I could be back in a job making money instead of —"

Doug was laughing, hands in his pockets and striding along. His chest hurt with the insincerity of the chuckle, but it worked.

"You jerk," Cheryl said, hitting his arm.

"No wonder those ads have you cowering," he said. "You're a sucker!"

Olivia, catching only the end of it, sang, "You a sucka mothafucka!"

They all laughed, leaving the mall and stepping into a cab that seemed to be waiting just for them.

Eileen walked through the silvered halls of the space station. The octagon designs on the walls shifted when she looked at them, and when she touched them, there was an icy feeling that traveled up her arm. She wasn't supposed to be here.

She rounded a corner and started to hear voices. One she recognized, one she didn't. The one she didn't slurred a bit.

"...can't sell them separately. It's a package deal, I'm afraid."

"Eleven dollars is juss too esspensive," said the unknown voice. "The chemical elements of the unitss are worth seven dollars, topsss."

Eileen came to a door that the voices seemed to be coming from and stood as still and as quiet as she could.

"Well, there's more than the production costs," said the voice, an irritated edge creeping in. This jogged Eileen's memory — it was her old field liaison, Oscar! *What was he doing here?* "There was the cost of shipping, of collection — and it's not like you'll be melting them down for the chemicals."

A strange little chuckle. "No, we prefer them whole. It iss true." A pause. "Nine dollars."

She leaned closer to the door.

"I've been instructed not to go a cent lower than ten," he said. *Good for you, Oscar, be firm with — whoever that is.*

"But these are a discontinued model," said the voice, going up an octave, almost wheedling. "Old stock. You don't even need these."

Eileen almost held her breath waiting for the answer. For some reason, it seemed to be important.

Oscar didn't reply.

There was a frustrated sound. "Fine. Ten it iss. You humans are good salespeople."

Humans?

Oscar laughed. "We better be. Our culture's been centered on trade for centuries."

"Ourss has been centered around obtaining food. Thatss the problem. So hungry."

"Talking about that, do you want to open one up to celebrate the closing of the deal?"

"An excellent idea. Thought you'd never asssk. I am particularly fond of the clone flavor."

Oh god oh god thought Eileen. She looked frantically for a way to open the door. As her fingers were scrabbling at the cold metal she noticed how young they were, slight little sausages. *Why am I a little girl?*

"Here you go," Oscar said in a jovial way. "A young boy. Do you need a knife?"

Jeremy! Eileen screamed silently. She pounded on the cold metal door, but not even a sound resulted. Her arms were helpless little-girl arms., getting icier and icier.

"Not with such tender meat, I'll just use my — how do you say? — clowes?"

"Claws," said Oscar, the rest of what he said drowned out by a horrible rending and cracking and slurping.

Eileen closed her eyes so tight, pounded against the cold wall. Pounded 'til her fists were numb, and she realized that she was pounding against the cement ground.

After she awoke, it took a few seconds to remember where she was. The alcove under the bridge was a different place in the light of dawn, and she lay for a few seconds on her side, looking out on the water and listening to the cars rush overhead. She sat up, too suddenly, and coughed up a blob of phlegm nearly the same color as the concrete it landed on.

She suddenly understood where her nausea was coming from. *A night of breathing unfiltered air. Disgusting.* She pulled her head mask on, and when she was fairly sure she wasn't going to vomit, sealed it up. Immediately her vision sharpened, her breathing cleared.

What an awful, awful dream, she said. She muted the car noise and turned up the water, letting it soothe her.

She wondered why her brain had dialled up Oscar in her dream. She couldn't really remember much about him other than his voice — although she *had* actually met him in person. She couldn't recall his face, but he had an average build with hair parted in the middle, a little restless as he had conducted her final interview.

"Could you explain to me, in your own words, the historical reasons for the unrest currently plaguing the African regions?"

She hadn't known it was her final interview, which was good because she would have been much more nervous. These were tough questions, and history wasn't one of her strengths.

"Well," she said. The interview had taken place in a very fancy building that she hadn't noticed before. "A lot of these countries — regions," she corrected, as he looked up sharply, "Couldn't repay their loans to the UCIC." She paused, hoping he wouldn't ask her what it stood for — *United Corporate something something?* He didn't. "And some of them refused to make the changes that were necessary for streamlining — instead of handing over power to service providers, the governments hoarded the money. Instead of paying back the loans."

"Uh huh," said Oscar. He had seemed bored, almost, but like he expected her to go on.

She suddenly remembered something. "I was with a friend, and we were watching TV once, and this report came on that showed that a person in Cuba — one of the… regions that had defaulted — got free medical care. She started crying, because her dad was in the hospital, but they could only afford third-tier services. But this old man in Cuba had his own bed, and people were smiling…"

"How did you feel about that," Oscar asked, suddenly focused.

"Well," Eileen said, wishing she knew what he wanted to hear. "It seemed unfair that they would use the money for that when they owed it to us." She glanced at him, but he was looking at her, so she looked away.

"But how did you *feel*," Oscar repeated.

"I was pretty mad," Eileen said, reluctant to admit it. She didn't like being angry — it was bad enough that she was half a woman already, she didn't like to sound like a man. But Oscar had nodded and made a note, then moved on to another subject.

It was his way to ask a whole bunch of questions, all in the same indifferent tone, although later you usually realized that only one or two mattered. She was glad he was smarter than her, though, especially after the mess in Zimbabwe — his analyst's voice had been incredibly calming. He made it make sense. She had been ready to throw in the towel.

Oscar seemed a long way away now. There had been a lot of talk about keeping in touch with the others in her unit, but it had been just talk. Now, in light of what Paul had said, she wondered if the others had felt ashamed of what they did.

Eileen didn't know what to think. At the time it had seemed like the only thing to do — helping the economy stabilize would help everyone. An exciting job, good pay, and she'd certainly travelled more than anyone else she knew, even if she couldn't talk about it.

Although from what Paul said, it sounded like he had been on the other side.

Well, maybe working for both sides would mean she'd helped one no more than the other. *Leave it to the big brains to figure out the rest.*

She stood up, feeling no trace of wobbliness thanks to the drugs the suit fed her. She focused on the mail icon and blinked twice.

"Hello, Eileen," Paul's voice said. "I'm going to be very busy all day today, so I've left this message to fill you in on what's going on. You are now uplinked via a baffler, so you have access without revealing that your suit's in action."

A half-dozen icons appeared on the periphery of Eileen's vision, tiny stacks of paper identifying them as documents.

"I've prepared a few dossiers for you to peruse while you wait. They're pretty much everything we know about the Self technology. The one that'll be most relevant to your assignment is the one on caching."

There was a pause, a murmur, and then Paul's voice again. "We don't know exactly when we'll need you, so just be ready. Take care." There was a click.

Eileen nodded to herself, pleased with how polite Paul was. She would rather be moving now, but she settled down on the concrete again and looked at the documents. She'd never been given this much information before, and it both flattered and worried her. *What did he expect from her?*

Self Ownership — Covert and Public, Self Process — Long Term Effects, Self Caching — Theories and Data, Self Weaknesses — System Flaws… Eileen opened up the Caching one, as Paul had suggested.

The artificial intelligence used to create the operations of Self and the running of Frisco is the only "entity" that knows how the bodies of their clients reach the cache or where the cache is. This extreme secrecy is necessary, representatives of the Self consortium claim, to prevent vulnerability to attacks or hostage taking. Despite the lack of data, common sense points to a few likely possibilities as to where the post-transfer bodies are stored:

1. Nowhere [Destroyed]
2. Deep Sea
3. Orbital Station
4. Foreign Regions
5. Underground

Eileen sighed. All of them sounded likely to her. She wished Jeremy were here — he had the cleverness of her brother Leo in him. She remembered the time they'd been at the park, when Jeremy couldn't have been more than nine. They'd just set up their spot — put a big umbrella down and were about to get started on their picnic — when a big silver toy tank rolled up to them.

At first, Eileen had been amused and pointed it out to Jeremy. Jeremy looked at it briefly and then looked around. Then the tank's cannon had spurted red goopy streams at them.

Eileen had leapt to her feet, trying desperately to remember from her training what color napalm was. Then she heard the laughter, saw the little brats, one of whom held up his fist and yelled, "Humans one, clones zero!"

She had looked at Jeremy, and he'd said, "Kids from school." But he was focused on the tank, tapping something into his watch. Eileen thought he was in shock, and patted his head and cooed something meaningless.

Most of the red goo had hit the picnic basket but none had got in, so Eileen opened it up and got out the sandwiches and drink-boxes. She opened one up and tried to hand it to Jeremy, but he was still tapping on his watch — smiling now, though.

Eileen followed his gaze just in time to see the remote-controlled tank dip over the curb and into traffic. The kid who had yelled at them flinched as his toy was crunched by a truck. Jeremy took the drink-box from Eileen's stunned hand.

She watched the little boy suck away innocently and was doubly impressed — he'd not only achieved his goal, but he didn't need to crow about it. He had settled the score — clones one, humans one — and that was the end of that.

The sun was now high in the sky. The shaded area was shrinking, the line of sun having crept undetectably towards her. She was struck with the compulsion to get out and about — just sitting here, reminiscing, was driving her crazy. But she didn't want to risk it in daylight.

Positioning herself as far away as possible from the line of sunlight, she sat cross-legged and told her suit to slow her metabolism down to the minimum but to alert her if any messages came through.

The light around her flickered and became murky, but the only indication that anything was happening was that the line of sun was now noticeably sliding towards her. Her suit kept a digital clock in the bottom right corner of her vision, the minutes ticking off like seconds.

It was too bad that slowing down time didn't make you younger. Not that she cared about being old — compared to Mary, she had adjusted to being a crone with no effort at all.

"I can't believe those bastards didn't warn us," Mary had said one day after debriefing, nose almost touching the mirror as she looked at her crow's feet. They were the last ones in the locker room.

The last few missions had required a lot of speed, and the accelerated metabolism had taken its toll. Eileen had shrugged, sealing her locker and punching in her code. "The contract said something, didn't it?"

Mary snorted, grabbed at her makeup kit. "'Unknown effects of the experimental technology,' you mean?" She took out her flattener and turned it on. "They made it sound like cancer or something. Not *this!*"

She slid the flattener back and forth, roughly. "I mean, with cancer they just put you under and scoop it out. I've had it twice. But these wrinkles — god!"

Eileen didn't say anything. She felt, in a strange way, relieved by the old woman's face that stared back from the mirror. She watched Mary root through her makeup kit and was glad that she wouldn't have to bother with all those things any more. It meant that her spinsterhood wasn't so noticeable, so pitiable — to a person on the street, she might have been a widow.

"What are you smiling at?" Mary snapped, patting on rouge like she was banging out a carpet.

"You," Eileen said. "You're still beautiful, and you still complain."

"Hmph!" she retorted, placated.

And, it turned out, wrinkles or no, she was married a year after she left. Mary always got what she wanted, and she was never satisfied.

After the sun plopped into the water, Eileen told her suit to speed her up. Her clock slowed down, but before she could start to venture out from her hole the suit gave her an error message. "Recalibration in progress…"

It *had* been a long time since she'd been in the suit; she'd entirely forgotten the five-minute rule, one of the basics. She sighed and sat down again, uplinking to *My News* to kill some time.

A huge-bosomed girl of 18 or so appeared and spoke directly to Eileen. "The Self silver package is now free!" the spokesgirl said with an excited lilt in her voice. "Self has decided to make their popular package available to everyone who wants it, regardless of income," the spokesgirl hugged herself in an ecstatic gesture that nearly made her breasts pop out of her t-shirt. "The silver package includes all the basics of the bronze package, plus!" The spokesgirl ticked off the features. "…A choice from nearly 50,000 personal appearances… a dozen free teleports per day… free reality-adjustment counselling… and much more!" she breathed.

Two choices appeared for Eileen: SEE STACY TOUCH HERSELF and GO FOR SELF.

Eileen disconnected, flustered.

Stacy winked at her. "Brian, before you go — if you go for Self now you get a free private chat session with me. I love Texans..." Eileen disconnected again, this time successfully. She was a little confused at how *forward* the newswire had become since she had last uplinked. *Hadn't the spokesperson been an older gentleman? A sophisticated man with a spark in his eye, quite attractive...* She opened My Profile. *Ah ha!* she thought. The baffler that Paul had set up to hide her identity had identified her as Brian, an 18-year-old Texan male.

It was quite dark now, and the suit had completed its recalibration, so she made her way onto the bridge proper, giving her humble refuge a final look. The headlights whisking by slowed to a leisurely pace as her suit revved up.

She headed into the city, such a different place than it had been when she was a child. As she sped down the hill, she reflected that only the geography remained unchanged, only the hills and the mountains. South to Hastings, dodging the piles of human waste that festered there. It was hard not to hate them, although she tried — they were the symbols of failure, the thin thin line between brilliant speculators and reckless idiots. She stopped at the foot of one of them, a woman of about forty, wondering what market crash had left her penniless and friendless.

The heap, cocooned in plastics, opened her eyes and looked at Eileen. "Mom?" she mumbled. "Too early for school." Her eyes closed again. *Always been lazy, I guess*, Eileen thought. She looked at the littered street and the vacant storefronts, even the smashed glass was dusty and old — this street had gone from being skid row to a trendy loft strip back to skid row again.

She ran away, towards the east, amazed at how much of the city she hadn't seen for the last decade. She started for the house she lived in as a teen on Commercial Drive but, on a whim, veered into an alley when she spotted a fire escape. She climbed up to the pebble-encrusted roof and freeze-framed the security camera she found there. She walked to the edge and looked down on a valley that used to be choked with green until developers had segmented it off and filled it with houses, houses now boarded up and locked down.

There was green, though, in another direction, in the distance. She zoomed in on the old train yard. There were healthy patches of flora along the ground, vines curling up the sides of the rotted boxcars. That was strange.

She sat on the edge of the roof, letting her black legs hang over the S of Safeway. It reminded her of how, when she was young, her aunt had drawn lines over the S to make it look like a dollar sign. Something to do with the company buying up the fruit markets along the Drive. She hadn't thought of Aunt Marcie in years. She had gone to fight in South America and had never come back, just like so many people lost in the shuffle of the tumultuous '20s. Marcie had never been a family favorite, anyway.

Eileen stood up and wandered around the rooftop fitfully. *All dressed up and no place to go.* Since giving it up, she would often fantasize about being back in the suit. Rude clerks, bullies at Jeremy's school, that fat guy in her neighborhood who refused to clean up after his dog — they cowered and repented in her mind's eye when faced with blacksuited Eileen.

She fluttered out her knives on the pebble-topped roof and lunged, swooped, twisted, pulled — imagined intestines dragged after her like a ribbon. *Who's intestines, Eileen?* a voice inside her asked. *If it's an AI running the show, there're no targets. What's a mission without targets?*

Eileen stood there, flicking her knives. Doing nothing but thinking was tiring her out. Feeling like a useless old woman, she lay down on the tar and pebble bed and asked her suit to sedate her.

Nicky awoke to the sound of the shower. "Oh shit!" she blurted, still so sleepy that raising her head was an effort. She looked over at Simon, who was totally asleep, his mouth slightly agape. *He wouldn't know.*

She sat up, pulling the sheet up with her. "How much time do I have left in my water account?"

"You have five minutes, 20 seconds," her watch chirped back.

She got up and pulled on her housecoat, looked back at Simon. One full leg had kicked free of the sheet.

When she figured 20 seconds had past, she knocked on the door. When she didn't get a response, she figured she'd go in rather than wake Simon.

Andre was mostly covered by the shower curtain but seemed alarmed anyway.

"I've only got five more minutes of water for the day, OK?" she said in a conversational tone.

"Oh shit," he said, turning off the water immediately. "I didn't know it was on a timer. Sorry."

"S'OK," Nicky said, leaving the bathroom and closing the door.

Simon was awake, staring at her through slitted eyes. "Good morning."

She sat on the edge of the bed, keeping her housecoat on. *Wonder where my clothes are in this mess?*

"What were you doing in —" he nodded towards the bathroom.

"The shower's timed. He didn't know."

"Ah," said Simon, touching the back of her housecoat. "Well, you shouldn't have to put up with that." He threw off the blankets and put on his pants, yanking them on over his bare butt.

"It sucks. I understood it during the density crisis, but now…" she said.

He was pulling on his t-shirt as he walked out the door.

Nicky was too sleep-logged to manage anything but a quiet "bye." Andre emerged from the shower fully clothed, only a slight glint in his hair to show he'd ever been wet. She got up and swished by him into the bathroom, cut off his apologies with the click of the door behind her.

She stepped into the shower and angled the head away as she got the temperature right, breathing in the steam. When the water rose past her toe, she scrabbled her finger around the drain until she dredged enough of her hair out for the water to escape. She looked at the clump, realized that she wouldn't have been able to tell if Andre's short curls were entwined somewhere, and leaned out to drop the clump into the garbage can.

She washed her nether regions first, slightly sticky with last night's misadventures. Her hungover brain was getting flashes: she had let them do what they wanted — and they had wanted a lot, as hungry as she was for the friction, this way, that way, up and in, out and down; when Andre had come, she pulled his head down on her pussy and pointed Simon's aching cock at his pal's ass. *It was so cute how boys always pretended it was the first time...*

The squirt of the KY-Pro, Simon's averted eyes and careful strokes, Andre's hot quickening breaths on her rawness, *fuck. That was hot.* She soaped her body leisurely, a smile on her lips. She remembered about the timer just in time to get shampoo lathered into her hair. *Click.*

Nicky stood looking at the showerhead, blinking soap out of her eyes. "Fuck," she moaned, looking at the mound of lather on her hands. She was trying to decide if she should get a pail of water from the sink, or just shove her head under the faucet, when the water clicked back on.

She quickly finished washing her hair and enjoyed another few minutes before she turned it off. She towelled off and left the bathroom door open to let the steam dissipate.

Alone in her room, she looked through her drawers for something to wear. Not quite shorts weather, so after a pair of unremarkable panties — she fought and won the battle not to dress sexy — went with some purple jeans and a blouse. She looked at herself briefly in the mirror, deciding not to braid her hair just now — *c'mon, who cares, the guy doesn't even wear underpants.*

Feeling quite ambivalent about whether she'd find them or whether they'd split — either had its issues — she wandered downstairs, feeling a bit of a stranger in her own house. She heard someone whispering in the living room and when she entered she saw it was Simon poking a bit of a stick into the fluke's cage and baby-talking them. Andre was sitting on the couch, looking at a prism knick-knack from her coffee table.

"Hey," Simon said, his smile bright and skully.

Nicky smiled back. "Don't feed them," she said as she pulled his hand away from the cage. She noticed his hands were dirty. "How'd you get so dirty so fast?"

"Fixing your shower," he said.

"Oh, you did that! Thanks!"

"No problem — just a little lever on the outside of the house," Simon said.

"They hardly do spot checks, anymore — just tell them you don't know anything about it if they ask you."

"Know anything?" Nicky said, creasing her brow in puzzlement.

"Like if they come by…" he said, trailing off as he saw her grin. "Tricky Nicky is right."

"Does anyone else want tea?" she asked, looking at Andre.

"Yes please," said Simon.

"Uh… sure," said Andre, looking up from the prism.

They seemed to be talking about something serious when she returned with the cans. "So are these the ones that JK was talking about?" Simon said, pointing to the cage.

"No, those are my flukes… just ratdogs I sell to tourists." *They're getting a little big for the cage,* Nicky thought as she looked at them jostling each other. "I can show you the other designs when we finish these. I try not to have food in the lab." Which was a lie, but she needed to gather energy before she allowed them into her inner sanctum.

She sipped her tea, trying to think of the last time someone other than JK had been in the lab. She had almost shown that guy she had picked up at the Terror party, but he had had a lot of body mods and she was worried he'd want stuff done for free once he'd seen her set-up. Or at least that's what she'd told herself. *He was a freak, anyway…*

"This is a nice house," Andre said, setting down the prism with a click.

She shrugged, smiling at his need to make conversation. "It's amazing what a 30% vacancy rate will do to rents."

"Higher than that now… 55? 60?" Simon said, glancing at Andre.

"Sixty," Andre said.

"How do you know that?" Nicky challenged. "You guys just got here, and now you're experts?"

Andre shrugged uncomfortably. Simon said smoothly, ambiguously, "It's one of the highest on the continent. That's why we're here."

Andre glowered at him. Nicky looked from one to the other, remembered their secrecy in the train yard. "You guys, man," she sneered, "spy versus spy." She went into the kitchen, her stomach having ordered her into forage mode. She knew there was nothing in the fridge, so she looked through the cupboard and found a package of Reese's Oreos.

She brought them back to the living room. Andre declined, but Simon dipped his dirty hand in, licking his lips. She sat down on the quilted armchair.

"So you sell those, that's how you get by?" Andre said, pointing at the flukes.

She nodded, washing down the cookie with a flood of tea.

"Smart cookie," Simon said, taking a bite of one. He ignored Nicky's wince and continued. "What happens if they die?"

"Well," Nicky said, rolling up the bag and slapping her hands clean. "If it's near the beginning of the month, I'm fine. I can just buy some more materials and bake up some more. But if it happens at the end, then I'm fucked." She sucked a tooth, contemplating it. "Actually, I could probably put it on credit. But the place where I buy gives a substantial discount for liquid funds."

Simon nodded, looking serious for once.

"And what about you two? Who's keeping you in spray paint and wine?"

Simon smiled, looked at Andre. Andre's lips were practically glued shut.

Nicky rolled her eyes.

"So," Simon said. "Can we check out your set-up?"

"Not until you answer the question!" Nicky said, folding her arms.

"We're helping set up a birthday party for this rich guy," Simon said.

"Someone's paying you to throw him a party," Nicky said, not budging.

Andre nodded and Simon shrugged. "Not a party for him, but... more or less."

"Uh huh," she said skeptically, giving them looks that let them know that she didn't believe a word of it. She led them upstairs anyway, climbing up on the chair and pulling the ladder down. She had them go first.

"Don't touch anything," she said as Andre went up, the tendons in his wrists working. Simon was taking his time, so Nicky helped him with a swat on the butt.

When she got up there, she was conscious of how crowded the place was with three people. Simon was looking around approvingly, touching the metal counter, lifting the beakers. "Cool."

"Break it and I break your face," Nicky said, sliding by him to call up her mythic fluke designs.

"You got genomes on that thing?" Andre said, pointing at the computer. He was looking intently at her equipment.

"Yeah," she said, running the in silico Cyclops fluke. It barked and ran around, its little tongue lolling. Then she ran the other two, and they romped and played together, as much as the small cubespace the computer projected would allow. "These guys are ready to go."

127

"Why haven't you made them, then?" Simon said. He stuck his finger in the holo for the flukes to interact with. "You don't have any of the lifedough?"

"Lifestuff. No, I have enough of that," she said, feeling tired. "I just don't want to grow them until there's, you know, somewhere for them to go."

"And you could do it here?" Andre said. "You wouldn't have to get another place to make them?"

"No, I'm pretty lucky," Nicky said. "I've got a full service lab here. I picked up stuff from my school when it was —"

"Yeah, JK told us," said Simon with a lazy smile.

"He told you that?" said Nicky. Her confusion, added to the proximity of the men, made her begin to feel a little disoriented.

"And you could add the uplinking?" Simon asked Andre.

Andre shrugged. "Yeah, she's already got cubespace. It'd be easy."

"What the fuck are you guys —"

"Hey Nicky," said Simon. "How would you like a job saving the world?"

"You coming to bed honey?" Cheryl called from the bathroom.

"No, not yet," Doug said, shuffling things around in the junk drawer. "Cheryl, do you know where the coke that Janice gave us is?"

She came out of the bathroom, towelling her hair. "It's in the liquor cabinet. You're not going to do that now, are you? That's not going to help you sleep."

"Just a few lines," Doug said. "Trying to do a bit of work. Brainstorm a few ideas."

"All right," she said. "We'll have to break in our new toy some other night."

"Break *me* in, you mean," he said, thinking about the size of the whip.

She laughed on her way to the bedroom. "Good night."

Doug entered the living room and deflated on the couch, allowing the thought in that had been trying to get in since he'd left Dr. Bodmodz: *the tattoo wasn't a simple prank..*

He felt a peevish irritation at his original simple explanation being shot down, that his life getting more complicated. He turned on the television. A rough-faced man was tightening bolts on an exoskeleton. "Look, we just can't take him. The corpses are on our tail. We'll be lucky to get out alive ourselves."

The shot spun around and focused on a woman in anguish. Her rebel hairstyle and jumpsuit struck Doug as absurdly clean. *He has stubble, she has carefully applied makeup.*

"We can fit him in the shuttle," she was saying, touching a man's arm. "He can go with me, in the shuttle."

The man was sickly, but wan and handsome. He turned his arresting green eyes on the man with the stubble. "Please," he said with a little cough.

"We need all the room for the shipment. Do you know how many people will die if we don't get these to Mexico? Think about Frida, about Diego —" he cut off to look at the sickly man, a curl on his lip. "Our people. *Real* people."

The woman burst into tears.

"I'm sorry, Susanita," the man said, applying himself to his work, wrenching viciously. "This is a war."

Doug lurched up from the couch and opened the liquor cabinet. He found the balloon close to the back and the mirror kit lodged up against the side. *Good.* He'd been worried Olivia might still have been using it for her dolls. He brought them back to the coffee table and sat down in the nearest armchair.

The ad was one of those atmospheric ones, with a gradual close-up on a blank can. There was a whisper of strings. Doug opened up the package of coke, which was made to look like a smuggler's balloon, and tapped out a small quantity on the mirror.

Doug removed the razor with its Coke-bottle-shaped hole in the middle and chopped up a few lines, partly obscuring the "Coke goes better with Coke" tagline. The promo item had come with a straw, too, but it'd been lost years ago, so Doug had to carefully snort with his bare nostril.

The show was back on again, and Doug watched it for a second. The sick young man was being stowed aboard the shuttle by the woman, and they shared a last look full of longing before she shut the compartment.

Doug looked at the mirror. Three lines left, the one closest to the one he'd just had a little ragged but really not bad. There was a small grease stain where his nose had touched the surface. He used the razor to slide the next line a little further away from the rest and then leaned down, keeping one eye on the TV.

"He's gone?" the gruff man asked, his stubble almost a beard now. The woman nodded, her face sad. "I'm sorry Susanita," the man said, touching her arm, his tone conciliatory. "We can't take the risk. I don't like it any more than you do."

Doug's bloodstream was beginning to perk up. He spun the TV perspective around so he got a top-down view on it. Sometimes if you pulled back enough you could get a glimpse of the surrounding film set, and this always amused Doug. *Nothing right now...*

The scene changed to a tight shot of the stowaway. His eyes were furtive, and he was communicating with someone. *Oh, those treacherous clones*, Doug thought as he did another line. *Not even the rebels can trust 'em.*

Doug turned off the TV, sick of it. It was a shame they had to make a crappy TV series of a good movie, although Doug knew that the success of the Harmless Cranks movie made it irresistible. The original movie had been able to depict the terrorists' tragic and doomed revolt in a way that the series never came close to.

I shoulda gone into TV, show those useless pricks how'ts done, Doug thought, his thoughts attached to a powdery white jet. *That's creative work, work that makes people think instead of making people think something.* Doug realized he was sitting in the dark.

"Lights up," he chirped, a little amazed to find there was still a line left on the mirror. He knew he shouldn't, but he tidied up the scraps with the razor and had one last mighty snort. He noted with satisfaction that the mirror was completely clean, smiling and nodding at himself.

"Oh yes, that's right," he said, forgetting for a moment everything except the fine sculpture of his nose. "That's a nose that knows how to clean up its dinner."

He got up and put the bag and mirror back into the cabinet, closing it with a quiet click. Slapping his hands together, "OK, gentlemen, it's time to get to work."

He sat down on the couch, turning on the TV and getting it to scan. While one part of his brain absorbed the color and noise, another part wished he was in the TV industry and could justify this as work. *It's kind of my work*, he said, *at least what happens to my work.* A few seconds later, before the channels climbed to the porn floor of the broadcast range and truly distracted him, he turned it off.

OK, he thought, his head flopping against the couch, *work for real.*

He constructed the report in his head, imagining Harris sitting across the way from him. *Better, Harris is that plant.* Doug got off the couch and sat down in the armchair. His body language firmed up slightly as he addressed the tall and stately plant.

"I've looked into the Infiltrators subculture, as you requested, and I've turned up some interesting data." He paused, and nodded. "Oh, neither did I. No one was more surprised than I that your fucking wild goose chase would lead me anywhere other than around in circles. As it turns out, they rather ingeniously provided me with a way to contact one of them." Doug paused, nodded, rubbed his nose, and listened attentively to the Harris flora. "No, naturally, it's absurd to think that they — of course, that's why — look!" Doug said, agitated. "This contact — could very possibly be an impostor." He nodded. "Probably. Yes, you're right. But still, the sophistication that they —" A long pause. "Listen you earless motherfucker, you don't know —" Doug stared for a few seconds at the plant and then sighed. "I'll have my desk cleaned out by the end of the day."

He propped his angular chin on the flat of his palm. *That didn't go well.* He looked at the plant, decided he couldn't bear pretending it was Olivia and breaking the news to her — even if he could use the practice, it was way too tall. *Even when you were hot shit,* a voice inside him said, *you never had the Infiltrators in your scope. No coolhunters ever did — they were either too clever or never existed in the first place. Someone's fucking with you.*

He thought about the scrambled face, the easygoing hello, the innocuous surroundings, and realized he was grinding his teeth. Who would want to do this to him? Who had he ever —

Lauden.

Of course. *Holy shit. Lauden! Still pissed off about the Ripper affair. He was there that night, he was — fuck, he even got him drunk!* Doug started to snicker. *The "i" tattoo — couldn't he have come up with something a little more subtle? Still, all in all, way more cunning than he had given him credit for.*

He looked at his watch. Past midnight, but what the hell.

He scrolled his watch back and re-established the connection he had disconnected so hastily in the tattoo shop. In the few seconds it took to resolve, he wondered why he'd been spooked so easily. *Well, they* had *been close enough to practically tattoo my ass...*

The same office was beamed onto the surface of his eye, and the same man was in there. This time, though, he was looking out the window.

"Doug!" he said in a welcoming voice that didn't entirely nullify the coldness of his slowly shifting mask.

"Lauden!" Doug exclaimed sarcastically.

The man didn't respond, just stood there.

"Get rid of that stupid mask, Lauden," Doug spat, irritated that he would continue with it.

"Ah... there it is. Lauden's your co-worker," said the man. He folded his arms, and said in a calm voice, "My name's not important, Doug."

"You sure it's not Prime Infiltrator?" jeered Doug.

"Quite sure."

Doug, using hand controls, zoomed in on the desk. It was covered with files, but they were gibberish. "These aren't even real. They're props."

"They're encrypted," the man's voice said. "I have quite a few visitors here. A lot of these documents are sensitive. The one on you, for instance." A hand, gigantic with the enlargement, picked one up.

Doug pulled back, got the man back in the shot.

"Wife Cheryl. Daughter Olivia."

"Very good Lauden. You've paid attention sometime in the last 20 years we've worked together," Doug said snidely. But a voice in the back of his head was saying: *this isn't Lauden. Lauden could barely handle coolhunting fieldwork, never mind this performance.*

"Born '99. Entered the workforce in '16." The man looked up. "Still a few years before the labor laws were phased out... did you lie about your age?"

"No," Doug said. "It was part-time, officially. Freelance."

"So you didn't lie?"

Doug was amazed at how quickly he answered questions for this man and had to force himself not to elaborate. "No."

The man put the documents back on the desk. He leaned against it and stared directly at Doug — or that is, his blurred and rippling head faced him silently. Doug had to remind himself that he couldn't be seen, that the man was only seeing a little icon bobbing about in mid-air.

"That's too bad."

"What?" said Doug. The coke was really failing him tonight. He felt frantic and outmaneuvered by the situation.

"I was prepared to pay you a lot of money to lie."

The statement hung there like a fart, and Doug couldn't resist sniffing. "How... much? And about... lie about what?"

"Well," the man said, rounding the desk. He spread out his fingers and pressed them down on the side of the desk. "We have a discretionary fund. That is, a fund for discretion." He laughed a bit.

"What was with the tattoo?"

The man laughed again, a slightly different tenor. "A little dramatic, I suppose. But we wanted to test you. If you hadn't figured it out, we would know that you weren't much of a threat. Not that you're much of a threat now — we're just at a rather precarious juncture."

Doug wished he had a drink, his throat was raw, but he didn't want to move. "How much?"

"We're willing to pay $500,000. To keep quiet about what you saw at the party. No reports, no summations."

Not enough, not enough. He summoned an indignant tone of voice. "A half a million. I see that come and go in an hour. And you want me to keep valuable information from my friends and colleagues?" Doug was sweating freely now, thankful the man couldn't see him, trying frantically to keep his shit together.

"At the party, what was it that you saw —" the man started.

"Forget the party," Doug sputtered — *'Cause oh god, I sure have!* — his voice climbed an octave. "You want me, a veteran of this highly competitive, cutthroat industry, to give up information on the most elusive and sought-after subculture in history for, for," *Keep it together, keep it together,* "less than a million?"

"A million? You haven't got a million dollars worth of —"

"Ridiculous! This conversation is over." Doug felt for his watch.

"Wait, wait," the man said, holding out his hand. "We could... we could manage 750."

Yes! Yes! Yes! "No. I couldn't. I couldn't betray my co-workers."

The man looked up — or at least his head tilted. He sighed. "Doug, this is just business. And don't play the puritan. You guys are parasites, milking communities and cultures for every drop of profit you can squeeze out of them."

Doug didn't know what to say. "I can't risk everything for less than a million. I have my family to think about."

"It's more than we usually pay."

Doug stared at him.

"You don't think this is the first arrangement we've made, do you?" the man said.

That grated too, even though it wasn't said in a gloating way — even though it was probably true. Coolhunters would probably be pretty easy to bribe — after all, they were just selling information. Doug stayed silent for a few more seconds. "All right."

The man turned around and made a few adjustments with the documents on the desk. "That's it done. The money is deposited into your account, listed as a performance bonus from your firm. I'd ask you to erase my connection from your watch. Not that I haven't enjoyed your company," the man said.

Doug wasn't thinking anything but *seven hundred and fifty thousand fucking dollars. That's gold baby!* "Uh huh."

"Goodbye, Doug." the man and his office winked out.

Rubbing his eye frantically. "Lights brighten." Tapping at his watch: Balance $752,982.12. *Holy shit holy shit.*

Doug bounced up. *Quiet — Olivia's sleeping,* warned a sane part of his whirling brain. "Holy shit holy shit!" he whispered as he ran up the stairs to his bedroom. "Gold! I've struck gold!"

He turned on the lights. "We're going to Frisco!" he said. The heap of blond hair and lumpy blankets shifted slightly.

He crawled up beside his wife and gave her a spastic squeeze. "We're going to Frisco, Cheryl —"

One eye opened.

"— and we're going gold!"

Both eyes. "Doug, I hate it when you do coke before bed," she mumbled, turning her head away. "Turn off the lights."

He laughed, maniacally even to his ears. The lie came easily to his lips. "Honey, I got the word from Harris that head office wants me in Frisco tomorrow. All the lead analysts, actually. And I got a bonus that means we can go in style!"

Nothing for a few seconds, then: "Tomorrow?"

"Yeah. I'm sorry it's late notice honey, I — wanted it to be a surprise." He flipped over on his back and looked around the bedroom, thinking to himself that this could be the last night he'd spend here in a long time. When he looked back, Cheryl was propped up on her elbows, looking at him.

"A surprise," she repeated. "I *thought* there was something weird going on."

"Well, I was waiting for a few things to come through," Doug said, plucking at her beige bra strap, guilty and jubilant. He checked his watch. "The Self office opens at six, so we've got a few hours."

Cheryl stood up and slipped into her housecoat. "Well, we don't need to pack," she said. "But we should empty the fridge."

Doug nodded. "Get a locksmith to secure the place. Put the house up for sale. Wonder if we'll get any good offers this time of night?"

Cheryl laughed. She looked at him flick through his watch and rubbed his bald pate. "A whole new life," she said dreamily. "Oooh, this is exciting!"

When she was leaving the room, Doug looked up with bright eyes. "Don't go banging stuff around, though… Olivia should get a good sleep." He connected to a locksmith. "Yes, I need to lockdown my residence… yes, I'll hold."

"Oh sure, Olivia gets to sleep," Cheryl said with a smile, closing the door quietly.

Could be her last sleep. Doug took a deep breath, sitting on the side of the bed, listened to the hold music.

As it turned out, the earliest the locksmith could be there was 5:30, so Doug managed to snatch a few hours of sleep regardless of the coke and excitement in his bloodstream. When he awoke, it was to the sound of Cheryl closing and locking their toybox.

"Got some sleep, eh?" she said. Her hair was tousled from trips into closets and crawl spaces in the last few hours.

"Time is it?" Doug said, looking at his watch.

"Just after five," Cheryl said, shoving the toybox against the wall and sitting on it.

Doug sat up, looked around. "You tidied up?"

Cheryl looked at him with her dark eyes, chin in her hands. She smiled and shrugged. "In case we come back. You know how I hate coming back to a messy house."

Doug nodded, thumped his feet on the floor. He knew better than to say that they wouldn't be coming back — everyone prepared for these things differently. Any future anthropologists would be disappointed, though. They liked things messy as a crime scene, like Vesuvius and Pompeii.

"I'm gonna rouse Lady Olivia," he said.

On the way to her bedroom, he noticed a box labeled FAMILY PICS+STUFF half out of the closet. He lifted the flap with his foot and saw the old picture of his grandfather playing the sax on top. He picked it up.

Cheryl appeared behind him, touched his waist. "I scanned in a bunch of the old pictures," she said.

"Good thinking, sweetie," Doug said, automatically, his eyes fixed on the browned cardboard frame, the smell of it, the things that wouldn't be digitized… he put it back into the box, almost roughly.

"I'm going to make some breakfast," Cheryl said, pushing the box away out-of-sight.

"Okie-doke," said Doug, smiling absently at her as he entered his daughter's room.

Olivia was a tidy little package on the bed. "Lights on, gradual," said Doug, standing there, watching the shadows on his daughter's face lessen and lessen, the butterfly flutter of her eyelids. *The last time I'll see that.*

He looked around her room, determined not to let the melancholy darken his good luck, his moment of triumph snatched from the jaws etc., etc. As the light neared full illumination he noticed the walls were covered by the Pole Position logo, flashed on everywhere, overlapping even, a hideously garish orange. *That album must have come with a flasher.*

"Daaad," Olivia whined, flipping and hiding her face. "Too eaaarly."

"How would you like to skip school today?"

Her head flipped back, her eyes narrowed. "JJ, right?"

Doug smiled. "No joke. If you're up and dressed in five minutes, you don't have to go to school." Then he turned and strode from the room, trying not to look at the orange cartoon ass that the Pole Position logo stuck out at him.

Down in the kitchen, Cheryl was spraying N'Oil on a piece of toast. She added it to the already sizable stack and gave him a questioning look. "Whattaya think?" she said. "I was about to start on something more ambitious, but I didn't know if you should go into this thing with an empty or a full stomach."

Doug nodded, fear seeping into him as he recalled the countless articles and entire programs dedicated to preparing oneself for Self — he'd deliberately ignored them. But there was nothing to be done at this point, so he plucked a slice with nonchalance he didn't feel and took a bite. "My tummy says — full stomach," he said through a mouthful and was rewarded by a slight lessening of the creases on Cheryl's brow.

Olivia came in, dressed in her little white turtleneck and said, "Four minutes, 24 seconds." Cheryl held out a glass of orange juice at her, which she dutifully drank and voluntarily took a slice of toast. Her bangs were combed down and covered her third eye tattoo — Doug wondered if the kids at school had teased her.

"UPS Locksmith," Doug's watch said, the voice tired and impatient. Doug's heartbeat quickened, and he took control. "Shoes, jacket," he ordered Olivia, taking the half-finished glass from her as he pointed her to the door. "Come on up, there in a minute," he said to his watch.

He offered the glass to Cheryl, but she shook her head. He finished it in three quick swallows and put the glass in the sink, taking her hand and pulling her to the door so that she didn't try to wash it and put it away.

Pulling on his corduroy jacket, he opened the door and hurried everyone out. He shut the door just as the elevator's soft ding announced the arrival of the locksmith.

"Where are we going?" demanded Olivia, finally.

"On a trip," Doug said, trying to smile mysteriously.

The locksmith approached, gave them a civil nod. "Service delivery for Doug Patterson," he said.

"That's me," Doug said, thumbing and eyeballing the proffered devices.

The UPS guy looked at his devices and nodded. "So it is. Frisco special?"

"That's right." He snuck a look at Olivia as surprise grew on her face, winked at her.

The UPS guy gave him the verbal contract about the procedure, and Doug dutifully nodded while really listening to Olivia's excited whisperings to Cheryl.

On the elevator ride down, Olivia asked what package they were buying.

"Gold, of course," Doug said. Olivia nodded her approval. Everything was as it should be, and Doug felt his heart leap a little at the idea that he had squeaked by again, another passing grade that could have been a fail.

As they left the elevator, Doug noticed a little flash behind him, and before the doors closed, he saw the Pole Position logo on the elevator wall. "Olivia!" he scolded, prying the flashbox from her hand.

She rolled her eyes. "I get five Pole Points every time I score a blank wall."

"Pole Points?" said Cheryl. "What are you talking about?"

Doug wished he didn't know. He peered out of the lobby doors, saw a taxi coming to pick them up.

Olivia tutted impatiently. "So-so-so, if you do a hundred, you get entered in the contest to win a date…"

Doug pushed through the door and walked towards the taxi. The SkyTrain passed overhead, pulling out of the station. As he ushered his family into the vehicle, he noticed something trailing behind the SkyTrain. *Ropes? Vines?*

"And what would you do on a date with these guys?" asked Cheryl with a smirk, looking at the picture of the band on the flashbox.

Doug slammed the door shut and told the taxi grill where to go.

"Kiss…" said Olivia, sticking out her lips.

Cheryl laughed merrily, and Doug managed an uncomfortable smile. "Nine-year-old girls don't kiss boys," he said, trying to keep his tone light.

Olivia kept quiet, looked at the picture on the flashbox. She remembered how Jill had bragged that she was gonna get a hoochie-mama body once her family got to Frisco. "Then I'm going to find Patricio P.P.," Jill had said, putting her hands on her hips and sticking out her bony chest, "And I'm gonna say 'C'mon, PPP, show me your bum!'" The four or five girls who were listening had exploded in giggles.

One of the older boys had seen her and imitated her chesty declaration to his pals. Jill had run to the washroom then, but couldn't outrun the catcalls and hoots of derision. It hadn't mattered, anyway — she was gone the next week. Olivia wished she had known they were leaving ahead of time. She felt a bit cheated that she hadn't gotten to brag or anything.

But she didn't want to complain. Dad had been acting funny lately. Even now, he was staring out the window, when there was nothing to see but grey mountains. They stopped at a red light and she noticed a big plant, so big it was drooping over onto the sidewalk. She noticed plants a lot more since last term — they had done a class project on how plants help people breathe, because they eat carbon dockside. The teacher was saying that if we all grew plants outside, they'd eat the smog right up! Olivia had planted the one she grew in class outside her building, but she'd forgotten about it.

They'd stopped at the place they were going to, and they got out. It was getting bright outside, but there was still no one up. They went into a pretty boring-looking store and her parents started holding hands, and looking at each other with lovie faces. Her mom held onto her shoulder, squeezed it occasionally.

A young man came up and led them over to a desk. They all sat down, and Olivia was annoyed that it was one of those really high chairs that made her feet dangle like a stupid kid.

"First customers of the day," the young man said. He had a smile that showed gums and great blond hair that looked soft. "Before we get started, we have a short cartoon that's made especially for our younger clients," he said, nodding at Olivia. "It basically explains the process and the trip ahead, and it's less boring than the legal mumbo jumbo we have to get sorted with the parents. What do you think, kiddo?"

Olivia, on being addressed directly, could only nod silently. *Less boring is good,* she guessed.

He nodded as if pleased and impressed with her answer and her watch bleeped her the message that there was incoming media, would she like to view it? She set the opacity and the volume to 50% — she wanted to keep an eye on this stuff — and ran the cartoon.

"How To Enjoy Your Self!" was the title. Mickey Mouse marched into the frame, wearing a golf shirt and his characteristic smile. "Hey kids!" he squeaked. "I hear you're going on a trip… a trip unlike any trip in history!" The scene behind him changed to a herd of cattle. "Neither cowboys —" said Mickey in a ten-gallon hat, "nor astronauts —" said Mickey in a spacesuit against a backdrop of stars, "have experienced the adventure that you're going to go on today!"

Dad was looking through the document. "What's the difference with platinum again?"

"Well, for an extra $1,500 per month per person, your body is cleaned daily, the muscles are stimulated so that they don't atrophy —"

Dad had been shaking his head since the money was mentioned. "Do you do pedicures?" Mom said in a sarcastic tone of voice.

The man laughed, and it coincided with Mickey laughing. "Not yet, ma'am, not yet… maybe in the next version."

Olivia focused back on the cartoon. Mickey had his hand poised on a lever beside a glass box. Goofy was inside, pressing his nose against the glass to see what Mickey was doing. "It's not really that complicated," Mickey said. "What happens during the upgrading process is this — " Goofy's nose jerked back from the glass when Mickey pulled the lever down. A funnel at the top of the box shuddered and sucked the ghost right out of Goofy's body, leaving the empty body to collapse on the floor. The body started snoring, Zs rising from his big nose.

The point of view followed the elongated ghost as it slid through the pipe attached to the box. "Goofy's mind (what there is of it, hee hee!) is transferred from his meat body to an entirely digital body — a body that never gets tired, or sick, or has to use the washroom!"

Olivia liked the sound of that. She hated having to ask to go pee in the middle of class, it was so embarrassing. She briefly listened to Dad talk about how much memory and storage they got, but lost interest.

Goofy's ghost took a few more twists and turns before it spurted out the end of a pipe onto the boardwalk of an amusement park — frozen at the moment of twilight, throngs of crowds stilled mid-stride. "And there's nothing stopping you from customizing your new Self body once you're here — your imagination's the limit!" Goofy, solid again, tapped his nose and ears into smaller versions, made his skin a few shades paler, and plucked a pair of sunglasses from midair. Mickey walked into the frame and did the same, and they put them on in tandem.

Mickey snapped his fingers, and the amusement park lurched to raucous life. Minnie scurried up and gave him a smooch. Pinocchio and Tinkerbell each grabbed an arm of Goofy and escorted him into the sunset. Before he became too small to distinguish in the crowd, Goofy turned back and said, "Enjoy your Self! Hyuk!"

The cartoon ended, and Olivia looked around. Her dad was still looking at the contract, scrolling through the text, but both the young man and her mom were looking at her.

Dad looked up, nodded. "OK, let's get started. You guys ready?"

Mom nodded. Olivia nodded, hoping having her spirit sucked out was as easy as having her cavities sucked out.

"All right, I'd have each of you focus on the passport seal you see in front of you," the young man said. A retinal beam went on from somewhere in the room, not her watch. Olivia saw a little book appear in front of her with her name on it. It had a little round symbol that pulsed slightly. When she looked at it, she felt dizzy and a little like she was falling.

"Bon voyage," said the rep, and the lights went out.

"I'll have a tequila sunrise," declared a fresh-faced cartoon kid, looking around at the people in the bar with bright-eyed pride. He hopped up on a bar stool beside Paul.

The kid was your classic Fresh Off the Boat — the cartoon body favored by people getting to choose a body other than their own for the first time, corn-colored tufts of hair above freckles and a gargantuan grin. "Can't believe it! All looks so real," the kid said, sliding his hands over the bar.

Paul looked up at the TV. Still black.

"Whatcha watchin'?" said the kid. The bartender handed him his slender glass and the kid went to pay him with a Ristwatch.

"S'automatic," the bartender said with a patronizing smile, and the kid slapped his forehead and laughed. A second later he was drinking the drink and smacking his lips appreciatively. Paul noticed he'd generated a straw without missing a beat, almost too easily.

"So issit the game, or what?" the kid asked again, nodding towards the TV, looking everywhere at once.

"It's not very interesting," said Paul. He might have allowed him a guest peek into the black screen, but the straw thing had him a little suspicious.

The kid shrugged, nodded at the documents he had laid out on the bar. "Bringing your work home with you?" he said.

Paul shrugged, a subtle mimic of the kid's gesture, curious to see what he'd do next.

The kid looked annoyed. "Don't talk much, do you?" He hopped off his bar stool and took his drink. "Nice talking to you," he said, a little too loudly.

Paul looked back at the TV — not pitch black any longer, there was the hint of predawn blue on it. He put a call through. The moment it connected, the kid looked at him with an insectile suddenness. Although Paul knew that the kid couldn't listen in, it chilled him a little.

"So what's up," he said to the person on the line, keeping an eye on the kid. He was working the room with his goofy grin, spurring knowing and superior smiles in the other patrons.

"Doug and his family are at the office," said the voice.

"And how long have they been in there?" Paul asked. He lifted a hand to the TV and pulled down the menu, made a few selections, pinpointed a place on a map. The grey morning sky on the TV righted itself and the rooftop view was replaced with a blur of streets and cars. *Attagirl,* Paul thought, impressed by Eileen's responsiveness.

"Maybe two minutes."

Paul wondered how long the transaction would take. "Try to get in closer, see what's going on through the front window. Try not to get spotted — don't worry about the salespeople, they can't see beyond the room."

A few tables away, the youngster had engaged someone in conversation. He was also a young man and was showing the kid whatever it was he was watching and making enthusiastic gesticulations. Paul quickly flicked through to rawview, and the bar became dataflows, swarms of representational information. The kid, as Paul suspected, wasn't a person at all: he was a black hole, sucking information through the tiny hole that the sucker's guest access had allowed him. He flicked back to normal view. The youngster was nodding and smiling at his mark's chatter.

"They're leaving now," said the voice.

Paul was stunned, forgetting the youngster for a moment. "But the pickup van's not — that doesn't make any sense!" He glanced up at the TV, and, sure enough, there was Doug and his wife and daughter walking away from the Self office. "Hold on."

On the screen, a white van bearing the Self logo slowed down. Doug and his family walked offscreen as the white van was backing into the alley.

"What the hell?" said Paul.

"I don't know," said the voice. "You want me to follow them?"

"No, don't bother," Paul said, "It's a miracle if he didn't see you already. I guess he got cold feet. Fuck. Great time for it."

He disconnected and tried to figure out what to do with Eileen. He'd assumed Doug and his family would be loaded into the white van, and she could tail it. *Goddamn it, it was perfect! What's with you, Patterson?*

He switched over to Eileen, determined to salvage what he could. The van, surely, would go to the body cache, or a drop-off for the cache. "That white van," he said to her in a voice that resonated with assurance, "follow it."

It was like letting a rabbit out of its hutch. He watched the visuals whip by for a few seconds, then disconnected.

The bartender stopped in front of him. "You need another drink," he said. Paul nodded tiredly.

The kid was still at it, listening to some woman with a hat, and Paul realized what was going on. Paul selected a business card, one that said:

Paul Harris
Data Security

and quickly gulped the shot the bartender had given him. He nodded at the bartender, flicked the card up into the air, and ported away.

The card arched up, over the heads of the patrons, and landed directly in the kid's shirt pocket. No one seemed to notice.

The Self van retracted its ruffles back into itself and started its engine. Whatever it had picked up in the alley had been entirely curtained by the ruffles, even from Eileen's rooftop vantage point.

She scanned the vehicle, her suit identifying it as being of Beijing origin and collecting 28 discrete items of information — dents, scratches, mud patches, rear-view angles — which would reduce the chances of losing it.

The van was entirely white, even the windows. The only thing distracting from its curves was an embossed Self logo. Eileen cranked her suit up to 500% as it pulled out, immediately noting a pair of notches on the roof that her angle had hidden before. A few seconds later her suit had identified them as slots for 'copter pickup. *Stick to the rooftops, then...*

The next building was close enough to hop to, although she had the suit take over her legs and confirm that the distance was small enough — silly to take chances, especially when she was so bad at guessing distances. She remembered one incident where she had tossed grenades on manual — they had hit the wall and rolled back. Mary hadn't let her live that one down for a long while. "Eileen throws like a girl," she teased, making everyone laugh.

The next building had a glass rooftop covering an Olympic-sized pool. *Must be nice*, Eileen thought as she jogged, watching the one swimmer cut through the water below. Her suit noted her focus and whispered, "Difficult hand-to-hand kill. Eighty-four meters from present position. Suggest projectile weapon."

Eileen sighed, her feet tapping somewhat musically on the glass floor. The next building looked like a far jump, and her suit sped up her run in preparation for it. Halfway through the air, after she'd glanced down at the Self van, she saw she wasn't going to make the next ledge. Terror jabbed at her like a clumsy killer, but then her suit raised her hands so that they slapped on the rungs of a ladder at the same time as her soles did. The suit fed her a relaxant and climbed her up to the crumbling building.

She was running again, feeling even more like she was on automatic, like she was driving in a car parallel to the Self van. The drug, as usual, disoriented her — her brain knew she should still be gasping, but her body denied it, accused the brain of overreacting.

Another jump, this one less dramatic, landed her on a cement platform complete with helipad. The suit saw the guard first, or rather the squiggly motion of his cigarette smoke. His puffs were furtive, one hand holding the door to the little stairwell house open.

Oh, hurry up and finish! thought Eileen anxiously. His unruly hair reminded her of Jeremy's.

"Easy hand-to-hand kill. Twenty meters from present position," whispered the suit. The suit, on auto with a mission priority of stealth tailing, shot her full of adrenalpro and lifted a flat hand in preparation for the fatal blow to an armed target. Her vision split between the Self van and a silhouette of the target that suggested green attack points and colored his weapons red.

The adrenalpro got Eileen's body and brain communicating again. She spotted the ladder and took manual control of the suit, which slowed to a stop a few feet from the smoker. The part of her vision tracking the van started to crowd with warnings immediately — she knew she just should have killed him, but she couldn't, not with that cowlick.

"Boo!" she said, feeling ridiculous, but not coming up with anything better in time. She revved up the suit, and as the man spun around in slow motion, she went the other way, getting to the ladder and starting down just as his cigarette hit the cement, sparks flying. He had his back to her, hadn't even drawn his gun by the time she was on the ground.

Her suit was screaming about the van now, barely a bright speck on the horizon as she again took to the sidewalks. "Yes yes," she muttered, "It'll be fine." As it turned out, the van was idling at a stoplight and she was half tempted to get up on top of it. *And wouldn't it be a pretty picture if the 'copter swooped down, you lying there like a black bear on a snow bank?* her wiser half chastised.

Although she didn't know what she *would* do if it were picked up. She couldn't very well grab its wheels. Ideally she'd get inside the van, but there was a good chance of it being booby trapped and it most certainly was surveilled in some way. As she lurked in the shadows of a nearby alley, feeling incredibly conspicuous, she realized it made more sense to follow in a car.

Still cranked up to full speed (she made a promise to herself she'd slow down as soon as she got in the car, save her energy) she dashed down the line of cars stopped at the stoplight, finally finding a pickup. It was one of those souped-up, chrome-piped tricksters, but it suited Eileen just fine — she tumbled into the truck bed and dropped out of sight just as the light turned green. When the truck started rolling, she slowed down to normal speed and got into a position where she could keep an eye on the white van and not get spotted.

As she got comfortable, she noticed that the box in the corner of the truck bed she had thought was for storage was actually a dog house. And that the dog house contained a pair of mean-looking eyes. Before she could get worried, they passed over a bump, and the house's plastic door glinted.

"Oh my," Eileen sighed. *A lot of excitement this morning. Hardly need any adrenalpro.*

The dog bared its teeth, but Eileen just tapped a foot against the door and smiled at it. Or that is, tilted her smiling mask at it. Dogs were actually often trickier than humans — they weren't surprised as easily and their target points were smaller and harder to get at.

The Self van was a few cars closer now. The pickup driver, invisible to Eileen through the opaque back window, was in a hurry, and whoever was driving the Self van wasn't. It had, according to her data, kept such a consistent speed that it was likely to be on autopilot.

The dog smushed its nose against the plastic, and Eileen was struck again with the unfairness of it. When a lonely person bought a pet, they fed it and loved it, often they came to accept it as part of their family — those were totally normal things. But when a lonely person buys a little baby boy to care for, to love — even if that boy is her flesh and blood — well, that person is depraved somehow. *And the boy isn't a real boy, he's a mockery of life cobbled together by people too smart for their own good.*

She looked at the dog, ignoring the kill data. It was an ugly-cute thing, all drool, froth, and yellowed eyes. It made that half-jerk chin move that marked it as debarked — one of the few genetic tweaks that had worked. Most didn't. Eileen remembered hearing a neighbor gush about her modified terrier — "No more poop-and-scoop!" — with a kind of trepidation. At first she thought it'd been because it looked like one of the dogs on an episode of *Rabid Fire,* that she was being paranoid. But then she heard the little clean-freak had cujoed on some kid.

There was that one company — Monsanto, wasn't it? — that had guaranteed stable behavior. If your pet cujoed, they'd pay for the hospital expenses, dispose of the old one and deliver a new one of similar type and value. It was expensive, but a lot of people swore by the subscription method. Then it came out that they were using the waste animals for extreme hunting games, and a lot of pet owners were outraged.

Ahead was a tunnel, the concrete painted to look like it was a ring of fire. WELCOME TO HELL, the text above it in old style letters read. Below it: {NOW DON'T YOU WISH YOU LISTENED TO PELE?} The ads directed at drivers were often confusing to Eileen — she hadn't been a driver in years —

and it always made her feel old. Jeremy took to explaining the campaigns to her when they were out and about, and she listened and smiled dutifully, but it fell flat as a dissected joke, either seeming convoluted or obvious.

As the Self van entered the tunnel, Eileen sped up to 250% and crouched at the ready. A tunnel would be a perfect place for a surreptitious drop-off. She told her suit to look for irregularities in the road that might suggest an opening. The yahoo who was driving her truck was changing lanes and speeding up, and Eileen was anxious that it would draw right up to the Self van — it was possible that she could be spotted by the Self driver or the van's surveillance. She tutted, irritated in the same way that she'd be irritated by a taxi driver who was driving in a reckless manner.

But she wasn't a little old lady in a taxi at the mercy of the driver. She was a killing machine, and, she resolved, it was time to start acting like it — otherwise she'd never get Jeremy back. She'd left the little old lady back in her house in Sunset Beach. She told the suit to tell her the most efficient way to commandeer the vehicle. A few processing seconds later, it showed her how.

"Take the tire iron from its enclosure," it whispered, showing how it was stored underneath a flap on the truck's flatbed. Then it placed a crosshair on the truck's back window. "Set speed to 312% and push the tire iron through the glass at this point. Withdraw tire iron, remove window, enter cab." It showed her how, first jabbing through the glass, then slapping the flat of the iron so that it cracked, then sketching an X to allow entry. "88% chance of instant kill. Run program?"

She checked to see why the percentage was so low. A few items scrolled up: 22% of Ford Prowler owners opt for safety glass; 31% opt for automatic driving, randomizing the driver's placement; 28% are "very likely" to have additional passengers. The suit asked her if she wanted to plan for these contingencies.

Eileen shook her head no. The van slid out of the tunnel into the sun, its white brilliance making her wince. She had the suit confirm the discrete identification marks, mulling her plan over as it checked them off. She hated doing anything under 90%. Beside her the dog was knocking itself into the plastic door, its fangs audibly clicking against it, almost as if it knew what she was planning. Then she had an idea.

She slowed down to normal speed, watching ahead. They went through two green lights before they hit a yellow, and there was a moment of anxiety as it looked like the Self van was going to get through on it. But it did stop, and the moment the Prowler's wheels were still Eileen went to 500%. Moving quickly but calmly, she slid up the doghouse door and hooked two fingers under the dog's collar.

The dog's legs jerked slightly as she pulled it out, gently. Its eyes were still set in that misted-over bite-lust, and its jaw was beginning to jerk with ghost-barking. Eileen grabbed the fur on its back and lifted it to the top of the cab, positioned it where the suit had thought the passenger would be and gave it a shove.

Its legs splayed as it slid down the contoured front windshield onto the hood of the car. Eileen breathed a sigh of relief — she'd worried it'd slide right off and maybe not even be noticed by a distracted driver. But it was already bouncing to its feet, mad as ever, ghost-barking like crazy.

She lay down in the bed, watching the doors. For a few maddening seconds, nothing happened. Then, the driver-side door crunch-clicked and began to swing open. *From here on in,* Eileen thought, *it's done — just a question of messy or clean.* She watched the back of the head of a long-haired burly woman get out of the truck, her chastising yells a molasses slur. One, two steps around the door and Eileen slipped her legs over the truck bed. As her feet clapped on the asphalt the woman followed the gaze of her pet, but Eileen was in the cab and pulling the door closed before her expression had a chance to form.

And just in time, too. The opposing light was yellow.

Which one's the accelerator? she panicked. She looked over at the woman and saw that she was heading for her dog. *Good.* She put her hands on the wheel and tried to remember when the last time she had driven was. And then, there was a sudden boom.

She ducked and turned her head, expecting the window to be shotgunned at the very least, but it had only been the elongated sound of the door finally shutting. "Oh!" she exclaimed, switching back to 100%, slapping down the lock on the door as if scolding it. She glanced to the side to see that the woman had escaped to a traffic island and was staring at the truck with hopeless ire, holding her dog to her chest.

Good reaction time, she thought as the light turned green. She cautiously accelerated, and after a few seconds she was able to relax. She glanced at the rear-view and noticed that the woman was talking into her watch, and she had a moment of anxiety when she tried to remember if Ford was the company that was able to make your car blow up or stop working if stolen by thieves. She asked her suit.

"According to Ford's FAQ, Ford offers a variety of antitheft options that range from simply disabling the vehicle to flooding the cab with lethal gas."

"What percentage of female buyers aged 18–34 choose them?"

A few seconds later, as if reluctant, the suit admitted that 18% purchase these options and only 3% of these were lethal. Eileen was further encouraged by the lack of options she saw in the cab — no autodrive, no scentmakers, not even a surround system — the owner seemed to be a simple girl, a girl after her own heart. She was glad she hadn't had to kill her.

Paul looked around the room. It was a stone chamber with a statue in the middle, a giant goddess figure with the head of a dragon and improbably sculpted physique. He walked around it, looking away from its lascivious grin and glinting emerald eyes to look into the body-length mirror she leaned on like a shield.

He surveyed the body he'd been assigned: he had a marine's brush cut and a rigor mortis smile, and a slight tick in his square jaw. One big muscle. *Pretty classic,* Paul thought, looking around the room. *Beats meeting at a restaurant.* He looked around the environment one last time before walking out steel doors that sprung open at his approach.

This was a hallway lined with weapons with little ornamentation except for a shield carved in the ground with crossed test tubes. Not dwelling on the decoration, Paul strode along the hall, passing a .45, a radiation waver, a sniper rifle, a bone melter, a grenade launcher, a plasma gun, a yakuza special, a massive taser, a Molotov cocktail — *there it is.* He reached for the bottle, and it leapt into his hand.

Thus armed, Paul continued down the hallway towards a pair of wooden double doors. They creaked open of their own accord and Paul walked out, a smile on his face as he thought about how lucky he was to have followed his intuition and given the cartoon kid at the bar his business card.

The doors boomed shut behind him. "A New Challenger Enters Castle Frankenstein!" intoned a voice. Paul looked around quickly, taking in the short hallways lit by pairs of globes that shot electrical currents between each other. He cautiously jogged down one slope, and the wall near him exploded in an acrid smelling burst of stone. He quickly retraced his steps, hearing behind him "I'm gonna burn you a bellybutton!"

He tried the other way, his heart beating like crazy, his footfalls echoing through the grey hallway. Around the corner he saw a yakuza special lying on the ground and stopped in his tracks. He listened for a second to see if he was being pursued but didn't hear anything. He wondered if he should pick up the more powerful weapon — the spinning blades would be way more useful than the cocktails in such close quarters. *But I might not be able to carry both, and I've got to keep the Molotov...*

Paul ended up sidling around the yakuza special and continuing, entering into a grand hall dominated by a huge banquet table. He was just wondering how the diners — slumped-over skeletons — had died when the stone arch above his head rained down grey debris. *Shit,* Paul thought, spinning around wildly. A second later, the ground pinged, and Paul started running for the opposite end of the banquet hall. *Sniper.*

He'd just located the balaclava-clad sniper, when a bullet slammed into his shoulder. *Damn.* He leapt up on the table and then back down, zigzagging as he targeted the sniper in a balcony box high above. He let a Molotov fly, his heart sinking as it missed the balcony entirely. As it smashed and covered the wall in flame, another bottle appeared in his hand.

The sniper laughed scornfully. "Nice weapon, newbie. Stay still while I frag you."

But a few more zags later, Paul had reached the wall and was safely underneath the box. The ground around him pockmarked as the sniper futilely tried to beat the angles.

"I just had the fucking rocket launcher, too," complained the sniper. "All right then, newbie. You're not worth fragging, but I'll come down anyway."

Paul, his chest heaving, noticed the skeleton nearest to him had a crown. He nodded fraternally at the king, whose skull seemed to be smiling at him. *The goblet and scepter are nice touches,* Paul thought, and then an energy vortex appeared at the feet of the king. It regenerated wherever it touched, sliding up the skeleton and fleshing and clothing it.

"Wow," said the sniper, who was suddenly beside Paul. He pointed with his rifle at the king, who was getting a handsome face to go along with his purple robes. "How'd you activate that?"

"I…" said Paul, deciding he didn't want to admit he had nothing to do with it and thus render himself dispensable.

The king stood and yanked an Uzi from his robes in one fluid move. He fragged the sniper, who thumped silently to the ground and dissolved into a cursing green pool of bones. He targeted Paul, and Paul waited for it, feeling the stupid bottle in his hand and wishing, instructions or no, that he'd gotten a decent weapon.

"You Paul?" said the King.

Paul nodded.

"Good. I'll meet you in the mirror room." The muzzle flashed, and bullets thudded across his body.

After dissolving into slime and a brief blink of blackness, Paul respawned in the room with the goddess statue. *Guess this is the mirror room,* he thought.

151

A second later the king came in, and Paul noticed his black-clad chest was emblazoned with the crossed test tube crest he'd seen earlier. He had the Molotov in his hand instead of the Uzi. He reared back with it, and for an anxious second Paul thought he was about to be fragged again, but the king whipped the bottle at the mirror.

It smashed and covered the entire mirror with its gasoline flames. Once it had melted a hole big enough, the king walked through it. After a moment, Paul followed him. On the other side of the portal was what looked to be Hell. *Oh, boys and their toys,* Paul thought. *How little things change.*

Paul glanced back at where he had come from and saw that a creature with a scaly reptilian body and the head of a full-lipped maiden held the portal on this side. Ahead, the king was standing at the edge of a precipice, his arms crossed as he gazed out over the scene below. As Paul joined him, he noticed a tiny pointed tail had poked out from under his purple robes.

Paul decided to sit down on the edge, swinging his legs as he watched the lovingly crafted scenes of torture and damnation below. A few seconds later, the king sat also. Paul noticed he'd sprouted stubby horns and had a swarthier complexion.

"So why the Molotov?" Paul asked.

"It's a crap weapon," the devil-king said. "No one chooses it voluntarily."

Paul nodded. "I noticed."

The devil-king snorted. "I was kind of curious to see if you'd make it across the Grand Hall. DarkTrousers had been waiting there for two days."

"Two *realtime* days?"

The devil-king nodded. "Yeah. He sucks. Fucking camper. I don't even know why we let him in." He shook his head, wearily. "I don't actually even think he's a clone, fuck what Razortime says."

"I guess there's no way to prove it in Frisco," Paul said. A piercing scream drew his attention below, where a rack had done its work too well and torn someone in two.

"Yeah, we have to go on nominations," the devil-king said. "But it doesn't really matter. He'll never make elite. He can run around Frankenstein all he wants, I don't give a shit."

"So is it elite that made the cartoon kid I saw at the bar?"

"Yeah," the devil-king said. "The hickbots."

"Hickbots. Very clever," Paul said. "Institutions and banks have been trying to make themselves uncrackable, to make the protection airtight. But with people's personal data, the focus has been on making it easy to share. So you've exploited this by having these hickbots crawl from bar to bar, getting people to show it a little data." Paul nodded admiringly. "It's like asking to see someone's driver's license for the photo, and memorizing the birthday and address as well. Except thousands of times a day, with no chance of getting caught."

The devil-king smiled, showing pointed teeth. "Yeah, it's a hack elegante. I didn't come up with it, though. Why'd you ask to see me?"

"The first guy I talked to mentioned the members of your crew," Paul said carefully. *And knowing my 12-year-olds, I figured Jericide, elite member of the Replicantz, had a decent chance of being Jeremy Ellis, Eileen's innocent little boy.* Paul smiled as he said truthfully. "And I'd heard of you. Based in Vancouver, originally, weren't you?"

"Once upon a time," Jeremy said, looking out across Hell.

Paul hid his smile, telling himself to be careful — he was used to his scrambleface concealing his reactions, but this environment wouldn't allow it. He looked down. A small rotating circle of sodomites, connected each to each by flesh, were ministered to by a cloven-hoofed guard who whipped when they slowed or when they didn't slow. He hadn't seen it loop yet — it was good quality work. He glanced at Jeremy, who seemed to be unconvinced by his flattery. "OK. I won't insult your intelligence."

"Oh good," said the devil-king.

"I'm researching signs of subversive activity in Frisco."

"Yeah, we knew that Data Securities stuff was bullshit," Jeremy said, a grin curling. "Well, the Replicantz won't be selling the hickbot for a few months. You can have our cast-offs when we're bored with them, like always. Gotta tell ya, though, you'll be paying through the nose for it."

"No," Paul said, amazed at the eloquent vehemence inside the 12-year-old mind. "I'm not interested in the hickbot technology. I'm interested in what it represents. I mean, you're obviously not a genuine subculture, but in a few years you might be…"

"What the fuck you mean by that?" Jeremy said, standing.

"Well, come on," Paul shrugged, staying where he was. "You're a bunch of kids hacking around. It's hardly something on the level of Code Warriors." He swivelled to face him, remained sitting. "They had a manifesto."

Jeremy expelled air from his mouth. "Man, you're so full of shit. Who fucking cares about some manifesto? Those losers were strictly internet, man." He wheeled around, his cape swishing. "A bunch of script kiddies with good PR, that's all. What did they do? Get on MTV. Big shit."

Paul agreed, but drew it out a little further. "Are you any different?"

"Fuck yeah!" Jeremy said, his petulant anger looking strange on his regal features. "We're clones. People treat us like we're fucking mistakes, man. Factory rejects. Out there we're too few and far between, but in Frisco we're a force to be reckoned with. The haters can't fuck with us here."

Paul noticed a well-worn quality to the outburst, but there was unmistakably passion as well. *How high up is this kid, I wonder?* Out loud, Paul said, "Prejudices die hard."

Jeremy pulled a shotgun from his cloak and loaded it with a snap of his wrist. Paul expected the meeting to be cut short. Then Jeremy stopped at the ledge, took aim and fired on a bone pterodactyl. The person who was riding it managed to squeeze off a plasma burst as he fell into the pit, but Jeremy sidestepped it, and it only lanced his cape.

"Lots of things die hard." Jeremy tossed the gun on the dirt and rejoined Paul on the ledge. "Funny thing is, we can make a body with a bellybutton on it and pass as spawned here. But we don't want to be like them. They're scared of Frisco, scared of the limitless power they have. They're scared they'll become inhuman here. But we're used to being monsters."

Paul nodded, feeling the excitement of discovery he felt when chancing upon a raw vein of new blood.

Jeremy turned towards him. Paul felt the boy's eyes staring out of the man's face and then heard it in his voice: "So I don't give a fuck what you think of us. It doesn't matter how you classify us. We're going to be a force in Frisco."

"I believe you," Paul said, sincerely. "But how are you going to keep your identities secret? What about... your parent?" He had almost said Eileen.

Jeremy jumped on the pause. "Yeah, parent is the right term," he jeered. "Sometimes you liberals are worse than the haters."

"Do your parents know what you're doing?" Paul said, *liberal* a burr under his skin.

"No. We all have a few different skins for different occasions." He displayed his devil-king appearance. "This is my business suit, for instance. Obviously when I hang out with my grandma I'll look different. It's not an issue now, since she hasn't moved here yet... anything new scares her." He shrugged, weary and accepting.

Paul smiled inside at the idea of Eileen being scared, at how badly each of them misjudged the other.

"So I'm waiting until I get enough money to customize a house for her. I thought it'd be quicker but there's been a lot of groundwork to cover here."

"She's probably pretty worried," Paul probed.

"I know." An uneasy look passed over his face. "It'll happen soon. We've had a lot of opportunities come up that we couldn't pass up, stuff that'll make us wads in the future." He nodded with his chin at the people being whipped in the pit. "This, for instance."

Paul nodded, as if he'd known all along that it was a real and not just well-crafted holos. "You guys didn't do it all yourselves, did you?"

"No no, the team of designers did all the visuals. We just did the back end. We can do stuff like Castle Frankenstein, basic stuff like that, but… well, you can't see it, but a lot of this stuff is really twisted. So they came up with the idea and the torture implements and came to us. They needed to know how to override a guest's ability to port away or adjust their sensory input."

"I've never heard of that," Paul said, suddenly nervous at the fact that he couldn't port away. He looked behind him to see how far it was to the portal. Pretty far.

"Good. If the Friscops knew they'd patch it, so it's got to be pretty underground."

Paul mentally noted the slang for Frisco Systems Operators.

Jeremy nodded at the pit below. "You see how busy it is now? It has a capacity for twice that — Hell's supposed to be crowded, after all. So it's nowhere near capacity, but… it's still made us plenty of money."

"Does it ever strike you that you might be able to do things with a broader impact with your skills?" Paul said.

"Of course," snapped Jeremy. "Making a playland for these sickos is strictly for the money. We've got plans."

Paul raised a skeptical eyebrow.

Jeremy took the bait. "We're launching a pirate ship."

"A pirate ship? You mean, for the bay?"

Jeremy nodded, his grin absolutely devilish.

"What will you do with it?" Paul asked.

"What do you think? What pirates do best," Jeremy said, his eyes sparking to life. "Loot and pillage."

155

Nicky leaned back in her seat, feeling the sun on her face. She pedaled leisurely along the street with only an occasional car to avoid, thinking about how perfectly the world suited her — *go on, go to Frisco. Us meek shall inherit the earth.* She spotted a vine crawling up a traffic light pole, and she braked.

She didn't get off her bike, just sidled up alongside the pole. Pulling one of the baggies out of her side satchel, she plucked a leaf and sealed it up, then spoke into her watch. "Sample E21. Corner of Cordova and Princess. Healthy, three-foot-high plant growing from patch of earth up a concrete pole." She pulled it gently away from where it was clinging, amazed at how secure it was.

A car, its light long green, idled nearby. Nicky gave the blacked-out windows an annoyed stare until it moved on. She was glad for the mask that Simon had bugged her to wear, not for his reasons but because it was a fairly inconspicuous disguise.

"It's not the same as walking around at night," he had said, his eyes big and entreating. "You pull in more air when you're cycling. And during the day, the smog's always worse."

They had been eating — she had invited him and Andre to dinner to celebrate her new job saving the world. "But what about these miracle plants," she had countered. "Won't they counteract the higher levels?"

"Maybe someday," he had said, somehow fitting an entire tomatochoke in his mouth at once. "But now there's no way that a few string beans are going to filter the exhaust of a billion Mexican cars."

Andre had mumbled something about how that made it sound like it was the Mexicans' fault, when all that had happened was that they were driving as much as us.

"I'm just saying… oh, fuck it," Simon said, throwing the mask on the coffee table. "Don't wear it, then."

"I'll need a new pair of lungs before I'm 60 anyway," she said lightly.

"Yeah, that makes sense. Spend $100,000 on a pair of lungs because you didn't want to wear a $10 filter."

He had dropped it then, and they spent the rest of dinner discussing Andre's time in Mexico. He had been helping out with ZapataTV, although after a while he'd become disillusioned and left. "It was just a job," he had said.

"Hey, no bashing jobs," Nicky had said, refreshing everyone's tumbler of red wine. "Remember what we're celebrating!"

"I'm celebrating a talented addition to the cabal," said Simon, lifting his glass.

"Yeah," said Andre, with a rare smile. "That's it."

Nicky had clinked without voicing the part of her that was saying, *I'm celebrating getting paid.* They were odd, these boys.

Nicky rode off, her eyes in search of more samples, her mind mulling over Andre and Simon. They seemed naively hopeful and worldly at the same time. She had expected them to change after the night they'd fucked — to drop the pretense of being mysterious agents on a mission. To become hard-headed, rough, mean: the norm. But instead they'd involved her in this odd scam they had.

"…So you just do what you do, and he pays you for it," Nicky had said later that night, trying to figure it out through the wine fog.

Simon nodded. "Yeah, well, did you hear about the ad swoop in Detroit?"

Nicky hadn't.

"Good, I'm glad. That means it didn't work. Ford had bought up every inch of advertising — every billboard, every poster — to promote some new fucking car. Just because they can, because Detroit is so poor. So me and some friends went and adjusted some of the advertising, so it drew attention to Henry Ford's admiration of Hitler. Paul saw what was going on and got in touch with me, said he wanted to fund me." Simon leaned over to double-check that the wine was finished. "Shit. At first I thought he was. like, from Nissan or something. But he's not. He's just this political activist, kinda, with a lot of money. So he gave me a bunch of cash, and I was able to hire some of the best graf writers in the city to bomb the fucking place. It was awesome."

"That's how we met," Andre said.

"Yeah, well," Simon said with a smirk. "I hired some crappy writers too."

They all laughed.

"Fuck you, *bossman*" said Andre.

Simon convulsed with hilarity, fell over on his side and knocked over the empty wine bottle. Nicky had been happy and proud to be with them that night, in such a frivolous mood, and even now with her cynicism awake she knew they were more interesting than most people she'd met.

She hadn't seen a sprig of green for a few blocks, so she set her eyes to scouring. There was a good-looking sample twined in the fence of Pleasant Acres, and she rolled her bike onto the sidewalk to clip it.

After she'd bagged it, she noticed the security guard standing outside his guardhouse. He gestured *c'mere* with his finger. Nicky got on her bike but didn't otherwise move. *Was he going to hassle her for taking a sample?*

She got on the road and started riding towards him. *Hey! Wasn't that the prick who electrified that old homeless lady? No, he's on the night shift...*

"I've got to fine you for having a vehicle on the sidewalk, miss," he called out.

Fuck! It is him!

She decided that she'd keep riding, cautiously pumping faster and faster. When the guard realized what she was up to, he yanked out his taser.

She felt her heart in her throat, but she kept riding, pushing the button that wasn't her brake button, watching the guard's finger for any movement.

He was patient, and she was barely ten feet away when his finger twitched. Her finger also twitched as it left the bunnyhop button, and her spine jarred a little at the sudden springing up.

I can't believe I'm not frying! Flying not frying! The joy flipped into terror as she descended and became surer than sure that the bike would smash itself and her, leaving her easy pickings for that sadistic little man, *why was she always doing such stupid...*

...such marvellous, exciting, hilarious things? she finished after the bike, with an impossible gentleness, splayed down to the earth but didn't slow a whit.

When she got home, satchel and pockets puffed out with sample bags, her bike wouldn't roll up properly. She smiled when she identified the obstruction in the spokes as taser wire, and she extracted the mangled and dirty souvenir. She held it by its prongs and said, "You won't be electrocuting anyone else anytime soon, will you?

She walked through the big house, which seemed bigger and emptier now that Andre and Simon had come and gone. It had felt the same when Kathy had left, however, but knowing that didn't make the melancholy go away. *There's always room for loneliness!* Nicky thought, making herself smile.

They'd stayed for a few days but then had left to go back to their tent. Or so she presumed — she hadn't asked because she hadn't wanted to seem nosy. She didn't know what kind of relationship they had — her getting this job made for a strange social progression: strangers to lovers to co-workers.

There was nothing in the fridge, but she found a Skippy sandwich in the cupboard. She smacked through it, looking at the wine bottles they'd left behind, the bulging garbage bags awaiting her attention. *Shit, I better get my ass down to the depot,* she mentally groaned, then a happy thought interrupted her. She had money! She, like normal people, could call the garbage truck and pay for a pickup! Regardless, she was tempted to ride down with her bike. *Bet it'd take five minutes max,* she thought, reveling in how the simple machine shrunk geography.

Wishing she had something better than pickle juice in the fridge to wash down the sandwich — *I'll buy orange juice tomorrow, haven't had that in ages* — she slapped her hands crumbless and headed up to her lab. Her watch announced a call and she was worried for a second it was her new boss, calling early for some reason, but it was her mom. She took the call. "Hi Mom!"

"Aren't you chipper!" she said, her voice gratified and surprised.

"Yep. I got a job!"

"A *job!* In — Vancouver?"

"Yeah. Biological work I can do from home." Nicky dragged over the chair and climbed up the ladder to her lab.

"Biological work? What company?"

"It's for this eccentric billionaire," Nicky said, having already thought out how she would spin it. "He does public art projects."

"Anyone doing biological work in this day and age must be eccentric!" said her mother, her voice still pleased. "Have you met him?"

"No, not yet. We did the interview by e-mail. I was recommended." Nicky stood the taser wire in a test tube like a strange flower.

"E-mail! How formal."

"Yep," she said. "He's going to touch base with me tonight. They've set up…" Nicky thought of something. "Hey Mom, I can patch you in visually! My cubespace is set up for Frisco!" Almost immediately she regretted saying it — her privacy defenses had momentarily dropped.

"Oh!" her mother exclaimed. "Well, just a second, I'm in a bath here." There was the schloopy sound of someone emerging from water.

It was hearing her mom's equal hesitation that made her relax a bit. She scanned the room for anything damning, didn't see anything, scanned again. "Let me know when you're decent, Mom." She took off her jacket and satchel, setting them on the counter.

"Come in!" Mom sing-songed.

Nicky snorted at her corniness, getting her watch to talk to the computer. A few seconds later, her mom's living room appeared in the small cube. It was a replica of the one in Vancouver that Nicky had grown up in, so she knew what each tiny framed picture and knick-knack was without having to zoom in.

"Well!" Mom said, getting up out of her armchair. She looked up and around. "This looks like a real lab! And oh my God you're huge!" She leaned back to contemplate her daughter, hands on hip. "This must be what I look like to the Chinese villagers in my mah-jongg game!"

Nicky growled and stuck her face up to the box.

Mom lurched back and squealed, dropping to her knees and yelling something in another language.

"What does that mean?" Nicky asked, laughing.

"I don't know, it's just what they scream before you step on them," she said, getting up, dusting off her knees by habit. She looked around some more. "So you got all this equipment from the school? I had no idea that it was so much!"

Nicky surveyed her gleaming counter, her antique test tubes, her EasyBake oven through her mother's eyes. "It's basically why I got the job, because I can do everything they need here."

"That's great, Nicky. Art-related, too, how perfect for you. Just great," and the two of them glowed in it for a few seconds. "I hope he's a nice man. He's coming today?"

"Yeah," Nicky said, checking her watch, glancing at her sample bag involuntarily.

"I'll let you get to it then. I'll head back to my bath. One of the best things about Frisco is that you can talk in the bath without worrying about dropping your watch in by accident."

"OK Mom, I'll call you soon."

"Bye," she said.

She emptied her sample bag into a small pile on the counter, thinking about her mom in the bath, calling all her relatives one after the other. *What does she do with all that time? Without sleep to break up the days?* She resolved to be more understanding about her mother's constant calling, wishing all the calls could be as mutually satisfying as this one was.

Noting the sample number, she put the vine clipping into the EasyBake and set it on reverse. A few seconds later it dinged and, after checking the oven to make sure it'd degenned completely, she scanned the data and grouped it with the verbal information she'd collected on site.

After doing a few of them, she began to wonder if there was a way to gang them up but decided to just do them one by one — she had a while before her boss got here, so she wouldn't try anything too fancy just yet. But it was exciting to think about learning how to use the tools of her trade — not just craft now, but trade — inside and out. Being paid for genetics… Professor Cho would be green with envy.

After she finished, she did some research, following where the data pointed. Pretty much on the hour, her watch bleeped.

She put him through to the cubespace right way. "Hello."

The little man with big shoulders nodded, his hands behind his back. "You're Nicky?"

Nicky nodded.

"I'm Paul," he said, looking around the lab. Nicky returned the favor, noting that Paul had no environment and appeared to be standing on her silver counter. Because of this, he took up all of the cube. If her mom had been figurine-sized, he was doll-sized. He was wearing a casual golf shirt and slacks, with a shifting blur where his face would have been.

More cloak and dagger, Nicky thought, *although he pulls it off better.*

"So Simon and Andre have told you what you'll be doing?" he said.

"Basically," she said, nodding. "Very basically. They said that you need biological work done — analysis, duplication — and that it's connected with JK's project somehow." She looked at Paul, saw his blur bobbing up and down in a nod. "They were pretty vague, though. It's all very mysterious," she said lightly.

Paul chuckled, his hands in his pockets. "Well, good for them. They're taking it seriously. It's the first time in a long time I've worked with agents this directly…" He seemed to be thinking about something, then looked at her. "Well, may as well get started. How did you do with the sample collecting?"

Nicky patted the pile on the counter. "There's a lot happening out there. I collected 20 without trying too hard."

"That's great. And did people give you any problems…?"

"Not in collecting samples," Nicky said. "Some people watched me, but that was it."

Paul's blur bobbed excitedly. "It's a different world from even five years ago. You would have caught a lot of security static. They would have gotten rid of the plants, too."

Nicky looked at the taser wire sticking out of the vial. "There was a bit of trouble with one guard, but it was more because of my bike than me taking samples. But I bounced over him."

Paul laughed, almost a cackle. "Older guy?"

Nicky tried to think back, picture his face. "Could have been."

"Wonder if he'd remember the bike strikes of the '20s. We ran through the streets in packs then. And you bounced over him?" He laughed again. "Terrific. I'm so glad to hear bikes are taking root again."

Nicky wondered if he had something to do with JK having it, but didn't want to ask and appear foolish. *He isn't responsible for everything.* "So I took ten of the samples and degenned them. The data looks pretty consistent." She moved the spreadsheet to the cube, and it appeared in his hands. He stretched it out and scanned it, nodding.

He looked at the spreadsheet for a few seconds, pulled in another file and compared the two. "Would you say the patterns indicate that the airborne spores were less successful than those with live carriers?"

"Not enough data," Nicky said immediately, feeling the anxiety that gripped her during trick questions in school. "It should also be noted that the collection methodology biases the data — I took routes that live carriers would be liable to take."

He looked at her, nodded, looked back at the spreadsheet.

She felt silly, like she overreacted. He wasn't necessarily looking for diamond-hard data. "More anecdotally," she started, and when he didn't cut her off for being irrelevant, she continued. "Lilacs that I found on a traffic island are more likely to have been airborne. And the shirt I wore to JK's party was covered with spores, but I swept them off onto a pile of dirt near my place and they didn't take. They were pretty sticky."

"Hmm," he said.

A few seconds passed, and Nicky plucked up her courage. "It would help if I knew the desired results of the experiment…" School had drilled it into her that the client always had a desired result — it was just a matter of working back from that.

Paul continued to look at the data for a few more moments, then set it aside. Nicky waited for the confidentiality speech, but it never came.

"I'd like to make the city wild."

Nicky bit her lip. "Wild?"

"Vancouver used to be a rainforest. I'd like to invite the wilderness back."

"Oh." Nicky wanted to say something else, but couldn't think of anything other than: *How very flaky.* She was glad she got paid for the sample collection up front. *Nice while it lasted, I guess.*

Paul had turned back to the data again. "This is working fine. Ideally, it'd be trees, but there's not enough time."

Alarm bells sounded in Nicky's head. She imagined a ticking bomb buried somewhere, ready to blow Vancouver back to the stone ages. "Time?"

Paul stared at her, and Nicky tried to smooth out her face. *It's so unfair*, she thought. *He gets to see me but I can't see him.*

"You know, I don't really see any resemblance."

"Resemblance?" Nicky said.

"Max. Your uncle. We were both Harmless Cranks." He crossed his arms.

"You were a friend of my uncle?" Nicky said.

"Well, we were colleagues. Comrades, I suppose. Did you ever meet him?"

"Yeah." It was one of her first memories, a family gathering, a big man with hair on his knuckles. "Once."

"We never got along," Paul said. "After we stopped the moon billboard, we were constantly fighting. Fighting about how to fight. He wanted to keep pounding away. I wanted to get under the skin. We both had our supporters, and we splintered off."

"It's funny, the movie says that you disbanded," Nicky said. "But I know that wasn't true, because Max disappeared."

"Max was assassinated in the most effective way — he was disappeared. Maybe he went to fight in Cuba? Maybe he went underground? No solid answers, and so no solid opposition. But he was killed — nothing else would have stopped him."

Nicky said nothing, a little disoriented to hear this cold explanation of murder from a man in a golf shirt.

"When I vetted your background, I was pretty shocked to learn of the connection. He always maintained he had no family. I was a bit shaken, actually. I often… think of your uncle."

Nicky nodded.

Paul raised his hand and shook his head. "No, that… makes it sound like I reminisce fondly about him. The truth is, the bastard is in my head, squatting in there, questioning my every move. It must have been the meetings, the post-moon meetings we would have. We argued until our throats were raw, and our brains were numb."

Nicky started to degen the rest of the samples, just to do something with her hands. "My father hated him, too." She shut the EasyBake.

Paul sighed. "I didn't hate him. Although I felt a… guilty vindication when he was disappeared. I felt like I'd been proven right, that he took unnecessary risks. But now, I almost feel like it was just bad timing. If it had been ten years earlier, things would have been different. The newspapers still reported on corporate activities, government still had some vestiges of power —"

"Max hated the government too," Nicky said.

"Yes, oh yes, I know," Paul said wearily. "Although that damned movie focused on that for political reasons. But my point is, timing plays a big part."

"All right," Nicky said. "But if you want me to work overtime, I'll expect time and a half."

Paul laughed. "Fair enough."

Having finished the rest of the samples, she took the spreadsheet from Paul and flowed the new data in.

When she passed it back to Paul, he said, "This is wonderful, Nicky. Much more than expected. We'll have a lot to talk about tonight — I'm meeting with JK and Simon and Andre."

"Lucky you don't have to sleep," Nicky said.

"Ha," he said, minimizing it and stuffing the spreadsheet into his pocket. "I'm sorry to have talked so much about your uncle. It's been… years, actually, since I've been able to talk to anyone about him. I'll get Simon and JK to fill you in on the rest of the project."

"It's OK. It doesn't bother me," she said. Nicky didn't understand whether he meant it was too dangerous to talk about her uncle or whether her relation to him had made it possible. He had an awkward mix of frankness and evasion that almost seemed unintentional.

Andre and Nicky sat opposite each other at the window table of Starbucks. Nicky was having a hard time because she didn't want to stare out the window at the umbrella box — they were supposed to be *discreet*, as Simon put it — and she didn't want to stare at Andre. Their conversation ground to a halt so quickly that not much grinding had been required.

Andre was sitting there, sipping his ChocoLatte, the translucent tattoo strip around his wrist unusually visible. She had only caught glimpses of it before. The little bones and ligaments slid back and forth as he tilted his cup.

"Brother I knew did his whole body like this," he said, seeing her gaze.

Nicky nodded. Embarrassed at being caught, she looked back to the box, which read, "Tilley's Disposables: Try an Organic Umbrella!" Finally she turned back and said, "He must have been unique looking."

He snorted. "Oh yeah. Big brother, too. Bodyguard for Jah Pimp. He was a friend of my sister's. There was one time at a barbeque in our backyard when he took his shirt off, freaked everyone out."

Nicky imagined watching bits of chewed-up hot dog sliding down a see-through esophagus to a big belly. "Must have been a hit." She noticed someone across the road plucking out an umbrella, looking at it, putting it back. "Damn!" Nicky said. "It's free, for God's sake!"

Andre smiled. "They're kinda strange looking. And it doesn't look like rain."

Then one person grabbed one on her way onto the SkyTrain, and another two helped themselves. "As soon as one person does it…" Andre said.

JK had had the idea to make the spore-carrying umbrellas, and Simon had wanted to see what the best method of dissemination was. Andre and Nicky were assigned the hands-off method, which suited her fine — she had been up most of the night slaving over a hot EasyBake, making the sample umbrellas.

A few seconds passed, and Nicky pulled her eyes away from the window, scanned the café to see if they'd attracted attention. Not that she could see. She and Andre weren't the most innocuous of couples, but a glamorous and noisy threesome was drawing most of the looks. She looked back at his tattoo. "So why did he do it? His whole body?" she asked.

He shrugged. "He said it was 'cause white people were gonna stare anyway, so give them something to stare at."

"Huh," Nicky said, feeling weird and white.

"But…" Andre drummed his fingers on the table. "It was also just to show that he was paid. That kinda body mod…" he shook his head. "Serious cash."

The table of three beside them was talking about body mods. "Rachel, if you want it, just do it! What *is* the problem?" Nicky wondered if their conversation was spurred by her and Andre's.

"Do you feel like people stare at you here?" asked Nicky.

"Yeah, they stare…" Andre's head tilted, his eyes looked thoughtful. "But it's different. Less fear here. More curiosity. There's no black folk here. Back in Detroit, they stare like they *know*. They know what you're about — you'd rob them, kill them, given half a chance… that you're probably a lazy African. Shit like that."

Nicky felt a twist at "lazy African." It was one of her dad's favorite phrases when she was growing up. It was his opinion that they'd be doing a lot better if the "lazy Africans" phased out their governments and got with the program.

"Hurts us all," he'd say after doing the household budget. He never directly blamed the Africans for her stingy allowance, but the insinuation was there.

"Do you think… it'll be better in Frisco?" she said and immediately wished she hadn't.

He snorted. "What do you think?"

"Well I mean… you can choose any appearance you like in Frisco."

Andre threw up his hands. "How many black folk can afford to move to Frisco? And even if a black man's rich, he can't just switch — all his business contacts know he's black. All his friends know he's black. So if he switches, everybody thinks he's ashamed of who he is."

She nodded and looked at Andre. "If I had the money to go to Frisco, I'd go to Detroit."

Andre laughed. "You don't want to go Detroit. Believe me."

Nicky shrugged, glad he was smiling now. "Not just Detroit. All over. Halifax. Miami."

"Oh," Andre said. "Do you know how much it *costs* to fly to Miami? Over $10,000!"

"Really?"

"Yeah," Andre said. "My aunt lives there, so I hear about it from my mother. 'Just because the rich people use up alla the fuel on flying around in space, how come I gotta pay that kinda money?'"

They laughed loud enough to attract the attention of the three loud-talkers, one of whom gave them a *keep it down* look.

"Hey, Andre," Simon's voice said.

"Yeah," Andre said into his watch.

"We're finished here," Simon said. "How are you guys doing?"

Andre gave her a *what's this guy talking about* look. "We aren't doing anything. You were giving them out by hand, and we were just watching."

"Yeah yeah. OK well just count your units and we'll meet back at Nicky's all right?"

"Yeah."

Nicky took a few more sips of coffee and they left, walking out and pulling on her coat at the same time. Andre didn't have a coat, just a thick cable-knit sweater on its own. "What if it rains?" she asked him, chinning at his sweater.

"I'll just open my brolly," he said in a passable English accent.

They were halfway across the road when they realized there was nothing to count. The umbrellas were all gone.

They headed up the stairs to the SkyTrain. While they waited on the platform, Nicky wanted to ask him how he felt about the tension between the Jamaicans and the Africans. But right now, his face was expectant and placid as he looked down the track, and she didn't want to stir up the waters.

"You know," he said. "I bet it took them longer to give them away by hand." He smiled. "I told Simon that, but he didn't believe me. The boy thinks he can charm the world."

"Oh yeah?" said Nicky, smiling.

"Hell yeah. It's ridiculous. The other night, we were working on this piece? And this security guard sees us down the alley and yells and starts running. I jam the cans in my bag and start walking away, fast, and I see that Simon is standing there, waiting. *Waiting.* This smile on his face."

Nicky could see it. "What'd you do?"

"I grabbed him by the hair and pulled him along. Eventually he came."

"Was he mad?"

"Not when he saw that the guy had a gun. He knows you can't argue with that."

Nicky hoped it was a taser but didn't ask. "Aren't there security guards in Detroit?"

Andre looked at her as if she was crazy. "Of course. That's how he got into so much trouble there, wrecking all those Ford ads. If Paul hadn't paid his fines, the debtor vans woulda got him. For sure. He'd be working 14-hour shifts in some sweatshop somewhere as we speak."

The first sound Doug heard was the sound of timbers creaking. The half-light of the room he was in allowed him to see a few dark shapes, but he managed to get off the hammock he was lying in by touch. When on the ground, he realized that the rocking wasn't just coming from the hammock. Spotting a thin line of light tracing a doorway, he made his way over to it and felt for the knob.

It opened onto a poop deck beneath a blue sky ribboned with clouds. *Holy shit. It all looks so real.*

Doug shaded his eyes from the sudden light and noticed something odd about his hand. Before he could fully register it, he noticed two skeletons lying on the deck, a larger one and a smaller one. *Well, that's kind of grisly,* he thought, shutting the door behind him. At the sound of it shutting, the small skeleton's head turned his way and shrieked horribly.

"Olivia!" said the larger skeleton, who propped herself up on her elbows and backhanded the small skeleton's shoulder. "Don't."

"But it's, it's —" the small skeleton said, pointing her tiny bony hand at Doug, shaking in exaggerated terror. "A skeleton!"

Doug looked at his body. Sure enough, it was fleshless. He tapped his foot bone on the deck, and it made a clicking sound. *Jesus.*

"We're just getting some sun out here," Cheryl the skeleton said. Her jawbone wagged slightly as she talked — not like a cartoon, opening and closing with every word, but in a more realistic fashion.

"Looks like you've got a little too much sun," Doug said, his voice sounding completely normal to him.

Olivia burst out laughing. "You look funny, Dad."

Doug looked at his long, bleached arm bones. He rolled them in a wave, clapped (well, clicked) his hands, and did the Running Man. Olivia screamed with laughter. In the middle of one dance move he tripped over a loose plank and fell. He felt no pain until Cheryl screamed.

Lot of screaming going on today, Doug thought absently as he pushed himself up with one arm and clambered to his feet. The other arm had busted off at the elbow and lay on the deck.

"Mom, it's not *real*," said Olivia.

Cheryl was looking at him through her finger bones, her whole body tense.

Doug tried to move the missing limb and the bone flopped around like a horrific fish on the deck. He made it give the thumbs up, and Cheryl's hands slowly dropped from her face. He stooped down and picked it up, unable to resist getting it to wave at Cheryl, who was waiting with her arms crossed. "The hand bone connects to the elbow bone…" he sung, putting it in its place and hoping for the best.

A little ghost with a doctor's bag appeared at the joint and looked at it, assessed it, and said. "$75."

Numbly, Doug nodded, thinking *stung already*. The Doctor opened his bag and went to work. A second later, after a whirr of activity, the Doctor waggled a finger at him and disappeared.

"What are you nodding at, Doug?" asked Cheryl anxiously.

"Nothing, nothing," Doug said, making his tone light. He moved his arm. "Good as new. Boy, this is quite a ship we've got, huh?"

He walked to the edge and looked over, watching the waves glint and ripple. He was impressed with the level of randomness, which was also evident in the sails snapping above. He tried to remember his nautical terms from his childhood ship simulations. *Which was port and which was starboard again?* He couldn't remember, so he pointed up at the cup that topped one of the massive timbers. "That's the crow's nest. It's where you keep watch for land."

He strolled to the front of the boat, his hands clasped behind his back. Without looking, he turned to his daughter, who was close on his heels, tapped his jawbone with a finger. "I wonder if that mermaid is still strapped to the front of the ship?"

"Mermaid!" Olivia said. She leaned over the edge, Cheryl scrambled to hold onto her waist, looking back at him with black sockets. "Hey, there is a mermaid there! It's wood though." She looked at her father. "Howja know that?"

"Oh, your dad knows a thing or two about ships," Doug said, affecting a captain's swagger. "I'm going to my quarters," he said, heading to a small shack that contained the wheel.

"Can we go swimming later?" Olivia was asking Cheryl. Doug looked back — Cheryl was already shaking her skull, gripping her hand. He was relieved. There was something about that water that freaked him out. There was no way they'd program an environment that infinite. A person who fell into that randomness would never be found again, he was sure.

"There's probably sharks," Cheryl said.

The shack had stairs leading down. There was a musty smell below deck that Doug appreciated even without a nose, just like he saw a small gaslight without the advantage of eyeballs.

"Sharks don't eat skeletons," Olivia scoffed.

Doug turned up the lamp and opened up the shutters in the roof that let light through its grill, appearing completely at home to his wife and daughter. He sat down at the desk, putting his feet bones up on it.

Cheryl made an amused sound. She noticed a large, leather-bound book and opened it.

"That's the *Captain's* Log," Doug said, "and I'm —"

"Shh," Cheryl shushed. "March 28th, 2036: The Patterson family, Doug, Cheryl, and Olivia, are at the end of their long journey to Frisco. In four hours they'll be arriving in the harbor."

"Four hours," Olivia moaned. "Boo." She walked away from the desk and gravitated to a large oval mirror with an ornate silver frame.

"Oh, there's something else appearing," Cheryl said. A scratchy sound was coming from the book. "Olivia discovers the magic mirror."

"I've got skin!" she said. The little skeleton was tilting the mirror this way and that.

Doug and Cheryl went over to the mirror and sure enough, the reflection showed all three of them as androgynous human beings with blond hair and white smocks.

"What're you smiling at?" said androgynous Cheryl. "You look just as weird."

"You look at the part you want to change," Olivia said. "Look at your eyes." They did, and as Olivia tilted the mirror they slid from blue to snow white to coal black. Doug stepped away from the mirror, and the two skeletons looked at him.

Doug looked down at his smocked arms. "Are my eyes still black?"

The skeletons looked at him and nodded, quickly turned back to the mirror. Doug went back to the desk and sat down, enjoying the squishy feeling of flesh on his bones again. He flipped through the Captain's Log, but finding nothing else of note on the lined pages, he went upstairs.

There wasn't much in the little shack except for the wheel, so he went out and stared at the horizon. It was slightly wavy with the heat, but there was nothing land-like. That suited him fine. He leaned on the railing and looked out at the sky, enjoying it more for how different it would be if they had come on a bronze or silver package. Dead, non-essential spaces like the sky would be covered with commercials — the clouds, at the very least, would be logos. The soothing rush of water would be replaced by snippets of new pop jingles.

He breathed in the salty air with satisfaction, relaxed like he hadn't been in weeks. Months. It felt like something was melting inside his chest.

"What are you smiling at?" Cheryl asked when he emerged.

"Those cheekbones."

Cheryl touched them self-consciously. "I felt like trying something different. I'd usually change my hairstyle, but I like my hair the way it is."

"So do I," Doug said and leaned in for a kiss.

Cheryl leaned away. "Eeee."

"What do you mean eeee?"

Cheryl pushed him towards the ladder. "I feel like I'm kissing Undra Massimos. Go get on something Dougish."

"I thought you wanted to try something new?" he said, grabbing her hips and puckering up.

She fended him off. "Not — that — new!" she said.

Doug lifted his hands in surrender and climbed down the ladder. *Not that new,* Doug thought fondly. *That's Cheryl to a T. All the choice in the world and she chooses cheekbones.*

"OK, I'm done!" said a tiny Indian woman in a belly dancing outfit. She flashed Doug a brilliantly white smile as she passed by. Stunned, he watched her climb the ladder and realized that Olivia was the same height as before but with alarmingly mature endowments. Without words, he tore his gaze away and went to slump in the captain's chair.

He listened to Cheryl's outrage with relief, happy that one of them was capable of it. The shouting drifted away to other parts of the boat, not lessening a whit. *Thank god she acts as conservatively as I feel.*

He got up and wandered over to the mirror, smirking at the jelly-jowled androgen in the mirror. *I can look any way I want* duked it out with *I should set a good example for Olivia* in his head. The latter won, if only by default, and he started with his fingers, giving himself the same piano ticklers that he'd never applied to that art.

A few minutes later he'd got everything but the hair looking Dougish. There were a thousand length and color gradations, but it went from brush cut to totally bald. Nothing in between. He went to look for other styles that were conspicuous by their absence. The black hairstyles jumped from a short 'fro to a comically massive one — suitable only for white people at parties, Doug decided. What you couldn't get was the well-kept but large afro preferred by Africans — funny that domestic rebels like the Harmless Cranks had already spun into heroes, while their foreign allies were still unmentionable terrorists.

He sat in front of the mirror for another minute or two as a bald man. He felt it looked like he had cut off his monk's fringe in a fit of shame. It wasn't right. So, with a sigh, he chose hair.

He climbed up the ladder and went to find the others. The sun had started to set. He found Cheryl sitting on a big heap of white sacks beside the prow.

"Is that Doug under all that hair?" she said, slapping the spot beside her.

Doug looked at the sacks before he sat. The sacks had weathered printing on them, which he read. "'Samuelson's Unrefined Flour.' Mmmm, mmm. Dinner is served."

Cheryl ruffled his full head of hair. "Nope, I don't like it. Very un-Doug-like. You think there's scissors on this boat?"

"I doubt it," he said, conscious of his dead tone.

She looked down at the flour sacks. "Are you hungry, Olivia?" Cheryl yelled at the sky.

"No," came the brusque reply from the crow's nest.

"Just as well there isn't any food here," Cheryl said in a chipper voice.

Doug recognized this as one of the times when Cheryl kept them all afloat and decided to make it easier for her. He put his head in her lap and stretched out on the flour bags. "I'm gonna close my eyes for a while, Cher."

"How much longer?" came the voice from the crow's nest.

Doug checked his watch. "Few more hours, honey," he said.

"Lots of time for you to choose something *nice* to wear," Cheryl sing-songed.

No answer.

"We're not leaving this boat with you looking like that," Cheryl said as a statement of fact, scratching Doug's neck.

Doug closed his eyes, hoping that the drifting would help him sort out his tangled ball of feelings, tease free the strands of gratefulness from those of anxiety.

He opened his eyes. Cheryl had found her own spot on the flour sacks, and when he sat up he saw the glint of her eyes in the dark. She sat up too.

"You really *can't* sleep," she said, clearly amazed. "I remember hearing that and thinking 'Yeah, right. Just wait until I have a day where I'm running around all the time, picking up Olivia, cooking —'" She stopped. "It's weird."

He put an arm around her. "We'll get used to it," he said, feeling recharged and strong again.

He stood up, took her hand, walked along the edge of the ship. The moon and the stars were spectacular things, slightly larger than life. Each crater was distinct. Doug wondered, *If they had gotten the billboard on it, would the Frisco moon have it also?*

Cheryl noticed his gaze and said. "A while ago, I had a nightmare that Frisco was all cartoons. The moon had this really ugly face, this green cheese face." She laughed.

"You were worried about Frisco?" This was hard to absorb. He had always assumed that she, like everyone else, was excited about the move.

"Not *worried*," she said. "Just a little… I don't know. It's a pretty big adjustment. A new phase in human history and all that."

Doug nodded vaguely, remembering how the high concept of upgrading had been silted over by granular marketing messages — special deals, low financing rates, new features, more options. He himself hadn't really considered what it would be like since then. Ever since the possibility had dawned on him that he may miss out on it, and destroy his family's prospects in the process, he hadn't been thinking about the big picture. On this ship, the past few months seemed a smear of grey, a needless binge of terrified self-pity. Doug was amazed and disappointed in himself.

"I mean… no more sleeping. No more waiting for Flo to leave before we can hump," Cheryl continued.

"Ah, Flo, I didn't even say goodbye." Doug said. He wouldn't miss his wife's period, but he would miss the stodgy and coy nickname and how hungry she was for sex afterwards. "What are you looking forward to here?"

Cheryl said immediately. "Working. Getting out of the house and into the real world. I can't wait."

"Really?" Doug said, surprised at her vehemence.

"Oh honey," she said. "I was so bored. Remember that day in the mall? When you were talking that silver package nonsense? I just about lost it. I've been pretty short with Olivia, too, last little while." She looked at him guiltily. "I've been acting out in general."

He smoothed down her hair, remembering the last time they'd had sex — he thought she seemed harder, less playful, than usual. "Well. I'm glad to hear you say that. I'd thought it was me."

"I'm sorry," she said, pushing her hot face into his chest.

"Don't be sorry," said Doug, wishing he could confess, too.

They sat there, rocked back and forth. "This is weird," Cheryl said. "I'm crying but I'm not stuffed up." She wiped her eyes. "Puffy?"

Doug looked. "Nope."

"How do you think Olivia will do here?" his wife said.

Doug realized by the tone of her voice that Cheryl considered Olivia's disobedience her failure as a parent. Her guilt and fear made her incapable of thinking lightly, creatively.

But he was capable of that. Doug looked over the side of the boat. Slight curves of light flashed on the surface. It felt like they were moving faster, lent a sense of urgency to the problem. "Why did she choose that body, do you think?"

"It's that stupid video," Cheryl said. "By Pole Position. There's a part where the singer in it Olivia likes goes off with this belly dancer. 'Dance Me Up'? Something like that. I was making dinner last week, and she watched it at least a dozen times. I knew I should have said something"

"Hmm," Doug said, starting to smile.

"It's not funny, Doug," Cheryl said. "We're in a completely new place. No one knows us. She looks so different — no one will even be able to tell that we're a family!"

"I know what to do," he said.

A few minutes later they were agreed, and they headed to the base of the crow's nest.

"Olivia," Doug said.

"What."

"You know that your physique is not appropriate for a girl your age and size," he said, his voice reasonable.

There was a pause. "So."

"So your mother and I feel that you shouldn't start off in your new school with a body like that. Other kids will make fun of you."

"I don't care about the stupid kids."

"There's also the fact that your mother is worried that people won't think that we're a family, because we don't look alike at all."

There was no answer.

Doug continued. "All we want you to do is for you to have a body that's normal for a girl your age. On your 15th birthday, we'll let you wear any breasts you like."

"15!" came the scornful retort from the crow's nest. "That's six years away! What if girls my age have big booties and tits already?"

Doug looked at Olivia. "Well, if more than half of your class has… that kind of body, then it's OK. We just don't want you going in on the first day like that."

There was a silence. Then: "10."

"14."

"12."

"13. That's it, Olivia."

There was silence, and Doug was satisfied. He'd started extra high, knowing she was her father's daughter. *13 was normal anyhow.* A few seconds later, Olivia climbed down and, without looking at either of them, went below deck.

When she returned she had the physique of a nine-year-old. The belly-dancing costume had shrunk appropriately. "They felt weird anyway," she said defiantly.

"She's still —" Cheryl made a gesture to her face that communicated *skin color*.

Without answering, Doug took Cheryl down to the mirror and made some adjustments themselves. When they emerged, Olivia was on her knees on the flour sacks, looking at the sunrise through a telescope. She looked reassuringly like a little girl again, the disinterested glance she spared them looked deliberate.

She did a double take. "I thought it was a tan at first," she said. "Well, they'll know we're a family now."

Doug put his Indian brown arm next to Olivia's. "Perfect match."

"Where'd you get the telescope?" asked Cheryl.

"It was in the crow's nest," she said, handing it over. She swung her legs against the flour sacks, perfectly placid. Doug felt a swell of pride: *still got the knack for creative problem solving*, he thought. *The art of compromise and keeping the client happy.*

"Kinda sucks," Olivia said, handing it to her mom. "Doesn't even zoom."

Cheryl looked in it one way, then the other. She twisted the end.

Doug looked at his wife in the sun, her black hair and brown skin glowing.

"I think I see something," Cheryl said. "Land."

The trolley car dinged and lurched forward, pulling them away from the docks. Doug threw a look backwards at his ship and appreciated its majesty amongst all the dinghies and speedboats tethered there. The bull-necked men who'd tied it up complimented him on it, although they must get gold immigrants here all the time.

As they started up a rather narrow hill lined with little houses and stores, a tour guide stood up in the aisle. "Well," he said, "looks like a lot of silver folk here today... you all come through on the free package?" A couple of nods. "Good for you, unbelievable deal."

The tour guide was a blustering fat man with red in his cheeks. The collection of gorgeous movie star passengers looked odd — too excited for their new beauty, too attentive to this tour guide character. Doug looked at his family and thought that they stood out from the silver types by their restraint in their choice of appearance.

"Welcome...to...Frisco!" the tour guide said grandly, and there was a smattering of applause. "Most of you know it was created as an emergency measure after the quakes but since that time has had countless trillions of dollars invested in it to ensure that it's the finest reality money can buy."

A guy sitting by himself in the seat ahead of Doug laughed, looking at something outside the window. The tour guide noticed it and smiled. "Those of you with gold or platinum packages have watches with a knob on the side. If you enjoy advertisements, like this man obviously does, you can turn it to the left and see what the silver and bronze people see."

Doug did so, and the windows in the quaint houses showed a tiny three-second adblip for Budweiser of a blond woman squeezing a fat man's bottom. Doug looked back at the tour guide and noticed that his formerly tan uniform was a multicolored montage of dozens of logos.

The trolley car was cresting the top of the hill. "An unparalleled experiment in corporate synergy, Frisco is a collection of different nodes only limited by imagination." From this vantage point, Frisco lay before them as an El Dorado — a hilly, colorful paradise, the Golden Gate Bridge finally golden. Doug tried to remember the last pictures he'd seen of San Francisco, some news bit about how the new Self servers being built in the ruined city were capable of weathering tectonic blasts, never mind any of Mother Nature's other nasty tricks. "These units could fall into the sea and not go offline," the techie had said, and Doug recalled his clamped jaw and battered helmet — it had reminded him of a fireman, for some reason, the same grim heroism — but he didn't remember the images of the city behind him. Frisco's images had supplanted San Francisco's in the public consciousness. Like the daughter of a movie star becoming more popular than her mother — fame, free of pudge or withering.

There were two or three dead ringers for movie stars around Doug. "Isn't that Kathleen Depp?" he murmured to his wife, and she elbowed him. She always found it in bad taste to point out bad taste. Both she and Olivia were dutifully looking out the window.

"There's the church we saw," she said to Olivia, pointing out the mysterious white structure. It had no cross, but there was no mistaking its significance.

When the gasps and rubbernecking of the trolley passengers slowly died out, the tour guide slammed a lever back and the trolley car continued on its way. Turning his back to the front window, he continued his spiel. "This is New Castro Street," he said as the trolley gathered speed, not unlike a roller coaster.

This part of the city was lively and, unlike the facades of the stores on the way up, looked filled-in. There were people strolling along the sidewalks, looking at menus in front of restaurants, gazing in well-stocked clothing store windows. Doug noted that the mannequins were the same as they were back home, despite it being as easy to create a lifelike dummy as it was to create a blank-faced one.

Gasps of horror and pointing drew his attention to an old man, struggling across the road, directly in the path of the rollercoastering trolley car. Understanding finally dawning on him, the tour guide himself glanced around and sprang into action. His whole body lurched as he slammed the lever back and there was a terrible screeching as the trolley car braked.

Doug watched it with a professional interest — the old man's glasses smashing horribly against the window of the trolley car; the agonized look on the tour guide's face; the white knuckles of the faux movie star ahead.

Olivia looked at him stricken and sick. Cheryl, meanwhile, looked away from the old man and licked her lips at Doug. Doug checked their watches — Olivia, like him, was set to bronze while Cheryl was gold. Doug twisted his knob.

"— crème brûlée." The tour guide was saying, all traces of agony gone from his face. "The finest chefs in the world. Just because you don't need to eat doesn't mean you shouldn't treat yourself." The old man was nowhere to be seen.

Doug looked at what the tour guide was nodding at, a quiet-looking restaurant with a small sign: Midas' Feast. The passenger in front of him was laughing again, so he turned his knob back to bronze. The club was replaced by a lottery store ("Get a Lotto More Out of Life!") and the old man reappeared ahead, tended by cute little badgers who had strapped an IV of Coca-Cola to his arm. There was a tiny red and white helicopter on the road now, its blades still whirring.

They walked him to the side of the road, although with every step he gained more pep, and before returning to their 'copter, one of them jumped up to place a pair of rhinestone sunglasses on his face to replace his glasses. The tour guide saluted the little mascots as they lifted off, then started the trolley car again. As they rolled by the old man, he waved, but then turned to ogle the bottoms of two sexy ladies over his sunglasses.

"Why are they waving at him," Olivia was saying contemptuously. "He's not *real*."

"Who's not real, honey?" Cheryl asked, looking around.

"People on bronze got a rubbernecker ad," Doug summarized.

"Ah," said Cheryl, not interested. "We should remember where that restaurant was, honey."

Doug nodded, amused that his wife was still thinking geographically. He turned to Olivia. "When did you know it was an ad?"

"Right when I saw him," Olivia said, opening and closing her telescope. "Why would someone be walking like that? There're no old people here."

Doug nodded, proud. Contempt for shoddy advertising — and the people that swallowed it whole — were the seeds for a career in marketing. *A lot more stable than coolhunting*, he thought, the anxieties of going back to work seeping into his brain. *At least Chan can't flaunt his age any more.* But even without a stomach, he still felt butterflies starting to flutter.

"Port to a restaurant like Lucky's, and you can dine with Mafioso right before the turf war starts — and bet on which gang will win," the tour guide was saying as the trolley car trundled by a flashing sign. Two fedora-wearing men emerged from a black Oldsmobile and went in. The last one, carrying a violin case, shot a dark look at them as he entered the restaurant.

"This reminds me of something," Cheryl said. "Disneyland."

"Well, I wouldn't know," sulked Olivia.

Guilt flit across Cheryl's face. Last year, when Olivia's friend Paula was going, they couldn't afford to send her.

Doug smiled. "Would you rather visit there, or live here?"

"Both," Olivia said.

Doug smiled and ruffled her hair. "Demand the impossible, negotiate from there."

A few seconds later, Olivia turned her head and listened to something Doug couldn't see. He tuned into bronze, and a little girl in pigtails and hot pants appeared in the aisle.

"...Plus, Frisco Disneyland has so-so-so nice acts like Pole Position and

Underwhere," she was saying, her eyes shining and beautiful, her skin as dusky as Olivia's. She didn't look at Doug.

Ah shit, he thought, amazed at how fast the pitchdrones were at zoning in on keywords like Disneyland. *Have to do something quick or I'll never hear the end of it.*

"Isn't it cute, Cheryl? Olivia's got an imaginary friend."

Olivia heard but didn't acknowledge this.

"Thought talking to fake people was dumb," he said lightly, with a smirk.

She twisted her knob to gold, giving him an annoyed look.

The tour guide had just pointed out the petting zoo and Science World. "And this is just a little taste of the attractions in Frisco," he said, putting the brakes on. "You can get off here or stay on for the business and residential districts. Remember, those of you with porting-enabled packages can simply say your destination into your watch."

A few people got off here, and Olivia stretched out. A couple across from them consulted with each other and then disappeared. It was less disconcerting than Doug would have imagined. More people got on, and Olivia had to give up her space. "Why don't they just port there?" she asked Cheryl in a whisper.

"They only have a few ports a day," Cheryl murmured back.

"All aboard," said the chubby tour guide, settling into the driver's seat and grabbing the lever. With a clang and a yank, the trolley car sped up so that the surroundings blurred into streaks of light and color. Doug appreciated the fact that this conveyed a sense of many exciting places and things to do without having to actually create them.

The colors slowly drained away as the trolley car slowed into the business district. Unlike New Castro Street, this place had only a few people walking around between buildings that stretched up further than the eye could see. Doug supposed that most people coming here ported from place to place. "This is the business district," said the tour guide.

"See you two tonight," Doug said, brushing unfamiliar cheekbones with his lips on his way to the exit. Another man, dressed far more appropriately than Doug, went out ahead of him. Doug, wishing he hadn't worn a casual sarong, stepped on the sidewalk and looked back to see his family watching him. Smiling, he raised a hand goodbye and walked purposefully in the same direction as the other man until the trolley car had warped out of sight.

His smile fell, and he asked the man beside him for directions.

Eileen's spine-plug was chafing, but she resisted the urge to scratch it, keeping her hands on the wheel. The suit wasn't really made for sitting — running, yes, leaping, sure, but something about the angle of sitting stretched the material in an awkward way. She didn't want to touch it and risk dislodging it — she suspected that sudden disconnection from the stream of drugs and electricity would kill her. *So what happens after I find Jeremy?* She shifted in the seat and tried to think of other things.

Although a little nervous driving at first, she'd been fine ever since she followed the Self van onto the highway. She was rather pleased — it'd been at least a decade since she'd been behind the wheel. *How'd that jingle go? "You-never-forget, how-to-drive!"?* Something like that. It certainly felt like an instinctual memory.

Gliding along the highway, she almost wished the Self van would speed up a little. It didn't even change lanes. Based on its regularity, her suit was now 90% sure it was on autodrive. Which made sense. She passed under another toll, wondering if the camera charging the vehicle's owner was also keeping her aware of Eileen's location.

Nothing like driving with music. She thought for a second about getting her suit to play something, but she couldn't think of anything specific. The truck had a radio in it, so she turned it on and had it scan. It hit an oldies station, playing something that sounded familiar, so she locked in. She didn't know the band, but she enjoyed the guitars — one heard them so infrequently these days. *What was that stuff that Jeremy was listening to? Clone Drone? Sounded like foghorns, so negative...*

She resolved that once she got him back she'd introduce him to different types of music. Scattershot jungle, for instance, the soundtrack of her youth — although when her father had taken out his old silver CDs and shown her yellowed and cracked pictures of punk shows, it was all in vain. She couldn't have cared less.

The Self van was making its way towards the off ramp, and Eileen was surprised to find out they were in New West already. She had checked out houses here years ago, but it had seemed too far at the time, too suburban. But it had certainly grown up nicely, with lots of stores along the street and nice-looking communities, not nearly as much traffic. She wondered if she'd made a mistake buying property in the city, maybe Jeremy would have fallen in with different kids, neighborhood kids instead of those online gamer types —

She heard a metallic thudding from the flatbed behind. While dosing her with adrenalpro and accelerating to 500%, her suit informed her that her vehicle had been shot 18 times by a rapidly approaching helicopter. There was very little traffic on the road, which Eileen was grateful for. She opened the door and hung off of it, seeing the cab's window flower with round bullet punches, and dropped her feet to the ground. It was moving too fast, so her suit took over with electric impulses to the appropriate leg muscles.

A small fire had started in the cab by the time she let go of the door, a black cloud curling from the plastic seat. She had her legs speed up a little — they were a blur under her, as if she was riding a black magic carpet — and cut in front of the truck into the lane the Self van was in.

Her suit fed her images of the 'copter behind, which was still firing on the truck with an array of machine guns that curved right around its belly, like the teeth of a smile. The Ford logo was emblazoned on the side with a jokey ad about its new security package: *Have you stolen a Ford lately?* She supposed she was lucky it wasn't one of those new freelancers — they wouldn't have sent out a remote-controlled bird, wouldn't have wasted bullets on the truck's flatbed.

Keeping in the Self van's blind spot, she was able to slow down enough to take manual control of her legs. She heard the crunch and, a while later, the explosion of the truck. She hoped that no one was in the way, but that was really the 'copter's lookout.

She focused on the van, which was making a turn onto a fairly busy street. She asked her suit for proximity to a Self office, and it indicated that it was a few blocks away. It wasn't worth taking to the rooftops, so she zigzagged through the streets — she couldn't avoid being seen, not in broad daylight and on a street as filled with shoppers as this, but by moving erratically she could avoid being seen twice. As the emergency procedures of her training had told her, *people will want to believe they are seeing things.*

She was doing fine until she saw the power low indicator begin to flash. Then she stood still and stared at it, the small icon of a hollow battery flashing on and off in the corner of her vision. A teenage boy in sniper glasses pointed her out to his friends, and she ran on, her legs feeling so numb they might as well have been on automatic.

The power source was low. Dangerously low. And the suit didn't run on a battery pack — *she* was the power source. She had nearly used her withered old body up. *How much time before...?* She couldn't bear to ask the suit. Her operations handbook had not described the battery icon — it was something youthful agents didn't need to know. She forced herself to focus, to keep moving, zoom in on the alley that the Self van was now backing into with the steady *beep, beep, beep*.

This alley had a little jog in it but was otherwise unremarkable except for its pyramid of boxes. The boxes, her suit told her, were the same size and coloring as the other Self boxes she'd seen. The New West office was fairly identical to the Vancouver office, with different brick to blend in with its neighbors. She thought the representatives, who were nodding perkily at their clients, may have had different hairstyles, but she realized she didn't care enough to ask her suit to compare.

Across the road was an alcove with a black door, a small sign identifying it as a gaming portal relocated to Frisco. She stood against it and attracted little attention. The van's ruffles were out, blocking the view of the alley. Eileen reviewed her options: this was obviously another pickup, and she needed to conserve her power. She couldn't follow it on foot. She couldn't steal another car without considerable energy expenditure.

Focus! Eileen you silly old woman focus*!*

The ruffles were retracting, and the van was revving up.

Can't lose the target. Eileen waited until the tires started rolling to accelerate. Once it had cleared the alley, she stepped up onto its bumper and scanned the handle-free back doors for a crevasse. Nothing. She scanned it again, increasing the zoom. Nothing — literally nothing.

There were no doors. The apparent breaks in the white metal were only a centimeter deep.

Eileen pulled herself up on the roof, wincing as the thin metal shell blurped inwards, but nothing else happened. She lay down, looked up at the sky, and thought about dying.

The small battery flashed on, even when she closed her eyes.

The warning sign didn't come in the form of an iconic battery for Paul — he presumed that was some digital flotsam at his end. He was, after all, watching Eileen's progress on the surface of a small pool of water. To the other people walking through the church garden, he looked meditative and serene.

The warning sign for Paul came when the Self van headed back the way it came. As soon as it got on the on-ramp to Vancouver, Paul felt dread uncurl in his stomach. *It's just shuttling between the two offices.*

He bit the bullet and opened a connection. "Paul here. Look, it's like we suspected — the van's a decoy."

"Hellllooo Paaaaul," said Eileen.

If he didn't know she was lying on the top of a van, he'd have thought she was drunk.

"Sorry," she continued, more normally. "I just slowed myself down to conserve power. Your information wasn't very good."

"I know, I know, but we had to follow it up to know for sure. I'm going to make it up to you, Eileen. I've got a hot lead on the cache," he lied, "But I just need some time to put it together. Is there somewhere you can go in the meantime?"

There was a funny sound. "Oh, sure…" she said, making the funny sound again. Paul realized it was her laugh made eerie by the digital filter in her suit.

"OK great Eileen," he said. "Just hold tight." He waited a second, but she didn't say anything else. "Talk to you soon."

He disconnected. *She sounded bad.* "Shit," he hissed, and a passing monk clad in white raised an eyebrow.

"Sorry," Paul said, even though he was pretty sure the monk was environment. As he watched the figure stride away, his hands behind his back, the hair made him think of Doug. *Why had he gone to the Self office and then walked away? Did they say something in there that freaked him out?* He never would have imagined Doug would pass up a chance to get to Frisco. He needed him here, following up the dozens of leads he couldn't follow up himself — he was on the verge of losing his advantage here.

Between that and wasting time with this Self decoy, the only thing that had gone right was Operation Brolly, as Simon called it. *That's one of the great things about diverse tactics*, Paul thought, scooping a pebble up and disconnecting the pool, the highway signs Eileen was seeing rippling away. *Something has to work eventually. Like with the monkeys and the keyboards.*

Simon had glowingly reported the dissemination of close to a thousand umbrellas, and Nicky confirmed a corresponding explosion of flora. Evidently, Tilley was taking credit for it, claiming that a commitment to the environment had always been a part of their mission statement. That was fine. If the preliminary results from the seeds were half accurate, Vancouver would be an urban rainforest in time for the symposium.

So many things still to do. Still, it'll be worth it — the 150th birthday should be a special one. Paul listened to his brain mutter as he walked around to the front of the church. *Get another bicycle supplier set up; it'll take care of itself then, the momentum's right. See about clearing the SkyTrain tracks. Get back to the Budapest crew — oh shit, and the Bolivians.*

"Mental note," Paul said, and his small angel appeared above his shoulder with its feather quill poised. "Budapest and Bolivia," he said walking through the large double doors, his voice echoing slightly. Another monk, this one refilling the holy water, gave him an identical disapproving eyebrow. This time he didn't bother apologizing, just found a pew near the back and sat down.

You'd think that since they've bothered to make a temple for themselves, they'd make a couple of different types of monks instead of cutting and pasting. He looked around at the people who sparsely populated the church, wondered if they cared. They were average Friscans — either 20- or 30-something in appearance, dressed in whatever their fashion applets had generated for them today. There were more women than men. What was unusual about them was that no one had their hand to their ear to indicate they were taking a call — there was no communication service in the church.

Another cut-and-paste monk walked by, holding a small flame cupped in his hand, and Paul's ire was whipped up again. *We had an infinitely varied environment on Earth, and we painted over it to draw our little stick figures.*

"Whoa, you look like you're in a good mood," a voice beside him said. A young man in sunglasses and a crooked smile was sitting on the pew. "Who died?"

"We did," Paul said.

"Oh no," he said in a mournful voice, his face decaying like a ripe fruit in front of Paul.

The kid was clever, but how deep did it go? "What do you think when you see that?" Paul said, pointing at the two monks, one at the altar and one cleaning stained glass.

"That whoever was doing skins was fucking lazy," Jeremy said, returning an eyeball back under his sunglasses. "But that's the way it is here, man. It's not just the skins," he said, spitting teeth as he said it. "It's the architecture too. And the security. That's why there's so many holes for rats like us."

Paul looked at him, expecting he'd have changed his zombie face for a rat one, but he was back to normal. "Just laziness, huh?"

"Well," Jeremy sighed. "OK," he started, wearily accepting Paul's seriousness. "It's like this. I've got a friend who does skins for environmental characters. He gets shit-all for it, and they're always on him — they want, like, 75 a day — so he can't spend time on the details. So he churns them out. He's made some wicked squidmen for an Atlantis environment, though."

"So it's not just laziness," Paul confirmed.

"No, it's also the evil corporation that's oppressing him," said Jeremy in a jeering tone.

"You believe in evil?" said Paul with surprise.

Jeremy folded his arms. "No. But you do."

Paul laughed a little. He was quiet for awhile, then looked around them. "Doesn't this feel like we're in a mob movie: Do you believe in Evil?" he said, stressing the E.

Jeremy chuckled. "Yeah, that's why I said we should meet here. It's dramatic."

There was something in the way he said *dramatic* that struck Paul; there was an enthusiasm there that pierced his jaded veil. "It's not that corporations are evil. They're just boring."

Jeremy smirked. "So true."

Paul was feeling his way here, gently touching the walls in the corridor that could lead him into Jeremy's confidence. "But boring in a serious way. I like variety. More than that... I have this theory that diversity is an incredibly important thing. Maybe more important than good or evil. The less diversity we have the fewer choices we have — the fewer methods we have to find happiness, justice, love. The fewer examples on which to base our lives."

Jeremy shrugged. "Suppose..."

Paul stopped here, worried he was talking over Jeremy's head. He remembered the speech Jeremy had given him in Hell and tried to forget that this was a 12-year-old boy. "Corporations have a vested interest in reducing diversity, since they function most profitably when they can mass produce their product, cultural or otherwise. They say we should shed our skins, that the biological code is too buggy. Time to scrap it and start from scratch. But maybe they're not bugs, but features?"

Jeremy nodded here, looked thoughtful. "Bugs can become features... that's what it's like with clones, too. I've got... this sensitivity to stimuli. I can like, shut down if I get too much. But it also gives me a focus, and that's how I got so good at coding. They thought it was biological, something in the Lee's Region part of my brain, so I wasn't worried about getting overstimulated when I upgraded." He made a soft snorting sound, glanced at Paul.

Paul looked interested, nodded. "And?" He looked around then, to give Jeremy some space. Some more people had come in, and there were three identical monks busying themselves now.

"I went in on bronze, 'cause it's free. I had a keygen to upgrade to gold. But you know, there's a lot of ads."

Paul nodded.

"Now I like ads, I'm not some '20s rebel type," he said throwing a little twist of a smile to Paul, "But there's a *lot* of ads. I was hanging around the pier on my first day. I was having a great time — it's like... you know when you're eating really good food, and you just keep eating? It was like that. I stared at the water, it had a Coke wave in it. Oh yeah. I walked into a bar and this beer song is blasting. Awesome. I had a few free Peanutz and the taste reminded me of a Budweiser."

"Peanutz often have that effect," Paul said with a smile.

"Well, yeah, OK," he said, taking off his sunglasses and rubbing his nose. "But this was like... well, maybe I was just thirsty."

"You've got a little indent on your nose," Paul said, shocked.

"Phobos's work," Jeremy said, holding out his arms as if his whole body were a custom-made suit. "He's amazing. I'll tell you about Phobe later," he said, his body turned towards Paul. "Anyway, I drank a Bud, and three girls came up to me. *Naked* girls."

Paul smiled at his excitement. "The Budweiser girls." People were standing up around them, and so did they. Music started, and Paul noticed a group of monks coalescing near the back.

"Yeah so they were touching me and...stuff, and even though no one else could see them, I was still embarrassed. So I took off."

"You took off?" Paul said.

When he looked back, Jeremy had put his sunglasses back on. "So-so-so, listen," he said, his guard back up. "I've seen lots of naked girls — my boy

Strength hooked me up with this." He looked around in a stagy way and waited until the half-dozen monks walked up the aisle. Then he pulled a pair of sunglasses from his back pocket and passed them to Paul.

They tingled in Paul's hand. Their construction was fairly rough and blocky, but he could make out a brand name: XRS. Looking at Jeremy, he slipped them on.

"Just don't look at me, guy."

The church was full of naked people. Paul immediately put it together. "X-Ray Specs."

"The holy grail," Jeremy said reverently.

Paul looked around. Ahead of him a woman's bare back curved with her penitently lowered head. He discretely leaned forward and checked out the couple sharing the pew with him. The man's penis was a perfectly proportionate and sculpted 12 inches, confirming Paul's suspicion about the average choices. More interestingly, her pubic hair was exceptionally bushy.

"Welcome, brothers and sisters, to the Church of New Beginnings," began one of the monks. As curious as he was, Paul forced his attention to the front of the church. Almost immediately, he wished he hadn't — the monks were inherently celibate. "Ahhg," he said, pulling off the hackglasses and hiding his revulsion at their smooth groins in a cough.

He handed them back to Jeremy, who was snickering in delight. Then he put them on to look at the monks. "Oh, *man!*" he said, pulling them off as if he'd been burnt. "That's just wrong." A few seconds passed, and then he said, in a thoughtful way, "But you noticed they had belly buttons? No genitals, that's fine, but God forbid someone mistakes them for *clones*."

Paul nodded, watching him rile himself up and then put a lid on it. *He'll use that later, for energy.*

"...the promised land in many ways people still feel a need to look for... meaning, for... something beyond what our five senses offer," one of the monks was saying, his face beaming. Now that he could see clothes, Paul noticed that the speaker had on a white smock while the others had on grey.

"What is this?" Paul asked.

"The AI who deal with Frisco generated this spirituality thing," Jeremy said. "They used some human-needs algorithm. Bogus, if you ask me."

A box, white and embossed with the Self logo, was brought up to the altar. The monk in white held it aloft. "A beautiful object, with no entrance or egress..."

Jeremy exhaled noisily. "They do the same thing every time. They blab about the stupid box for a while, and then show you that nothing's in it. Normally, when things are this boring, I just flip to bronze," Jeremy said. "But this is the only place there's no difference."

"Huh," Paul said, realizing that the makers of this place, the makers of Frisco, were conscious of the importance of silence. At some level, they realized the constant barrage of ads was something to be escaped from, and he took heart in their inconsistency. And there was something about that box that reminded him of... the van! The white van Eileen was following. *Wow. That was spooky. Could the AI have a symbolism or an aesthetic, a taste of its own?*

He looked at the monks, then at the other people. "Are these people here for the service?"

"Not likely," Jeremy said. "There's a few minutes at the end where you can petition the monks for changes to Frisco. I myself don't like to beg —" He stopped talking, noticing an angry look from his well-endowed pew mate. "Whatever, footlong," he muttered but then looked at Paul. "Wanna... d'ya wanna... come over? Like to my place?"

Paul nodded, charmed by his awkwardness.

"Port us to 3ffe:b00:c18:1:290:27ff:fe17:fc0f," Jeremy said. "Do you agree?"

Up at the altar, the monk broke the box in two like he was breaking bread.

"Do you agree?"

"Yes."

They were in a small foyer. Jeremy, a foot shorter and unmistakably himself, plopped his chubby bum into a chintz chair and picked up a telephone receiver. It was a push-button model, but by the speed he dialled the number, he was used to using it. He ignored Paul completely for a few seconds.

"Oh, hello," a woman said from behind Paul. "You must be one of Jeremy's friends!"

A small, sprightly woman stood in the doorway, holding a plate of cookies.

Paul, trying to reconcile this white-haired Eileen with the blacksuited assassin, took one.

"I'm Jeremy's FakeGrandma. Are you here to play some games?"

"Uh...."

Jeremy slammed the phone down.

"Jeremy!" scolded Eileen.

He sighed. "Sorry FakeGrandma." He took a handful of cookies, and she smiled. "We're going upstairs to play some games."

"I thought so," she said, looking at Paul with a twinkle in her eye.

Sidling by Eileen nervously, he followed Jeremy as he pounded up the stairs. He took a bite of the cookie, but it was tasteless and doughy.

Jeremy's bedroom door had a bright sign that said "Gamerz only!" on it, and a hotel doorknob sign. He flipped that to Do Not Disturb and held the door open.

Paul gave a stately nod and stepped in.

Jeremy shut the door behind him. "*Stay a while… stay forever!*" Jeremy said with a well-practiced evil voice, as he pushed by Paul. He dumped the cookies into a wastebasket and seated himself in front of his cubespace, kicking the power supply on, clearly lord of his domain.

"So you got out of the bar with your pants intact…" Paul prompted, seating himself on Jeremy's bed.

"Right, right," Jeremy said, leaning back in his chair, which clickity-clacked to accommodate. "I've seen lots of naked girls, so it's not like I was scared of them — Phobe keeps saying that, but he's a spaz — I just wasn't used to them touching me. Looking yes, touching no. It was a personal space issue."

Paul nodded. Plenty of men of his generation, weaned on guiltless cathode masturbation, had a difficult transition to having sexual partners. The Joystick Syndrome. *Technology giveth, technology taketh away.*

"So I'm out of the bar, walking down the street, and they're *following* me. I start running, they start running, bouncing up and down…"

"Sounds awful," said Paul, somberly.

"They had these grins… like they wanted to *eat* me. Squealing. I started to think it was something Jupiter had set up to ambush me — they're like, second best after us — so I freaked. Fuck it, I said, and I gave my watch the port address Phobe gave me. But they're always changing it, so I ended up at the old address."

"You gave a hex address."

"Yeah, makes a lot of shit easier like when you're trying to sync up stuff from device modules —" he stopped when he saw the blank look in Paul's eyes, his smile half-ashamed, half-cocky. "Doesn't matter. Yeah, I punched in the numbers and went straight into the void."

"Because the address didn't exist," said Paul.

"No, you can't port to somewhere that doesn't exist," said Jeremy patiently. "It was cleared out. Totally empty."

"So you're floating in a black —"

"Bluish green. Cold, too." Jeremy had pulled some code up in the cube and massaged it absently, his gaze distant.

"Cold?"

Jeremy looked at him directly and nodded, as if he didn't understand it himself. "Chilly. And then the dead space — everywhere — was filling up. I turned them off but they just kept popping up."

"What kinds of ads?"

Jeremy looked away. "Uh, well, I guess because of the Budweiser ad, they were all — sex stuff. Full frontal popup attack."

There was a knock at the door and the code squirted under his hand like mashed potatoes. "Uh — empty trash — come in, FakeGrandma!"

The door opened, and FakeGrandma came in, a plate of cookies before her. "Thought you boys might like some more!"

Paul smiled. "Funny, we were just talking about cookies popping up."

"No thanks, FakeGrandma," said Jeremy.

She went away with a hurt smile.

Jeremy sighed and shut the door. "I'm just too fucking good." He threw himself in a huff at his formachair, all the weight of the world behind him. "All the details are perfect. I could have at least made her cookies a little better than they really were."

Paul smiled wryly. *Let him talk.*

"Originally, I made my room a little bigger than it really was, but then I changed it back. She'd notice. Actually, I left one thing." He got up and opened a closet door. Flames, screams, and an awful stench exploded from Hell. "For when I was working on it a lot. I should close it up, really. We sold it the other day for a silly amount of money."

"Always nice to have a back door," said Paul, ignoring the bragging.

"I'll plug it when she gets here. I want everything to be exact, perfect. By the way," Jeremy said, thumbing at the door, "I didn't put too much time into FakeGrandma. She's nothing like that…"

You don't know the half of it, thought Paul, suppressing a smile.

"She's…" Jeremy's voice hitched, his nostrils flared, and he turned toward the lump of code. In a matter of seconds Jeremy's hand had gone from squeezing it to shaping it gently into a polygon. When he looked back, his face had a calm smile on it that chilled Paul. "She's quite different. An outstanding woman."

He just manually adjusted his mood. Paul himself had tried it when he had first arrived, but hadn't liked the feeling. *Mind you*, Paul reflected, *I'm hiding my feelings now.* "Is that who you were calling when we first arrived?"

Jeremy spun the code and split it into two, before he answered. "Yes."

"But she's not answering."

"I think... she might have... gone on vacation." Jeremy's sure handling of the code slowed.

"Oh," said Paul, waiting.

He shoved the code back into storage and looked at Paul resentfully. "Look," Jeremy said. "If I was willing to let you come with the pirate ship, will you find her for me?"

"Find her?"

"Well... it's not like she's *hiding* somewhere. The worst that could have happened is that she fell or...." The hitch again. "I could go back myself, but it takes at least two weeks for them to process the fucking request —"

Paul nodded. "And if anything is found on the voyage...?"

"All booty shall be shared equitably," Jeremy said.

"Then it's a deal," said Paul smoothly. "I have several agents in Vancouver who can look into it."

"It's probably —"

"Nothing, but it's good to look into it."

Jeremy had pulled out the code again, was massaging it. "Thanks."

"Great, you're back," Chan said within seconds of him porting in. "That sleeping cult assignment has turned up amazing stuff."

"Super, just give it to Ryan. I'll take a look at it before our Monday meeting," Paul said, sitting at his desk. *Now get out.*

"Apparently, they go into some kind of stasis, see visions. A common 'dream' is working in a factory, on an assembly line. There's some wing nut going around talking about how it's symbolic of how we've become enslaved to machines —"

Paul was nodding, trying to keep his voice calm. "Sure, OK, interesting. Just give it to Ryan."

Chan looked at him so blankly Paul had a fleeting notion he'd left his scrambleface on. "We have to *move* on this," Chan said adamantly. "7% have heard of it and over .1% actually practice it. We've gotta do more mining *now* or we won't have the jump on the competition."

He stared at Chan until the young man looked away. "I'll take that risk, David."

Chan was gone. *Pique port*, Paul thought. *Poor peep.* He stopped the giddy alliteration, tried to clear his mind. He'd just come straight from Jeremy's, no time even for a drink. *These young kids tire me out, always with their jump on the comp, jump on the comp. That's why Doug would have been perfect to take over here, goddamn it. He's mellowed, got a bit of perspective. And he's too self-obsessed to pay notice to my private projects...*

Ryan was there, his smile apologetic. "Someone here to see you."

"Who?"

Ryan shrugged. "Walked in off the street."

Paul gave his assistant a dark look. "Well I can't —"

His door opened, and a slim Indian man walked in. "Hello, Mr. Harris."

"Doug?" Paul said, immediately recognizing the voice.

Doug nodded.

Ryan grinned and disappeared, his trademark Cheshire move.

"I was just thinking about you! Welcome to Frisco, Patterson!" Paul got up and rounded his desk, gave his oldest employee a hug. *How the hell did you get here?* Paul thought as he patted Doug's back.

"Thanks," Doug said, an embarrassed but pleased smile on his face at the unprecedented warmth.

Paul stared at him. "When did you come in?"

"Our boat docked an hour ago."

"Huh." *Maybe he went back to the Self office? But I would have been notified...* "Well, here you are." He sat down at his desk and pulled out a document. "About damn time, too."

Doug just nodded.

"Take the trolley car in?"

"Uh huh."

"Good. It gives you a better sense of the place. Instead of porting all over right off. Olivia must have loved it, eh?" Paul nodded knowingly.

"Well..." Doug said, tilting his head. "She's... harder to excite nowadays. You know the pretweens."

Paul laughed roughly. It was the laugh that made the Harris persona. "I better! We'll go under if I don't."

Doug was smiling, but his eyes were distant. *Jesus,* thought Paul. *It's either Jeremy and Eileen not knowing the first thing going on in each other's lives, or it's Doug knowing too much. Parenting, it's lucky I...* he let the thought trail off. He couldn't quite muster a complete dismissal, yet there wasn't anything tangible enough to call regret either.

"I just wanted to thank you," Doug said. "For giving me the space to… tie things up at home. Most people would have fired me."

Paul nodded solemnly and realized that Doug had a full head of hair. He decided not to comment on it. He looked at the document he had out, pretended to study it. "Whattaya know about pirates, Doug?"

"The computer kind or the yo-ho-ho kind?"

Paul looked up, grinned. "Both."

The elevator doors opened.

"You're not authorized to be on this floor," it told them with a voice that sounded like it had a cold. "Security is on its way."

Nicky gave JK a look as they walked down the hall.

JK grinned. "Sure, and Opening Emergency Door Will Sound Alarm, too," he read from the sign on the door he proceeded to open.

A horrible screech made Nicky think the sign was serious. Her heart leapt, but it turned out to be just ancient hinges. They entered a stairwell and started up. Nicky looked at the ivory tiles. "Jesus, even the stairwell is high class. How'd you know about this place?"

"I used to live here with my folks. Maybe three years ago? They lived in one other place before they went to Frisco." They'd gotten to the top of the stairs, and he was having trouble with the door. "Don't tell me they've locked —" It opened a bit, and then he got his shoulder into it.

First time I've seen him use those muscles, Nicky thought as the door flew open and JK stumbled out with it.

The stairwell, tastefully lit as it was, was flooded with natural light. JK stood framed in the doorway, hands on the hips of his overalls, surveying. "Yup," he said, looking back at Nicky, the sun making bright disks of his glasses, "You'll find this plenty inspiring, ah bets."

Nicky shaded her eyes and stepped out into a park, an amazingly extensive one given that it was on top of a building. Looking at the door, she saw what had obstructed it: one of JK's bushes, mostly uprooted. Wandering around with JK, she saw that that wasn't the only one.

"Wow," she said, taking off her shoes. "Did you seed here?" She wiggled her toes. *Mmmm, grass.*

"Nope!" JK said, rummaging through his bag. "These are the children of Operation Brolly. Maybe the warehouse party. Good air, good soil, good wind…" He pulled out some sample bags. "I'm just going to take some clippings, but you should check out those trees over there."

Nicky headed in the direction he nodded, eventually seeing the trees he was talking about. They were mostly camouflaged by JK's bushes and vines, but other than that, she didn't know why he wanted her to see them. She put a hand on a rough-barked branch.

Never been able to resist a good tree, she thought. She dropped her shoes at the base and clambered up awkwardly. She was glad of her calloused toes, reflecting that the last time she climbed a tree she didn't have that advantage. No little-girl dresses to worry about, either. *Where was that? Probably at Trout Lake, before it went gated.*

Midway up the tree she found a comfortable seat. From this vantage point, she could see that the park wasn't that big, it just had a clever layout that made it look big. From here, too, she could see the smogcatcher lines and an adjoining pool that even from here looked brackish.

She swung her feet vigorously, and there was a sudden move at the base of the tree that drew her eye. A raccoon, as big as a dog and as unafraid, had its paws on the base of the trunk as if undecided on whether to go up or not.

"Hi there," said Nicky, hoping it wouldn't take a fancy to her shoes.

Uninterested in conversation, it pushed off, its paws audibly hitting the ground. Its big bottom rolling back and forth, it ambled off, giving her shoes a wide berth. When it disappeared into a bush, she gave out a hoot of delight. "I saw it!" she called. JK's chuckle drifted over.

How the hell did it get up here? she wondered. It was hard to imagine it scaling the shiny tower that she saw on her way in. *A raccoon!* She hadn't seen one of the little robbers since her childhood — she hadn't been fond of them then, however. She was bitter that the scavengers had lived while her Shamus had been wiped out along with the rest of the cats. Her teacher had caught her whipping stones at a raccoon in the alley.

"One hissed at Shamus once," she had sullenly explained to the principal.

"Well, raccoons didn't kill him," the principal had explained, by now old hat at dealing with kids with the Feline Fury syndrome. "We did." Nicky hadn't been interested in the explanation: that the clawless and affectionate breed of cat that became the most popular also turned out to be genetically susceptible to a certain disease.

"I wanted one with claws," Nicky had said, staring at the Bikes Kill! display, a mangled run-over wheel. "But my mom got me one of the other ones instead."

"Well, sure," he said with a crooked smile. "She valued her curtains."

It had put Nicky off pets for a long time and probably onto genetics. Even now, she didn't view what she made as pets, and she never made two identical.

"Mental note: raccoons the size of bears," she said to her watch. *That'll cost a lot, but I'm not paying.* "Bears the size of squirrels," she added, smiling to herself.

"Told you you'd be inspired!" said JK from below.

"Bears will be fun — I've never been able to afford the higher-priced genomes."

"Oh, we probably won't be licensing any of them, if my plant work's any indication. We've been paying for the raw materials, nothing more. Well, the umbrella template, that was a little obscure. I think they got someone in Norway to do it. An organic sculptress. So which one did you see?"

"Which sculptress?" said Nicky, confused.

"Which *raccoon*."

"There's more than one?" She looked at the bush it had disappeared into.

JK was stooping to investigate something on the ground. "There's a whole gang of them. Might be a family. Haven't seen any babies, though."

Nicky liked that. "Gang. Gang o' 'coons."

JK sat down. "Isn't it great, Nicholas? That we get to actually make all this stuff, and it doesn't just sit around in art galleries?"

Nicky felt a thrill go through her, just as it had every time she thought about it since Paul asked her if she wanted to do it. "Or sit around in cages in our living rooms, for that matter..."

"I was so glad you wanted to do it," JK said. "I kinda knew Paul had it in mind since the beginning."

"I just thought he wanted me as a lab techie," Nicky said. "I had no idea... I still don't believe it."

"It's because you don't work the angles. You don't have the angling mindset. You're straight ahead," he said, tapping the center of his forehead with the flat of his hand and pointing straight ahead.

'Cept when I'm bilking tourists, she thought, thinking of her ratdogs.

"I'm going to take these samples and analyze them and do a second batch of seeds that'll combine these fertile plants with ones that are really attractive to insects."

"Attractive to insects, huh? Real shapely bulbs?"

"Naw. They smell like rotting meat. Didn't want to use them at the party," he said.

"'Oh, basil! Ah! Are those roses? Hey, is that a corpse I smell?'" Nicky imagined.

JK laughed. "Mmmm..." He licked his lips.

"So you'll put together the stinkiest and the horniest seeds..."

"Pre-cisely." He lay down on the ground and looked up at Nicky. "I've never been able to cross-pollinate my own plants before — it's always been one-offs."

"I've never been able to afford to let my animals go," Nicky said. "I've always had to sell them. That doesn't feel much like art. It feels like retail."

JK nodded, looked at the bush suddenly. It rustled again, but nothing emerged. "It's funny. I can see the park how it used to be here." He squinted, looked around. "Underlying how it is now. A carefully manicured place for people who could afford it. I still liked it. I used to come here at night and smell the plants."

"I'd get my chlorophyll fix over by Pleasant Acres," Nicky said, noticing something in the crook of the tree branch above. She got to her feet, carefully, and investigated. It turned out to be a bunch of old leaves, but it made her remember finding a nest in a tree once… *or did I see that in a movie?*

"Birds," she said into her watch.

Nicky crouched on her branch and slipped to the ground, stumbling just a bit. JK made a nod towards the exit, and she agreed.

"Birds are good," JK said. "They'll spread the seeds."

"My animals are not simply ways for your little weeds to get around," retorted Nicky.

"Ha!" JK said.

When they were going down the elevator, Nicky asked JK if he'd seen much of Andre and Simon.

"They're not still living at your place?" JK responded, surprised.

"Not really," Nicky said, deciding that an occasional sleepover didn't count.

They walked through a lobby guarded by aggressive signs and the stares of security cameras. Outside the building, a van idled.

"Wow, the neighborhood is really going to hell," JK said. "They would have never dared drive their van here last year." There was a pair of black-clad security guards talking to a stooped and ratty man. As they passed, Nicky thought there was something familiar about him.

"Doug Patterson," the woman was intoning. "Your debt has been purchased by Microsoft America. Are you capable of paying it off today?" He stared blankly at her, and suddenly Nicky stopped in her tracks.

"You're that guy at the party, the drunk guy who talked to me," she said, looking at his face, his balding head. He turned to her voice, but his eyes were vacant.

The guard ran through the rest quickly. "In that case Microsoft America has requested that you be relocated to a factory of their choosing so you may begin to work off said debt thank you for your cooperation." They led Doug into the van, and he went without a sound. The security guard's black sunglasses pointed their way for a moment, then looked away.

"Looked like someone you know?" JK said as they walked away.

"It definitely was the guy I met at your party — didn't you see him with the..." She made a gesture on the top of her head.

"No, but," he shrugged. "I heard my friend Kerry was there, and I didn't see her either."

"No, it was him. I remember his name. Doug. We were talking about the mountains." She heard the van starting up behind them.

"I guess he just wandered in..."

"No, he was with someone. A girl I've seen around. And he was dressed like he came from work."

"Maybe he got laid off. Companies have to strip down for Frisco," JK said. "Or so I've heard. Actually, I've heard that 20-hour work days are the norm for a lot of Friscans. Four hours of leisure and then it's back into the fray."

"Huh," she said, looking back. The van was tiny now, rounding a corner.

Nicky got used to working with her tiny boss pretty quickly.

"You're sure you don't mind?" Paul was saying. He'd set up the cubespace with a comfortable armchair and a small fireplace, and his scrambled face (more like a smudged thumbprint at this size) looked in her direction.

"Sure I'm sure," Nicky said, twisting and kneading the in silico bobcat she was working on in another cube. They had partitioned the big cube into two smaller ones, set them a few feet apart on the silver counter. She was having trouble with the stomach. "It's nice to have someone around."

Over the last week or so, Paul's visits had become more and more protracted. At first it had made Nicky nervous to have him around — she was worried that she'd sour the deal — but she enjoyed the conversations so much that eventually the feeling wore off.

"I'm glad to hear you say that," Paul said. "Usually, I hang around in bars in Frisco. Just to be around people. But I've never been much of a bar person."

Nicky nodded.

"I know this sounds kind of weird, but being around you soothes me. I'm around a lot of personalities that get my back up. Talking to you calms me down."

Nicky looked at the little man in the cube. *What am I, a sedative?* "Ohhhhkay. Try not to fall asleep."

"Don't take that the wrong way," he said, waving his hand.

"Can't you just automatically adjust your mood?" she said, making a level-sliding gesture.

"Well, yes, but… it has a weird cumulative effect on your… spirit, in my experience. I think it's just that I can talk freely with you. It's been quite a few years."

Nicky saved the bobcat, set its diet to vegetable, and ran it. She watched it grow, watched muscles ripple and atrophy, and checked the time when it died. It was fairly average. "So… what's changed?"

He had been scanning a yellow document in his hand. "Hmm?"

She set the program to run a thousand bobcats, and the cubespace divided into subcubes. A thousand tiny babies started to grow, considerably slower than just one — it would take a while, but she'd have better stats. Having Paul in the cube slowed it down a little, but that was OK.

"What's changed that you feel like you can talk freely?"

"Well," he started. He put the document away and folded his arms. "For years, in the late '20s, there was genuine danger in doing what I was doing. People were disappearing. The corporations were nervous and as trigger-happy as a post-coup general. My tactic — which differed from your uncle's — required I dedicate a lot of time and energy to establishing myself and distinguishing myself in my company."

"What was your company?" Nicky asked.

"In data security," Paul said.

Nicky knew a stock answer when she heard it — she had a few of her own. "What happened to talking freely?" she said, not looking up from her work.

Paul leaned forward in his chair, put his elbows on his knees. He began, "I've…" He stopped, tutted as if frustrated by himself.

"Oh, stop," Nicky said. "Don't tell me if you don't want to."

"The truth is," Paul said, running his hand through his hair, "I haven't had to exercise this kind of secrecy in years. It's just habit. It's not like I have coolhunters camped outside my house any more. Infiltrators have become mythic."

The bobcat aging was almost half done, and Nicky watched the status bar creep along. "You almost sound sad about it."

"Well, there was an excitement and camaraderie — I was working with *people*. For the last ten years all I've done is shuffle money around."

"Curry Time," her watch said.

"Just a sec," she said, both to Paul and her watch.

Climbing down the ladder, she forced herself not to hurry, trying to think of Paul like any other house guest. *It is pretty flattering, though.* She answered the door and took the cardboard box, waiting for the better part of a minute while the delivery girl fumbled with the payplate. *'Course, maybe he's telling me because I'm of no importance.*

"Sorry, I'm new," the girl said, finally offering it to her to touch. Normally, getting a delivery would be an enjoyable novelty for Nicky, but she found herself impatiently smiling and reaching to close the door. "Thanks for choosing Curry Time."

She nodded and closed the door, the delivery girl's watch bleeping insistently.

When she got back up to the lab, the bobcats were grandfatherly. She set the box on the lab counter and opened it up. She spooned up her daal in silence, occasionally glancing at Paul, who seemed engrossed in whatever he was reading. When she was using the naan to sop up the juice, the bobcats died, and the computer intoned the death march.

Paul looked up at this and chuckled. "Oh, what'd ya get?"

"Curry special."

"Huh…" he said, nodding. "Do you cook at all?"

"From scratch? No, not really. Too expensive. I usually pick up dinner plates from the Safeway."

"I used to like cooking. Never got around to it much…." He wiggled his fingers in front of his face. "I loved chopping garlic. The smell would stay on my fingers for the whole day."

Nicky wondered what whole garlic looked like. Paul's reminiscence reminded her of her father, though, who complained unless Mom cooked once a week. She had hated Sundays. She had never connected the two before, but Paul was probably the same age as her father.

She focused on the bobcat data. The simulations, on average, had lived nearly as long as her first one. So the new grinding teeth and innards took — they worked biologically as herbivores, but was their aggression innate? Or learned? "So it looks like I've got a working design for the vegetarian bobcat," she said. "I left the claws."

"Good, good!" Paul enthused. "And they're native to this area?"

"No, not this strain. The local ones rejected the stomach."

"Still, bobcats! Can you imagine it? You come to this place on the edge of the world, a place you've hardly even heard of in the shadow of stunning mountain vistas. You travel around it in a light rail car, looking down on a city overgrown with plants of every description. At night, you catch glimpses of glowing eyes in the bushes, which bound away before you know what's happening!"

Nicky smiled, tantalized both by the vision and his enthusiasm. "You mean the SkyTrain?"

"Yes — did you know it's the only functioning public transit system on the west coast?"

She shook her head. "Is that why it's happening here?"

"One of the reasons… I've lived here for many years, mind you," he said. "I relocated in the '20s."

"From where?" Nicky saved the bobcat and cleared away her takeout boxes, using the bag to wipe up some crumbs.

"Before that, I was living in New York City," he said. "Spent two years working with a group on public spaces issues. Ended badly."

Nicky was running a sterilizing wand over her counter. When she got to Paul's cube, she said, "Excuse me," as if she was vacuuming under his feet. He barely nodded, lost in thought.

"What happened?" Nicky asked.

"Well," Paul started. "the woman I was living with at the time was a librarian at the New York Public Library. She'd been working there for a year when the Barnes & Noble buyout was announced. It was the end of her world."

"Did she get laid off?" Nicky asked, scrolling through her list of animals-in-progress.

"Well, yes, but that wasn't the problem. It was… more that that particular library was one of the last public libraries left standing. They had thought that the major cities would have one public library left, supported by individual donors — but charitable donations sharply dropped off after they couldn't be written off. Obviously most sensible librarians retrained as dataminers or booksellers, so by the time the New York Public Library was being sold, those that remained were hardcore."

"And your… this woman wasn't one of the sensible ones," Nicky said, trying to remember what she knew about libraries. She remembered seeing an historical thriller where the killer was a librarian, but you never guessed because he was so mild-mannered. *Something to do with renting books?*

"No, Anne wasn't sensible. She — I remember a time…" he laughed, leaning back in his tiny chair. "We were at the border between Canada and the US, while there still was one. The guard asked us one too many questions, by Anne's standards, and she leaned out the car window and started asking him questions: 'Why is it that *people* have a harder time getting across the border than *biohazardous waste*?' That kind of thing. Man, did we get all our holes searched that day," he said with a rueful chuckle. "They ended up turning us back, too."

Nicky smiled, although she didn't really get it. She wondered if this Anne would have problems with her making animals — she remembered seeing something about the anti-Frankenstein movement. She liked the idea of someone who would lean out of a window and sass someone like that, though. "What… you don't have to tell me if you don't want to but… what happened to her?"

Paul wasn't listening, he was pawing through a directory. "I don't even have a picture to show you," he said in the same sad burr of a voice. "What happened? Well. The librarians, the ones that were left, were pretty committed. We made a stand at the NYPL doing public demonstrations — with the two lions out front it made for pretty good images to feed to the media. We lobbied Barnes & Noble, and when that didn't work, we trashed their stores."

"You trashed them?" Nicky said, alarmed by the casual way he said it.

"Not all of them," said Paul. "Just the half dozen or so that had opened up within walking distance of the library. They had the same architecture as the public library, the same reading lamps and tables…"

"Wow, it's changed…" Nicky said, thinking of her last visit to B&N Media to buy a movie for her mom's birthday — they'd been blasting Underwhere's latest. She didn't remember seeing a book section.

"Of course it has. They were only like that until people forgot what libraries were like. Like predatory pricing — once the competition's out of the way, the prices shoot up. Now people remember them as relics of another age, a thing out of place in our world. Which is how they treated Anne's death, as a tragedy in the classic style, the story of a woman born in the wrong time. But it was a statement, not a tragedy. The pictures of her lying on the stairs between the lions with her arms stretched out, the blood trickling from the open veins in her wrists. She even dyed her hair white, put it in a bun. Her attempt to be the Every Librarian, I suppose."

Nicky had totally stopped what she was doing. The part about the blood made the curry sit badly in her stomach, but she could see the picture, for some reason in black and white, Anne's hair looking like a wig on her young body.

"They made fun of her hair on a talk show," Paul said, sighing.

"That's awful," Nicky said, wishing again that she could see Paul's face.

"You put anything out of context, and it seems ridiculous," he said. "Even a beautiful gesture."

"And people are pretty stupid about hair to begin with," Nicky said. "I met this guy who was balding on top, and he didn't want to get it patched. I thought it looked pretty neat. But evidently, people at work were really harassing him about it." In her mind's eye, she saw his vacant stare at her before he was led into the van and had a sudden notion that he was fired for it.

"Huh. Yeah, I know someone like that. Doug's the last balding man in the world. I respect him for it."

Nicky's heart leapt. She thought back very carefully. She ran through the scene earlier today in her head. "The balding guy I know got picked up today by a debtor van. I'm almost positive it was the same guy. He looked really spaced out, though. They called him Doug something."

"What? Not Doug Patterson."

"Yes! Doug Patterson. That was his name."

Paul stood up. "Where did you meet Doug?"

"A party. Actually, it was JK's —"

"*Doug* was taken by a *debtor van*? But he's —"

"Well — *a* Doug was taken by a debtor van. He'll be halfway to a Microsoft America factory by now."

"His body will be, anyway," Paul said, pacing, lost in thought.

Nicky watched the tiny man walk back and forth, muttering to himself, and went back to her experiments. When she looked back, he was gone.

By the time he got home, Cheryl was white. Doug didn't say anything about it, just looked around their new apartment. It was about the same size and appearance as their place in Vancouver, with an extra room. Doug looked in.

"I figure that could be the study," Cheryl was saying, looking in with him.

The room had semi-opaque crystalline walls, a featureless cube. "Gets a lot of light," Doug joked.

"You just touch the walls," she said, demonstrating. As she moved her fingers across the surface, it cycled through the color spectrum. "The whole place looked like this when we arrived. Looked like something out of a science fiction movie," Cheryl said.

Doug thought briefly about how so much of Frisco was inspired — or perhaps limited — by the gutter genre. "Lots of work," Doug said, nodding at his wife appreciatively as they left the room.

"I figure I'll leave that room to you," Cheryl said. "If we don't end up using it much, we can delete it. It'll decrease our monthlies by," she consulted a spreadsheet that appeared in the air. "$542."

Doug nodded, a little dazed, and went to sit on the couch.

"This householder app's really easy to use," Cheryl said, crumpling it up into nothing. "Pop the numbers in and you're there. It accesses your accounts and makes recommendations."

Doug nodded, feeling himself getting numb.

"Well? How was work? Did you get a hero's welcome?"

"Yeah. It's all a lot to process," Doug said, curling up on the couch. It was softer than their old one and a lot cleaner. "So, no cleaning here, eh?" he said, not sure where to start with work.

"No," Cheryl said. "Although the manual says that you have to defrag every so often, or there can be problems. It's just a switch, I did it today."

"Problems?"

"Just 'problems.' Kind of ominous, huh?"

Doug forced himself to chuckle.

"Just as well, there's not much time for cooking and cleaning. I sent out my resumés today. Presume the old bastards will want me back, but I'll have to renegotiate my salary. They'll ream me if I don't have other offers. Plus, looking at the finances… best if we hit the ground running."

Doug knew he should have felt relief, but instead he felt a sinking feeling at her enthusiasm. "We're not that badly off. You can take a while to get used to all this. Relax."

"*You* relax," Cheryl said. "I've been sitting on my ass for the last *year*, Doug."

Doug nodded. He knew it had been hard for her. He just wanted… somewhere to go that wasn't so fixated on business. "Where's Olivia?" he said suddenly, thinking of the little leg-hugging girl he'd left behind in Vancouver. Rudely, his brain reminded him of her new and unwelcome maturity.

Cheryl's smile was bittersweet. "She's in her room. She had a pretty rough day." She sighed. "Oh, I feel awful, but I'm glad she did."

"What happened?" Doug said, sitting up in the couch.

"She came in crying. She said everything was fine until someone asked her why she was, you know, Indian. When she told them it was because of that Pole Position video, they laughed and started picking on her. Evidently," she shrugged, "Pole Position was last week's candy. So they mocked her, danced around, and mooned her like the singer does…"

"Oh. Well, that explains why you're —" He plucked his own skin.

"Yeah," Cheryl said. "I thought it would make her feel better."

"I won't be changing it," Doug said. "It's the hit of the office. Harris thinks it suits me, that I look very Imperial Raja. Singh in accounting is my new best friend." A paper clip creature popped up from under the couch when he said Harris and tapped its comically outsized watch. *Three hours 'til your meeting with Mr. Harris!* It said *sotto voce*. Doug ignored it.

"Somehow I knew that would be your attitude," Cheryl said with a resigned look. "She wants to switch schools."

"Absolutely not!" Doug scoffed.

"Why?" said Olivia, standing there suddenly. She was sniffling, holding a stuffed Sugar Crisp bear. She looked even younger than she had in Vancouver, but Doug was too angry to have sympathy.

"You don't eavesdrop just because you can, young lady," Doug said. "Go to your room!"

Olivia's face moved from defiance to misery to defiance. Finally she burst out crying. The bear hung limply from her tiny fist.

Cheryl gave him a look, and when Doug looked back, a level panel had appeared above Olivia's head marked Parental Mood Override. With her eyes, Cheryl slid down the anger and sadness levels. Olivia's tears dried up.

"Honey," Doug said. "Go on. I'll be up in a minute."

She blinked at him with big blue eyes, and disappeared.

"She's being manipulative," Cheryl said.

"That makes two of you," Doug shot back.

Cheryl shrugged. "She was getting hysterical."

"She was *crying*. And where did she get that teddy bear? The gold package is supposed to be ad free."

"It came with the bed," Cheryl said.

"Great," Doug fumed. "I'm going to the study."

He shut the door and went to sit in the middle of the room. It was quiet in there at least. Doug opened his mood panel. His anger was dangerously high, according to it. But it was dropping by tiny increments. He breathed and watched it drop.

A few minutes later he came out and went upstairs. He knocked on Olivia's door. There was no response, but a few seconds later he opened the door anyway. The growling hitching of pop music blasted out, but he braved it and shut the door behind him. *If I don't have any eardrums anymore, why does it still hurt?* Doug wondered.

Olivia turned it off, but otherwise didn't look up from what she was reading.

"What's that?" Doug asked.

"*You* could have told me." Olivia said. "You were probably laughing at me too."

"I could have told you? About Pole Position, you mean?"

"I thought you were a coolhunter," she said bitterly. "You could have at least told your own daughter."

"I don't deal with specifics like that, honey. I just analyze trends —"

"Whatever," she said, going back to her document.

Doug looked at the glowing text. It looked like poetry for a moment, but when he read it, he knew they were lyrics.

"Yeah under our skin we're all the same, baby/Port over here and dance with me maybe —" he read aloud until Olivia minimized it.

"I'm studying," she said, folding her arms. "That's the cool group. Reptilian Eyes."

"Do they have strange-looking eyes?" Doug asked, amusing himself.

"I haven't seen the video yet," she said, glaring at him.

"Well, you'll be up to speed by tomorrow," Doug said. "Are you going to bother with trifles like homework?"

"I've got all night," Olivia said. "School doesn't start until eight."

"Lucky you," Doug said. "I've got to go back in a few hours."

She shrugged. "At least you don't have to go back to the meanest kids in the world."

Doug sighed, smiled, shook her shoulder, thought about how Chan had made a crack about his "tan."

"Why Daddy?" she said plaintively. "I hate this school. Can't I —"

He shook his head, forced himself to meet her eyes. "You gotta be tough, Olive. There're kids like that in every school."

"Yeah but — if I could just start over I —" She saw Doug's slowly shaking head. Her eyes narrowed. "I can't wait until I get a job. I am so out of here. One of the girls at school already has her own apartment."

Doug, pretending that didn't wound him, stood up. "Let me know when you have some marketable skills," he said with a light smile. "I'll help you write your resumé."

The new arrivals were milling around the dock. A whole shipload of them had arrived a few minutes ago — luckily, after Doug had found Harris and the pirate.

"I wondered how silver and bronze people got here," Doug said, taking in the cruise ship with its ribbon-garlanded gangplank. "There's a lot of them."

"Such typical tin men, too," said the pirate. "Check out Mini and Maxi over there."

He chin-jutted at a man at least ten-feet tall with a tiny companion riding his shoulders. "There's always some joker who maxes out the height option. I think —"

Whatever the pirate thought was lost to the dings of the approaching trolley car and the increased roar of the crowd.

"I rather like the — festive attitude," Harris was saying, his arms crossed. He was scanning the crowd avidly. "Look at that person there with reptilian skin. That wasn't available when I was coming in."

"It's some kind of promotion thing," the pirate was saying. "Some crappy boy band. You get a free album."

"Reptilian Eyes?" Doug asked.

"Yeah," the pirate said, as if reluctant to admit it.

"Not even a day here, and you're already on top of things," Harris said. "Told you he was the best I've got," he said as an aside to the pirate Doug was meant to hear. Despite being conscious of his boss's ego petting, he felt his chest get lighter.

The pirate grunted, unimpressed.

"This is Jeremy, Doug — he's our latest and greatest. He's in pretty deep with the Cracker scene in Frisco, and he's going to be taking you on a daring data raid." He glanced at Doug with an arched eyebrow. "You up for it?"

With a spiel like that, you must really want me to go... He nodded. "Beats hell out of sitting at my desk…"

"All right then, I'll leave you two to your adventure," Harris said, winking at Jeremy. He ported.

Left alone with the burly man, Doug felt a little intimidated. The pirate was a caricature in virility — chest hair bursting out over his shirt collar, biceps stretching fabric, a dagger hilt poking from a waist sheath.

Jeremy caught him looking, and he yanked out the dagger. It glinted in the sun. He shaved off some hairs from his log of a forearm. "Nice, huh?" he said. "The original didn't have it, but I made a few mods. Didn't even have a patch."

Doug was surprised out of his nervousness. "No patch? What's a pirate without a patch?"

"Exactly!" Jeremy shoved the dagger back. "Basically a dirty sailor."

"But you decided against the wooden leg," Doug said.

Jeremy smiled a grizzled smile. "Overkill. C'mon, I'm a young pirate."

Doug wondered *how* young. It didn't really matter, but he found himself trying to guess anyway. *He reacted like a kid to the boy band, but he knows a lot more than an average kid about pirates... could just be an unaverage kid, though.*

"OK, let's get our passports stamped," Jeremy said, straightening up from his languorous lean against the building. "Take off your watch, otherwise they'll be suspicious. They don't get many newbies at the passport office." They walked towards a small shack set in a little from the docks.

Doug looked at his watch self-consciously and took it off. "I guess I won't need to flip to silver or bronze."

Jeremy gave him a scornful look. "You don't even need it for that. It's just because Ristwatch is part of the Self consortium. They're planning to add more features to it — someday — but they want people to get used to it for now. Didn't you notice how useless it is? All it is is a volume control. You can't change the station, just the volume."

Doug nodded. Jeremy had a point, but his wrist still felt funny without a watch.

There was someone else at the passport office. "I was told last week that I could leave this week," a middle-aged woman was saying. "My aunt is in the hospital."

A man in his fifties in a peaked hat held up a finger. "I'm accessing the audio from your last visit to the passport office," he said in calming tones. Then, a different voice from his mouth said: "There is a processing time while your body is retrieved and revived, one week for platinum and up to two weeks for the other packages." Then the officer said in the woman's voice, "OK, that should be fine." The passport officer smiled politely after the recording ended. "It says here you have a silver package."

The woman huffed and stalked away.

"Have a nice day," the man said after her. "Next." His calm eyes looked over to Doug and Jeremy.

Jeremy put a passport on the counter, dug through his pockets while the counterman picked it up.

"I'm leaving," Jeremy said, pulling out a small remote control with one button. "And there's nothing you can do about it."

The counterman's smile never wavered. "There can be processing time of one to two weeks —"

Jeremy clicked the button and froze. A smile spread on his face.

The counterman was stamping the passport. "One to two seconds, more like," the counterman said. He held out a hand to Doug. "Passport."

Much to his amazement, Doug had it in his hand. He passed it to the middle-aged man who was gesturing impatiently.

"Now you see why you don't need the watch?" the counterman said as he stamped Doug's passport. "Power of the mind…"

"I'm feeling a little under the weather," said Jeremy in the measured and calm tones of the counterman. "The passport office is closed for maintenance."

The counterman thrust the passport back at Doug, grabbed the remote out of Jeremy's limp hand, and mashed the button down. Jeremy's hand shot out and grabbed the remote from the counterman's hand.

"Let's go," Jeremy said, walking away.

Doug looked back at the counterman, the smile slowly returning to his face.

They walked towards the dock. Another trolley car dinged its departure in the distance. The dock had pretty much emptied now, and the *SS New World* was gliding away out to sea. There was a ship coming into the space it left, one pretty much like the one Doug had come in on. He scanned the horizon for something that looked like a pirate ship.

"There we are," Jeremy said.

A half-dozen other men were waiting for the ship, with striped shirts and wind-tousled hair. "For your own safety, please do not interfere with the docking process," one of the men said, the words odd out of his mouth.

Jeremy showed the man his passport, and he nodded. He motioned to the other men, and they set up the gangplank. Doug showed him his passport as well.

After it had been set up, the man said. "Come back soon, Doug Patterson and Jeremy Ellis." Jeremy ignored him completely, but Doug thanked him as he jogged up the gangplank.

Jeremy immediately went below deck, and Doug followed him. By the time he'd entered the captain's quarters, Jeremy was already on his knees. Something about the way he was peeking out the porthole struck Doug as young.

"They're just standing there... why aren't they —" Jeremy's body relaxed. "OK, they're untying it." He looked at Doug with a grin. "Whew."

"Whew."

Jeremy looked out the porthole again, less intently.

"That was kind of close. I nearly lost it when the passport guy was shutting down — they definitely investigate that stuff."

"That's a pretty neat device you've got," Doug said.

Jeremy shrugged. "Still nearly fucked it up."

"That would have been awful!"

"Seriously."

"I woulda had to go back to the office!"

Jeremy rolled his eyes. "The deal with Paul would have been screwed, too. I know you're just here to make sure he gets his share of the booty. But I guess he's too busy to come himself. Which is fine, as long as he keeps his side of the bargain."

"Ah," Doug said, stifling a smile as he recalled Harris's words. *I want you to soak it up — every piece of lingo, every value, every subcultural nuance. This Replicantz thing is going to be hot. I don't want to spook him, so I've told him I want in on some data he's stealing. I can't imagine it'll be that valuable, but act like you really want it, be disappointed if you don't get it.*

When the dock started to recede, Doug sat on a hammock and looked around. Identical in every detail to the ship he'd come in on — the mirror, the imposing captain's desk, the rust around the porthole. It seemed like a long time since he'd been there, but it had been just over a day. *Not sleeping played havoc with your conception of time.*

Jeremy had installed himself at the desk. He had his patch flipped up and was poring over code floating in mid-air. It reminded Doug of the first time he'd seen people work code in a cubespace, how much like sculpture it seemed. Doug wondered why Jeremy hadn't made the eyepatch transparent — maybe the costume wasn't just for the outside world, maybe it was meant to heighten the identity of pirate in himself. Or maybe he just hadn't thought of it.

Jeremy made an irritated sound, unbuckled his dagger and set it on the desk. While he was doing so, he noticed Doug looking at him. "What?"

"What's the plan, Cap'n?" Doug said.

Jeremy went back to his code. "The plan is… that you give me a couple of minutes of peace to double-check this."

"Aye aye," Doug said, sauntering out of the room and up the ladder. The squall of seagulls and tangy smell hit him and he inhaled deeply. He felt relaxed, in control, even though Jeremy was running the show — it was a familiar feeling, almost cozy. He wanted Jeremy to be in his element, so he could watch and learn. The ego he lost now would be repaid with interest when he laid out the details of a fresh subculture for his client. But it was important to be subtle — Cheryl often accused him of topping from the bottom.

When he was young, he thought it was something everyone in the business world did. He thought about the incident with Lauden.

"I told our contact that I'd hold off 'til next week before we sell the data," Lauden had said. The subculture in question had been a group of kids who collected DVD discs — an artsy-fartsy bunch who had imagined there was a beauty in the degenerated and warbly recordings, who traded cables and player units as big as suitcases. "There's a big convention next weekend, and they don't want the media rush."

Doug remembered nodding his head, although he was quite speechless. *I'm supposed to believe that he's put months of research into this and is willing to risk it being scooped by another agency because of what he told a* contact? Doug became convinced that Lauden was ready to cross over to another agency. While Doug hadn't done much of the work, it didn't excuse Lauden making him look like an ass. He had been busy establishing himself around the office rather than helping out his partner, which sucked, yes, but it wasn't like Lauden complained.

So when the Friday meeting rolled around, Doug had spent Thursday night printing out the report — they still had to submit hardcopies in those days. Still, he'd been grateful for the solidity of it when Harris had looked to Lauden, and he had been able to remove it from his briefcase and slap it on the table.

Lauden's eyes had widened with surprise, his mouth had opened, but all eyes were on Doug. "The Rippers. Retro-cool, gentlemen," he started. "Not as easy to immediately turn a profit on, but it'll pay off in the long run. Remember the craze for convex screens a few years ago? That they made the image 'warmer'?" He had had them then. Lauden hadn't said anything — what was he going to say? That he was *sitting* on a property? He'd be fired on the spot. His mouth remained tightly closed all meeting, in fact, he hadn't said anything to him for three years after that.

Not that Doug had noticed. There was a good ten-year run without any hitches, where he was turning over ace after ace. It was only when he was approaching thirty and there had been a year of bad leads — *not to mention that psycho kid who had whipped flameballs at my fucking car...*

After the attack — a contact gone sour — he had a couple of weeks in hospital to stare at the walls. Lauden had come to see him, along with a bunch of guys from work, and it had made him reassess his original judgement of his co-worker. Apparently, he had been serious about holding off on the report. But why? In the end, it was to everyone's benefit for a subculture to be mainstreamed. A subculture isolated some vibrant part of human experience, and all coolhunters did was make that available to the masses. That Lauden took the whiners seriously enough to violate protocol — but still did his job — convinced Doug that he was dangerously weak-minded.

Doug had the occasional twinge when he remembered the anger on the face of the kid before he loosed those flameballs.

Butcha gotta break a few eggs, he thought, leaning his elbows on the edge and looking at the silhouette of Frisco. *Microsoft didn't build Frisco by listening to people's complaints, did they? Hell, look at the pyramids...*

Jeremy's shadow, stretched over the wooden planks, jolted Doug back from his thoughts. He walked over as Jeremy placed a small object by the mast of the ship. It was squat and gold and made Doug think of a kettle.

"OK," Jeremy said, taking a big breath.

"So are we going to start steering for the edge of the world sometime soon?" Doug said. "I told my wife I'd be home for dinner."

"No, the wheel on these crappy ships don't actually work," said Jeremy. "They're practically on wires."

"Oh, I know they don't usually work, I just thought you'd have made some mods," Doug said, casually dropping the slang.

"Yeah, we've done that. Soon as you steer it off course the winds whip up, though. We tried to go under, but there're reefs."

"You've gone… underwater?" Doug said, horrified at the idea of entering into the void willingly. "What's there?"

Jeremy changed his mind and put the gold object on the other side of the mast. "Not a fucking thing. We went down in subs, we had bottomfeeder bots comb the entire fucking thing — we were sure there'd be something. What a waste. Took a whole *week*."

"And now?"

"Now… we try to go over." He looked at the gold object.

Doug prodded, wanting to know what the hell they were getting into. "And this kettle is going to —"

"It's a *lamp*."

Doug nodded, hoping that Jeremy's coding skills were greater than his visual art ones. "And this lamp is going to do what, exactly?"

"Well, it'd take all day to describe what it's going to do, *exactly*." He was getting nervously snappish. He rubbed it a few times and then set it down on the battered wooden planks. "Let's just say it should get us where we want to go."

Doug looked at the crude sketch of a lamp, smoke pouring out of the spout, and started to get worried. "It's not going to do anything serious to the boat, is it?" he said, hearing the greedy slurp of the water grow louder, as if anticipating a meal.

"Just relax," Jeremy was saying, but he sounded far away.

The smoke was white and poorly rendered and quickly filled up his field of vision. *Least it doesn't make me cough.* The smoke was so white now, without gradations, and his own body was so perfectly visible, that Doug felt like he was floating. This, added to the fear and irritation, was starting to make him feel nauseated. *All in your head, Patterson, remember — you don't have a body.* Despite that, his gut roiled.

"Sorry about this," came Jeremy's voice. "I didn't know it'd take so long to process. In the simulations there's just a puff of smoke and then it starts up."

"Why do you have to have it smoke? What's wrong with a fucking progress bar?" Doug shouted.

"Progress bar," Jeremy snorted. "All right, gramps."

Doug bit his tongue. *Little shit. Little showboating —*

"Hope it's not frozen…" Jeremy's voice had dropped its cockiness.

Frozen? Doug's stomach flipped. *Whatta fuck is Harris sending me with this — he couldn't crash the system, could he? I mean what would a system crash do to me?* Before his panic rose into hysteria, he called up his mood panel and slid his fear level down. *Oh god that's better.* Before he closed it, his surroundings started to fade back in, like an old-fashioned television, and his fear climbed again. *Jumping at my own shadow now,* he chastised. Doug, now quite calm, was interested to see that when his anger jumped, his fear dipped.

"Well…" he said, looking around. The ship was still the ship and the sea still the sea. He breathed a sigh of relief. He looked around for Jeremy and saw him staring up, a grin on his face. With some trepidation, Doug followed his gaze and saw a black flag. The Jolly Roger.

"My, how terrifying," Doug said, noting that instead of crossbones there were two test tubes. "Did we have to do all that —"

"Take her up," Jeremy called to the flag, and Doug saw the skull eye wink — or rather, saw the socket close in a skinless mockery of one. "You might want to sit down." Jeremy said.

Doug stared at Jeremy as he sat down on the weathered planks. He opened his mouth to speak and a sudden lurch and a whoosh of air knocked him down beside Jeremy. Struggling up on his elbows, he looked to see what the hell was going on.

The way the sails were moving made Doug think at first that they had cracked and were blowing away, but the repetitive way they moved up and down made him realize something else was going on. He looked at the bow and saw that the heavy lumber was bending as if made of rubber — he looked at the sets of sails, one bent that way, and that another. The explosive gusts, the lurching movement of the ship — *they're wings. He's got the sails acting as wings.*

"Have you noticed there are no planes or jets in Frisco?" Jeremy said.

"Uh… no, I haven't actually." *I've been here for a total of thirty hours, so forgive me if I haven't done a transportation option survey.*

"That's 'cause they don't want us poking around in the attic."

"How high are we going?" Doug asked, looking up at the perhaps-not-limitless sky.

"High as we can," Jeremy said. "High as they've built it."

They rose for a good little while. Doug looked over the side. The vague blur of land wasn't getting any smaller. "Do you think we're still rising?"

"No," said Jeremy. "We've gone past that set of clouds three times," he said. "I'm pretty sure we've hit the loop, but let's check it out." Jeremy pointed, and the flag winked again.

As they approached, the clouds looked blocky and low rez, but as they got closer Doug realized that they weren't clouds at all, but huge masses of interconnecting white boxes. Jeremy lowered a rope ladder and it thumped hollowly on the bizarre structure.

He flipped up his patch and clambered over the side. "All right, you hold down the fort here," Jeremy said excitedly.

Doug nodded, relieved. He steadied the ladder as Jeremy climbed down. The pirate put a gentle boot on the box-structure, tested it, and finally stepped. Doug realized his heart was in his throat, imagining Jeremy falling through to the ocean below. Jeremy was bouncing up and down on the cloud. "Solid," he called up.

"Doesn't look solid to me," Doug called down.

Jeremy sat down and yanked one of the boxes out of the structure. "Holy shit."

Doug looked down. "Holy shit what?"

"Are you *looking* at these *dataflows*?" Jeremy said, his voice tremulous and high pitched. "Holy fucking shit!"

"I'm looking at you staring at a white box."

Jeremy made an annoyed sound.

Doug watched him for a while. He knew that codeheads could spend hours and hours doing their thing, barely taking breaks for naps or food. And now that they didn't have to sleep or eat? *Could be here a very long time, Patterson.*

He felt like he did when he was a teenager going out with his cousin, and Jack wouldn't go home until long after Doug wanted to, but it was Jack's car. He looked down through the clouds at the city and zoomed in on it. He wondered if Jack was in Frisco.

He sat down on the deck, leaned against the side. He had an interesting idea. A very interesting idea indeed. "Hey, Jeremy, I was wondering —"

A box tumbled over the side to Doug's left.

"Port back to your boss with that," Jeremy's distracted voice called. "You can thank me later."

"Well, uh… could I borrow that little device you used on the passport guy?" Doug asked, steeling himself for the rejection.

Instead, the little black remote flew over the side. Doug picked it up and looked at it, reading a label on it: *The Ol' Switcheroo.*

Paul sat at his desk, staring at the box.

On the dataflows view, he saw a box bursting with information, a dense and frenetic opposite to its serene package. He was picking through it, and though an organization man himself, his mind reeled at the ingenuity of Self operations.

Once a person had their mind digitally copied in the Self outlet, their physical bodies — with brains in a drone-like stasis — received instructions via their watches to walk out of the office and randomly around the city.

Paul was in awe of the next stroke — after a few days, debtor vans were automatically issued requests to pick up the people. Not only was this a brilliant use of already existing infrastructure, but it also showed an incredible understanding of human nature — that the debtor van security team would mistake stasis for dementia, and that the public at large would simply assume that there were more homeless people these days.

Bodies are a by-product of the process, and the AI's figured out a profitable way to utilize that by-product. But the fact that it knew not to directly transport them to sweatshops — that's pretty cunning, Paul thought, a little apprehensively.

"Paul," Chan said, suddenly standing before him. "Have you had a chance to look at the Dreamer file?"

He resisted an urge to cover the white box. "Get out."

Chan's eyes dropped to the white box

"You don't port directly into my office! Get out!" bellowed Paul.

Chan vanished, startled.

Although he knew that Chan couldn't have understood what was in the box, it reminded Paul of how valuable the data was. Self's standing offer to outbid anyone on information concerning itself was a pretty good safeguard — but it assumed that the only motive people had was a profit motive. *And that's only one among many.*

Another safeguard was that the data in the box only detailed the operations and pointed to the control center. The real motherlode of data was cut off from the network, only accessible by a physical interface. And few people would have the ability to get this access.

Paul, however, was one of them. He put a call through.

"Eileen," he said, trying to keep the excited tremor out of his voice. "I know where the bodies are."

Eileen was tired of it all.

Part of it, she knew, was going into low-power mode so often. But her emotions weren't too out of sync with her sluggish body — she had been dazed ever since discovering that the Self vans were decoys. On an endless circuit from one office to the other, delivering and picking up nothing, signifying nothing.

She would have given up then, pulled the plug out of her spine and hoped for the best, except that Paul had convinced her to hold off.

And now I'm on the slow boat to Hell. It was a hovercraft, actually, and she had been on it for almost a day. At least with the plane and that truck, she had been able to power down. But the hovercraft bounced just enough to convince the suit that she was in potential danger, and it consequently kept Eileen chock full of stimulants. *Why did I listen to him?*

Paul had made a convincing case — he said that he was on the tail of the real location, said that it was vital that she stay on the job, otherwise the bastards that had kidnapped Jeremy would get away with it again and again.

The hovercraft thudded and sent a nice jolt of pain fingering up her back. Part of her brain registered that there was something different with that thud… *something drier?* She stood up, or as far as she could, and looked again for something window-like. But there was nothing. She could be back in Vancouver for all she knew. For all she knew, they could be hitched up to the Self van.

"Heh heh," she wheezed. After almost a week of stasis under the bridge Paul had jolted her awake. His voice had lost the earnest sincerity of his plea to stay plugged in — he was all business now, an excited edge to his voice that worried her. He didn't seem the type to get excited. He told her he'd set up transportation, and five minutes later a black truck stopped on the bridge, its back doors open.

Pretty much since then she had been in one box or another, her only company the suit. Her suit was able to tell her the exact latitude and longitude, that this hovercraft was almost 20 years old and steered by autopilot, and that her power reserves were critically low. Eileen was actually used to the blinking battery in the corner, didn't consciously see it. She was numbly astonished that she wasn't dead yet. It reminded her of the time on a road trip with a gas car, when she and her cousin had coasted on fumes to the only gas station left in Ohio.

Don't get that with those electric cars, she thought. *When they're out, they're out. Guess I'm more diesel than diode.* She had a little laugh at that. She wished Jeremy was here to enjoy that. *He'd roll his eyes — it's his age — but he'd think it was funny.*

"Agent," said her suit.

Had she imagined that? "Hello?" she said.

"You're nearing your destination, agent," Paul said. He sounded even more guarded than usual. She didn't like how he wasn't using her name any more — it was as if he was trying to put distance between them. As if steeling himself to lose her.

"All right, Paul," she said, deliberately using his name.

"Please be professional and avoid using any names. I'm going to be along for the ride, seeing what you see. I've also got an expert with me, an expert in bypassing security systems. We've got to follow his instructions to the letter or else you won't complete your mission."

"Will I find —"

"Your primary objective will be reached," he said, cutting her off.

There was no other communication until the hovercraft whined to a stop. She opened the hatch and climbed out into the dark. She hopped down from the machine onto stony and scrub-patched ground. She did a 360 scan. There was a brightly lit compound, her suit told her, half a mile northeast.

"Head towards that," Paul said.

Eileen started to run, keeping her speed at normal, hoping that Paul wouldn't urge her to rev up. "Your coordinates are hardly exact," she said to distract him.

He didn't respond.

She should have been happy to be out of the hovercraft, but she didn't feel much of anything. There was a dim familiarity to the approach, though, and she realized that the terrain and the glowing compound reminded her of missions in Africa. *Though I'd never be going in alone there,* she thought.

She could make out a small building, a bus and a structure in silhouette that she didn't recognize. She got the suit to run possibilities.

"Boeing Spaceliner 2031- AU," it told her.

What the hell was a spaceliner doing out here?

"OK, get over that fence and make a beeline for the spaceliner." Paul's voice said. She could hear him consulting with someone else. "We don't know what kind of security to expect, so exercise extreme caution."

She smiled at that, remembering the joke that "exercise extreme caution" is code for "exterminate with extreme prejudice." She revved up as she approached the fence. She'd always been good at climbing fences, ever since she was knee-high.

Her suit easily absorbed the electrical charge — there was hardly enough to kill a small animal, which she supposed was the idea. The barbed wire at the top was as meaningless as parsley sprigs with a fancy dinner — a purely decorative touch. She climbed down the other side, as opposed to leaping down as she would have had there been any targets. *Spare the bones, when I can.*

Heading towards the spaceliner, she was a bit spooked by the absence of sentries. Her suit scanned fruitlessly for human movements, and the only sound was the *chit chit chit* of her feet on the grit as she ran. She approached the back of the spaceliner, hoping the three giant pipes wouldn't explode to life, a potential danger her suit was alerting her to.

"It's not set to fly for another half hour," Paul said, seeing the alert. "There — you see the stairs? Go up them."

Eileen did — instead of the accordion walkway that usually leeched off (or fed) passengers to aircraft, a stairwell had been set up for ground access. She rounded the staircase cautiously, making sure there was no one on the stairs, and then sprinted up them. Light streamed through the open door of the spaceliner.

She vaulted off the last step and through the open door, landing in a crouch with her palms to the floor. The part of her that was sure it was a trap and waited for bullets to tear through her was disappointed.

"Relax. Go to normal speed. Agent? Relax."

Eileen felt her chest inflate and collapse, inflate and collapse, hearing the sound of her breath above all else. She thought she was hallucinating at first — that her sporadic sleeping had caught up with her. But her suit was in on it, too — it was seeing targets everywhere, drawing crosshairs over people as fast as it could process. The entire spaceliner was full of people, sitting buckled into their seats.

"Agent! Relax. They can't see you."

Eileen stayed where she was, still and silent. It was true that no one was looking at her. It was true that no one seemed agitated by a figure in a blacksuit with a painted face leaping through the spaceliner door. She stood up slowly.

She turned off her suit's insistent assessments of the people around her — the crosshairs were so dense she had problems seeing their faces. The people in the spaceliner were well-dressed. Their faces were composed, relaxed. If she had been watching this on TV, Eileen wouldn't have noticed anything unusual.

"There should be an empty seat... 33A," Paul was saying to her. "There it is. Get into it."

Eileen made her way down the aisle. 33A was a window seat. 33B was occupied by a woman in her forties, a fashionable comb in her hair. She stood there, waiting for the woman to do something, but she didn't do anything but breathe evenly and stare straight ahead.

"Just get in, agent. Squeeze by and buckle up."

God, how I hate micromanagers. But she did what he said, stepping over the lady's knees and sliding on the complicated harness. She'd never been on one of these spaceliners, but she was damned if she was going to wait for Paul to tell her how to do it. As it turned out, it was fairly obvious — tab A into slot B with a winch at C and a loop round at D — and no sooner had she settled in than the door hissed shut.

"Fantastic! Good work, agent," Paul said. He was laughing. "That was tense there — oh god. OK, it'll be all automatic from here."

There was nothing for a while, just the sound of the engines starting up. She looked around at her fellow passengers. *Not too different from your average flight,* she thought, *everyone looking straight ahead.*

"Welcome to flight 0001, out of Nunavut," came the voice in her ear. "This is a non-stop flight to the body cache circling the earth. Those who are cybernetic killing machines are requested to go offline until the seatbelt light is off. Regrettably, there is no in flight movie, as most of your brains are locked in stasis," Paul continued. "But we hope you'll enjoy your time with Self Spacelines."

By the way Paul had been goofing around, Eileen assumed he knew exactly what would be going down once they docked. But now she wasn't so sure.

"OK, take a left here…" he said. "Actually, no. Take a right, that looks like a terminal down there."

Eileen stopped. "You don't have a map."

"No, we —"

"What are you looking for," she said.

"If we can get to a terminal, we can do a search for who's stored here," he said. He sounded nervous. *Damn it,* Eileen said. *Smells like a double-cross.*

"That box down the hall —" he went on. Eileen queried her suit, and the box was identified as Maintenance Storage in big red letters. "Ah," Paul's voice said, chastened.

Eileen got her suit to run a check for datafeeds, and a faint glow lit up from inside the wall. She followed the way the glow was flowing. A few twists and turns later in the white-walled rat's maze and she was in front of a terminal. "Here's your terminal," she said. "Do you need a direct connection?"

There was a pause. "Yes."

She yanked out the keyboard — it was useless, the passwords they used on these stations would take days to input through a keyboard — and shoved her index finger into the socket. "Patch it through to your hacker," she said, her vision flickering slightly with the new connection.

"Fantastic. You're a pro," he enthused.

"I know that," she snapped. She was still annoyed he had had her running around without a map. "Is your hacker in yet?"

There was a pause. "No." There was more silence. "No, he says it'll take a little while. Agent, after we have the data regarding your mission goal, we will have to apply that."

Yes, she translated, *once they knew Jeremy was here, she'd still have to find him.*

"It makes sense to use this time for some reconnaissance. Do you agree?"

"I do," she said, satisfied by his tone.

"If you trace your way back to where you boarded the station, we can see what happens to new arrivals. How they're stored and such."

She was already running. "Agreed." Eileen had actually thought that would be a good thing to do from the beginning, but Paul had started giving her directions after the spaceliner docked.

She arrived back in the octagonal room where they had deplaned. The door back to the spaceliner was sealed and locked, so she headed down the hallway where her docile fellow passengers had filed down. Walking now, she looked into an open doorway. Her suit immediately compensated for the darkness inside and identified four targets, prone on single beds, one against each wall.

Moving down the hall, she found another identical room. They reminded her of hostel rooms, plain but hardly unliveable. Didn't fit the lavish image of the space station resorts, but the guests weren't complaining. Eileen remembered wanting to go to a space resort when she was a teenager. They had broadcast MTV from the opening of a rock themed resort, and the gravity was kind of spotty — the VJ interviewing Prince kept floating away. Eileen hadn't wanted to go nearly as much once they had stabilized the gravity — that had seemed to be the fun part, to her.

A naked man ran out of a room. *Well — maybe there's still some fun left after all.* She chased his firm buttocks down the hall, drew up alongside him. He was in his forties and very trim, a neutral expression on his face. She looked down at his business, which was flopping and bouncing around.

"Now, now, agent," Paul said.

Eileen had forgotten he was there, seeing what she saw. *How embarrassing.* She looked ahead. The corridor ended in a glass wall with doors in it. Through the glass, Eileen saw more naked people running. Someone whisked by that might have been on her flight, but she couldn't tell for sure without the clothes.

She followed the man through the door and onto the running track. It circled a huge weight room, where naked people of every description were working out in a sweaty, bland, methodical way. Keeping out of the way of the runners, she watched one old man pull at a handle until he couldn't pull any more. Then he immediately walked to another machine and sat down at it.

She could hear Paul laughing. "This is brilliant. Getting people to maintain themselves. How perfectly cost-effective!"

"Are you kidding?" Eileen said. "The spaceliner, the station — this costs billions!"

"Yeah, but these are just the platinums. The elite clientele. They've got the other bodies making enough money for ten of these stations."

Something about that bothered her, and Eileen tried to figure it out as she watched the people. Every so often, someone would leave the track, and someone would leave the weight room. No one seemed to be waiting for machines — maybe they had a secondary choice. She started towards the other side of the room, there was a door there

nothing

Her surroundings faded in. She was sprawled on the ground, one of the oblivious joggers nearly stepped on her. "Agent, what was that?" Paul was saying.

Eileen knew what it was. *My battery.* But she was so close. She wasn't sure what Paul would do if he knew. "I don't know."

"Maybe you should go back to the terminal. Maybe they've got some defenses we haven't detected yet."

She walked towards the glass doors, standing aside for the three incoming nude joggers. The resolution faded in and out, and she hoped Paul didn't notice. She felt ashamed of how weak she was.

"Get out of there, agent. They might have a field in that room that's affecting your suit."

She ran down the hallway. The resolution thing happened again, but it wasn't so noticeable with only the white walls. "It makes sense they'd have defensive measures. We just expected it to be spider sentries or something," Paul was buzzing in her ear.

Eileen knew better. The more money an operation had, the more power, the less security measures it needed. That despot in Hawaii, for instance, had the giant mechanical spiders that had terrified and captivated viewing audiences — he was weak. That was the only time she'd ever seen them. But they were just bigger, scarier guns, reliant on the skill of the operators.

With soft bellies to boot, she said, remembering her satisfaction at laying two of them to waste. *You've had a pretty good run, Eileen.* Her vision was doing very strange things now, and a red warning was flashing SYSTEM SHUTDOWN. But she was right in front of the terminal, and she was able to slip her finger in the socket more from touch than by sight.

She really felt the surge through her then, like you feel a soft breeze when you're sick. She could hear Paul's voice, but it was breaking up. She felt so tired but knew there was only pain ahead — once the suit was inactive, the accumulated abuse she'd given her old withered husk would soak in, soak into her bones and probably melt them too.

Her head was dropping, dipping down and up. The suit had stopped mainlining her drugs. She could already feel an ache in her joints — pain was coming, rolling down the tracks, not sounding its whistle. She sat down against the wall, sliding down so her finger stayed in the socket.

What will they do with my body? She had an image of her stiffening corpse being leaned against the weight machine, her hands placed on the handles just to fall off, and cackled to herself as the darkness rushed in.

The two of them walked along the path for five minutes without saying anything. Doug took in the trees around him, inhaled the pine smell. *Well Patterson,* he thought to himself, *you've finally made it to the mountains.*

"So," Harris asked with a grin. "Whattaya think of my new office?"

"It's great," Doug said as the path skirted a ledge that showed a valley deep and green. "It's not a bad size."

"Yeah, I'm not exactly tripping over boxes here, am I?" Harris's laugh was big, as big as the valley, head tilted back.

Doug raised his eyebrows at his boss's uncharacteristic hilarity.

"It's just a fake, of course," Harris said, plucking a leaf from a tree and rubbing it. "But it's an exceptionally good one. It's inspiring."

He handed the leaf to Doug, and Doug dutifully inspected it. He flipped it to the veiny side and watched a tiny bug run around on it. When he looked up, his boss was looking at him with the same interest. Doug felt his anxiety start to rise, had to prevent himself from adjusting it. Harris looked away.

They were going uphill, and Harris took the lead.

What does he want, anyway? thought Doug. He had finally settled into a routine — his work was intense but challenging and Olivia had managed to lose her loser status at school. Without dinner or sleeping to bring them together, Cheryl and Doug hardly talked… and had yet to make love. He had talked to her about making a trip to the Marquis outlet, but their schedules hadn't clicked yet. She was totally occupied with job interviews, four or five a day.

"So, about this Replicantz business," Harris threw back. "Your report didn't recommend when we should sell the data."

There was a crack of thunder that made Doug jump. "Well," he said, hoping Harris didn't see his flinch. "It's just a preliminary report."

"Yes, yes," Harris said impatiently. "Ah, rain."

Doug felt the drops, bigger and bigger, hit his clothes and hair. He almost wanted to suggest porting out, just to change the subject, but he saw Harris was enjoying it.

"So should we sell the data, Doug?"

"Preliminary findings are strong, but we need more research," he said, feeling as if Lauden was moving his mouth.

Harris stopped and turned around to look at him. "Did my bullshit detector just go off?"

"No," Doug looked back at Harris. "It's too young, they're going to do bigger things…" Doug babbled. "I just," he dropped his eyes. "I don't really know."

"Good," Harris said, with a funny smile Doug hadn't seen before. "That's good."

They crossed a bridge that connected two outcroppings, and Doug watched the raindrops hit the black oily wood planks. Harris leaned on the guardrail, looked over the edge. Doug did the same.

"The fact that you're questioning yourself, that you're weighing things beyond their immediate market value…" Harris smiled. "That's what I need."

Doug didn't know what to say. He didn't agree — it just made him weak, ineffective…

"I want you to run the agency for me, Doug."

Doug took a deep breath and looked off at the charcoal sky. He gripped the guardrail with his long fingers and felt nothing. No exaltation and no fear. "Well."

"I've got another project that deserves my full attention," Harris said, turning to look at him. "So you'll be in charge."

The rain was really coming down now. Doug felt the drops stream down his cheeks, slightly amazed at how much he'd changed, how the promotion just seemed to complicate things. Then, feeling a small item in his pocket, he remembered that he had options. He felt the burden lift.

"Finally, a smile," Harris said, staring at Doug. "Took a second to sink in, I guess."

Lightning jagged across the sky and drew Doug's attention to something metallic and large on the other side of the valley. He zoomed in on it, and it looked to be a space station, crashed but largely intact.

Harris noticed his gaze. "Oh, that's just a sketch," he said. "For something I'm working on."

The bobcat leapt up on a parked car hood and roared at the passersby. Screams and pandemonium ensued, the sidewalk frothing with people. The camera pulled away to include a concerned-looking anchorman watching the panicked crowd. He looked into the camera.

"Robson Street shoppers were terrorized today by a feral animal," the anchorman said. Behind him, the bobcat pounced at a baby carriage, then froze in mid-air.

A new shot of a young woman clutching her purse. "I… couldn't believe it. I thought it was one of those ads at first, but then it just ran away, and I realized it was a real animal. It's like they're taking over…"

A different shot of an old man with a baseball hat: "I was *this* close to it. I got my gun out, but I couldn't get a clear shot. A lotta folks were in the same boat — we all were talking about it afterwards… I don't remember what it looked like exactly, I just remember the teeth, these needle-sharp teeth."

"Stadium," the SkyTrain said. "This stop is Stadium."

Nicky looked away from the news report. She knew that nothing like the re-enactment could have taken place — she had made the bobcats with just enough aggression to be able to fight if they were cornered, to defend themselves.

A sophisticrat across from her caught her eye. She was the only other person not watching the news, staring at a book instead. Nicky tried to see what the cover said, but the angle was wrong. The girl, about Nicky's age, smoothed back her bangs and turned the page gently. Nicky figured she'd read more paper books if she didn't have to be afraid of it falling apart or of pages missing. She hated that. Plus, like any antiques, they were expensive.

She imagined what it must have been like to be able to go to a library and get any books you wanted. New ones, too. What an amazing thing for someone poor like her. It reminded her of Paul's story about the last library, the way his voice had gone all quiet. Thinking about that made her think of her special project, and a kind of ebullient joy bubbled up her spine.

Soon, soon. She looked back up at the news. The eyewitnesses had finished their litany of horror, and it had returned to the anchorman.

"No fatalities have been reported yet from the bobcat attacks," he said. "But residents of Vancouver and the surrounding areas are advised to stay in their homes. Sandra?"

Sandra, dressed in a gold bikini, grinned into her mike. "Thanks Dave. I'm reporting from Frisco where the folks at Self have some rather exciting news." She waved around her, and the camera shot took in a pool surrounded by beautiful people wearing only the scrambled fuzz added by the network. Sandra watched a couple slide down a blue waterslide and splash into water colored a bright gold. "As you can see, there's a new attraction in Frisco — these beautiful pools have opened up all over to celebrate the 0.9% financing offer on the Self gold package." She stopped a burly short-haired man as he ran after a squealing girl by poking her mike in his face. "You look like you're having fun."

"Oh, it's great," he said, sliding his hand through water-slicked hair. Another man snuck up behind Sandra. "When I was growing up, I always wanted to be out in the sun and the water, but the smog, you know," he said with a shrug.

Sandra, seemingly unaware of the man fiddling with something behind her back, nodded sympathetically.

"It's time for me to have some fun in the sun!" he concluded with a grin.

Suddenly Sandra's bikini top came off, and as she clapped her hands to her breasts, the two men grabbed her and carried her towards the pool. "This is Sandra Loomis reporting from Friscooooooo!" she managed before hitting the water.

Dave reappeared, smiling and shaking his head ruefully, the bobcat still frozen behind him. "In other news today, a Showdown at the Waterfront. Security fended off boatloads of Africans who attempted to sneak into Vancouver last night." Cut to a pitch black scene with popping sounds and screaming.

"This station, Main Street Science World." Nicky got up. The sophisticrat girl removed a rectangular piece of paper from the back pages of the book and used it to mark her spot. Nicky recognized the colorful bookmark as paper money. *Neat*, she thought, watching the girl straighten out her lapels with a sidelong glance as the doors slid open.

She left the SkyTrain with one or two others. As she made her way down the stairs, she noticed that the doors hadn't closed. A few more people left, looking annoyed, and Nicky guessed it was a delay. More and more delays, more and more station closures. She hoped Paul knew what he was talking about when he said that the system just needed a "few modifications." She could see his little hands framing his argument. "Get rid of the advertising, get some way to clear the plants off the track, and we've got an automatic monorail that'll inspire the world," he had said, rubbing his little chin.

When she got down the stairs, she headed to the train yard. A few blocks away, she noticed the half-finished billboard. She looked carefully at its silhouettes of two dancing girls, an unidentifiable shape in the corner where the logo would be, deciding that it was no further along than when she had seen it last. It was eerily frozen, kind of beautiful in its vagueness. It was surprising, being prime space on the side of a building visible from the SkyTrain and from the road. *Not that too many cars were on the road,* Nicky thought, looking around.

She noticed a cyclist approaching, and she kept walking, smiling to herself. She wondered if it was JK or Simon, she couldn't tell from that distance — but when he passed, she realized it was neither. It was no one that she knew at all.

As the blue-jacketed cyclist pumped further away from her, she tried to unravel her feelings of indignation and excitement. Whatever they had started had caught on, become bigger than themselves but also out of their control. Just like when she had freed her animals, the dozens of hopping, flying, running beasts that she had crafted.

"Nicky built an ark," JK had sung, while her heart sank lower and lower and the menagerie fled from the train yard. He noticed her mood and patted her on the shoulder. "Gotta let go. They were never yours," he had said, and at first she thought he meant that Paul had paid for them to be made. But now, having seen glimpses of her animals all through the city, she realized that he must have gone through the same thing every time he let his spores fly and let them become part of the world.

"She doesn't want to go," Nicky had said, approaching the giant butterfly that still sat on a perch of twisted metal. Its green and yellow wings twitched slightly as Nicky held out her wrist as a perch, but it didn't move. She wanted to lift it, but she felt JK's eyes on her and looked at him guiltily.

"Have faith, Nicholas," he said, his eyes soft with compassion.

There was a flutter, and the butterfly flew away.

As she approached the train yard, she wondered why there weren't more animals there — it was relatively free of humans. However, there wasn't much cover or food, only an occasional scrub brush littering the dusty ground. She had seen more than one security guard poking at a raccoon up a tree in a gated community, on the other hand. *'Coons don't care that they're not wanted,* she thought, happy that she had succeeded in increasing their speed without affecting their loping walk.

Maybe the elephants would come back, she thought as she approached a boxcar and whacked on the door with the flat of her hand. *To die in the train graveyard.* Although the way things were going, there might not be any wild ones left. JK had told her that he had seen one being placidly lead around on a leash by some rough-looking teenager.

The boxcar door opened and Simon stared out, blearily.

"Sleepy Simon was a pie man," Nicky said, smirking at his bedhead. "Whatteryou doing? There's only 93 days until the symposium, you know, there's no time for sleeping." Paul had started the countdown at 100 and called it "the final stage." It made her wonder how long he'd been planning the gathering of dissidents, artists, and scientists.

Simon sat down in the doorway, let his legs dangle. "I know it. I was up all night last night bolting those stupid blades onto the SkyTrain. They better work."

"You have a meeting with the East Van Anarchists in a half hour, Simon, at the —" his watch reminded him politely, and he slapped it quiet.

"To cut the vines? Won't they notice?"

He leaned back into the boxcar and grabbed a Starbucks, cracked it. "Yeah. But we were able to generate a work order in their system to do it." He took a sip of the steaming coffee. "Paul's got someone who can make their system do anything. It's been all automatic for ten years now, even the advertising contracts. He's getting the system to refuse any new contracts — to say there's no space — so once this month's run out, that'll be it."

"Huh," she said, finding no ads hard to imagine. *Where would people look?* She remembered the sophisticrat she'd seen today and had a bizarre image of a SkyTrain car filled with people reading books.

"93 days," Simon mused, taking another sip. "And I'm already being run off my fucking feet."

"Really?" Nicky said. "I haven't been doing much more than before."

Simon shrugged. "Yeah, but you're the talent. And he doesn't own your ass."

Nicky felt a tingle when he said "talent." "Yeah, Andre told me about Paul paying off your fines."

Simon nodded, took another slug of coffee. "Ahh, I'm just venting. I just hate having a boss. He never holds it over me. If he wanted to, he could have just bought the debt rather than paid it off, but he didn't." He pulled on his hair. "And it's an amazing project to work on. Show me someone else who's organizing a radical gathering to mark the 150th birthday of the corporate entity."

Nicky raised an eyebrow. "Well, I'm sure the corporate entity's mom is planning something…"

Simon laughed, showing his skully teeth.

"Why does Paul care so much about this?" Nicky said, hoping she didn't sound stupid. "What happened in…" She did the math. "1886?"

"There was this big court case that ruled that a private corporation was a natural person. That it had all the rights of an individual but none of the responsibilities." He looked around the train yard. "Actually, it was a railroad company. Santa Clara County vs. Southern Pacific Railroad."

"That sounds… weird," said Nicky. A lot of law-making and governmental regulation sounded strange to her, though.

"Yeah… it took over a 100 years, but eventually corporations grew to the point where they were more powerful than governments, and decided they owed it to their stockholders to dissolve the old and inefficient mechanisms of democracy."

"I guess you thought about this stuff before you met Paul," Nicky said, hoisting herself up on the ledge of the boxcar. She saw a rabbit scamper behind a train husk across the yard.

"Yeah, you know, I wasted a couple of years in school," Simon said. "For a long time I wished I could have been around in the '20s, that's when all the action went down. That's what I find interesting about Paul. He lived through that, but unlike most of the people that were active then, he's still involved." He nodded. "It'll be interesting to meet the man in person."

Nicky looked at him sharply. "What do you mean?"

"Paul's going to be here. For the symposium."

Nicky blinked. "Here? But…who comes back from Frisco?"

"Paul does, I guess. He had to set up his business in Frisco, but I guess he's got someone else doing that now."

"What exactly is his business, anyway?"

Simon nodded, squinted at her. "He's never offered that information."

"And you've never asked? Nosy bastard like you?"

He smiled, shook his head. "I'm kind of… scared to. I know it's gotta be a profitable business, if he can do all this stuff on the side. And therefore…"

Nicky waited, looking at his thoughtful face.

Simon jumped to the ground, slapped the side of the boxcar. "Yeah. Yeah, I'm going to ask him. Face-to-face." He looked at his watch. "Gotta scram."

"Where you off to?"

"Meeting up with these old folks. Anarchists. They're working on places for people to stay, food, showers. There's going to be thousands of people here, so we need to make sure we have the basic infrastructure in place."

Nicky nodded, liking how certain Simon was about that.

He ducked into the boxcar and grabbed his knapsack, pulled it on. He took a few steps and turned. "Sorry I have to leave," he said.

Nicky made a face. "I come all the way to hang out with you…"

He grinned, already walking away.. "Bullshit, you didn't come to see me. I know who you came to see. Good to talk to you though, Nicky."

Nicky watched him walk away, his feet crunching in the gravel and dust.

When Simon was out of sight, she jumped down and hurried over to a green-doored boxcar. The door was rusty, so it took a couple of lunging yanks to get it open.

"Hello there…" she called into the dark interior. She didn't see anything at first, but then there was a glint of an eye. Then they padded into the light.

"Sorry I had to keep you locked up last night," she said, stroking back Ben's baby mane and scritching his ear. Frank dropped to the ground and wound around her legs, almost knocking her over. "Wow! You're getting big!" Nicky said with a laugh. Frank looked at her questioningly, and she gave him a pat on the head. He pushed up on her hand and purred in a way that sent a tingle down her spine. *My lions.*

She had hit upon the idea when she was looking at pictures of the New York Public Library, after the story Paul had told her had stuck with her for a few days. The two stone lions that flanked the entrance, she discovered, were called Patience and Fortitude. Pat was an OK name, but Fortitude was a little pretentious. She read a little more and discovered that the guy who popularized the library was the same guy who discovered electricity. So she named them after him, instead.

She walked a little away from them and smiled as she heard their light steps following her. When she could feel them close on her heels, she turned around and held her hand in a certain way. Ben, without hesitation, came around to face the way she was, stopping directly under her hand. She waited for a second, but Frank didn't come around to her other hand. She pushed Ben's head, and he settled into a crouch.

"Good, Ben, good…" she said, removing a package from her bag and opening it. She double-checked that it was tofu jerky before she gave him his treat — she didn't want him to get a taste for meat. She looked over at Frank to see if he was seeing this. He was watching, but he seemed content to lick his grey fur clean.

"Frank!" she said, and he got up almost guiltily and trotted over to her. Even with opaque eyes, his face had an expressive and friendly look. He was the playful one, the stupid one, and she couldn't punish him. She had a while yet, anyway. Ninety-three days or so to teach them to stop at her sides.

What would Paul think of them? she wondered suddenly. She imagined herself, flanked by the stone-colored lions, facing Paul — his face pale and unscrambled, his body weak from being in storage, his eyes most certainly piercing. *Would he be old, as old as Dad?* She thought of what she might say, but everything sounded stupid. The ball of excitement and nervousness spun in her stomach as she imagined his reaction to the lions. *Would he be creeped out? Flattered? Both?*

She sat down on the ground and played with Frank. While they wrestled, Ben sat to the side, aloof. When the SkyTrain approached, she stopped to watch, holding Ben's paws still. As it crested the curve, she could see the blades bolted on the front, rusty salvaged metal throwing off sparks here and there.

Doug got home from his meeting with Harris and hung his jacket up, a smile playing on his lips. "Hey Cheryl!"

Cheryl's voice came from the study. "In here."

Making sure he had it in his pocket, Doug went and stood in the doorway. She was flipping through different documents, a harassed look on her face.

He leaned against the doorway and looked at her. "Find anything yet?"

"Well," she sighed. She looked up at him. "What're you smiling at?"

"Just happy to see my wife," Doug said. Other than the desk that Cheryl was sitting at, there was no furniture — the place was still at its default settings. Doug went and looked over her shoulder.

"A couple offers," Cheryl said. "Four."

"That's great!"

"Yeah. They're all entry level, though. I'd be starting at the bottom."

"Hmm…" Doug walked in front of the desk, stretching his arms. "I got a promotion today. Harris made me boss."

Cheryl smile was bittersweet. "Congratulations," she managed.

"Yep," Doug went on. "I'll be making enough to support the whole family."

Cheryl's eyes flashed. "While I stay home and take care of Ms. Mucky Muck? Is that where you're going with this?"

"I'd love to stay home and hang out with Ms. Mucky Muck."

"Well fucking bully for you, Doug!" Cheryl said, getting angry.

Doug slapped both hands on the desk and stared at his wife. "Don't you wish that we could switch places?"

Cheryl made a tired sound. "Doug, go away."

Doug took the small remote out of his pocket. "Yes or no."

Cheryl put her hand up. "Yes! Yes, are you ha—"

Doug pushed the button. "—py," he said, his face curling angry.

Cheryl grinned from ear to ear. She got up and approached her husband.

Doug was looking at the device. "The Ol' Switcheroo? Doug, where did you get this?"

Cheryl took the remote and put it back in Doug's pocket. "Never you mind." She put her other hand in his other pocket and fiddled around.

"Oh!" said Doug.

Cheryl pushed all the documents off the desk and Doug onto it.

"Oh!" repeated Doug, now horizontal. They both laughed.

Cheryl straddled him, pinned him down with one hand. "Tell me I'm a genius," she said, moving her hips.

"You're a genius, Doug," Doug said, biting his lip.

Cheryl stopped unbuttoning his pants, raised her eyebrows.

Doug grinned. "I mean: You're a genius, Cheryl."

Paul flicked through the black and white channels until he found something good.

Ever since he'd had access to the space station's controls, he'd spent an hour of every day just watching the elite of the western world — as they slept, as they ran, as they ate. For some reason, seeing them eat was the most disturbing — watching their jaws move so mechanically, the packets of processed nutrition chewed up and ingested. Right now, he watched a room of four sleep.

Without so much as a yawn or a stretch, a teenaged girl sat up, stood, and jogged out of the room.

So much jogging! Was it even good for you? Isn't it hard on the joints?

He put a call through. "Jeremy! Paul here. Question for you: I've got control of the station. If I land it, you say that there's no chance of it being destroyed?"

Jeremy's audio came through, raucous music in the background and his voice, muffled. "You ever think maybe I might be busy?" Another voice chimed in: "Yeah, he be busy motherfucker!"

Paul smiled. He imagined that Jeremy was king shit of his crew after cracking Self. If he wasn't before.

"Shut up Phobe," Jeremy yelled. The music quietened. "So-so-so, this is how it is. A meteor hitting the station wouldn't do anything to it. It's unshakable, just like the servers in Frisco. Just watch what you land it on."

"'Cause that shit's flatter than a pancake!" Phobe giggled.

"OK, great. And we could restore their brains?"

"Yeah, you know how we transferred your agent in the space station to Frisco? With the terminal he was plugged into? That terminal can also take those bodies out of stasis, either with a tone or a retinal flash. Just be careful with mine, OK? Make sure it gets extra special attention."

"*Extra* special!" piped up Phobe.

"Naturally," Paul said, his mind working away. "And remember the rule of thumb in information securities: the quieter you are, the richer you'll be. Take care, guys." He disconnected.

Jeremy's oblivious mention of his agent reminded Paul that he hadn't seen Eileen's body in any of his channel-surfing sessions — her blacksuit would stand out, surely. *Maybe they took her suit off and stored it wherever they store the clothing.* He flicked through the channels, stopping on an old woman using a weight machine. *That could be her...* he thought. But there was the odd message that the suit sent back after they transferred Eileen's mind: *battery dangerously low, disconnecting...*

It made Paul think about the consequences of a body's death. As he understood it, the mind in Frisco would continue on. But it also meant that they were effectively trapped in Frisco. Each body-death ensured a loyal customer. So did births, for that matter. If Self offered a baby option to Friscans, it certainly wouldn't be reverse-compatible with the obsolete biological system...

Paul put Eileen out of his mind, and flicked on. On the screen, an old putty-faced man huffed away at a rowing machine. He looked vaguely familiar to Paul. *One of the AT&T&Bell execs? Matt something?* Paul tried to imagine, as he had tried several times in weeks since conceiving his plan, how he would address someone like Matt. He knew they would be appalled at the conditions in which Self kept their bodies — he thought that most of them would be upset at the idea that the bodies of their colleagues and friends who weren't platinums were being used as complex gears in factories overseas.

But how to spin it for maximum effectiveness?

No! Not spin it. How to tell the truth — so they see the big picture. Put it in context. Show it for the horror it is.

Paul watched the beads on the putty-faced man's forehead turn into streams. *Probably the first time that guy's broken a sweat in decades.* He looked at the man and tried to imagine talking to him.

"Capitalism needed an endless supply of cheap workers to continue its endless growth, so at some point it had to end. Europe exploited North America, North America exploited South America, South America exploited Africa — eventually there was no one left to exploit," Paul started, looking at his notes, immediately feeling like this line of rhetoric was going to alienate most of his audience. As if responding to him, the putty-faced man stood and went to a weight machine that faced away from Paul.

Paul flicked to a camera that framed a woman who was doing sit-ups, her breasts jostling with the movement like jelly sacks. He continued. "And even the assassinations and warmongering of corporate interventions could only maintain the status quo for so long. The magic of the free market would be revealed as black magic, dependent on slavery and inequality in order to function. But before the pyramid scheme toppled, technology stepped in and put a new twist on it. It didn't replace human labor with machines. It used humans as machines." He watched her angular face bob up and down a few more times, trying to decide if she would care that her neighbor's body spent its waking hours removing glass particles from a circuit board or spraying glue on the sole of a shoe bound for Mexico.

He flicked through a few more channels, until he got one that showed a wide shot of the gym, and addressed the crowd as a whole: "Now the snake has begun to eat its own tail in earnest, sending the species into a new spiral of degradation."

The only answer was the squeaking of the weight machines.

Paul sighed. He'd never been good at speeches. *And they'd never listen,* a voice inside him hissed. *Best to just start fresh. Clean the slate. Send the station into the sun.*

Paul flicked through the channels faster and faster, looking for the one thing that would shut the voice up. He found it. The camera was trained on four beds, one occupied by himself. He was a little trimmer and shaggier than he had been the last time he'd seen himself, but it was undeniably him. So destroying the station, even if he had been so inclined, would also destroy his body. It wouldn't mean death, but it would certainly limit his options.

The last decades had required betrayals and self-denial and deception, and the voice wanted revenge. But the voice also knew what he knew — by destroying his enemy, he'd be destroying himself. He couldn't kill them — but he intended to shake them up. When the symposium had begun, he would land the station in the hills of British Columbia. Then he'd restore their pre-Self minds and invite them down to Vancouver. And in their naked state, physically and otherwise, they might be receptive to the gathering of free organisms — biologists and radicals and artists — and allow themselves to be transformed as Vancouver had been transformed.

Or not. At the very least, he would arrange things in Frisco to take maximum advantage of the mayhem. Mr. Harris would make some uncanny predictions, make a few well-informed investments… it wouldn't be wise to present Self with the data Jeremy had found, even if they did follow through on their promise and give his agency the coveted Self account. But plenty of coolhunting agencies would bankrupt themselves in a second for it, so brokering the data once he'd had his fun wouldn't be a problem.

"Mr. Harris," Paul addressed his sleeping body, "That's what you call a win-win proposition."

The house fell quiet, and Eileen sat on the bed, her hands bunching up the blanket. She and Jeremy were supposed to go for a walk when his friend had left, and it sounded like he was gone. *An awful noisy boy,* she thought, glad she couldn't hear exactly what they were shouting about.

Good that he has a friend, though. Not just that, but Jeremy wasn't suffering at all in this stimulus-rich world — in fact, to her astonishment, he seemed to be thriving. Apparently he even had a *job*, making specialized environments. She didn't know what she thought about a boy his age having a job, but... she didn't know much about anything in this place.

It doesn't smell right, she thought. Her old room had smelled of old apples, not roses. *And this blanket is too smooth.* But overall, she was amazed at Jeremy's skill. When she had appeared there after her suit shut down, she had thought for one wild moment that it was a dream, that it had all been a dream. When Jeremy had burst in and hugged her, crying, she had known something was wrong — if it was her dream, why was he so upset? Even knowing that something was strange didn't change the relief she felt when he was in her arms. She pressed him hard against him until the tears came, the dirty water of the last weeks finally draining from her.

There was the expected knock at her door.

"Grandma, hey Grandma... do you feel up for that walk?"

Eileen sighed and opened the door, went back to sit on her bed. Jeremy was there, a tentative smile on his face, lifting up a picnic basket.

"Packed some food. I figured we could go to the boardwalk."

He tries so hard, Eileen thought. Jeremy wasn't eating before she got there, but now he ate with her at every meal. She knew it was just to make her feel better, to help her adjust. He was the strong one, now. "Maybe... maybe in a little while, dear."

The picnic basket dipped in Jeremy's hand. Eileen's heart ached. He set down the wicker basket and sat beside her on the bed, concern plain on his face. Eileen didn't know what to say to him.

"I was thinking that maybe I shouldn't have made the house," he said. "Maybe it would have been better for you just to just... jump in."

Eileen shook her head. "No, it was... good. A good thing."

Jeremy sighed, his frustration obvious. "I mean, you won't know if you like it until you just try..." he trailed off.

"I know, dear," she said in a small voice, remembering the view outside her front door. After their reunion, Eileen had walked in a daze through her house, staring at herself in the hall mirror. Surprised not to see the blacksuit's painted face. Jeremy had followed her around the house, anxious. When she got to the front door, he had touched her shoulder and murmured a warning. But she ignored him and threw it open.

No stoop, no flowerbox. No nothing. The white blankness was far more shocking than any yawning blackness could have been. She had known, then, and had closed her eyes. *Frisco.* A second or two later she had heard him shutting the door.

It wasn't fear that kept her in her room for the next few days, as Jeremy assumed. Or not *just* fear. She went through a period of being angry at Paul for exploiting her, to being angry at herself for allowing herself to be exploited, to being angry at Jeremy, for not needing to be rescued at all. It had all been pointless.

Jeremy got off her bed and shook her knee.

"C'mon. We'll take the trolley car. If you want to go back at any point we can just port. C'mon."

"We will *not* port," Eileen said with a sharp look. "You're still grounded."

He looked away, guiltily.

He's too thin. He's lost his baby fat… or had he just deleted it? She couldn't believe it when she found out that he had been here having a grand old time while she had been running around like an idiot.

He had tried to call her, though, and at least that was something. She let herself be pulled up off the bed. Then Jeremy was pushing her out the bedroom door, putting the picnic basket on her arm.

"I need my hat," Eileen said, and Jeremy pulled it out of the picnic basket and set it on her head, leading her by the arms down the stairs. He had thought of everything, every possible excuse. He led her to the foyer, opened up the front door. He made a gesture towards it as if he was the butler and she the lady of the manor. She had to smile, but it was bittersweet. *He's so charming, when did he get so grown up?*

She peeked out the door. Jeremy had transplanted the house into an affinity neighborhood, a string of houses of people preferring a more traditional spatial environment. There was the battered wood of the old flowerbox. She drew herself erect and strode out the door.

She walked down the steps and looked around. It wasn't her neighborhood

— wasn't anything like her neighborhood — but when she looked back at her house, she was reassured. "You did a wonderful job on the house."

"I was thinking about doing the whole neighborhood, but I didn't have any pictures. There's places that'll do that for you, though —"

"No, no," she said. She looked around. A few houses down, a white-haired man came out of his house with his dog. They started down the street. "The houses are different," she noted.

"Yeah, well," Jeremy said. "There're ways to match up your house with similar ones, but this place was close to the trolley car."

"No, I like that they're different," Eileen said, looking at a garden with a cute little fence around it. "It reminds me of when I was a child."

"Oh. Good," Jeremy said. "Here's the trolley car stop."

The man she had seen coming out of his house was waiting, idly scratching his dog's ears. There was nothing on the street, no traffic at all. She looked at the dog, wondered if it was real — did he pay to have the dog's mind uploaded? Or was it something that was born here? She was itching to know, but she had never been good at talking to strangers.

"D'you know when the trolley car is due?" Jeremy said.

Bold as brass, Eileen thought, *wonder where he gets it. Must have been a recessive gene.*

"I'm sorry, I don't," the man said. He looked at Eileen with light blue eyes. "Just move in?"

She nodded and forced herself to speak. "Yes, just a few days ago."

"Welcome!" he said.

She smiled at him. "Thanks." A few seconds later, she added, "Do you like it here?"

The man cocked his head. "Frisco, you mean? Or this neighborhood?"

She shrugged, smiled at him. "Both, I guess."

"Well. My children are all here. I like being near them. I like being in a place that feels real." He looked around. "This neighborhood feels real. At the beginning I found it a little much. The jumping everywhere," he made his hand hop around, and his dog jumped up and licked it. He laughed, a low chuckle that soothed Eileen, and wiped his hand on the dog's yellow fur. *What a nice man.*

"You mean porting," Jeremy corrected.

Eileen shot Jeremy a sharp look, and he dropped his eyes.

The man nodded. "Yeah. I found *porting* quite disorienting. I prefer taking the trolley. I'm in no hurry."

Eileen thought about her suit, about what it gave her and what it took away. "Speed's overrated, that's what I think," she said.

The old man chuckled and scratched his dog's head. "Oh! I should mention it to you. There's a group of us in the neighborhood who are pooling our money. For snow."

"For what?" said Eileen. Jeremy looked interested.

"A big snowfall. On Christmas Eve, specifically." He grinned, rubbing his big weathered hands as if they were cold. "Sledding. Snowmen. Angels."

"Snowball fights," added Jeremy. "Cool. I know a guy who can do ice, too."

Eileen laughed her first laugh in Frisco, a small one. "That sounds ridiculous," she said. "Count me in."

Jim Munroe lives in Toronto's Annex neighborhood. He was managing editor at *Adbusters* before writing the novels *Flyboy Action Figure Comes With Gasmask* (Avon, 1999) and *Angry Young Spaceman* (Four Walls Eight Windows, 2001). His website has his stories, short movies, video games, and tips on do-it-yourself indie media making: www.nomediakings.org